THE RSVP

LAUREN BLAKELY

COPYRIGHT

AUTHOR'S NOTE

Several years ago, I released a book titled 21 Stolen Kisses. For many reasons, that book has been retired completely and has been off sale since early 2021. It will remain off sale forever. However, some of the getting-to-know-you scenes in that book served as the inspiration for character traits for Bridger and Harlow — such as their love of Broadway shows, the Skittle Toes, the bike crash into the cab, and the shirt obsession. All of those aspects of the prior story have been massively revised to fit this brand new storyline with all new characters.

ABOUT THE RSVP

Our days are full of secrets. Our nights are for seduction...

For the last year, I've wanted someone I can't have.

The man my father built his latest multimillion dollar business with.

He's a decade older than I am, and he's entirely forbidden.

The fact that he's never given me a second glance only makes me long for him more.

But the other night, across the room at a gala, everything changed. His broody gaze lingered on me and grew darker.

So I'm officially done being the good girl.

Tomorrow I turn 21. As a gift to myself, I plan to seduce my father's business partner.

Happy birthday to me.

DID YOU KNOW?

Want to be the first to learn of sales, new releases, preorders and special freebies? Sign up for my VIP mailing list here! You'll also get free books from bestselling authors in a selection curated just for you!

PRO TIP: Add lauren@laurenblakely.com to your contacts before signing up to make sure the emails go to your inbox!

Did you know this book is also available in audio and paperback on all major retailers? Go to my website for links!

For content warnings for this title, go to my site.

THE RSVP

Dear Reader,

Harlow and Bridger's forbidden romance begins with a prelude, **THE CRUSH**. If you already read THE CRUSH when it was released on its own, go ahead and start at **THE RSVP**! If not, then start right here and turn the page. The prequel is a key part of their romance — you don't want to miss it!

Xoxo
  Lauren

THE CRUSH

PROLOGUE

Harlow

I didn't hit the car on purpose. I wasn't *that* obsessed. I wouldn't have called it an obsession at all.

Besides, I'm not that devious.

I'd say I'm more crafty.

But a year ago, I was neither devious nor crafty. I was just a girl with the start of a crush.

Everything that happened that night was just the luck of the draw.

I wound up a little bruised—fine, a little broken—and intoxicated by a man I couldn't have.

1

THE MAN IN PURPLE

Harlow

Several Months Ago

The office door clicks open. I look up from the French news site on my laptop and sit straighter at the dining room table.

This is my chance to check him out. I'm home for the summer, so I've been grabbing as many opportunities as I can. Furtively, I turn my gaze as my new crush exits my father's plush home office, then strides across the polished hardwood floors of the living room, wingtips clicking.

Sounding like money.

Looking like a magazine ad.

I've been stealing glances at Bridger for the last week, ever since I returned home from the NYU dorms.

I've known him for years, but when I saw him a few weeks ago at a dinner my father hosted, my pulse surged and my skin tingled.

And a crush was born.

So, yeah, I love studying in the middle of my home, prepping for my next semester abroad. Just in case I can catch a glimpse of him.

And I'll have another one right now, thank you very much. From my vantage point at the imposing oak table, I peek at the man's gorgeous profile as he leaves, hoping he turns toward me soon so I can steal a glance at his outrageously blue eyes. I want to know what's behind them.

My father ruins the view, though, walking right behind him, a glass of Scotch in his hand, saying goodbye to the man he built his media empire with over the last five years. "Sorry to cut this meeting short," my dad says wryly. Everything sounds wry in his English accent. Part of his charm, some say.

His American daughter isn't fooled by his British charm.

Bridger laughs lightly as they walk through the living room, empty-handed. "No, you're not, Ian."

Dad wiggles a brow. "Fine, I'm not sorry."

At least have the decency to pretend.

Bridger nears the door, and I'm just not that interested in the subjunctive tense this second.

Not with Bridger wearing that tailored purple shirt that hugs his arms, those trim charcoal slacks that hint at a strong body, and no tie.

Never a tie.

Bridger's tieless look is so...*tingly*.

"We'll catch up tomorrow on the Spanish deal," he says, scrubbing his hand along his chin. Stubble lines his fine jawline. A faint dusting of dark brown hair, a seven o'clock shadow.

What would it feel like along my fingers? Against my face?

A shiver slides down my spine, and I suppress a murmur.

"Tomorrow for all things Spanish deal. But not too early, you know," my dad says.

What? No wink? How else would one know what you'll be up to?

I'm tempted to roll my eyes, but instead I seize the chance to inject myself into their business conversation, flashing a knowing smile Bridger's way. "Dad doesn't like to wake early," I say, innocently.

Like I don't know the real reason Dad will sleep in.

Like the real reason isn't coming over in a few minutes.

Cassie. Or Lianne. Or Marie. Or whoever the latest lady is that my dad's banging behind his fiancée's back.

Slowly, like maybe we're both in on the joke, Bridger turns my way. My pulse kicks. His eyes are dark blue, the color of the dawn before day takes over. They hold mine for a beat, then he looks away quickly. I'm hopeful enough to want to believe he's entertaining the same thoughts about dangerous kisses.

But I'm smart enough to know he's not.

"Yeah, I know," he says, then he's out the door.

Not even a smile. He's just gone. But what did I

expect? I'm simply his business partner's college-age daughter, ten years his junior.

I turn back to my laptop, ready to study.

Except...

With Bridger on his way, my father turns to me, checks his watch, then hums, like he's gearing up to make a request.

Whatever, Dad. You're not going to shock me.

I close my laptop before he speaks.

"Harlow, love, do you think you could study in your room?"

Translation—be a good girl, put your earbuds in, blast some music, and pretend you hear nothing while I fuck someone who's not my fiancée.

I fake a smile. "Of course," I say, swallowing down a spoonful of disgust.

"You're such a darling," he says.

I flash a bigger smile. "Thanks."

Then, he disappears up the stairs. Naturally. He must go beautify himself before the lady shows up.

She'll probably be here in less than ten minutes. Like I am going to stay in my room for the next several hours. I'm not even going to stay in this house.

There's a big city out there for me to escape into.

I grab my backpack from the dining room floor, stuff my laptop in it, and sling it over my shoulder. Maybe when I reach Big Cup, I'll tell Dad I left.

But then again, maybe I won't. Chances are he won't notice or care.

When I stuff my phone into the pouch of my back-pack, the sound of Beethoven's *Symphony No. 5* blasts from Dad's phone on the coffee table in the living room.

It's his fiancée calling. Joan's in Vermont teaching a symposium on classical music. Poor Joan. I like her well enough, considering I've only lived with her for the last two summer breaks.

His cell rattles again, the violin announcing her interest in talking to her fiancé. *Not my problem. Not my problem. Not at all my problem.*

I ignore it as I pad quietly to the door. It opens into an outside alcove. My bike's in there. I'm almost free from alibi duty.

Footsteps shuffle upstairs. "Harlow, love," he calls out.

I tense.

Don't do it. Don't ask.

"Can you grab Joan's call and tell her I'm in a meeting with Bridger?"

And he's asked.

I burn, but I say nothing as I reach for the knob, stuffing in my earbuds. Useful prop. But soon, I'll need Sondheim, Larsen or Miranda to cleanse my ears.

For now, the violin becomes more urgent. So does my need to go. I turn the knob.

The sound of footsteps grows louder. "Harlow, can you answer that, please?"

Flames lick higher in me as I weigh my options. Pretend I didn't hear? Just leave? Or something else. Like, hey, how about a *no*?

I hardly even live here anymore. I did enough of

this in high school. Why do I have to do it during college breaks too?

"Harlow," he calls once more from the top of the stairs, standing by the banister now.

The violin insists.

He shouts my name. Too loud to ignore. Hand on the knob, I carelessly turn my gaze to him, adopting a confused look as I point to my earbuds. After I take one out, I ask, "What did you say?"

He laughs, shaking his head. "Joan was calling. She'll call again. I'll just handle it," he says, waving a hand dismissively.

"How noble of you," I mutter, too low for him to hear.

He peers at me curiously, cataloging my backpack, my fleece. "Are you leaving?"

Genius.

"Layla called. I'm meeting her at the coffee shop. Good luck with your *Bridger meeting*," I say, sketching air quotes. I leave before he can say another word.

He can deal with his affairs on his own. I'm not his alibi anymore.

I open the door, step into the alcove. There, I tug on my helmet, then grab my silver bike, hoisting it by my shoulder. I leave the brownstone, rushing down the steps, fueled by righteous fire and rage.

He can screw his lady friend without any help from me. It's not like he has me around in the fall or the spring. He can't use me during the summer.

Slapping the bike down, I hop on in a flurry. I jump

off the sidewalk and right onto Eighty Third Street, then race west on the smooth concrete.

Maybe, just maybe, I'll catch one more glimpse of Bridger in the six o'clock sunset as I ride down Fifth Avenue. He'll be walking. He usually walks.

He's only a few minutes ahead of me.

I bolt south on the avenue, sandwiching my body and the bike between the parked cars and the cabs, the trucks and buses screeching downtown. Fast and furious, I want speed and distance. Far away from my dad and his habits. His women showing up at all hours. Him asking me to disappear.

Here I am, disappearing into the New York night.

It's just me and the lights and the sounds and the streets of the city as I dodge the bullets the traffic throws at me. I weave past a car turning into Central Park, and then, out of the corner of my eye, I catch a flash of purple.

My heart surges. Bridger's a block away. I pedal faster, darting past the cars to my left.

Maybe I'll just hop over to the sidewalk, roll up beside him and say hi.

There's a cab twenty feet ahead, pulling over to the curb.

Once I jam past it, I'll—

But my phone rings. It's Joan. Someone swings a cab door open five feet in front of me. The wrong side —the traffic side, not the curb side.

Heart pounding terribly, I try to swerve, and I'm this close to making it when the door smacks my elbow, and bam.

My bones rattle. My head rings. I'm toppling off the bike, my foot slamming into the tire, my head smacking the pavement, all of New York saying *fuck you* to me too.

Pain radiates down to my marrow.

Twenty seconds later, a man in purple is over me, lifting me up, carrying me to the sidewalk. Arms wrapped around me.

When the ambulance arrives five minutes later, he tells me he'll meet me at the hospital.

Everything goes in and out of focus except for the screaming in my bones. And the wild thought that occurs to me—maybe it's the pain or the adrenaline, but I'm not sorry I lost that fight with the car door.

2

ALL YOUR BROKEN BONES

Harlow

I don't call my dad on the way to the hospital. But after the nurse starts my IV, Bridger's standing by my bed in the emergency room, telling me, "Your dad will be here soon. I reached him." He sounds so cool, so in control.

Like he can handle any crisis.

Including finding my father while he's finagling.

And, evidently, getting into my room in the ER. I don't ask how he pulled it off. But that's what Dad's told me Bridger does. Pulls things off. Gets things done.

"Why do people open doors into traffic?" I ask, my voice trembling more than I want it to. I don't want him to think I'm weak.

A gentle smile moves his lips. "People are terrible. But you're going to be fine, Harlow. Ian is on his way."

I don't care about Ian, though, or how Bridger tore

him away from Marie or Cassie or Lianne. "Thank you for being there."

"I'm glad I was," he says.

I feel hazy. Warm all over. Whatever they put in this IV for my broken ankle is good.

"Come see me tomorrow?" I ask. Maybe it's a plea. Hard to tell.

The stuff in the IV is *really* good.

Bridger doesn't answer right away. His jaw tics. He's wavering. His blue eyes are chased with conflict, his brow knitting.

I'm not above a little begging when I can blame it on the drugs. "Please," I say with a frown. "It would make me feel better."

He nods, resigned perhaps. "You're a good negotiator," he says, giving in.

I tuck the compliment into my pocket as he gives me his number. "If you need anything and can't reach your dad."

"Thanks," I say, even though I've had Bridger's number for some time. Dad gave it to me long ago— *here's Joan's number, here's Bridger's number, here's the studio number.*

I've never used it, but now I have permission.

When a nurse comes in to tell me it's time to cast my ankle, he wishes me well and leaves.

* * *

My head CT scan is clear, so they send me home that night. My foot screams the next day, but painkillers shut that down quickly, and soon I'm feeling pretty good.

I entertain visitors nonstop in my living room. Layla appears in the morning, bearing lip gloss and nail polish. She's an angel. Ethan brings tulips and gossip about our Carlisle Academy alum—the former senior class president of the most elite prep school in Manhattan was just thrown out of Yale after three years. Joan sends bouquets of dahlias, then calls, too, asking how I'm doing.

"I've been better," I tell her, appreciating the motherly check-in.

After I get reacquainted with the joys of naptime, my brother FaceTimes from London, offering to catch a flight to New York to be with me. I decline but ask Hunter to tell me stories of life in England.

All day long, Dad swings in and out of his home office down the hall to check on me. After he orders a late lunch from my favorite Mediterranean restaurant, he tells me about the new storyline in *Sweet Nothings*, probably to distract me.

Or maybe to distract himself till he sees whoever again.

"And then Josie and Sam get all caught up in this whirlwind fling," he says. "We see them sneak off to the wine cellar and the library."

I have no interest in learning where his characters canoodle, but I feel too good to cut him off. "Great, Dad. Tell me more."

He unspools the next few episodes then checks his Victoire watch and pushes up from his chair. "I have to nip off. I have a thing." He shrugs, sheepish, and nods to the front door. "I'll be back later, but Bridger's going to stop by too."

"Oh?" I try to sound blasé.

I pulled off the nonchalant look, judging from Dad's *no big deal* grin. "Yes, he wants to make sure you're okay. Good thing he was there to call 911."

Dad leaves for his *thing*. The door has barely closed behind him when I grab my brush from the coffee table, run it through my hair again, then slick on lip gloss. I glance at my shirt—a cute slouchy top that goes with my shorts. Perfect.

A few minutes later, there's a knock on the door. "Come in," I shout. Bridger knows the code.

Bubbles bounce under my skin as Bridger unlocks the door. When the handsome, broody man strides into the brownstone, those bubbles speed through me. I am effervescent.

He holds a bouquet of gerbera daisies. "Hey there."

"Those are my favorite flowers." Did I mention that in the hospital last night? Have I ever said that at a dinner party, event, or gala where I saw him? I don't know.

He peers around the living room, checking out vase after vase. The room is bursting with blooms. "It's a florist shop in here."

"I might start a side hustle peddling flowers." I point to his arrangement as he sets it on the coffee table by the couch. "But I like yours best."

"Thanks," he says, evenly, like he has to be careful with me. Like he can't reveal any emotion.

Understandable. I've known Bridger James since I was fifteen and his upstart production company acquired the TV rights to *Sweet Nothings*. He was the wunderkind new producer who spotted a hit and made it happen with my dad. They became partners, then, in growing that property to global domination, turning the book series my mom had penned and Dad had inherited into a worldwide phenom as a TV show. The risqué, racy soap opera counts legions of fans, and it started in my home when the two of them worked late on the concept, refining it and then pitching it to a network. Now, they own a renowned TV production company together called Lucky 21 that's responsible for *Sweet Nothings,* its spin-offs and other top shows too.

Over the last few years, Bridger's hung around at my house late at night working, then shown up early in the morning collecting Dad for meetings. I've seen him at fetes, galas, parties.

But someone else has always been around. Now it's just the two of us, alone together for the first time.

"Want a seat?" I ask, gesturing to the other chair.

As he sits, I catalog his appearance—he's in his *work uniform.* Sharp pants, fine leather shoes, and a tailored shirt. Today's is a shade of deep, rich green.

"Nice cast," Bridger says, gesturing to the pink cast on my foot.

"Evidently the cab door had it in for me. Have you ever broken a bone?" I ask, quickly shifting away from my ankle injury.

"Many times," he says with a sigh, but it's a welcoming kind of sound, like *been there, done that.*

I sit a little straighter, eager for this chance to get to know him. "Tell me all your broken stories."

He laughs curiously, eyeing me like he isn't sure I mean the request. "Really?"

I'm not backing down. I want what I want. "Yes. Really."

Here in my home, the day after a nasty crash, with my father off doing whatever, his handsome, sexy, nearly inscrutable business partner wiggles three fingers on his right hand. "Broke these when the center stepped on my hand during football practice in junior high."

"You were the quarterback?" It delights me to no end, learning these details.

"Of course." There's a smirk on his face, like he couldn't be anything but the team leader.

"Were you good at football?"

He tilts his head, his gaze a little challenging, a touch cocky. "What do you think?"

"Yes," I say, feeling a bit fluttery. A bit naughty too.

"Good answer," Bridger replies, sinking deeper into his chair, looking comfortable or maybe even relaxed at last.

"How many games did you win? Touchdowns did you throw? Passing yards did you log?"

He raises an appreciative brow, whistling low. "Someone knows football."

I bob a shoulder playfully. "I know a lot of things."

His expression shifts, going dark for a second. Then he swallows and answers in a businesslike tone. "I did well," he says, like he rearranged his answer at the last minute.

I ease up on the Lolita. "What else did you break?" Surely, this is a less sexy comment. I hope it's enough for him to stay.

"I broke my kneecap a couple years later," he says, recounting a high school injury.

"How'd you manage that?"

"Playing soccer my sophomore year. I planted my foot wrong while I was twisting around to try to score, and then it snapped. Felt like it fell down to my shin." He shakes his head in remembered pain, wincing.

"That sounds terrible," I say in sympathy. "Did it really fall to your shin?"

He taps the side of his calf under his black pants to show me where his kneecap had landed. "It was knocked about two inches out of the socket." He blows out a sharp breath. "That hurt."

"That sounds like an understatement," I say.

"Yeah, it is."

"That's awful," I say, but I'm giddy for more of his stories, more of him.

Just more.

He regales me with tales of his high school sports, from soccer games to football plays, till I say, "Is that all you did growing up? Play sports?"

With a laugh, he shakes his head. "It wasn't all I did, but I was good at sports for a while there. Until I stopped playing," he says, and I file that detail away as I keep listening. "Plus, I think my mom just wanted to balance out all the show tunes and cabaret I'd grown up with. You know, just to give me a full sense of the world."

Is he for real? I nearly bolt out of the chair with excitement. "I love cabaret," I say, breathless.

He shoots me a doubtful look. "You do?"

"Cabaret, show tunes, Broadway, you name it," I say, enthused by this bond I didn't know we had.

"Yeah?" His tone pitches up, maybe with excitement too.

"I do. I could spend all night in the theater," I say, and that flirty purr returns to my voice, unbidden.

Dammit. I didn't mean to go there.

And I shouldn't have, because Bridger glances around nervously, checks the ornate and ominous clock on the living room wall—my dad had it shipped from his favorite shop in Knightsbridge—then sighs. "I have a meeting," he says. "I should go."

Please don't go.

But I know better than to sound desperate. "Of course. But you wouldn't leave without signing my cast, would you?"

There's tension in his shoulders still as he reaches for the Sharpie on the table, then checks out my cast. Layla and Ethan already commandeered most of the fiberglass real estate.

"*Hmm.* Not much room left," he says, analytically, checking out the options.

But I saved a spot for him. Kept it virginal. "Right by the toes," I say, pointing to the land he can claim on me. "There's a little space."

I wiggle them, showing off my bright red and

purple toenail polish. "My friend Layla painted them this morning. She calls them Skittles toes."

When Bridger meets my gaze, his blue eyes darken to the color of a midnight sky. "I'll just sign right here by those Skittles toes then."

As he scratches out his signature near my candy-colored nails, his fingers skim against my toes.

A whoosh rushes through my body.

This is the first time he's touched me.

I don't intend for it to be the last.

3

IS IT OBVIOUS?

Harlow

Three months later my cast is gone, and it's time to wear heels again.

It's a New York party night after all, and I'm not about to show up among the glitterati of Manhattan in flats.

"I still can't believe you're leaving me to fend for myself tonight," I whine to Layla after we bound up the steps in Dad's brownstone and turn into my old bedroom suite. She's only staying for thirty minutes at the party, and I feel betrayed already.

"I'm the worst. But trust me, I tried to get out of the charity board dinner that Mom is making me go to," she says, huffing.

"Too bad bailing isn't an option," I say, heading for the closet. But it would be poor form to ghost my—cough, cough—*own* party. But it's really *Dad's* party. His why-doesn't-everyone-congratulate-me-for-having-a-daughter-land-a-prestigious-semester-abroad-program party. All his friends and business associates will be here to kiss his ring.

Why else would they come? Because they care that I'm one of ten college students in the country accepted into this French program? Or maybe how studying in Paris for a few months will help with my dual degrees?

They care as much as they cared when Dad threw a party for his little valedictorian when I graduated from Carlisle Academy three years ago.

In my walk-in closet, I flick through the options and pick a little black dress. I slip it on, then peruse the shoes, running my fingers over a few shelves. I hold up a pair of red-bottomed black heels. "The ones Dad bought for me last month after he bought us orchestra seats for the opening of *Adventures of the Last Single Guy in New York*, and then finally turned up at intermission. But hey, he was, ahem, *late from a meeting*?" I grab a pair of silvery crisscross high-heeled sandals. "Or the ones Joan bought as an *aspirational gift* after I broke my ankle?"

Layla rolls her sky-blue eyes with a particular kind of carelessness, the kind reserved for parental BS. Then, she points a French-manicured nail authoritatively at the silvery pair. Layla makes fast decisions. "Those will make your legs look extra hot. Not that that's hard."

I bob a shoulder, glowing a little from the compliment. "Thanks, friend," I say, then I perch on the edge of the bed and slide into the shoes, methodically crossing the straps till they climb high enough to hug my calves. I rise, then jut out a hip, showing off the outfit.

She hums low in her throat. "Those should be illegal," she says with a whistle. "They go perfectly with the LBD."

Fine, fine.

Perhaps, I don't entirely hate the idea of the party.

Bridger will be there. And maybe, dressed like this, I'll look closer to twenty-one.

It's less than a year away.

It's a magic age.

Then, I'll no longer be in college.

I'll be his contemporary.

A frisson of possibility unfurls in my chest. I hide a grin from my friend. I haven't breathed a word about this storm of feelings to anyone. And I've never kept secrets from her. But this secret feels like mine. Like a private letter, locked in a box, hidden away.

* * *

Layla and I circulate dutifully downstairs, making small talk, a skill we've both been schooled in for years. Her since birth, me since my father became a big deal.

How is Jasmin doing in Tokyo?

Is Vikas enjoying his work in Washington?

Did you see the new sculpture at the Keller Gallery?

All the while, I graciously accept congratulations from all my father's friends and associates.

Thank you. I'm so fortunate to be going there.

Yes, it's going to be a wonderful challenge.

I can't wait to settle into my flat in the Sixth.

And blah, blah, blah. Layla makes a few laps with me, snagging a champagne flute from a cute server in black tie, tossing the guy a wink.

He smiles back, showing straight white teeth. Layla is such a sucker for great teeth. She should consider snagging the city's top orthodontist's client list sometime.

Once he's weaving through a pack of suits, my friend waggles a glass my way. "Want one?"

"No," I say, but it's too late. She grabs a second one from another passing waitperson and thrusts it into my hand.

"Layla," I say, but I take it anyway. It's easier.

She nods to the packed home. Easily one hundred people mingle in the living room, spill into the dining room. "Who are all these people?"

I lean closer, dip my voice. "Miss Such and Such, the VP of Sucking Up. Mister Whoever, the Director of Kissing Ass. And, finally, there's the Manager of I Have An Idea to Pitch You," I say, surveying the scene—smart dresses and blow-outs on the women, slicked-back hair and tailored shirts for the men.

"Ah, I was hoping to pitch an idea to *him*. The idea of me," she says, then points surreptitiously to a handsome guy easily fifteen years older than she is.

I shoot her a doubtful look. "Seriously?"

She just wiggles her brows. Then she looks around again. "Oh, the hot one's here."

I figure she's spotted another thirty-something guy, but when I follow her gaze my breath catches.

It's Bridger. He must have just arrived. He wears a royal blue shirt and charcoal slacks. He's leaning against the wall, not drinking either. Watching the scene unfold. Part of it but separate as he studies the people while tugging on the cuffs of his shirt.

Warmth blooms in my chest, a frothy, delicious sensation. I feel floaty, a little dreamy as I watch him. A young publicist beelines for him and his gaze shifts to *on*.

Then, Layla bumps my shoulder. "When were you going to tell me?"

Confused, I turn my face to her. "Tell you what?"

With an *I caught you* smile, she shakes her head in disbelief. "I can't believe you didn't say a word sooner. How long have you been hot for your dad's business partner?"

My stomach drops. And that secret didn't last long. "Is it obvious?" I ask. "To everyone, I mean."

Her smile is gleeful, a little wicked. "No. But to me it is because I know you. And damn, he's pretty." She nudges me again. "Go shoot your shot."

The idea is too much. Too tempting. Too dangerous. But I appreciate her efforts. "Thanks, but I don't think it'll work out," I say, since isn't that the truth. He's just not interested in me. Not to mention the *big* hurdle—I could never be with my dad's business partner.

Layla shrugs, then drops a kiss to my cheek. "I should vanish. Don't miss me too much." Then, low, under her breath, she urges, "Shoot, Harlow, shoot."

"Get out of here," I say, rolling my eyes.

But her command has gotten a hold of me. When she's gone, I spin around, hunting for him again, but he's chatting with a woman in a paisley blouse.

Bridger doesn't have a drink in his hand, and an idea takes hold. An opening line, if you will.

As I head to a group of network execs to put in more time, my father strides over, intercepting me. Joan is with him. She looks regal, her chestnut mane swept up in a chignon.

She smiles affectionately at me. "Let's raise a glass in a toast to our star," she says.

"Of course," Dad seconds.

He doesn't even have to clear his throat. He commands a room by his mere presence, playing the part he's mastered. A modern-day Gatsby, complete with the slicked-back hair and semi-permanent grin. His eyes gleam with fatherly pride. "To my daughter. I've never been prouder," he says to the crowd, then he wraps an arm around me. "Paris will be lucky to have you this fall."

I'm his prize, all right. I smile, the bright, shiny kind that charms his friends. Something else I learned from an early age. *Be nice to Daddy's associates and you can do what you want.*

"Thank you," I say to the crowd that's smiling at me but sucking up to my father.

Except Bridger. He doesn't need to suck up to my dad. He's his equal. Equal shares in the company. Equal say. His dark eyes meet mine as the partygoers lift their glasses and give a collective *Cheers.*

"Thank you so much," I say.

When the guests return to their networking, my father weaving back into the sea of black and white and gray, the paisley lady says goodbye to Bridger. Buoyed by Layla's shot of confidence, I'm determined to snag a few minutes of his time before someone else corrals him. So he can see me as a woman, not my father's daughter.

Like that, I pass my drink to a waitperson and go to him.

4

LUCKY NEW YORK

Harlow

When I reach Bridger, I flash him a grin. "Want a refill?" I ask, eyeing his empty hands, taking a gamble with my offer.

"No thanks," he says, then his gaze travels to my legs, a smile shifting his lips. "You're walking without help again."

A zing rushes down my back. He noticed my legs.

I gesture to my high-heeled feet. "And I have a cool scar," I say.

His eyebrow lifts. "You do?"

"On my ankle. I'm not sure if the bike cut me up or the cab. Either way, I got marked," I tell him, a little playfully, then I turn to the side, hoping he enjoys the profile view as I bend, pointing toward the vicinity of the inch-long jagged scar, still pink. "Right there."

As he looks down, he swallows. Roughly, maybe. Or

is that my imagination? "Yeah, that's some scar," he says, giving nothing away.

"Guess we're both cool now," I say, then tilt my head, weighing the next thing on my mind. "By the way, I didn't think you'd accept my drink offer."

He takes a beat. "But you made it anyway?"

"I wanted to see if I was right."

His brow knits in curiosity. I've set the trap. He's taking my bait. "I'll bite. Right about what?"

The next words come out cool, casual. Like I'm just this observant about everything. "You don't drink," I say.

There's a glint in his eyes. "You noticed?" He sounds mildly surprised, but I can't quite tell if he's making conversation to pass the time or because he enjoys talking to me.

But now's my chance. I meet his blue-eyed gaze straight on. "I notice things," I say, nervous and thrilled over the admission.

He's quiet for a few seconds. Then he says, in that measured, even tone, "Yeah. You do."

It's an observation. Maybe a curiosity. Almost impossible to read.

"I do," I say.

He scratches his jaw, then says, "So NYU, and now a semester in Paris." Like he needs the conversational shift. "You picked well."

"Don't worry," I say, a grin teasing at my lips. "I'll be back in December. You can't take the girl out of New York for long."

"Lucky New York," he says, and I want to cup those

words in my palms for the rest of the night. The rest of the year.

I smile, buoyed by his response as I work out a reply to keep this going when Dad shoulders his way past me.

The buzz-killer nods at the man I'm in lust with.

"Bridger, I must steal you away. Lionel from the UK office is here," Dad says.

Yes, of course Lionel from the UK office would attend my celebration.

I grit my teeth in annoyance but just smile like the good daughter. Even though Dad doesn't even say a word to me. He just whisks Bridger away and that's the end of that.

* * *

Later, I'm still feeling bold from his *Lucky New York*, like I've been shot up with a feel-good drug. Something that makes me feel bigger than the world. I slide into bed, under the covers, touching the wooden box of letters I keep on my nightstand. It's safe. Then, I place the phone on my pillow, just inches from me. I run my finger along the necklace I wear every day, feeling the shape of the *I* that hangs from it.

I for the French word *intrépidité*.

Then, as if champagne is bubbling through me— but it's not, not one bit—I tap open my text messages. At last, I have a reason to use that number.

I'm brave. I'm intrepid.

Harlow: I notice other things too. Like how good you looked in your shirt.

Then I hit send, a little high, a lot on top of the world.

As I get ready for bed, I check for a reply.

Nothing.

After I slip into a pair of sleep shorts, I look once more.

Silence.

I close my eyes, but sleep is so far away it might as well be in Indonesia.

In the morning, I wake to a blinking icon. I catch my breath.

Bridger: Thanks. Bespoke makes great shirts.

Hmm. Well, it's not what I wanted but it's something. It's more than a *thanks*. Maybe it's even an opening.

Once I'm up and out of bed, I find my dad in the kitchen, brewing a cup of tea and nuzzling Joan's neck.

"Morning, love," he says to me when he pulls away from his fiancée.

"Hello, Harlow," Joan says with a slightly embarrassed grin, like they were caught doing more than neck kissing.

I've seen so much worse, honey.

"Hi Joan. Hi Dad," I say breezily, then head for the fruit basket to grab a peach. When I finish it, I say, "I'm going for a bike ride."

It's my first time in the saddle since I broke my ankle, and my scar makes me feel intrepid as I ride.

THIS COLOR WOULD LOOK GOOD ON YOU

Harlow

A week later, I'm shopping in the Village with Layla and Ethan at a trendy boutique. He needs a sexy shirt for our last weekend in the Hamptons. Layla needs a barely there top. I need nothing—I'm not trying to impress anyone at our final party before we fan out to universities around the world next week for our senior years.

When they head to the dressing room, I wander around the men's clothing section, running my fingers over the shirts.

Then, my gaze catches on the brand name on one tag.

Bespoke.

I glance around, furtive.

This would be risky. A little wild.

But the risk fuels me. I hold up the teal button-down shirt in front of me. It's too big, of course. It's a men's large.

Grabbing my phone, I angle the camera just so.

I don't show my face. Instead, I snap a pic of the shirt fabric laying against me.

That's all. Before I can think better of it, I send it with the caption: *This color would look good on you.*

I tuck the phone away, resisting its insistent pull for the next hour. But when I'm nibbling on a chickpea dish at a sidewalk café Ethan picks for lunch, my phone buzzes.

Immediately, my chest zings.

It has to be *him*.

When I grab it in less than a second, Ethan smirks. "Hot new date?"

I scoff, but then I sizzle when I read Bridger's note. *Thanks for the fashion tip.*

It's just a chaste note. It's just a thanks.

But it's also a *response.*

I feel elated and defeated at the same time in equal measure. "Just a friend," I say, then set the phone facedown.

Layla arches a perfectly groomed brow. She's not taking this one lying down. "Just a friend?"

"Just a friend," I repeat, since I'm not sure that he's anything more.

"Are you sure?" she asks, staring at me, like she can extract the truth with her eyes.

"Is there a reason Harlow would be unsure?" Ethan asks curiously, jumping in.

"I'm positive," I say firmly, then flip my hair off my

shoulder. "So, what do we want to do first when we hit East Hampton on our final weekend?"

Layla's blue eyes say she knows what I'm doing but her mouth says, "The beach, of course."

Ethan shakes his head. "No, *the pool*. Your pool is unfairly obscene," he says, emphatically.

"But is something obscene truly unfair?" she counters, like they're having a philosophical argument.

Thoughtfully, Ethan taps his regal chin, the perfect match to his classical nose. He's a looker all right, all blue-blood, Upper East Side, matinee-idol pretty. He's attracted all the guys and gals in college.

As they debate the semantics of obscenity, I hide a smile rising inside me.

Maybe this text is *just* the start of something.

* * *

On Sunday night, we cruise home from the Hamptons in Layla's sweet sports car, exhausted from the sun, the water, and our last time together for a while.

"I'll miss you all," I say after she pulls up in front of my brownstone and gets out.

"I'll miss you more," she chimes in, throwing her arms around me.

"I'll miss you the most," Ethan says, not to be outdone.

"Group hug," I declare, and we smoosh each other until tears are rolling, since the end of summer is always sweet and bittersweet.

Finally, I tear myself away from my friends and say goodbye.

Later that week, I'm in my room packing my suitcase for my semester abroad—clothing, a few books, a couple keepsakes. My father ordered his limo driver to take me to the airport tomorrow. Dad's so extra, but I can't complain.

I FaceTime Hunter, even though it's late in London. "You better come see me," he says. Hunter has an English mom and mostly grew up in London. But his accent is less posh than Dad's.

"Same to you," I say. "You'll only be a Chunnel train ride away."

We chat some more then I say goodbye, and after I zip my last bag, I flop back on my bed, checking the time on my phone. Eleven.

My phone blinks with a text from my dad. He's downstairs, but he always texts me goodnight.

I'm off to bed. Sleep well. Joan will be back in the morning. Xoxo

I smile faintly, a vague sense of appreciation for his note floating past me as I drift into sleep.

But in the middle of the night, I'm dreaming of takeout cartons of Thai, and Vietnamese, and tacos. My stomach growls, and I wake with a hungry start.

I blink my eyes open.

I wish my mother were here to send me off. Even though I remember her less and less, I still wish she were here, especially since Paris was *our* dream. She loved the city she lived in when she attended college. We'd visit as often as we could, traipsing around museums, lingering in chocolate shops, playing in the Tuileries Garden. Even after so many years without her, there are moments when the missing coils inside me. But then it unwinds seconds later. It's weird, grief. Weird the way it lingers sometimes, like a trailing scent of faint perfume long after the wearer has left the room. Sometimes you notice the scent. Mostly you don't.

My stomach growls again. I focus on the practical matters rather than faded memories. I didn't eat dinner, so I go downstairs.

The brownstone is eerie and still, as it should be after hours. I pad quietly to the kitchen. In the fridge, I snag hummus and carrots. As I dip a carrot, I hear footsteps and turn my head.

Seriously?

I learn two things in the next few seconds.

My father has a new lover.

And she sleeps topless. She wears only boy shorts. Her magnificent tits fly free as she walks past the dining room table, toward the kitchen before she stops short, startled.

"Oh my god," she says, her hands shooting up, covering her breasts.

I grit my teeth, swallowing down my disgust. I show nothing. I am the portrait of unflinching as I lean against the kitchen counter. Impervious.

"Hungry?" I ask as I crunch into the carrot.

Even in the dark, I can see her face turn red. "I'm so sorry."

But she's not moving. Perhaps her bare feet are stuck to the floor of the entryway.

"I had no idea you were going to be in the kitchen," she says, stumbling on words.

I smile. All plastic. "That's clear."

She spins around, rushes off.

I finish the carrot in the silence, then return to the upstairs bedroom. I can't wait till I don't live here anymore. If I could *never* set foot in this house again, it wouldn't be soon enough.

When groans slink up the stairs and curl down the hallway, I grab my headphones, punch up the sound-track for *Ask Me Next Year,* a little-known Broadway musical, and let it help me blot out the sounds of my father's sex den below.

The next morning when I go downstairs, still humming the bittersweet tunes, I brace myself for a run-in with the new lady. But the amply endowed woman is nowhere to be seen. Instead, my father is brewing tea and listening to NPR's morning report, dressed for the day in a polo shirt and beige slacks.

He turns my way and smiles. "Ready for the big day?"

"Yup," I bite out.

"What's wrong, poppet?"

I've had enough. I've swallowed years of lies, and I'm done. "I'm not here that often," I tell him. "Just summers and breaks. So, do you think you could ask your sleepover guests to, I dunno, wear clothes when they wander around the house at night?"

A slow grin spreads across his face, and he rolls his

green eyes—the same shade as mine. "Poppet, it's nothing. You have all the same parts."

That's his argument? "So if you were queer, and had a half-naked man as a guest this would be *not okay*. But because you're straight, it's *okay*?"

He furrows his brow, trying to work out my logic. "Is this about orientation or identity?"

I huff. There's no point. He doesn't get it. I grab a bagel and bite into it, ripping off a hunk.

As I chew, the front door creaks open and Joan sails in, just arrived from Boston. "I couldn't miss sending you off to Paris for the semester, sweetheart," she calls out, kind and oblivious.

My throat squeezes. *My father fucked someone else while you were out of town. Her tits are perkier than yours.* Instead, I say, "Thank you for coming."

I know better than to tell her the truth.

When I was thirteen, and my father was married to Roselyn, wife number three, I let slip at the dinner table that his friend Graceanne had spent the night a few weeks before. I'd thought she was simply sleeping over in the guest room.

The next day, Roselyn checked into a *spa*. My father sat me down in the living room and told me I needn't have concerned myself about Graceanne. After all, he and Roselyn had an arrangement. *An understanding.* "Darling, I know you're trying to be helpful, but it's better you don't get involved. Roselyn doesn't need to know about my guests. It'll only upset the delicate balance of an adult relationship."

But that left me more confused. "Okay, but you said that woman was your friend. Graceanne?"

He'd patted my knee. "Exactly. Just a friend. So we don't need to tell Roselyn these things again. They can send her over the, well, the edge." A fatherly hug. An unspoken warning. "Best to just keep things that happen in the house...*in the house*."

Let sleeping dogs lie.

Roselyn moved back in a month later. "She's so much better now," my dad had declared. Like her stint wherever she'd been had erased the memory not only of his cheating but of my big mouth.

They stayed together for another year, then my father left her. I knew what was coming when he switched from a rainforest scent to a spicy one. He always picks out a new cologne when he's ready for a new woman.

Perhaps Roselyn had upset his delicate balance, because he soon moved on to Mariana, marrying her for a few years, then changing his cologne again when he met Joan.

I'd learned my lesson. It wasn't my place to breathe a word. There would be no more accidental mentions of *friends*.

So I keep quiet now. Even when my dad wraps Joan into a warm embrace, cooing, "Love you, darling," I just keep smiling. I could nab a statuette in Hollywood with my cheery smile.

When we slide into the back of the town car, my father takes her hand, and bile rises in my throat. I stare out the window, fingering my necklace as the limo swings south on Fifth Avenue, en route to the airport.

I count down the seconds till I'm out of the country and far, far away from him.

Though, admittedly, I'll miss seeing the one person I liked bumping into around my father.

The man whose shirts I adore.

But missing him is ridiculous. This is just a foolish little crush. Bridger's shirts don't matter, our bonding over Broadway doesn't matter, and my wicked feelings don't matter.

I vow to get over him while I'm in Paris.

* * *

Mostly, I do just that in France. It helps that my father mentions offhand in an email that Bridger's started seeing someone. Someone named Emma he met online.

I ignore the burn in my chest. I ignore it for all of September.

Then, I no longer have to ignore the feeling because it fades on its own. Maybe from lack of oxygen? Not seeing a man will do that to you, I suppose. I barely think of him from thousands of miles away.

Fine, André *does* help distract me. The French art student I meet mostly takes my mind off Bridger as we wander through museums together and visit dance clubs with our friends.

Except, maybe we're wired to want what we don't have since sometimes when I kiss André in my flat in the Sixth, I think of the man in the purple shirt. Sometimes when André touches me, I imagine someone else's hands on my skin.

Maybe that's why this brief Paris romance doesn't last long enough for André to be my first. That, and art studies keep calling to me, leaving little time for my French lover...or Bridger.

There is too much beauty here in Paris to linger on one faraway man.

* * *

When I return to New York in December, I nearly turn down my father's email invitation to attend a *Sweet Nothings* gala.

I want to RSVP instantly with a *no*.

And that feels fantastic. Freeing even.

Until I read on, seeing the part where Bridger's single again.

Oh.

Well.

Maybe I *should* go to the party. Just to confirm this wicked little crush is out of my system after all.

I change my reply to a *yes*.

But when I go, Bridger's wearing the teal shirt.

Harlow and Bridger's love story begins in THE RSVP.

THE RSVP

1

MAYBE NOW

Harlow

I'd be lying if I said I didn't miss Paris, but it is good to be back in New York.

The poets and writers will have you believe that nothing aches like longing for a lover. But I'm here to say, the hole in my heart was for these two humans—Layla and Ethan.

I craved friend time so much while I was in Europe. And I want to gobble up every second with them now that I'm home again.

We're in the spacious kitchen of Layla's family's Upper West Side four-story brownstone—her mom is off in Greece for most of December—and I'm holding a pretty blue box with a silver ribbon around the center. Layla turned twenty-one while I was in Paris for the fall semester of my senior year of college. Since I committed the mortal sin of missing my best friend's birthday, I'm making it up to her as best I can.

"It's from a store in the 6th that's on every travel influencer's under-the-radar list, so naturally, everyone knows about it, and it better be the best damn chocolate ever," I say as I thrust the box at my friend. I unearthed the jewel among chocolate shops on the corner of Rue de la Huchette, near where I lived for the last three months. "It called out to me. It said *please bring me home to Layla*."

Layla hugs the box to her chest. "Good thing you listened to it."

Ethan clears his throat, side-barring to Layla. "Better make sure she snagged the good stuff before you say that," he teases.

"Please. I always get the good stuff," I say. Then, since I missed Ethan turning twenty-one too, I snag a gift bag for him from the counter.

With grabby hands, he digs into the tissue paper, extracts a skinny silver tie, then cracks up. "It's what every aspiring rocker wants."

"See? I always take care of my loves," I say as he loops the tie around his neck and knots it loosely.

"And I got *this* for us to celebrate," Layla says, then brandishes a bottle of champagne from the kitchen counter. In a swirl of black cashmere and blonde hair, Layla yanks open a drawer and grabs a cloth napkin. Ethan tugs on a cupboard door and snags some glasses. It's a familiar choreography, the way we know each other's homes. We've known them since we met in first grade way back when.

Layla hands the napkin to Ethan, who covers the cage on the bottle with it, then pops the cork with panache. He hands the bottle to Layla and she pours two glasses, then arches a brow my way over the third. But I decline, opting for a boring LaCroix I grab from her Sub-Zero instead.

I'll be twenty-one soon enough but legality's not the point.

I pour the bubbly water, then the three of us toast. "To a great winter break," Layla says, the liquid glistening under the light of the chandelier that illuminates the kitchen island.

"To countless holiday parties with lots of gorgeous people," Ethan puts in.

"Hear hear," Layla says.

I lift mine higher. "And I'll drink to saying no to all the parties my father invites me to. It's the start of a new era."

We all toast to that.

* * *

Even though I'm home, I don't go *home*. The last time I ran into one of my father's lovers in the middle of the night, I learned it's better to have my own place.

So after I catch up with my friends, I head downtown to Chelsea to the apartment I rented and will share with two English majors for my final semester.

This way, it'll be easier for Dad to conduct his affairs.

I mean, cheating on his fiancée has to be simpler

when he doesn't need to either enlist me to help cover it up or kick me out of the house when his lady of the month arrives.

Still, I'm intrigued by his email that arrives as I'm unlocking the door.

Do I want to attend The Annual Silver and Gold Sweet Nothings *Affair?*

It's the holiday party for his world-famous television show that's become the toast of the globe. The show my father built on the backs of the bestselling novels he inherited from my mother when she died.

No, thanks. I won't be going. I don't need to lean in to his ego.

But, he adds, the fete will be held at The Museum of Modern Art. In the sculpture gardens.

I'm tempted. I'm definitely tempted. I never could resist a museum. Art is such an elixir.

As I walk down the hallway to my apartment, I read on.

There will be people there that you should meet, Dad adds.

Fair point. I *should* meet people in the art business. That's true. I need to think about what I'll do in six months when I graduate.

Then, at the bottom of his email, he finishes with *Bridger will be there. You can cheer him up since his girlfriend broke up with him.*

I nearly drop my keys in my hurry to type "yes."

Shutting the door, I set a hand on my chest, trying to calm my speeding heart. There's so much in this email. So much possibility.

My father's business partner is single.

His handsome, intriguing, doesn't-fit-into-the-crowd, only-ten-years-older-than-I-am business partner.

My once-upon-a-time, wicked little crush.

The man who carried me to an ambulance when a cab hit my bicycle last summer. The man who checked in on me the next day at my home. The man whose shirts I complimented after my send-off-to-Paris party.

The incredibly off-limits, sexy-as-sin, inscrutable man who runs a multimillion-dollar company along with my father.

Bridger had a girlfriend while I was in Paris.

Now he's single.

And he'll be at the *Sweet Nothings* party.

I'd thought I was over my one-way crush. Surely, I am. I can't harbor feelings for this long just because he's handsome. Or because I pictured him once or twice when I was with someone else.

Then again, why the hell is my heart jittery? My pulse spiking? And what is this fizzy feeling racing through my body?

Maybe I'm not over him. Maybe the crush is zooming back to me on its return trip.

I'm a few months older.

A lot wiser.

And I'm a woman who wants to know what's become of a once great and powerful crush.

So much for saying no to my father's invites.

I RSVP instantly.

In the morning, as I head to the campus for a meeting with my faculty advisor, I pass a shop in the West Village and do a double take.

The store is the one I went to a few months ago with Layla and Ethan before I left for Paris. As they shopped, I stole away to the men's section, found a shirt that reminded me of Bridger, and sent him a photo.

My breath catches again just thinking of that.

I open my phone, click on my texts, and return to that last thread with him. There's the shot of me holding up a teal button-down, the caption reading: *This color would look good on you.*

He replied with a simple: *Thanks for the fashion tip.*

That was all he said. But still, I run a finger over the text, and I hit the like button for the first time on his reply.

* * *

The next evening, I get dressed in my apartment in Chelsea, feeling a little wound up as I zip up a simple dark red dress. Soon, I'll know if time has doused my desires, or if this bouncy feeling is infatuation all over again.

I touch up my mascara and dust on some blush, I adjust the gold necklace I always wear, with its letter-shaped pendant—*I* for the French word, *intrépidité*.

A gift from my mother.

My contribution to the gold theme tonight.

I step into a pair of short boots and grab a coat, then I leave, the elevator whisking me downstairs, where I head out into the New York night. It occurs to me that I'm going to a party Bridger will attend, and for the first time, I'm leaving from someplace other than the home I once shared with my father.

That thought wraps around me like sweet smoke wafting through the air, a little tantalizing.

I catch a Lyft uptown, slicking on lip gloss when I reach Fifty-Third.

Well, he does need cheering up, and perhaps I'm finally the woman to do it.

2

SHIRT MEMORIES

Bridger

You're only as good as your last hit.

Every singer knows this. Every actor, every writer—hell, *everyone* in the entertainment business should live and die by this mantra.

I've been hunting for a new hit for years.

It's December and we just wrapped another season of *Sweet Nothings*, so I spend the afternoon in my office overlooking Central Park, flipping through pages and more pages. Some of those pages are a script for a drama that has "streaming hit" written all over it. *Anti-Heroes Unleashed.* It's unputdownable. I lob in a call to the writer's agent and discuss terms.

I'd call that a very good nine-to-five, thank you very much.

But in this business, one good day does not make your career. I glance at the clock on the wall. I need to take off soon for an event. I'm honestly not sure I want to go to it, but that's most events. There's a chance, though, that David Fontaine could be there. If I could just grab a word with the guy...

His new show *The World Enough And Time* is blowing critics' minds. The darkly comic TV show about an ex-CIA agent gone undercover premieres this Thursday night.

I want our company to land his next show. *Badly*.

Snagging Fontaine would be a challenge—bigger than any I've encountered before, given his impressive resume, as well as his notorious pickiness. But I like to combat pickiness with patience. Fontaine doesn't stick with one production company for long—maybe because he hasn't found the right one.

Or maybe because the right one hasn't found him.

Yet.

My new intern, Jonathan, raps on my office door. Clears his throat. "Hi Mr. James."

"Come in. And, like I said, you can call me Bridger."

Jonathan strides over to my long wooden desk, waggles his iPad. "Thank you, Mr. James. I read *Savage Love* at lunch. I prepped my coverage for you."

"And?" I ask, leaning back in the chair, hoping he can get to the point soon. Yay or nay—that is all.

Jonathan swallows nervously. He does everything nervously. He'll never fucking last like that. But he's a friend of one of the producers at *Sweet Nothings*, and blah, blah, blah.

"I think the rising action is great," he says, fidgeting with the cuff of his shirt.

"The rising action?" I counter.

"The beginning...of the story," he explains, awkwardly.

"I'm familiar with what rising action is."

"And it's good," he says, then goes on for a full minute about what happens in *Savage Love*, and I want to interrupt, to tell him what an elevator pitch is, because the clock ticks ominously louder in my head, and I need to go home, shower, change, go for a walk, then get over to MoMA. Promised Ian I'd show up, and I always make good on my promises, no matter how distasteful I find events. "But I think it would be better if the love story started sooner," Jonathan says, finally finishing.

That snags my interest—the mention of the love story. I want a love story that grabs me by the throat.

"Remember this—the love story should always start sooner than you think," I say, then I stand and check my reflection in the window overlooking Central Park, assessing what I'm wearing. I'll change for the party when I'm home in a little bit. "You know what I want to find, though?"

"What, sir?" Jonathan asks.

"The next *Sweet Nothings*," I say, feeling the hunger for a hit deep in my gut. I won't stop hunting till I find it. "But we can't wait for a love story to start," I say, pausing to look at the wall clock, the ticking a reminder I need to go. "It needs to start right away."

Jonathan knits his brow. "Um, I'll keep looking, sir. I have lots of scripts to read this weekend," he says.

"Great," I say. Maybe he'll learn something here at my production company, Lucky 21. Maybe he won't.

But right now, I need to do the next thing on my list. Look sharp for tonight. I wish I enjoyed schmoozing. Dressing well covers how much I dislike it.

Once he leaves, I check the time again on my watch. It's six-thirty. My chest tightens, and it's borderline painful. I'm due at MoMA in an hour and a half. On my walk in Central Park, I can remind myself of why I show up at parties. Why I need to be present.

For the company. For the show. To do my job networking after hours.

I take off for my apartment in Gramercy Park, listening to a long-forgotten musical on the way, to numbers hardly anyone remembers or knows. Then, once I'm home, I strip out of my work clothes.

Under the scalding-hot stream of the shower, I picture the party tonight. The people who'll be there. The deals I need to massage. The things I'll say.

When I'm out of the shower and dried off, I head to my closet, review the rows of shirts, arranged by color. Blues, purples, pinks, greens, oranges.

I consider each one, as I put on black slacks, slip into wingtips. Then, I pick a new shirt. One I bought last week.

I look at my reflection on the closet door.

Huh. It does look good—this teal button-down.

3

MY DIRTY LITTLE SECRET

Harlow

On a cool December night, I enter the museum, check my coat, and follow the sign for *The Annual Silver and Gold* Sweet Nothings *Affair* in the sculpture gardens. You'd be hard-pressed to tell it's December since the outdoor heaters are working overtime to warm the air.

In seconds, my father spots me, heading straight for me by the fountain. He wraps his arm around me, dropping a kiss to my cheek.

"Hello, poppet, so good to see you," he says, then after we chat briefly about the traffic, the weather, how I look—*good, good, good*—he says, "Excellent. Now, there are people I want you to meet."

In no time, we chat briefly with Dominic Rivera, one of the actors on the show who loves art, then my father's introducing me to curators, educators, and auction house executives.

It would be overwhelming if I didn't grow up being introduced.

A woman with black braids in a stylish top knot and cat-eye glasses is a curator of expressionist art here. Her name is Amelie, and she meets my gaze with the particular intensity of someone about to cross-examine someone. *Me.*

"You want to work in the museum field?" she asks in a French accent.

"I'm considering it," I say, even though that's not entirely true. But she doesn't need to know I'm undecided. I don't know her.

She quizzes me about whether I consider myself an acolyte of the Marxist school of art history, the post-colonial one, or something else entirely.

"It's hard to imagine that social and economic circumstances don't influence the creation of art," I say, a response that would brand me a Marxist.

Except my dirty little secret is I study art because, gasp, I like art.

The shape of it, the look of it, the way beauty makes me feel.

But I'm supposed to like the *why* behind it. So I drop in terms like Feminist Marxism to show I paid attention in my theory classes. My grasp of the lingo seems to light up Amelie.

"Do you speak French?" she asks me in that language.

"I do. I studied there this past semester," I say, answering in French.

"Keep in touch then, Harlow," she says, then gives me her email, telling me to reach out if I need anything.

"I will," I say, smiling privately.

When Amelie catches the eye of someone she needs to chat with, I figure I'll make a lap or ten to find Bridger. I need to work on my theory of crushes now and their rate of decay.

Instead, when I spin around to look for him, I nearly bump into a silver fox. His arm is wrapped around a woman's waist, and he's laughing into her silky black hair.

"Oh, excuse me," I say quietly.

"No worries," the woman says with a laugh, then adds, "For the record, sometimes a sculpture is just a sculpture."

"Sometimes they are," I say, amiably. I don't want to make any little asides about Amelie or art history. That would be rude. I extend a hand. "Harlow Granger."

"Ah, Ian's daughter," she says, knowingly.

That's me. I used to be Felicity Dumont's daughter, but no one thinks of my mother anymore, of the worlds she built, the romance she captured in her tales of *Sweet Nothings*. "Yes, I'm *that* Granger," I say as brightly as I can, briefly touching the *I* on my necklace.

"I'm Allison Tanaka-Fontaine," she says, and instantly I recognize her last name—her husband's a sought-after TV writer. "I do some consulting for the museum. They wanted me here tonight," she says, apologetically, like she has to explain her presence here. She gestures to the man with her like she's about to introduce him, but he's peering toward the door.

"For what it's worth, I sometimes just like to look at art too."

I smile, feeling a strange kinship with her. "I'm the same," I say. "I like to look and to feel."

Her eyes twinkle. "Yes. I get that."

Then, they weave out of the party like spies, evading capture.

A few seconds later, Bridger walks into the gardens, adjusting the cuffs on his shirt.

He always does that at parties. Like his buttons could come undone.

Oh.

Oh my god.

That shirt. He's wearing teal. He's wearing the color I told him to buy. My breath catches, surely from the surprise of the shirt.

Not from anything else.

But my pulse spikes too. My mouth goes dry. I should have practiced what to say to him, but then Marxism happened, and now *he's* happening.

Chin up, heels on, I head to him, my stomach annoyingly cartwheeling with every click of my shoes on the concrete. Maybe it was foolish to think I could archive those feelings while I was a continent away. I kind of wish I could file them in a cabinet of the past. Because what the hell am I supposed to do with them *now*? But I don't turn around. I don't walk away. I go to him, needing the proximity to know for certain that this is happening all over again.

When I close in on him near the Picasso sculpture, he's scanning the place like a sniper, his gaze acquiring targets. There's an intensity to his blue eyes that's disarming. "Hi," I say to his side, and it comes out too breathy. Nearly inaudible.

"Hi Bridger," I say, trying again.

He startles, then shifts, his eyes landing on me. "Oh." There's a tinge of surprise in his tone. His gaze travels quickly, too quickly, along my body. "It's been a while," he says, recovering, arranging his voice to that even, professional tone I've known for five years.

"Yeah, it has been," I say, taking a breath to steady myself when I catch a whiff of his scent. Soap, something expensive, something organic, I bet. Something that touched his body an hour ago.

Something delicious.

The   scent   floats   through   my   nose, awakening...everything.

So much for time. So much for distance. So much for trying.

I'm not over him. Not at all.

"A long while," he adds.

Does he sound wistful, or do I just want him to sound wistful? "How are you?" I ask.

"How are *you*?" he counters, like he's avoiding the question. Or maybe like he's legit interested in how I am. A girl can hope.

"I'm good. I graduate in May. Six more months," I say, since what's more important than that? I'm *almost* out of here. Can I write it in the sky any clearer?

Bridger nods like he knew this already. "Ian did mention that," he says.

I wince, wishing he hadn't interjected my dad into

the conversation. But I'll just eject back out. "Paris was amazing. You've been, I presume?"

He nods. "I have. What made it amazing for you?"

Oh, that's nice. A question to keep the conversation going. "It was everything I'd hoped it would be," I say. "I had my own flat by the river. I sat in cafés drinking espresso and being broody as I read dark poetry."

That earns me a wry smile.

"And I lived at the museums and galleries."

"Sounds incredible. Those are terrific opportunities, dark poetry aside," Bridger says, like a man talking to someone who's *almost* his contemporary.

At least, I hope so. Or maybe I'm just reading things I want to hear into his words. Only, I don't want to talk about me any longer. My gaze drifts to the cuffs of his shirt. "I see you have silver cufflinks," I say. "Very subtle nod to the theme."

His eyes dart to my necklace then back to my face. "And gold for you."

A ribbon of warmth unfurls in me. He noticed. It's time to cut to the chase. "I heard you're not seeing Emma anymore," I say.

Bridger breathes out hard, a sigh, but it's nearly emotionless. "You heard right," he says, and he doesn't sound like a man who needs cheering up whatsoever. He sounds just fine.

"You seem content," I observe.

Bridger shrugs, one strong shoulder rising up. "We didn't have that much in common it turns out," he says, like it's just one of those things, no big deal.

"That's important, isn't it?" I ask, and I don't feel like

the girl who crashed into a cab six months ago. Or the one at the summer send-off party.

I feel like I was forged from Paris. Then I rose up from Chelsea. Once upon a time I was raised on Fifth Avenue, but I'm not the girl living in my father's house any longer.

"Common interests? Yes. They are," he says, emphatic, then glances around the open space, a little hamlet in the midst of the city. We're surrounded by stone and marble, by money and erudition. "So this must be good for you, art history and all?" He asks the question like he doesn't want to return to the party, like he'd rather talk to me.

Finally. I can read him.

I lean in closer, conspiratorially, stealing another hint of his cedar scent. "Can I confess something?"

He hums, a note of intrigue. "Sure," he says.

I tip my forehead toward the tree near us. We move around it, past its branches, farther away from the hubbub of people. He doesn't seem to mind getting some distance from the crowd. Perhaps this is a sign that the crush could be two-way.

No, that's too wild a thought.

But wouldn't that be something?

"What's your confession?" he asks, tugging on his cuffs again. Is that a nervous habit, maybe? Or perhaps an orderly one?

"I don't know what I want to do with my degree," I admit.

And wow. Did a weight lift from my shoulders? I think it did. I let out a surprised breath. "I..."

"First time you said that out loud?"

"Yes," I say, enthused, excited even to speak the words I was holding inside with the museum curator.

Everything feels lighter. "I don't know if I want to work at a museum, or visit a museum, or run an art gallery, or just wander into art galleries. I don't know at all," I say, then I glance away, worrying at the corner of my lips. "And I've been studying. I should know, shouldn't I?"

He shrugs casually. Gives an easy smile to match. "But *should* you?" It's like point, counterpoint.

His question is open-ended. He's asking. *Really* asking. So I really answer. "I feel that way a lot. I think I have some guilt over not knowing. Should I, Bridger?"

His dark eyes gleam, like he wants to share something. Wants to reveal. "Want to hear a secret?" That word on his tongue sends a charge through me.

I want to *be* his secret. "Tell me," I say, desperate for more.

"I didn't study business, or Econ, or even English lit like most people in my field," he says, and I feel like he's offering conversational appetizers on a platter.

I want to eat them all. "What did you study?"

"Psychology," he says. "And I'm not a therapist. I'm just...a producer."

"Just a producer. More like an entertainment industry force of nature," I tease.

A sly smile. He won't admit it in words, but that tilt of his lips says I'm right with my assessment. "But see, I'm not a psychologist. Sometimes you go into your field. Sometimes you don't. The key is learning to think.

That's what I learned in college. And how to strategize. Know what I mean?"

"I think I know what you mean. Strategy applies to any field. Thinking does too, of course," I add.

"Exactly," he says, with a satisfied smile.

"Then I hope I'm learning both," I say.

Maybe I can put them to use with him?

I hope, as we talk, that I'm being strategic with this crush that didn't end, that phoenixed out of the ashes tonight.

Bridger's eyes drift to the crowd. Something flashes in them. Reluctance? Annoyance? But mostly it looks like resignation. "I should talk to Jess Dudeck," he says, definitely resigned. "I'm supposed to work on a deal for Romania. There's a TV network there wanting to format the show," he explains. "That's when—" He shakes his head, a little embarrassed. "You don't want to know what formatting is."

"Actually, I know what formatting is. When they take the concept and adapt it for syndication in foreign countries," I say.

A smile. Like he should have known better. "Of course. You've always paid attention," he says, then his eyes drift down to his shirt, and since I'm pretty sure it's best to leave anyone wanting more, I find the will to go. But first, I lift a finger, run it briefly along the edge of his shirt collar. "Teal is your color," I say, then I walk away.

Floating.

Just absolutely floating on this crush that's come

slamming back into me. Only this time around, it feels like it could be more than a crush.

Maybe I need to put my strategy skills to use.

When I go to bed that night, it's blissfully quiet in my bedroom. My roomies are out. Here in Chelsea, in my sixth-floor apartment, I never have to worry about over-hearing my dad's affairs.

It's been a lovely week so far.

Quiet, most of the time, since my roomies are gone so often.

Almost like I'm living in the French countryside where my mom used to take me when I was younger.

I can sleep peacefully.

Except, I'm not tired at all. I'm wide awake, looking up shirts online.

When I'm done, I email Amelie, telling her it was nice to meet her, and I enjoyed our chat. I may not subscribe to the same points of view she had, but the talk was stimulating. Besides, you should thank someone who takes the time to ask about your inter-ests, then who offers to stay in touch. A vital business skill I learned from my father.

He's taught me a few things about strategy, I suppose.

* * *

A few days later, I'm meeting Layla and Ethan for lunch in the Village, so I make my way there early, stealing an opportunity to return to that boutique from last summer. I'm alone with Sondheim in my ears as I hunt through the men's shirts until I find one that speaks to me.

Ruby red.

I hold it against my chest, position it just so.

I snap another shot. Maybe there's a little more of me in it now. Just a hint of my throat, just enough skin to see the *I* on my necklace.

Then, I tap out a note: *Next time, try this color*, and I attach the photo.

He texts back a day later. One word.

Noted.

It's a nothing reply. It's nearly empty. But it feels like a bookmark. Like he's tracking my ideas, marking where we left off.

Somehow that's enough to carry me through the next few days of the winter break.

Trouble is, there's no chance I'll run into Bridger here in Chelsea. I won't bump into him in the kitchen, or the dining room, or the living room like I did during that summer break.

So when my father drops the news out of the blue that he and Joan called the wedding off, *and* he's taken up charcuterie, then invites me to a dinner party—all in the same email—I think strategically and say yes.

4

MUCH TO THE CHAGRIN

Harlow

The problem with the dinner is my father thinks he's a matchmaker.

I sweep into Dad's home with olives and cheese—because a polite guest brings a gift, even if she's the daughter of the host—and Dad tugs me aside and whispers, even though we're the only ones around, "Vivian would be perfect for Bridger."

He says it like he can't believe how fantastic this idea is.

When it's awful.

Why is he doing this? Is this because he left Joan last week? Or maybe Joan left him—he never clarified who was the leaver and who was the leavee. But he's keeping busy like *this*?

"Vivian as in the new junior agent at Astor Agency?" I ask, hunting for a believable reason why

Vivian is bad news for Bridger. Astor is Dad's lit agent for his solo writing, like the novels he's written in the *Sweet Nothings* world. None of his books have ever hit as big as the ones my mother penned—the ones Dad and Bridger launched to worldwide fame.

"Yes. Good memory," he says.

"Is it a good idea to hook Bridger up with someone at your agency?"

"Why not?" Dad asks breezily, like he can't conceive it wouldn't be.

Because he can't. Because Dad hasn't a care in the world. He's rich, he's good-looking, he's brilliant. He wants for nothing. He doesn't even have the decency to miss his newest ex-fiancée.

But I can't let this match happen. "Doesn't she also rep one of the writers on your show? Isla, I think?" I ask, a little desperately. But as arguments go, *conflict of interest* seems pretty valid.

"Even better," Dad says brightly. "More they have in common."

Dammit. Foiled.

"Just seems risky," I add, trying to mask my irritation, maybe failing.

"Harlow," he chides gently. "Remember what I've always told you?"

I seethe. As if I could ever forget the instructions he gave me long ago when he said: *Darling, I know you're trying to be helpful, but it's better you don't get involved. Roselyn doesn't need to know about my guests. It'll only upset the delicate balance of an adult relationship.*

I certainly won't step on his matchmaking toes tonight.

He grabs a fresh wooden board from the counter. "This arrived today from Sur La Table. You can help set it up. You have such a good eye."

And that's that. The match will be made. The food will be displayed.

And I, evidently, have an eye for arranging food. That's what my double major in French and art is all about. But I put that eye to use as I attractively arrange the olives and cheese on the wooden board, next to the grapes and crackers.

When the guests arrive a few minutes later, I deeply regret agreeing to dinner.

This is hell. I have to sit through this meal while my dad plays matchmaker with the pretty young agent.

Vivian's attractive in a standard New York City entry-level-professional sort of way—straight brown hair clipped back, a black sweater, chandelier earrings, and trendy boots.

As my dad circulates with a board of figs, nuts, and cheese, she makes small talk in the living room with Bridger about the supposed golden age of TV, and how the entertainment business is blessed with so many options these days.

Boring.

He seems to listen intently, but he says little, maybe because she talks a lot. He wears his five-o'clock shadow like a 1950s ad exec, and he looks like he spends his working hours on the phone, talking, negotiating, wooing. He also sports pressed black pants and a shirt the shade of a ripe raspberry.

But it's not the one I told him to wear and that pisses me off too.

After ample praise from his guests for his charcuterie skills, my father heads to the kitchen to assemble an encore, nodding not so subtly for Vivian to follow him.

Naturally, I follow, too, a few steps behind.

No one notices I'm there. Dad taught me to be invisible when it comes to adult affairs, so I use that to my advantage as I beautify the board.

"What do you think, Vivian? Is he the bloke for you?" Dad asks her.

Jaw ticking, I listen as I layer figs.

"Well, what's not to like? He's handsome, well-educated, and he's making bank. He could be the one," she says. I want to tackle her. Who cares if Bridger has money?

I damn well plan on making my own money when I am out of school. I don't intend to be dependent on anyone else's wallet. Besides, love shouldn't be about what someone makes. It should be about how someone makes you feel.

"There you go," my dad says, chipper.

I hate my father all over again, in a fresh, new, feral way.

But I try to tamp down my anger as the man of the matchmaking hour walks into the kitchen to pour himself another iced tea. Bridger helps himself to a pitcher from the fridge, and after he fills up his glass, he spies the board I'm finishing. He plucks an olive from the center.

After he bites into one, he rolls his eyes in pleasure. "Olives are my guilty pleasure," he says to me.

Yes. To me.

Take that, Vivian.

"Don't feel guilty about pleasure," I say, flashing a smile his way.

Vivian edges up to the board. "I better try one too," she says, then bats her lashes, reaching for an olive as well. There's a competitive tone, even a territorial one, in her declaration.

Something flames up in me—a thick plume of jealousy as she sets a hand possessively on his forearm.

Get off him.

But immediately, deep shame washes over me. He's not mine. I need to stop entertaining this crush with my supposed *strategy*.

I need to stop feeding it.

I need to stop feeding it, or it will never die.

All through dinner, I fasten on a proper smile and I play the adult game, talking to everyone else.

Not Bridger. Not Vivian. Not Dad. Just the three other guests, until finally, they're gone. Vivian is the last, waving at Bridger as she leaves.

"Good night, Vivian," he says, evenly. It's a friendly tone, one I instantly recognize. It's the way he spoke to me after my crash. Then at the send-off party. It's the way he's talked to me since I've known him.

Until the party the other week, when we stole behind the tree and he asked me questions.

When the door snicks shut, Vivian's gone. It's just the three of us, so I slide into chore mode along with the two business partners. As we ferry dishes to the kitchen, my dad gives a big-eyed look to Bridger.

"So, what did you think of her?"

Bridger gives an *I'm going to let you down* smile. "I'm not sure we're the right fit," he says.

Yes! Yes! Yes!

"I wasn't suggesting you get married," Dad says with a laugh.

"What's wrong with marriage, Ian?" Bridger counters, baiting my dad as he returns to the table to pick up stray forks and glasses.

I hope this clean-up lasts forever. I'm dying to hear the details.

"I suppose it's fine for some people, but I don't think of *you* as the marrying kind," Dad says, now loading the dishwasher as I rinse the plates.

"If she were right for me, maybe I'd be the marrying kind," Bridger says to my dad, a teasing note in his voice as he hands me a plate to rinse.

I take it, giddy to hear him talk so freely. I stay silent so they'll keep going.

"So when you meet the right woman, you'll be down on one knee?" Dad asks him.

Just like you, Daddy.

"I guess we'll see when I meet her," Bridger answers.

"Okay, mate. What are you looking for in a bird?"

Bird. Jesus. I stop biting my tongue, chiming in at last. "Dad, maybe consider saying 'woman.'"

"Young people. Always so PC," he says with an eye roll as he closes the dishwasher.

"It's not PC to call a woman a woman," I correct.

"What is it then?"

"The way you *should* talk, Ian," Bridger says decisively.

"See?" I retort with a cocky tilt of my head.

Dad laughs like he's just so amused by me. "Send them to college, this is what happens." He turns his full focus back on Bridger. "Good thing for Lucky 21 that you and I aren't the same generation," he says.

No kidding. Dad's in his late forties. Bridger is thirty. His birthday's in late March.

"Why's that, Ian?" Bridger asks.

"Gives us an edge that you're younger, since you know how people should talk these days," Dad says.

"You could learn too," Bridger counters, and wow. That's hot, how he talks to my dad, standing his ground. "And that might also be why we have different ideas of what makes a relationship work, Ian," he says, smirking, perhaps a sign that he knows more than the industry knows about my dad. It's no secret he's been married four times. But I'm not sure his philandering ways are common knowledge. But Bridger must know.

What does he think of my father's affairs? He can't possibly condone them.

"What makes a relationship work, then?" Dad asks, reaching for an open bottle of wine from the kitchen counter and pouring the rest into a fresh glass. "Shared interests? Common beliefs? A little humor?" He asks as if those are totally unbelievable.

Bridger leans against the counter, scratches his jaw. It's a power move, casually gearing up to win this poke-prod debate with my father. "All that," he says, then takes a beat before he delivers the punch, "and knowing all the lyrics to every song in *Ask Me Next Year*."

I swallow a gasp.

He says that last line with a wry smile.

I'd told myself my crush was over. I'd almost tricked myself into believing it. But inside, I thrill at the words. *I* know all the lyrics to the musical *Ask Me Next Year*.

Every single one in every single song.

Does Bridger know that?

Is that comment for me?

Dad laughs. "You win this round. You and your show tunes. You know, Harlow is a Broadway baby. She loves all musicals," he says, then checks his watch. "Need to make a call."

On that, he breezes out of the room, down the hall, and out of sight.

I don't move a muscle. I'm still vibrating here in the kitchen. Finally, I look up at Bridger, meeting his inky-blue gaze.

There's no strategy, only instinct as I, almost under my breath, repeat the chorus to the bittersweet ballad in the show.

"He Can't Be Mine."

Bridger turns to me slowly. "What did you just say?" His question comes out quieter than the dark night.

But I don't utter those words of longing again.

Instead, I say, "It played for two months in 1998." I'm

warm everywhere as my heart climbs into my throat. My insides are spinning. I'm sure my feelings are tattooed across my face, living, breathing ink marks saying *I have it bad for you.*

"And hasn't been revived since, much to the chagrin of musical theater diehards everywhere," he says, and his eyes sparkle as he stares at me with...wonder.

"Yes. Much to the chagrin," I add.

I can't stay this close to him without revealing everything, so I retreat to the living room and open a book I left on the coffee table the last time I was here. But the pages are full of drunk lines weaving in front of me. I can't concentrate. I'm tipsy just being near him.

5

SOME MORE SOME TIME

Bridger

I'm not thinking of her that way.

I'm not thinking of my business partner's daughter like that. I'm not feeling a thing for her.

But for the first time ever, across the living room, drinking my iced tea, I am.

I'm looking at her like...she's not his daughter.

I'm noting her, every detail. Lush chestnut hair, pink lips, a delicate throat. Pale skin.

Her green eyes are flecked with gold. Have they always been flecked like that? Has her skin always been so creamy? Her red sweater hugs her chest, and her jeans meld to her legs. She's tall in those black boots with a zipper up the side.

Was she always tall? Always lithe?

I don't even know. I probably shouldn't know.

But I know this—my chest is painfully tight, like

someone's turning a key in a jack-in-the-box, over and over. Tightening me. This feeling can't be healthy. This must be heartburn. Or a panic attack?

Except it's not.

It's something else.

Something all too familiar.

Something I know well. Something I shouldn't feel for Ian's daughter.

I desperately want to be unaffected by her clever reply, I absolutely want to let the hopeful note in it slide right off me like I do a thousand comments about a thousand things every day. But she's no longer the girl on the bike who I took to the ER one day last summer.

She's Harlow.

A...woman who likes the same obscure musical I do. A woman who chose her major for the same reason I did. A woman who isn't fooled by bullshit at parties.

I shouldn't say another thing to her.

I really shouldn't.

But the words take shape in my mouth as curiosity fills all my cells, and I do it anyway.

I toss back the next line in the *Ask Me Next Year* song, a question. "Wasn't it time?"

What are they even asking about in the song? What's the *it*? I don't know. I don't actually care. All I know is that the song makes me feel. Makes my chest ache.

Harlow looks up from her book, her lips parted. Her eyes are full of intrigue.

Then, like we're tangoing, she takes the next step, speaking the next line in the song. "Isn't it now?"

I heat up.

Stop. Just stop.

Instead, I ask, "What if it's all a dream?"

She exhales, a long, lovely note of excitement. Her cheeks flush pink. In a whisper, she utters, "But he can't be mine."

Words to live by.

I tear myself away from these forbidden thoughts. I swallow down my desire. "Yeah, so that's a good musical," I say roughly, then I make my excuses, saying I have an early run along the East River.

What the hell? Am I actually explaining my schedule?

"Have a good one," she says, and I bolt.

I walk home, counting the steps until thoughts of her are buried so deep you'd need an archaeological dig to excavate them.

I hope.

I fucking hope.

* * *

A few days later, I'm running along the East River Greenway. My nose is ice, and my hair is as cold as a tundra.

But it's a habit. So I go, and I run, and I refuse to think of things I shouldn't think of.

Of people I shouldn't picture.

Instead, I review the day ahead. I have a meeting with Ian at the office at nine-thirty. We need to discuss the plans for our newest *Sweet Nothings* spin-off—*After-*

noon Delight. Then, I have a conference call with our London office. After that, I'll dive into scripts, maybe make some more progress on the Fontaine situation.

Somewhere around Eighteenth Street, a voice calls out from behind me, mingling with the sound of pedals pumping and wheels whooshing. "Good morning."

And just like that, the ice age ends. Heat zaps down my spine.

I turn my gaze, slow my running pace. She slows her bike too, then stops near me. I pull up short.

Harlow smiles my way, sensual and indulgent. "Who would have thought you owned something besides pants and perfect business shirts?" she says, her breath imprinting on the morning air.

I try to keep the tone light. Keep it safe. "Can't burn off all those olives wearing a dress shirt," I joke. Joking has to help.

"Maybe don't burn them off," she says, then shudders as she tugs her sleeves down lower. Thank god it's too cold to talk for long. "I can bring you some more sometime."

Olives. She's talking about olives. But she's also talking about more. Momentarily, I let myself forget who she is. I let the ties that bind us fade away.

"Castelvetrano, please," I say.

"Noted," she says with a devilish smirk that turns into a smile.

I can't linger on it. I have to run. "Bye, Harlow," I say, then I resume my jog.

She pumps the pedals then pulls ahead of me. "Bye, Bridger," she calls out as she rides well past me, and my name on her lips sounds too good in the cold New York morning.

Too good to mention to her dad, in fact.

A few hours later, when I see Ian, I don't mention my encounter with his daughter.

My pulse isn't surging anymore, so why bring it up?

I don't say a word when it happens again a few weeks later.

I'm cruising by the United Nations headquarters, listening to Cole Porter, when a flash of silver blurs past me.

Then she slows, whips around, doubling back. She finishes her three-sixty by my side, wheeling along. "Hi, morning runner," she says from her perch on her silver Trek.

Is she here on purpose? For me?

The possibility thrums enticingly through me. But that makes no sense. Harlow couldn't be interested in me. Harlow's younger than me, the world at her feet. It's foolish to think she's intentionally riding at the same time as me on a path that runs up and down the city. Bumping into her is simply a New York coincidence. A city of eight million breeds coincidence. That is all.

"Good morning...*rider*," I say.

She turns the wheels slowly, keeping pace with me as I go. "You don't miss a run, do you?"

"I don't know, Harlow. Maybe I missed the last few weeks," I say, almost, *almost* suggestively.

Ah, fuck.

That was a flirting 101 mistake. Now she'll know I'm

aware that I haven't seen her. She'll know I've noticed when she's here, and I've noticed, too, when she's not.

When I shouldn't notice her at all.

"You missed your morning workout?" She tsks me. "Such a truant."

Glad she didn't latch onto my subtext. "Yes. That's me," I say lightly. Friendly.

"Hmm. I'm not sure you're a truant, though," she says, like she's musing on who I am. "I bet you're here every morning. On the dot. Like a religion." She takes a beat, her eyes twinkling. "Am I right?"

She's more than right. She's also more than friendly. *I think.* "Why do you say that?"

"You seem...let's just say, *the type*," she says, her tone confident, like a woman who knows what she wants.

The type. She's already pegging my type. Okay, let's do this. "What's my type?"

"The type of guy who works out every morning," she retorts, and a prickle of awareness slides down my spine. The sensation of being...known.

Then her gaze slides to my right arm. I'm wearing a long-sleeve workout shirt, but the cuffs are pushed up, showing some of my ink. "You have a tattoo," she says, pleased, like she's just unearthed a discovery.

"Yeah," I say, and this feels so personal. Not the ink —the talking about it. I'm not sure if I should talk about it with her. Hell, I'm not sure about anything right now, especially how to volley with Harlow. Conversing with Ian's daughter alone is a game, and I don't have the rulebook. I'm playing in the dark, so I improvise. "Don't you go to college downtown?"

"I do. Are you asking why I'm riding *here,* along the East River, instead of near where I live?"

Jesus. Could I be more transparent that I'm fishing for intel? *Like, have you been looking for me every morning like I've been looking for you?* I need to get a fucking handle on myself around her. "I guess I am asking that," I admit, but I stop there. Giving nothing more away. I need to figure out the rules to this flirting game, stat.

"I don't like traffic. Don't you remember?" But she's really asking, *How could you forget?*

That was shortsighted of me. She broke her ankle in Manhattan traffic seven months ago. I can't believe I thought she was riding here for any other reason than emotional necessity. "Have you avoided the streets on your bike since last summer?"

"When I can," she says, tone straightforward, not shirking away from the accident, just dealing with some kind of PTSD from that crash. "I don't want to take a chance."

"I'm sorry, Harlow. That's rough."

"It's okay. Life happens, right?" There's more to that remark, much more to unpack.

For now, I give a simple answer so I don't make another mistake with her. "It sure does."

"But it's safer here anyway," she says, her lips curving up again, a hint of a smile teasing me. "Because what are the chances a man in purple will save the day again?"

Her smile blooms fully.

The temperature in me spikes. I breathe out hard.

Harder than before. I wish it were the exertion. I wish I weren't thinking these thoughts about her.

And yet, my mind is wandering to so many places. My eyes will give it away.

I tear my gaze away from her and quietly say, "Let's hope you don't need that again."

There. That's...safe.

And I can look at her once more. When I do, she's glancing down at the phone in its holder on her handlebars. "I have French class in thirty minutes," she says.

I knit my brow. "I thought you were fluent."

"I am. But there's always something to learn so I'm taking French lit now."

"You know *Afternoon Delight* takes place there? In Paris," I add, in case she doesn't follow the details of our *Sweet Nothings* spin-off.

She's all Mona Lisa as she says, "I know, Bridger. I know."

I heat up again. Is it January or June? "Of course you know," I say.

A playful shrug. "But French lit waits for no one."

"French lit," I say, with a low whistle of admiration. "Enjoy."

"*J'aime toujours la littérature*," she says, and even though I don't know French, I get the gist of her reply.

I also like the way the words sound on her tongue.

Something I shouldn't like at all.

She tosses one more smile my way—I tell myself it's just a friendly one—then presses hard against the pedals and blurs off.

I should look away as she rides. Stare at the river. Gaze at the buildings. But I watch Harlow until she blends into the rest of New York on a cold morning in late January.

* * *

When I walk into McCoy's restaurant in midtown that afternoon to discuss *Afternoon Delight* with Ian, I feel like I have the start of a secret.

A dangerous one that would destroy our business if anything came of it.

Good thing my poker face is legendary.

6

MAYBE ACCOMPLICES

Harlow

On a Tuesday morning in April, I'm stretching in bed, alternating between texting my cousin Rachel about my upcoming trip to visit her and my aunt in San Francisco, and texting Layla and Ethan about my twenty-first birthday plans, when my phone pings with an email from my father requesting that I go shopping this afternoon—*to help him*—which can only mean one thing.

I'm both shocked and not.

I tell my friends I have to go, then I get out of bed and call my brother in London. He's the only one I can talk to right now.

Hunter answers right away on FaceTime, walking down a busy street in Bloomsbury, where he lives. Still dazed, still reeling, I wander to my apartment kitchen to start a pot of tea. "You won't believe what Dad asked me to do," I say.

He snorts. "Bet I will."

"Go shopping for jewelry," I hiss, incredulous.

Hunter cringes. "Are you bloody serious?"

"I'm deathly serious." I turn on the kettle, like all these routine actions will shake the surprise of the request away.

"Did you say yes?"

"Yes," I say heavily and then lean against the counter. "I feel like I should help," I admit, a little ashamed.

There's no shade from my brother. "I get it," he says with sympathy.

"How long do you think this one will last?" I ask as I spoon loose-leaf tea into a pot.

"It'll be what? His fifth?" Hunter asks, though he knows. Of course he knows.

Hunter's mom was his first wife. My mom was his second. Since she died nine years ago, he's been married twice and almost married—to Joan—once. But it's not the trips to the altar that matter so much; it's the mileage on the side. I've lost track of those affairs.

I sigh. "And I doubt this one will last. But I'll be the good daughter."

"You always are."

"I mean, what choice is there?" I ask, waving a hand around to my apartment. "He pays my rent. He pays my tuition. He pays for my life."

"You should go," Hunter says, resigned.

"I should," I say, remembering one of the letters my

mom wrote to me when I was younger. It's in the wooden box I keep with me here in Chelsea.

Sometimes, after Mom and I had a fun or interesting or unusual day together, she'd write me a letter and leave it on my pillow at night. So much better than anything from the tooth fairy ever was. Mom's pillow letters were unexpected little gifts, chronicling the day. I recall one in particular.

Dear Harlow,

Can I tell you a secret?

We were walking home from the store today, and we neared an older woman, hunched over, pushing a grocery trolley— one of those stand-up silver trolleys you only see in New York. Her oranges spilled out. Plunk, plunk, plunk. They rolled straight into the gutter. It was raining too. You ran ahead and handed her our oranges. "Here you go."

She thanked you and took the oranges. We continued on our way, and you were happy to have helped at that moment.

Here's a secret—you'll usually want to help. That's a natural reaction. But so often we don't know the kind of help someone requires. Other times, we offer the wrong kind, or the person refuses it.

But every now and then, the help we give is the help someone needs.

. . .

She's right. I just never thought that advice would apply
to my father, asking me to help pick out jewelry for his
fifth wife.

* * *

Later that day, I head into Katherine's on Fifth Avenue.
The store is sparkling with jewels and metal on every
one of its five floors.

My dad waits for me by the engagement rings. He's
bouncing with excitement by a display of Canadian
diamonds, the placards proudly touting in scripted font
that these stones are conflict-free.

He points to a pear-shaped solitaire. "Ethical
diamonds. Do you think Vivian will like it?"

I have no idea what she'll like. No idea whether she
cares about how diamonds are mined or if he's buying
an ethical one to impress me, since he knows that I
care. "Yes. It's lovely."

That's not a lie. Truly, it's a stunning ring.

"I'll propose this weekend. I want everyone who
matters at a party after. Will you come?" he asks, so
earnest, so real.

I matter to him.

And really, when I add up all he's done for me—the
bruised knees he tended to, the essays he read, the
dinners he supplied, the tuition bills he's paid—I
swallow my discomfort, and I say yes.

So does the object of my father's matchmaking. The woman he wanted to set up with his business partner accepts the ring when Dad proposes to her later that week, in Central Park, by the Conservatory Gardens, with a string quartet playing and a photographer capturing it all.

* * *

On Saturday night, I give myself a pep talk as I walk up Park Avenue, a box of fine chocolate in hand.

In another month, I'll graduate from college. I'll be on my own. Maybe my dad's affairs won't bother me then. Maybe it'll be easier to look the other way, like I've done for so long.

Like I'll do tonight, when I smile and say *congratulations.*

When I pretend he's not addicted to women.

One more night. Pretending.

I take a deep, fortifying breath, then it's showtime when I walk into Ava's Bistro, heading to the private room for the Granger party.

There, I see Bridger, his evening stubble lining his chiseled jaw, his forest-green shirt hugging his biceps. He's giving a bouquet of purple gerbera daisies to the happy couple. Vivian takes them, hugs them to her chest, then smiles magnificently at her fiancé's business partner.

My father claps Bridger on the back affectionately, then shifts his focus to another set of guests as Vivian sets down the flowers on a table.

Bridger spins around, searching, and—I hope —finding what he wants when his gaze lands on me.

For a few breath-held seconds, there's delight in his dark blue eyes. Like he's glad I'm here. Like I'm that person you glom onto when you don't want to talk to anyone else.

He's that person for me.

I take a step closer, caught up in him. He nods toward the flowers. His eyes darken. "Your favorite," he says, a tease of a smile on his lips.

My heart slams against my ribs.

He got them for *them*. But really, they're for me.

Could this be what I've been looking for? The sign I've been hoping to find on this flirtation road?

The man remembered my favorite flowers from months ago. "They are," I whisper, my voice feathery as I corroborate his observation. "Maybe I'll take them home tonight."

"Maybe you should."

Maybe we are accomplices. Maybe we both need this complicit escape from the madhouse of my father's engagement. Maybe it's not just me.

I don't look elsewhere. I don't care if I'm giving away what's happening inside me when I look at him, when I'm near him.

I tingle all over, then one more time when he makes the next move, asking, "How was your day?"

"It was good," I say. "How was yours?"

"Not bad. I went for a run," he says, with a wink in his tone.

I light up. "I went for a ride," I say.

I don't say the next thing—*I didn't see you.*

But I know what he's not saying.

I didn't see you either, Harlow. I looked for you. My days are better when I run into you.

My vague daydreams about him don't feel so vague any longer. They feel possible. And I know, in this second, it's time to make a plan.

7

DEBRIEFING THE CREW

Harlow

The benefit of Layla attending school in New York City too comes a few days later when she, Ethan and I are able to meet at a trendy new falafel shop on the upper edge of Manhattan.

I count down the hours all day until I can see them. Until I can tell them. I'm giddy to share with my best friends the plan I've concocted.

When I arrive at seven, I could burst with the details, but I've held in this secret for so long already. I can wait till I find just the right opening in the evening.

Once I'm inside, I spot Ethan. He's corralled a high-top table by the window, and he's as sharp as ever in jeans, a red Henley, and deliberately messy brown hair. "This is the best people-watching spot in the neighborhood," he says as I join him, kissing his cheek.

"Good. And nice beard," I say approvingly, patting his new scruff.

"Thanks. It works," he says, with a casual shrug.

"On everyone, I bet," I say.

He answers with *you know it* eyes.

Seconds later, Layla sails in, looking like a pinup, even in jeans and a polka-dot high-neck blouse.

Once she's seated, the server swings by, and I order a bubbly water, while Ethan asks for a martini and Layla a mojito. The server checks their IDs, then, satisfied, says he'll be back soon.

"The cocktails here are fantastic," Ethan adds as the server walks away.

"And yet you ordered the most boring drink," Layla says drily, chiding him.

"Please. Who ever said martinis were boring?" he asks with an eye roll.

"I say it," Layla retorts, and I half want to tell them to stop ping-ponging because I have *news*, but I also love to watch their verbal games. I always have. So I let myself enjoy the show as a spectator. There will be time to share soon enough.

"Because mojitos are *un-dull*?" he asks, with an arch of his brow.

"Mojitos are sexy," she declares, then licks her red lips, because of course Layla wears red lipstick.

Ethan shoots her a doubtful stare. "So let me get this straight. You think some gorgeous guy is going to pick you up because you ordered a mojito?"

Layla shrugs playfully. "Studies have shown mojitos attract older men."

He cracks up. "Well, then. Bring on the silver foxes," he says, then turns to me, an expectant look in his hazel eyes. He drums his hands on the table, like he's playing my walk-up song. "So, what do you want for your big day?"

"Let me guess. What every Upper East Sider wants," Layla says. "Access to the first level of her trust fund."

"But of course," I laugh, since they know how mine is set up—some of it I can access this year, but most of it when I'm twenty-five. Hunter's is the same way, though his payout on his twenty-first birthday was modest, so I'm not banking on these funds. Besides, I want to be my own woman. Make my own money. "Anyway, you know I just want to hang out with my favorite people on Saturday night," I tell them.

Layla squeezes my arm affectionately. "And Saturday night is all about you, Harlow. But will you even be able to stay up past your bedtime?"

Yes, I'm the Goody Two-shoes of the group. "Gosh, I sure hope so."

The server swings by with our drinks, and we thank him. When he's gone, we toast to twenty-one, then we recap our plans for my birthday. We're rounding up friends from Carlisle Academy, friends from college, friends from Layla and Ethan's various summer internships.

"First, we'll do dinner at J," Layla says, then shudders in excitement. "I think my mother's lawyer sold his soul to get us that rezzie."

"J is only the hottest new restaurant in the city. Have

you seen pics of the head chef?" Ethan asks, like the chef is the height of gossip.

"Tattoos and wild hair? The one who looks like the ultimate fuck boy?" Layla asks.

"As all good hot chefs should," Ethan says.

"Yes, I've seen his social." Layla mouths *yum*. "So, after we check out the chef, we'll head to Edge in SoHo."

"I got us on the VIP list," Ethan adds.

Seriously. My friends are the best. "I love you guys," I say with a happy sigh. Then, I can't hold it in any longer. "I have something to tell you."

They're both focused on me instantly, eyes wide, chins propped on hands.

Butterflies wing through me, and I sip my fizzy water. Then, like the star in a heist flick assembling the crew for a job, I say, "So, I had this idea for what I want to do this summer..."

I lay it all out, and when I've given them the blueprint, I eagerly ask, "What do you think?"

Layla blows out a long, appreciative breath, shaking her head in admiration.

Ethan stands, then goes full supplicant and bows before me. "I'm not worthy."

"Stahp, stahp," I say, but I feel like a rock star.

"So, when will you do this?" Layla inquires.

Not soon enough.

I gulp. "I'll ask tomorrow. I know where to find him. I'll even bring my own cake."

I have my birthday wish already planned.

8

DEFINITELY MOSTLY THE LINE

Bridger

Back in high school, when I hunkered down devouring books in my local library, I never imagined that more than a decade later, I'd be inking a deal for pretty perfume.

But I suppose it makes a strange sort of sense.

As a teenager, I loved books. Now, perfume may help sell a love story.

Lately, my life revolves around stories and scents.

On a Friday morning, I'm reviewing the terms of a partnership with a perfume company in Paris. Their eau de toilette will feature in an *Afternoon Delight* episode, and then the perfumer will release an *Afternoon Delight*-branded scent.

Smells like spice and seduction, the company has said.

After one last read, I send the contract to legal, then there's a rap on my door.

Probably Ian, since we have a meeting in ten minutes, but as I set my reading glasses on my desk, Jules, my new admin, walks in. She started as an intern and moved her way up, and she's packed with precision.

"Good morning, Bridger," she says quickly. She's never called me Mr. James.

"How's it going, Jules?" I ask, but she has nearly less patience for small talk than I do.

"I have the research you asked for on *Anti-Heroes Unleashed*. And some questions about Parisian locations for *Afternoon Delight*," she says, since the show is set there. "I sent them to your reading folder."

"Great. I'll look at them shortly." I glance at the clock. "Once I finish the meeting with Ian."

She nods crisply. "I also sent you coverage of *Plays Well With Others*, a novel by Hazel Valentine. I read it last night."

"And?"

"The love story starts right away." With that, she gives me a small smile. By now she knows what I want.

"Excellent."

"You get some football, some lessons in seduction, an interesting take on fake dating. It's definitely worth a look," she says.

"Good elevator pitch."

"It's sexy and sharp," she finishes, then nods again, like a cadet ready to turn on a West Point heel and go.

I hear a throat clearing in the hall, then a warm, English voice saying, "Did someone say sexy and sharp?"

Ian strides into my office and beams at Jules, who repeats the succinct pitch for him. "Sounds promising," he says.

She sees herself out, and once she's down the hall, he points at her. "She's a good admin."

I narrow my eyes. "Hands off, Ian." What he does after hours is his business. I just don't want *his* business interfering with *ours*.

He scoffs. "Please." He settles on my couch grandly, spreading out and setting his feet on the low coffee table. I wish he wouldn't do that. He knows that. It's not a table for feet. "I'm practically married already. You don't have to worry about me." He taps his fingers on the back of the gray cushion, like he's prepping to make a point. "As a matter of fact, Vivian and I are scouting for wedding venues this weekend in Connecticut. Checking out little inns and such."

That has to be pure Vivian. Ian would never get married at an inn when there are Yale Clubs, and posh hotels, and Michelin restaurants that host nuptials. "A B&B, Ian? That's not your style," I say, then add drily, "You must really like her."

He beams. "She's the one," he says.

"Glad to hear," I say, meaning it. I hope his new romance is everything he truly needs.

Vivian was wrong for me, but apparently, she's the woman of his dreams. Or so Ian tells me. I've heard that from him a few times before. Heard it about Joan. I heard it about Mariana, his fourth wife. I heard it retrospectively about Felicity too, from him, years later. How her death after a brief and unexpected battle with illness nearly destroyed him. How close he was after that to the edge of…well, life.

But I didn't know Ian in the aftermath. I met him a few years after he'd started to pick up the pieces again. I think he mostly did.

Mostly.

Definitely *mostly.*

Either way, his affairs are absolutely not my business.

But his shoes are, and I can't stand looking at the bottoms of them. I'm about to ask him to get his feet off the table, when he says, "But I don't leave till tomorrow." Then he smiles, a little conspiratorially. "Which is good, because I want to give Harlow a present before I go."

In no time, the clip of my heart increases.

I try to breathe normally. I fight off the images of Harlow that flick before my eyes. From his engagement party. The way she looked at me when she realized I'd remembered her favorite flowers. The way my chest fluttered annoyingly.

But what did I expect? I gave her flowers, and my blood went hot.

I shouldn't bother him about shoes when I'm thinking of his daughter like this.

"Oh yeah?" I ask, as nonchalant as I've ever sounded in my life.

"I got her a fantastic gift," he says, and I don't even need to ask him what it is. He proceeds to tell me.

My eyes pop. "Wow. That's extravagant."

He shrugs, but his smile's too big to hide his excitement. "Well, fine. It's really from Felicity," he says, but as if that detail hardly matters—that the big gift comes from his dead wife's books. Then he blinks, staring at his shoes. "Bollocks. Sorry, mate," he says, swinging his feet off the table. "Forgot."

He sounds genuinely contrite.

"It's fine," I mumble.

"Anyway, at least Harlow still likes me. Hunter, on the other hand," he says, shaking his head, frustrated perhaps that his son used to work on our show, then quit recently. "But girls are easier."

I would have no idea. And certainly, I have no comment on his parenting. I just have no comment.

No thoughts. No feelings. Nothing.

Ian's knee bounces. "I'll give it to her when I take her out to sushi tonight. She's going out with her friends tomorrow night for her official big day. *Of course.*"

He says it like she couldn't do anything else for her twenty-first birthday. Like *kids today*.

My jaw tics. Images of her dancing, laughing, flirting taunt me. She'll be out on the town with people her age, looking beautiful and young and tempting. Her hair swishing, her lips bee-stung, her eyes inviting.

A pang of jealousy stabs me in the chest.

I should really take up yoga.

Something. Anything.

Maybe learning to let go of my *no feet on tables* rule would be a start.

"I'm sure she'll have fun," I say, vaguely, distantly, because I should not—I really should not—have an opinion, let alone a visceral reaction about Harlow's birthday plans.

Jules knocks on the door again, pokes her head in, her brown eyes all business. "Your daughter's here," she says to Ian.

I flinch. I must have heard that wrong.

But Ian is beaming. "Fantastic. Send her in," he says. Then he turns to me as he rises. "That's a surprise. I didn't think I'd see her till tonight."

Yeah, it really fucking is a surprise. I push back in my chair. "I'll let you two—" but of course he's in *my* office.

And seconds later, so is Harlow. She's dressed in trim, black pants. Tight, but fashionable and still businesslike. Short black heels. A steel gray blouse—tough but feminine at the same time. Her lush chestnut hair is cinched tightly in a clip.

Her long, graceful neck is dangerous to my pulse. I want to touch the *I* on her chain, the skin beneath it.

I clench my fists.

"Sweetheart," he says, then brings her in for an embrace.

"Hi, Daddy," she says.

That's odd. Something about the way she just said *hi, Daddy* sounds a little...intentionally sweet.

And yet still sexy. Too sexy for my own good. I sit up higher in the chair, adjusting.

She holds up a white paper bag with pink lettering. Piece of Cake. "I picked up a cake. I thought we could all celebrate."

We. She wants *us* to celebrate?

I'm stuck at my desk. I don't dare move. My throat is dry. My body is hot. I wish he were gone. I wish I didn't want that. I close my eyes momentarily, then open them.

Ian smiles. "You know I can't resist sweets, darling. You got your sweet tooth from me."

"I did, Daddy," she says, and that's different too. It's like she's playing up their connection right now.

What the hell is she up to?

She sits down next to him on the couch—across from me.

My desk *and* a table form a blockade between us yet I'm still off-kilter.

"So it's good you're both here," she continues, her green eyes twinkling and eager.

"Why is that, love?" he asks, patting her hand, the indulgent dad today.

"Because I have something to ask the both of you," she says, brightly.

Then she meets my gaze, and the utter innocence of her smile is chased with complete mischief.

Like how she looks at me on the bike path. Like how she talked about *Ask Me Next Year*. Like how she murmured over the flowers.

I've no clue what's coming but I am dead certain that this moment is about to become a dividing line in my life:

Before she asks.

After she asks.

9

HAPPY BIRTHDAY TO ME

Harlow

They won't say no.

I repeated that the whole way up in the elevator, at reception, then again when I walked down the hall.

They won't say no.

Because...I won't let them say no. I've practiced my pitch.

Now that I'm here, I'll keep my request simple and direct, all business, the way they've taught me by example over the last few years.

I am determined as I reach into the bag and take out the small chocolate cake and then the knife I brought. Sleek and silvery. After I open the pink box, I slice the small cake, then set pieces on the plates I brought too, handing a piece of decadent, rich chocolate to Bridger, then to my father, then keeping one for me.

After all, requests go best with a gift of food.

First things first.

I square my shoulders. "So, I came for my birthday gift," I say, then purposefully backpedal to explain, "Well, I'm excited for you two to give it to me." I smile, a winning, practiced, Upper East Side grin.

My father tuts. "I was going to wait till we had dinner tonight, love."

He told me he has something special for me. He'll give it to me over sushi. But I have plans for another gift. One I'm giving myself.

"Oh, you don't know about this one," I say, mustering all the confidence he's trained me in. "Because it's something from both of you."

My father blinks, confused. I steal a glance at Bridger. A crease digs into his forehead.

Good.

I've kept them on their toes and that's important in a negotiation.

And so, I take the next step in my great heist. The prize? I glance at the man behind the imposing desk.

Him.

"I graduate in a month. With my dual degrees," I say, making my case, simple and clear. "And I've been thinking more and more about what I want to do after graduation. I'd like to work in business and art. But I'm trying to figure out exactly what that looks like," I say, and that's *somewhat* true. Mostly, it's strategic. "Since you're launching *Afternoon Delight* soon, I thought wouldn't it be perfect if you had somebody here who could help you research all things French and art for your show that takes place in Paris? And while I'm doing that, I could learn more about the business of television deal-making. Then, I can really understand if the entertainment business is going to be the right career for me," I say, folding my hands in my lap.

There.

I'm done.

I've made my simple elevator pitch, the kind these two have always said they want to hear.

Instantly, my father beams. He's such a pushover. His eyes shine. "Sweetheart," he says, utterly delighted. "There's always a place for you here."

One down.

He looks to his business partner, expectantly. Well, Bridger *is* in charge of the business side of things, so of course he has the final say.

He's stoic. Barely moving. He's a statue at his desk.

"But I'm in charge of creative," Dad adds. "Bridger would be working more closely with you. Would that be okay?" My father asks me, like it's my choice.

Yes, Daddy. That would be so very okay. "Absolutely," I say.

But Bridger is stony. Not moving. Just...breathing.

He's simply inscrutable. That both scares me and thrills me.

I want to break down his walls. Chip away at them. Discover who he is. Already, I've seen the cracks and I want more. I long for what's behind them. But the only way I can reveal that is if I get closer to him.

That's my plan.

He purses his lips and swallows visibly. Then he

nods, quick and decisive. "Of course. Welcome to Lucky 21," he says.

I tamp down the fireworks bursting inside me. "Thank you. I won't disappoint."

I reach into the bag, take out a candle and set it in the chocolate frosting on my slice. Then I light it with the lighter I brought.

"Make a wish, darling," my father says.

As the flame flickers, I look across the room at the man I've run into on the East River path many times over the last few months.

He tugs on the cuffs of his ruby-red shirt. His lips are a ruler.

But his dark eyes say he's hiding our secret—the secret of our attraction.

I blow out the flame and make a birthday wish that I'll seduce my father's business partner this summer.

* * *

Later that night, over avocado rolls and edamame, my father tells me I should arrange a meeting this summer with the attorneys about my trust fund access. "It's not much, the trust fund," he says. "But your mother set it up for you long ago. It was her idea. She loved you so."

"I know," I whisper around the lump in my throat. That, I have never doubted. I have always known.

Then he gives me a beautiful velvet box. Inside it is a key to a one-bedroom apartment on Sixty-Eighth Street with a view.

Paid in full.

I'm stunned, speechless.

But he has more to say. "I used the royalties from her last *Sweet Nothings* title for this place. It's gorgeous. She'd have wanted you to have it," he says, solemnly. The shine in his eyes makes me think he still misses her in his own way.

My throat tightens. It's like a gift from her too. "I'm overwhelmed. This is incredible."

He covers my hand. "And thank you for always... keeping *things* within the family," he says.

I don't move for a moment. This apartment is also some kind of payoff for having kept my mouth shut? Like he used her royalties from her last book to say he appreciates my silence? The silence he told me to keep or someone might go insane?

I don't know what to say, except an uncomfortable *thank you*.

Truly, I am grateful. An owned apartment is the ultimate extravagance in Manhattan.

Especially since I can put this to good use for my seduction plans.

10

THE DOUBLE TEXT

Harlow

Technically, this is my first job.

Babysitting the Bancroft twins down the block when I was thirteen doesn't entirely count. Everyone babysits after all.

Then, I read up on babysitting, took a CPR class, and learned the basics.

I don't know what to study before I start at Lucky 21. I suppose I've been studying the ins and outs of TV production for years, absorbing it from the air around me, in the conversations.

But I don't like to make mistakes. I don't want to mess this up.

As I head to the door of my apartment on a Monday in late May for my first day on the job, I reach for the knob when my phone buzzes.

I nearly jump. What if that's Jules? I report to her.

What if she wants me to show up early? If she does, I'd have to run.

I grab my phone, slide it open.

Dad: Are you sure you don't want a ride? I can send Jasper over right now. I don't need the car for another hour.

That's so very him. But no.

Harlow: Thanks, Dad. But I'll walk.

Dad: If you insist! I'm on set all week. Let me know if you need anything.

I tell him that I will, but I don't plan to need anything from him.

I take off, wishing I didn't feel so...unsettled.

Maybe the walk through the park will settle my first-day jitters. As I head across Sixty-Eighth Street —*my street*, something I'm still not quite used to—I talk back to my worries.

This is a summer internship. You've got this. You're smart. You're diligent.

But as I peer over the canopy of green trees in the distance, my gaze landing on the black skyscraper that houses Lucky 21, the nerves start up again, like little birds flapping their wings in me.

Oh, for fuck's sake.

These aren't job nerves. They're man nerves.

And I know why. Since I strutted into Bridger's office more than a month ago and made my wish, a few things have happened.

I've graduated from college.

I've moved into my own apartment.

I've visited my cousin, Rachel, in San Francisco too. She's my mom's sister's daughter, so it was good to catch up with another Dumont woman.

But I've only seen Bridger twice in the last month or so. The first time on the path, he barely slowed, but I still asked him how *Afternoon Delight* was going. "No complaints," he'd said. Then he glanced at his watch and said he had to go. He smiled convivially and ran off.

The second time I saw him on the path, he was on the phone. He pointed to his earbuds and mouthed *call*.

That's why my stomach is bouncing.

What was I thinking, engineering this internship? Maybe I've made a terrible mistake.

Maybe I'm just a silly girl.

Maybe I'm—

I slow my pace around the edge of the park when something gold comes into view.

Is that a birdcage over there by a bench? I walk to it. Tilt my head. It's gilded, a home for a bougie parrot. There's an equally fancy sign hanging from the bars in an ornate frame.

Better than TV—free to a good home.

I shake my head in amusement, then do what any good New Yorker would do. I snap a picture of it and post it on my social feed, titling it *TV for hipsters?*

As I cover the last few blocks, my nerves fade. Maybe I simply needed a distraction and photography did the trick.

When I reach the black building, I take the elevator up to the office I know so well on the fourteenth floor. There I give my name to the peppy receptionist—Christian—but he playfully rolls his eyes. "Hush, Harlow. I know you," he says.

Right. Of course.

I'm the picture of nepotism. Will everyone hate me? Think that they're here on merit, but I'm here on...well, I'm here on *scheme.*

Regret swirls in my gut. This was a bad decision.

Christian pops up from the desk and ushers me down the hall. "How is your morning so far, Ms. Granger? Can I get you a coffee? Tea?"

He's trying to wait on me. This can't be good. I can't have the people who work here thinking they need to tend to *daddy's girl.*

"I'm great, Christian. Thanks for asking," I say, and up ahead I spot Bridger's door. It's wide open.

"If anything changes, let me know," Christian says, then flashes a helpful smile, bordering on obsequious.

"You don't ever have to get me a drink," I assure him.

"We'll see..." Christian says, singsong.

I may not win this battle. And as we pass Bridger's office, I lose another battle, since I can't resist stealing a glance. I don't see him, though. I only hear him, saying, "I'll be there at three. Yes. We can discuss the credits then."

I wonder if he'll invite me to the meeting. Discussing credits seems like part of what I'm here for.

Seconds later, Christian sweeps out his arm, indicating a group of cubicles. "The interns," he says, then whispers, "You're hardly one."

But I am. I truly am. "I'm definitely one."

He rolls his eyes again and sails back to reception as a woman with immovable brown hair rises from a chair, then sticks out a hand. "I'm Jules Marley. Bridger James's administrative assistant. I'll see you to your projects," she says with robotic efficiency. "And I can definitely help you feel like an intern."

Thirty minutes later, I'm working on a...database.

I don't see Bridger all day.

Guess Jules was right.

* * *

When I arrive on Tuesday, Bridger's not in his office. Jules mentions something about an off-site meeting. "You can organize the production photos in the Dropbox folder," she says crisply.

"Great," I say, injecting all the pep in the world into my voice. "I'm happy to do it."

"Good," she says, then gives me the login and leaves me to it.

I spend the day sorting.

So fun.

* * *

On Wednesday, I get to—wait for it—check links.

Woohoo.

Okay, fine. Website links break. It's important to check them and blah, blah, blah, but this is mind-numbing work. When I'm rappelling down the rabbit hole of *Sweet Nothings* episodes links, my eyes turn heavy. My brain feels syrupy, and my mind drifts to other days, other places.

Then, I jerk my head. Where am I?

Shoot. I can't fall asleep at my cube.

I push back from my chair, glancing around to make sure no one saw me snooze for even a few seconds, and make my way to the lobby to grab a tea at the coffee shop there. I order quickly, and once I have an English Breakfast in hand, I spin toward the exit. But then I stop and stifle a gasp.

Bridger is swiping his ID tag through the lobby turnstiles and reading on his phone as he strides into the building. His dusky blue suit hugs his legs, caresses his arms, and accentuates his ass.

He's beelining for the elevator. Perfect. I'm cutting across the lobby with the same destination. I arrive ahead of him, and he looks up when he reaches me. The second his eyes land on mine, he squeezes his phone harder, as if to keep it from clattering to the floor.

"Hi," he says, businesslike, as if we didn't once flirt on the bike path. "How's it going, Harlow?"

I don't know what to make of him, but I have an idea. "It's...good," I say, since I don't want to complain.

The elevator arrives. He holds out his arm. I step inside. The doors shut. "How are you?"

"Just busy. Lots of meetings. You know how it goes here."

But that's the problem. I don't know how it goes here. Bridger's supposed to show me, but he's shutting me out, avoiding me.

"Actually—" I break off and swallow the rest because his phone rings and he lifts a finger.

"Need to take this," he says, apologetic, but also not. Relieved, maybe?

When we exit on the fourteenth floor, all I can do is watch his back as he strides down the hall in that tight suit, deep in conversation with someone else.

* * *

That night, I pace my apartment, staring out the floor-to-ceiling windows that overlook Manhattan as I give Layla chapter and verse of the week so far.

"Sounds like he's avoiding you," she says, confirming what I suspected.

"Why would he do that?" I ask, but I fear I know the answer—he's not into me the way I thought he was.

She scoffs. "Because, girl, he's hot for you."

I stop, press my hand against the glass. "What?" I whisper.

She laughs. "Did you think it was something else?"

I gulp. "Yes."

"Oh, he is *so* avoiding you," she declares.

That sounds too good to be true and too awful at the same time.

I don't want to be avoided.

I want to be included.

Maybe I just need to be pushy. With that resolved, I settle onto my couch, fiddle absently with my necklace, and ask her to entertain me with her stories.

"Like the one where my mom's trying to set me up on *another* date?"

I smile. "Yes, that one." I lie back and listen. Layla's relationship with her mother is complicated, but no matter how thorny it is, her tales of their chats still bring a pang of *missing* to my chest.

When we hang up, I get ready for bed, and I run my finger over the wooden box on my nightstand shelf. Inside are all the letters from my mother.

Every year, I miss her less.

And that hurts too.

* * *

When I reach the office on Thursday, Bridger's walking out, breezing past reception. "Meeting with Webflix," he says to Christian and me with barely a smile. "Gotta go."

Wait. No. No way.

"I want to go," I blurt out.

But the elevator door is closing on him.

"That man. He doesn't waste time," Christian says, admiringly, under his breath.

I grit my teeth and huff. "That's true," I say, trying to put on a smile.

Layla may be right, but if he's into me, it hardly matters since I never see him.

* * *

I walk home after the day's work, passing the bus stop by the park on Fifth Avenue. A banana lies on the bench, looking lonely. Then I squint, spying writing on the banana in ballpoint pen.

Tonight. You. Me. Black lace.

Clever. Maybe that was in someone's lunchbox? I snap a shot and post it on my social with the caption: **Sometimes you just need to spell it out.**

Which is good advice.

Really good advice.

Bridger usually arrives at the office at eight-thirty. That night, I set my alarm for earlier than usual.

* * *

On Friday morning, I make it across the park and arrive by eight-ten. I head for my cube. I beat Jules to the office. Then I flip open my laptop.

And I wait.

At attention.

Listening.

Ten minutes later, I catch the echo of footsteps on the hardwood floors. Wingtips. The sound of money. That's my cue.

I pop up, head down the hall, and meet Bridger at his door as he's unlocking it.

I'm not letting him slip away from me today. I want what I want—*an explanation.*

He blinks, those deep blue eyes full of questions. "Oh. Hi."

I don't fuck around. "Why won't you take me to meetings?"

He parts his lips, but for a few long seconds, no words come. I've caught him off-guard, and he blanches. "I didn't think...I guess...I...." But he's not the boss for nothing. Quickly, he recovers. "You're right. I should. You're here to learn. I need to be involving you," he says, each word slow and nearly painful.

Did I misread everything? Is Layla wrong?

"I'm meeting with CTM this morning about one of their writers. Do you want to come?" he asks, smooth and in control again.

A part of me wants to ask: *but do you want me there?*

I don't ask. We're having a business relationship for now. With the confidence I've honed for years, I raise my chin, and answer, "Yes. I do."

And I hope Layla's not wrong.

"I'll meet you at ten."

On the dot, we're outside the building and he's holding open the door of a town car for me.

I slide in.

Bridger follows, shutting the door behind him. The

air conditioning hums. The tinted windows seal us in. New York feels right next door and very far away.

"We're meeting with Mason Stein," he begins, then his gaze drifts to my leg. To my ankle. "Your scar's faded."

It comes out scratchy. And like a pleasant surprise.

Wait. No. A sexy surprise.

"Yes, it has," I say, turning my whole body to him.

He licks his lips, then gestures to my ankle. "I just noticed," he says, backpedaling. "That's all."

Before I can think better of it, I say, "It's okay...*to notice things*."

His breath seems to come out in a harsh pant, then he drags a hand over his hair and seems to shake off the fog. "We'll be meeting with Mason Stein, the agent for TJ Hardman," he says, regrouping as he mentions the romance novelist. "His agent is interested in striking a development deal for his books. I'd like him to land at Lucky 21."

That's genius. "I've read all his novels," I offer, feeling a little like I just discovered an ace up my sleeve.

Bridger's eyes widen. "All of them?"

"Every single one," I say, proudly.

"Which one lends itself most to a TV show? Besides *Top-Notch Boyfriend*," he says, since that book was made into a movie.

"*Look Me Up*," I say confidently. "The fake boyfriend relationship is told almost in little episodes. And it lets you get into queer content, which is a growing market."

"It is. Good thinking," he says.

When we reach CTM, he exits the town car first then offers me a hand. Like a gentleman.

Or perhaps an opportunist?

I take his hand. He curls his fingers around my palm. A whoosh rushes through me. This is only the second time we've touched. *Really touched.* My hand tingles first, then my whole body.

There's a taut moment when I swear his fingertips brush across my skin before he lets go.

"Thank you, Bridger," I say, then softly I add, "And thanks for having me."

He swallows after those last words.

Having me.

Maybe that was a Freudian slip. But maybe not.

He gestures for me to go first. I head into the lobby ahead of him, letting him look. Letting him watch me.

When we're in the elevator, he steals a glance at me then tears himself away instantly.

I rein in a grin.

In the CTM conference room, Bridger introduces me simply as "Harlow at Lucky 21." Maybe he doesn't want to draw attention to my newbie status as an intern. Or perhaps he doesn't want to use my last name and let on that nepotism is at play.

I'm not terribly bothered. But I *am* curious.

I say hello, then Bridger is all business with the agent, batting around possibilities. Then he turns to me and says, "Harlow has some thoughts on *Look Me Up.*"

Whoa. Talk about trial by fire.

"I love thoughts," Mason says drily, then waits for me.

I've been raised on pitches—selling is second nature. "The first episode would be true to the book, and you could cliff it when the guys see each other again," I begin, then sketch out the rest of what could stay and what could go from the enemies-to-lovers-to-pretend-boyfriends storyline.

Mason nods approvingly. "Interesting." He taps his chin for a few seconds. "We have lots of interest in development deals for TJ. But we'll be in touch." He takes a beat. "And soon."

Once we leave the offices and we're safely in the elevator, Bridger shoots me an approving smile. "He never says *soon*. That's good, Harlow."

"I'll drink to soon," I say, feeling a little giddy over it.

As we head to Amsterdam Avenue, Bridger reaches for his phone, but then his gaze drifts longingly to a sidewalk café with white tables and green chairs, somehow both homey and trendy. He raises a brow in a question. "I was going to call the driver, but any chance you're hungry? I skipped breakfast."

I'm not hungry at all. "Yes," I say instantly.

We grab a table in the parklet. I order a salad, and he chooses a risotto. After the server leaves, Bridger undoes the cuffs on his shirt, rolls them up once, then twice. I glimpse the faint black lines of his ink, something like leaves.

Someday, I want to ask about the art on his arm. But when he catches me looking, his expression turns unreadable.

Now's not the time for something so personal, not when I've just started making headway with him again.

Instead, I glance around so I don't seem so...*obvious.*

My attention snags on a woman in a leopard-print dress several feet away. She's chatting on the phone, like any New Yorker, all while walking a peacock on a leash.

In a flash, I grab my phone and snap a shot of the woman and her pet.

Bridger studies me quizzically. "You just took a picture of a peacock."

"What else does one do when someone walks a peacock?" I counter, feeling like I'm getting my Bridger rhythm back.

"Take pictures I suppose," he says, with a glint in his eyes. Maybe he's getting his groove back too.

"Then why didn't *you* snap a photo?" I ask. Maybe I'm a little saucy.

"That's a damn good question. I suppose I should have captured the moment."

"Do you wish you had a peacock picture? Maybe I could share mine," I say, teasingly.

A faint flush spreads on his cheeks. "Yes, please do that, Harlow."

With a smirk, I send it to him with the words, *Ask me why I took it.*

After he reads the message, he looks up, curious. "I thought we established why you took it. Because it's there."

"Yes. But I might have a collection too," I say.

That's met with an arched brow. An inquisitive grin. This is so much better than his avoidance. Maybe Layla *was* right.

"All right. I'll ask. Do you have a peacock collection, Harlow?"

"No. But I've been taking pictures this week of found things in New York. I post them on my socials," I say.

"Show me," he says. It's a demand. A hungry one. I can hear him saying it in other ways.

With enthusiasm, I click on my feed, turn my phone around, and watch as he scrolls through the images I took this week. The birdcage and its *TV for hipsters* caption. A book I spotted on a stoop of a building: *The Gentleman's Guide to Good Dressing.* Then, the banana.

"Black lace on a banana," he says, clearly amused. "Someone's having fun tonight."

"Yes, I bet they are," I say, then slide my teeth over the corner of my lip.

He watches my every move. "Yeah, I bet they are," he repeats, a little hot, a little husky. "How long have you been doing this?"

"I started this week."

"Any reason?"

To settle my nerves over working with you. To have something to do. A project, a focus, a story.

I keep that to myself. "They're like a puzzle. I'm trying to solve it," I say.

I'm trying to solve you.

The food comes, and we dig in. As Bridger lifts his fork, he says, "I wonder when you'll find the next one."

It's as if he's merely musing on the topic.

"Me too."

Then, after we eat, I return to the question of his

introduction. "Why did you call me by my name rather than introducing me as an intern?"

His jaw tics almost imperceptibly.

I continue, asking, "Or as Harlow Granger?"

His eyes lock on mine, intensely, importantly. "Because that's how I see you. As Harlow."

Not as an intern. Or a Granger.

He leaves that there with all its implications. And I take those implications home with me, tucking them close, keeping them near.

That night, I'm lounging on my couch reading, when my phone pings and Bridger's name appears. Immediately, I click over to his text, breathless with anticipation.

Then there's an image of a Post-it note on a street sign. Someone wrote *Get supplies* on it.

It's just supplies. But it's also *not*.

I reply.

Harlow: I hope someone got their supplies.

Bridger: I hope so too.

Then when I'm about to return to my book, another note pops up. A double text.

Holy shit. A double text.

Bridger: You never want to miss supplies.

Harlow: Never. It's a rule.

Bridger: One you shouldn't ever break.

Harlow: I wouldn't.

Bridger: I didn't think you would.

We're not talking about supplies. And I'm no longer wondering if he was avoiding me. I know he was. And now he's not.

Especially when he double-texts once more.

Bridger: You don't seem like a rule breaker.

I'm all kinds of turned on as I write back, *But maybe I am.*

11

AND I GIVE IN

Bridger

I give in.

I finally take up yoga.

I've got to do something with all these wild, dangerous thoughts of Harlow. Maybe the practice will help.

I make plans for Sunday morning with Axel Huxley. The thriller writer lives in my building, and he's become a friend over the last few years.

A devotee of the downward-facing dog, he's been urging me to go for some time.

"Yoga is the best. It keeps me limber so I can write literally till the day I die," he says as we head to the yoga studio around the corner from our Gramercy Park building, following the yoginis in tight pants, rolled-up mats tipped on their shoulders, leading the way.

"Bet that's not what you want to be limber for," I say drily.

"Which is what I was going to say about you. So, I'm surprised at your advanced age you haven't taken it up sooner?"

"I'm so old at thirty-one," I say, but the sarcasm in my tone hits me all wrong. I am old when I think about the woman I'm craving. Ten years is a lifetime. But the age gap isn't the biggest hurdle.

Still, I can't let Axel win the battle of barbs. "Speaking of advanced age, I believe you're still and always will be older than me?"

"And I believe I just came up with the name of my next villain," he says, then over enunciates, "Bridger," with a certain evil panache.

"Sounds good to me," I say.

He laughs, then we're quiet for a beat.

"So...who is she?" Axel asks as we cross the avenue. "The reason you're taking up yoga after all this time."

Shit. Am I that obvious? And if I'm that transparent to my friends, what will Ian say when he notices? *Hey mate, who's the new bird who's got you so tightly wound?*

My eye twitches.

"She's no one," I say.

Axel hums doubtfully. "But it sounds like she's someone."

She *is* someone. But I won't breathe a word about her to anyone. My feelings are too dangerous. Too forbidden. Too...wrong. There are entirely too many wrongs, starting with *she's an intern* and ending with *Ian would never forgive me*. He'd never trust me again, and you can't run a business without trust.

The company means too much to me. My work is my compass. It's the only steady thing I've ever known.

Feelings are irrelevant.

They're kerosene, and I don't need to fan the flames.

"Doesn't matter. It really doesn't matter," I say once more, for emphasis.

To remind me.

With a sympathetic sigh, Axel nods thoughtfully as we weave around a young family—a mom and mom pushing a stroller. "I get it," he says. "Some relationships just go...nowhere."

My buddy sounds resigned, possibly even sad. That's not like him. Axel's usually brash and carefree. "Speaking from experience?"

"Unfortunately," he says. "There was this woman..." Then he waves a hand, as if he's dismissing her from his memory. "She's not worth mentioning. Know what I mean?"

But that's not entirely how I feel about Harlow. My captivating Harlow is completely worth mentioning. There's a part of me that wants to tell Axel all about her. That wants to tell my mom. That wants to say something to someone, everyone.

Most of all, to her.

Instead, we turn into the yoga studio, and I try to let go of all my dangerous thoughts as I hold the warrior pose, sinking deeper into it, like I can battle all the wild ideas in my head.

* * *

On Monday, as I run along the river, I practice what to say the whole time in case I run into Harlow on the path.

If I see her, I'll say, "What should I wear today?"

Or, maybe, "Did you see that broken record player with the sign, *Doesn't work but might be fun to fix?* It's back on Thirty-Fourth. I took a photo of it."

And...

I groan over my pathetic lines, and my pathetic plans to talk to her.

Get it together, man.

I toggle to a new playlist on my phone and blast *Rent*. As I peel off miles, I don't think of her. I think of music, and stories, and the way I felt when my mom first took me to see this show when I was thirteen.

I felt like I was where I belonged. I was seeing a story unfold on a stage.

As my sneakers slap against the concrete, I send Mom a text.

Bridger: Remember the standing O the cast of *Rent* received for "La Vie Boheme?" That was a fun show.

Mom: Oh my god, that one was the absolute best. I'm singing it tonight. It's part of our set.

Bridger: I'm jealous of all the Canadians who get to hear you sing it.

Mom: I'll make you a bootleg.

. . .

Texting my mom about the cabaret tour she's on in Canada passes the time for the rest of my run.

That feels like a victory.

* * *

After I shower, I stand in my closet, towel slung around my waist, studying my options. The row of oranges—the sunburst, the burnt, the bright orange. The reds, from the wine to the cranberry to the ruby. Then the blues. I run my fingers along the half a dozen blue shirts, taking my time, imagining Harlow here in my home. Touching my clothes.

Picking one out.

Wear the robin's egg. It goes with your eyes, she'd say.

Just hearing her voice in my head sends a hot shiver down my spine. I breathe out hard, then wrap a hand around the fabric of the shirt on the hanger, like I can fucking hold onto a shirt for stability.

I reach for a navy one instead. But when I hold it against my chest and peer in the mirror, it looks wrong.

It's a boring color.

I should wear a bold shade.

I put back the navy and put on the robin's egg. It's not for her. Really, it's not. I need to stop by the set of *Sweet Nothings*.

That's why I'm paying so much attention to what

I'm wearing. It's the right shirt for a set visit since it's a power shirt.

When I reach the studios on Eleventh Avenue, I make my way to the writers' room. As I head down the familiar hallway lined with framed shots from the show —Cruz kissing Anna in his library in one season, Sam and Josie arguing in the wine cellar in another season, Cruz kissing Anna's twin the next season—one of the actors rounds the corner and lights up when he sees me. It's Dominic Rivera, who plays the wealthy, library-loving playboy. "Bridger! When are we going to give Cruz his own series?"

I smile at the star. "Maybe someday," I say. You never know. If the research shows Cruz can sustain his own show, he'll get his own show. That's when.

The actor's gaze drifts heavenward. "From your mouth to God's ears," he says, then flashes me his winning grin. "Then to the network's ears. Then to a green light."

I clap him on the shoulder. "Cruz keeps our writers busy, that's for sure," I say, then after a quick goodbye, I continue to the writers' room.

Before I reach it, I hear Isla, her voice carrying to the hall.

"Oh, my god yes, that would be so brilliant," says the young writer.

Then another voice. "Because you are brilliant, my dear."

Ian.

I grit my teeth. He can't call her dear. That's not okay.

I close the distance and turn into the room as she curls a hand on his arm and points to the laptop screen with her other hand. "Like this?"

He leans in closer, patting her hand on his wrist. "Yes, that is a brilliant punchline." He looks up and meets my gaze. "Ah, look who's here!"

There's zero recognition of the fact that he's standing *that* close to an employee. That he just touched a writer on the show.

But who am I to judge? I stand that close to his daughter.

I swallow my "*Be careful.*"

"Can you meet with the EP?" I ask him, all business.

"Of course," he says, then he smiles at Isla and waves goodbye. As we walk to the office, he glances back at the writers' room. "She's a clever one."

"Glad we have such talent working on our shows," I say, focusing on her job, not her fucking arm.

"Me too."

But it comes out a little too salacious, so I redirect. "How's Vivian?"

"Incredible," he says. As we head to our meeting, he waxes on about the woman he supposedly adores.

Maybe the Isla touch was nothing.

I put it out of my mind.

* * *

Later that day, while Ian's on set and I'm back at the Lucky 21 offices, there's a rap on my door. Sounds like

Jules from the double taps. "Hi, Jules," I call. "Do you have the *Afternoon Delight* scripts?"

"No. The head writer needs to rework some scenes."

That's no good. "They shoot next month."

"Hopefully it's plenty of time." She offers a shrug.

Sure, some shows do rewrites in a night. But *Afternoon Delight* is a new show. It should be spit-shined and battle ready. "Thanks for the heads-up."

"And your lunch is coming in fifteen minutes. Also, Harlow finished the database. I want to put her to work on cataloging old scripts from the show. They're in a password-protected file, though. Okay to give the password to her?" she asks.

My neck grows hotter. "Of course."

Give her anything she wants.

"Thanks," she says.

As she goes, I try desperately to erase thoughts of me giving Harlow everything she needs, but then I flash back to the pitch Harlow made about working here. Art, French, research. It's a waste to have her cataloging old scripts. That's busy work. Harlow's an intern —a fucking intern, and I'd do well to remember that every second of every day. She's also a damn smart one, so we might as well use her talents for the benefit of the company.

"Actually, Jules," I call out.

My assistant stops in the doorway, turning back. "Yes?"

"Could you send her the French translations from the show? And the artwork referenced in the scenes with the museum visits? Ask her to cross-reference them. Make sure they're all accurate," I say. That's a better use of Harlow's brain.

Jules's lips twitch like a rabbit's. "Of course."

She turns on her heel and leaves.

My lunch arrives shortly, and I eat alone as I review a contract. The only company I have is Patti LuPone as Reno Sweeney, playing faintly from my computer. When I finish, I turn on my tablet, then open a paper notebook. As I review the new coverage Jules sent me on prospective shows, taking notes on the pages, there's another rap on my door. Double again.

"Hi, Jules," I say without looking up.

"It's me."

Me.

How can one word turn me electric? I set down the pen, look up. Harlow's brown hair is loose and curling over her shoulders. Her pink lip gloss shines invitingly. She wears a pencil skirt. Black. It hugs her thighs too deliciously.

I don't even know what to say next, but I don't have to figure it out because she points at my desk as she closes the door. "You write in pen?" She sounds...enchanted.

"Just some notes on a script. Why?"

And why are you shutting the door? But thank you for that, because I want to talk to you for the rest of the day, and I don't want to be careful at all.

"That's cute."

I growl. "Writing in a pen is cute?"

"So are those notebooks," she says, walking over to

my desk, running her fingertips along the page I was writing on.

"I'm old school," I say. But maybe she thinks I'm old. Too old for her? Ah, hell. Why am I thinking this? Maybe because I touched her hand the other day, because I send her texts, because she shut the door, and I didn't stop her.

And because right now, she's smiling like she has a secret.

I'm a negotiator for a living. A goddamn dealmaker, yet I'm on edge with her and her fearless grin as she stares me down. She'd be terrifying in a boardroom. I'd lose every battle to her.

"What is it?" I ask, breaking the cardinal rule of negotiations by going first.

"I like your shirt," she says.

"Thanks," I manage to say through the desert in my throat.

She sits on the couch, crosses her legs.

The view. The gorgeous fucking view of her.

So help me god.

But I can't look away, especially as she glances at the emptied bag from lunch, spotting the name of a sushi restaurant on it. "What kind of sushi do you like?"

I laugh at the randomness of her question. Maybe she needs a tension breaker too. "All kinds."

"But you have to have a favorite, Bridger. Nigiri, roll, or sashimi?"

"Combo platter, as a matter of fact," I say, and tap my pen on the edge of the desk, trying to figure her out.

This is new for Harlow, this brand of office chitchat. She's never engaged in it before.

I don't want to stop. I don't want to stop a thing. "You like sushi?"

She gives a light shrug. "As long as it didn't swim beforehand."

"Vegetarian joke. Good one."

She gestures to my computer, to the music coming from the speakers. The soundtrack to the musical *Card Game* plays now.

"I'm not into the game..." she says, starting the opening line to the show-stopping title tune, the tiniest touch of sultry to her voice.

There it is.

A callback to the night in her dad's home, to our exchange of lyrics. To our first-ever flirtation.

And I'm not careful at all as I volley back, tossing a line about how games don't thrill me at all.

Her eyes meet mine—those beautiful green eyes that make my stomach flip. "So then why do I want..."

The next line in the song lingers on the tip of my tongue. I desperately want to serve it up, but it's risky.

I do it anyway. "To play games with you," I say, then the world blurs away.

There's nothing beyond those windows. Nothing outside the door of my office.

Everything I want is in this room.

Her eyes never leave mine. "It's a good question," she says, but that's not the next line. That's her commentary, and yeah, it's a damn good question for sure. Especially since her voice feels like a caress.

But if I stay here, I'll never leave this hazy cocoon of lust. I'll lock the door, push her against it, and kiss the breath out of her. I'll hike up her skirt, set her on my desk, and devour her. I'll never be able to keep my hands off her if we keep talking like this.

I clear my throat. "Do you listen to anything besides show tunes?" I ask, hoping that's innocuous enough.

"I do, but I keep coming back to them. And you?"

"I would have to say it'd be a rare day if I listened to something that wasn't meant to be belted from a Broadway stage." This is safer, so much safer.

"What do you like besides *Ask Me Next Year* and *Card Game*?"

"*Les Mis*, and definitely *Rent,* and of course *Sweeney Todd*. But my favorite ever is *42nd Street*. My mom was one of the understudies for Peggy Sawyer for one of the revivals some years back," I say, and this is curing my lust. Talking about my mom is not sexy at all.

"Did she ever get to play?"

"Many times. The lead always had vocal problems."

"Not the kind of thing you want to have when your name's in lights. Did you see your mom's performances?"

"Yes. She's a talent all right."

She also drinks too much. Lives too large. I keep that to myself, though.

"Do you have a favorite song from *42nd Street*?"

"The title track."

"Can you put it on?" she asks, but before I can move, she's standing, crossing the distance, stretching across my desk. She's inches away, and I want to grab her waist, haul her across the desk, and pull her into my lap.

I want to run my hands through her hair and kiss her neck until she's gasping.

Begging.

Panting.

She clicks over to the new tune. The familiar opening notes play, but she doesn't leave. She scoots up on the desk and perches on the edge, legs crossed, looking like sin and my downfall as we listen to the song in silence.

The three minutes end far too soon, and when they do, she hops off my desk and heads for the door. But before she opens it, she stops, then walks back to me, taking a deep breath. "I lied."

I blink, trying to reconnect to reality. "About what?" I rasp.

"I don't like your shirt." She tilts her head. "I love it."

She touches the cuff, fingering the material.

My breath hitches. This close, I can smell her. Vanilla and temptation. I fight back the urge to say *I wore it for you.*

Instead I say, as emotionless as I can, "I should get back to work."

Her eyes flash with a touch of disappointment, then she says, professionally, "Me too."

* * *

That night, I send her a photo of the record player.

.   .   .

Bridger: I took this photo for you.

That feels like a small victory too. I resisted telling her the depth of my obsession. Then, she replies.

Harlow: I took this one for you.

It's a shot of her crossed ankles, and it's the sexiest thing I've ever seen. And I give in even more.

Bridger: I'm keeping it.

12

THAT EXTRA INCH

Harlow

I start wearing skirts every day.

The man likes my legs. Might as well give him what he wants.

I zip up a gunmetal gray skirt that hugs my hips and hits at my knees.

Ah, who am I kidding? This hits an inch above the knees. Sometimes, you need that extra inch.

I check my reflection in the mirror, give myself an approving nod, then take off for work. Along the way, I reread last night's texts. I replay the last week, then the last few months.

Bridger seems to like to chat on the path, on the phone, at cafés. And while he seems okay to chat at work every now and then, he's definitely more reserved behind his desk.

Maybe I need to get him out of the office.

"Waitress" plays in my earbuds, but I'm barely listening to the festive tune. My strategy brain is working overtime as I traverse the edge of Central Park, feeling the clip-clopping of horses more than I hear it.

I could ask him to a show.

I could invite him to take pictures with me after work.

But is that too much, too soon?

I squint, thinking, then I think harder when I spot a flash of emerald green. Tailored pants, thick, dark hair —Bridger is fifty feet ahead, walking along Central Park South, headed for the office.

As if of their own accord, my feet pick up the pace. Wait. Am I truly doing this? Power walking to catch up to him?

No, I can't be that obsessed. I can't be that girl. But then Fate must love me fiercely because he stops to check something on his phone. My breath catches as I walk and I hope.

I do not run, and still, I reach him. Like that, I'm no longer miles from nowhere. I'm next to Bridger.

"Morning, Bridger," I say.

He looks up. A smirk already owns his lush lips. "You're everywhere, Harlow."

Does he think I'm a stalker?

But before I answer, my phone buzzes in my skirt pocket.

His grin widens, his eyes drifting to the source of the sound. "Like I said..."

As I slide open my phone, tingles rush over my shoulders. A picture pops up on the screen.

A strange one. A Tupperware container in the dark, with the lid flipped open. Inside it is a keychain with an Eiffel Tower tchotchke hanging on the silver circle. "Does this count? It's someone's geocaching. Well, their cache," he says.

He took another photo for me, and this feeling in my chest—like bubbles shook up—must be what effervescent is. "Where did you find it?"

"I was walking through the park the other night. Before a dinner party thing—I usually do that—and I spotted this behind a rock," he says, methodical, but a touch excited too.

There's so much to unpack there. So much Bridger intel. But I start with the easiest one. "This absolutely counts," I say. "Can I post it?"

"Be my guest," he says as the cars and cabs and buses trundle by. But as they move, we stay still outside the park, the early June morning wrapping around us.

I was right. Bridger lets go outside of the office.

"Then thanks for the invitation," I say, with a sexy smile. I post the picture quickly, then show him the caption: *I'll be going back soon. You?*

His expression shifts. Serious, concerned. "You're leaving?"

A line digs into his forehead. That's...a tip-off. "Not yet..." I say, then trail off, letting the possibility of my absence hang there. To torture him.

Fear can be a good motivator, after all.

"Soon?" The concern is almost too much. I want to abate it, but I want to toy with it too.

I'm a cat playing with her catch.

Am I lying? Not really. I might go back to Paris, so I reassure him with, "Not *too* soon."

He says nothing. But in the slight twitch of his lips, then how he purses them together, he's reassured. He's cool Bridger again, in control Bridger again.

I like all the Bridgers, but I especially like when he shows me his wishes and his wants. I like when *I'm* those wishes and wants. I shrug playfully, then toss out, "You should come with me."

We're not really going to Paris, but it's a trial balloon.

He laughs, like that's ridiculous, then starts walking to the office. "Should I now? Go to Paris?"

"Absolutely," I say. "I hear there are all sorts of things to find and photograph there. Chapeaus on park benches, discarded art in alleys, abandoned flowers in passages."

"Sounds like a story," he offers.

"A good story," I say, but I hold back other words. I don't say a love story, but I hope he hears it in my tone.

"You could tell that tale," he says.

"Maybe I will," I say.

The black skyscraper looms ahead. In a few minutes, we'll step inside the cool, air-conditioned building where we play our roles.

Boss and intern.

But sometimes, even within those walls, I just feel like we're a man and a woman. Like I do right now. "Or," I say, returning to the *you should come to Paris* vibe, then seizing it, just taking what I want, "we could go to a show here. On Broadway."

It comes out in a hot rush. I feel fizzy, dipped and coated in sugary hope as he stops at the corner outside the park and looks me straight in the eyes. Briefly, his tongue darts out, wetting his lips, like he's thinking. He takes his time, then speaks quietly. "Do you think that would be *obvious*?"

God. Yes. I want obvious. Badly.

But instead I tilt my head, play innocent. "What's obvious?"

"I think you know what I mean," he says, his voice low, perhaps a warning.

I don't want to heed it. "Do I?"

He nods, never taking his eyes off me. "You're a smart woman."

"I know," I say, the ions vibrating between us.

His brow arches. "Know that you're smart or know what I mean by obvious?" The current between us is electric, fully charged.

"If we go to a show, I would think it would be *obvious* how complicated this has become," he says.

Flames blaze up inside me. Anticipation clings to the air. This is the turning point. Keeping my gaze on his beautiful blue eyes, I don't ask. I state, making all my intentions crystal clear. "Do you know I know all the lyrics to *Ask Me Next Year*?"

He's silent, jaw ticking, as if he's considering what to say next or whether to say it at all. Then in a voice that almost wobbles, he says, "If they ever did a revival—"

"Bridger," I cut him off in a sharp whisper.

My father is staring at us, standing in front of the black building. His head is tilted, his gaze curious.

My chest hollows.

I step back, wave, and smile. "Hi, Dad."

The look on Bridger's face is blank. He's erased all emotions in an instant.

But the look on my father's face is delighted. "So it's going great? The internship?"

I shudder out a breath. "It is," I say, at the same time that Bridger says the same.

I'm sure we both feel the same utter relief.

I feel, too, like I'm getting away with murder.

13

BIG DESK

Harlow

The message blinks up at me the next morning as I grab my phone on the way to work. The hair on my arms stands on end.

Dad: Can you swing by the set on your way to work?

Did he hear us yesterday after all? Does he know? Another message lands with a sharp buzz.

Dad: My car will be waiting outside your building.

Dread crawls up my spine. I leave, the door shutting with an ominous clang.

My pulse spikes as I head down the hall, then it shoots out of control as I step into the tiny elevator car, surrounded by men in suits, women in sharp trousers.

They are the other denizens of this building. This fancy twelve-story building I could never afford on my own. I shirk to the back of the elevator, completely out of place.

The twenty-one-year-old interloper. The fake, the fraud. They live here for real. My gorgeous one-bedroom is entirely unearned.

My stomach nosedives as the elevator plummets. The rightful residents, those who probably earned their homes, shift their stances, scroll on phones, check watches.

I stare at the brass doors, throat tight. The elevator arrives at the lobby.

Ashamed, I hang behind, then head for the exit.

"Good morning, Ms. Granger," the doorman says.

"Good morning, Henry," I say, smiling, wishing I didn't feel like I live with a silver spoon in my mouth.

But I like my silver spoon too much to spit it out.

On the street, a gleaming black car waits for me. My dad's driver stands by the door, swings it open, gives me a good morning.

I say hello, with my stomach churning. Once inside, I check that the partition's up, then, I FaceTime my brother in London, where it's early afternoon.

He answers right away, his dimpled face appearing

on the screen, his brown eyes curious but concerned. He's in the office, a bank of TV monitors behind him. He's a producer at Webflix in London. "Hey, what's up, Lo?"

"Hi," I say, breath stuttering.

Instantly, he gets me. "Shit, what's wrong?"

I shake my head, a lump forming in my throat. "Hunter," I say, my voice low as the car pulls into morning traffic. "Dad called me to the set today. I have no idea why, but it feels foreboding."

He frowns sympathetically. "Look, working for Dad is brutal. It was for me. But he's always been different with you."

"I'm sorry," I say, like it was all my doing, Dad being harder on his son. "For how he was."

"It's not your fault. He just...he adores you."

That's the problem. I'm his princess. His good daughter. "I know, but he texted me to come in this morning, and now I'm freaking out."

"Why? I mean, besides the fact that he's a total wanker," he says, and I smile, agreeing, I suppose.

But I shouldn't involve another person in my terribly messy affairs. "Oh, I'm sure it's nothing," I say, breezy, trying to let it go.

"Harlow," he chides. "Why are you so worried?"

I need an answer. I need to cover up the terrible truth of my intentions. "I just don't want to mess up the internship," I say, and that's mostly true. I don't want to ruin the internship since it's my chance with Bridger. My *only* chance, and these feelings are no longer a crush. The more I know him, the more I care for him, the more I think Bridger needs me too. There's something tense in him. He's a tight coil of a man. He seems to need...unwinding.

I want to unwind him.

But what if Dad has figured me out?

I blink away the horrid possibility and ask Hunter how he's doing. "Have you met anyone who's excited you?"

Hunter came out as bisexual earlier this year.

"No, but I remain very committed to the cause," he says with a laugh. "Even though I've only managed a few snogs."

I laugh harder, feeling better after talking to him, as I always do. "Well, I hope you get more than snogs. When will I see you again? Are you ever coming to New York?" I ask in my little sister pleading voice.

He laughs. "Maybe. My boss, Bernard, has been saying he wants me to do some work with the Webflix team in New York. He hasn't said when, though. But I am heading to San Francisco next week to connect with some production companies there."

"Well, come here after," I suggest, since I'm helpful like that. "I'm sure Bernard will understand your sister wants to see you."

"I'm sure he will too. You know I want to see you," he says, with warmth in his brown eyes.

"I know." I pause, then ask, "Who are you meeting with in San Francisco?"

"A handful of sports and documentary producers.

One of them does sports adventure shows, and I'm totally chuffed to meet them. Maybe try to land one of their reality docs."

"I can't wait to hear about it," I say, but as the town car nears Eleventh, I feel like I've inhaled black smoke. I'm lying to Hunter by omission, and I feel like my dad. I can't be a little liar, like he is.

I practice the words in my head—*Hunter, I'm wild for Bridger James.*

Then, it's time to say them out loud. "I want to tell you—" I begin, but he's turned around, his attention caught elsewhere at work.

My brother swings his gaze back to me.

"I have to go. Chat later, Lo," he says, then blows me a kiss.

"Bye," I say, but he's already gone, and I'm here.

Summoned.

* * *

My father's rarely at Lucky 21, because he's either at home, writing and overseeing scripts, or here on-set.

Or here. In his throne room for his empire as the creative director, surrounded by his many Emmys for writing, and his shelves full of my mother's love stories. The spines grow larger, like billboards, as I head down the hall, my shoes clicking along the cavernous corridor.

I touch the *I* on my pendant, wishing I could remember her more.

But then, I've remembered enough, haven't I? *Be intrepid. Be brave.*

That's what she left me with.

And Dad?

His biggest life lesson is this one—best to leave adult affairs to themselves.

I'm an adult...ergo.

I turn my emotions around, tying them up in a neat satin bow. I march in, chin up, unafraid.

"Love!" he calls out, standing, coming around his desk, embracing me. "I brought you coffee. And I need your help picking chocolate for the wedding," he says, then points to a display of chocolate truffles on his desk, box after box of Lulu's Chocolates next to a cup of coffee, steam rising from the blue mug.

That's all he wanted? My input on his wedding favors?

"Of course," I say, thrilled to taste chocolate, rather than be reamed.

After I sample the wares, I pick a dark, raspberry chocolate, then Dad walks me to the door. "I'm so glad the internship is going well, especially since I'm going away on Sunday for a few days," he says.

"Oh. You are?" I ask, trying to hide my excitement that he'll be MIA but probably failing. "Where are you going?"

"Cape Cod. A little getaway for Viv," he says. "Maybe you can figure out the problem with *Afternoon Delight*."

"What's the problem?"

"That's the question. The script needs some work," he says, then drops a kiss on my cheek.

And I'm dismissed.

I got away with this flirtation, and the theft of his awareness feels wicked and wonderful.

Especially since I plan to keep getting away with it.

I spend the day doing a final check of the French translations for *Afternoon Delight* and double-checking the art references. Finally, I'm using my schooling here.

The day flies by, but I still want the end of it, when others start to leave, to come even faster.

Around six, I knock twice on Bridger's door. He's at his desk, bent over his tablet, a pen in hand, music playing softly.

"Come in," he says.

I don't want to come on too strong, though, even as I push on the door, closing it. But lightly, almost like it's closing of its own volition. Not mine. Once I take a seat on his couch, I start with something easy. "I keep meaning to ask...what kind of cabaret tour is your mom doing?"

His gaze swings to the shut door, then to me. "Her favorites. A mix of showstoppers and torch songs," he says, then lifts a brow. "That's an odd question."

"I was starting with a softball. Were you expecting me to come in and brainstorm a solution to *Afternoon Delight*?"

He sighs heavily. "Would you please?"

"Want me to read the scripts?" I offer. I'm not sure he'll let me. My dad would. But I don't want permission from my father. I want permission from Bridger.

"Do you want to?"

I shoot him a look that asks, *Don't you know me?* Because I think he does know me. I think he should by now. "Of course I do," I say.

"I'll send them to you," he says, then leans back in his chair, that sapphire-blue shirt making him look like a king, his stubble making him look...virile. "Soon, you'll be taking my job."

I laugh. "Watch out, Bridger. I'm angling for the big desk," I say, letting my gaze drift to his very big desk.

Big desk. Big desk. I swear those words flash in his eyes.

"Yeah, it's a good size," he says, deadpan and deliciously dry.

"Maybe I should read the scripts at your desk," I say, feeling all kinds of bold. Who knew a meeting with Daddy would wind me up like this? I feel a little topped off, amped up even. Like I can ski a black diamond, the wind whipping past my hair, snow flying in my wake.

"Feel free to set up camp. Stay all night," he says, and yes, hell yes. Everything *is* complicated all right, but he's not shying away from our office flirtation.

Give in, Bridger. Give in to me.

"Well, that's quite an invitation," I say.

"I've noticed you're good at invitations," he says.

"And how are you at RSVPing?" I counter.

Laughing, he shakes his head, like he can't quite believe I'm here. "I could be better," he says.

"You're telling me," I say.

Another laugh. Another *I can't believe what you're doing to me* sigh. Then, a look. It leaves me heady...this close to woozy.

But Bridger glances toward the shut door, wincing. We're not truly alone. Too many others bustle beyond that wood.

Music plays from his computer. *Company*, the Raúl Esparza production. "Do you go to Broadway still?" I ask, since I sense he needs a shift from invitations and complications. Otherwise, I'll be the one winding him too tightly, and I can't have that.

"I do."

"Do you have a Broadway crew? Theater friends?"

He shakes his head. "I mostly go alone," he says, then twirls his pen. Nervous habit? Maybe. "Not everyone shares my musical taste. But that's okay. I don't mind going solo. I'm used to it."

"Why?"

"You want to know?" He sounds doubtful but intrigued. I have the sense he doesn't talk freely about himself. Or maybe people don't ask. Perhaps he's so used to pitches, to *I have an idea for a show.*

Maybe he needs someone who wants to know him, *truly* know him, and also to listen. I'm that person. "I do want to know. Very much so," I say, backing off the flirt, playing up the earnest.

Because this is truly how I feel.

Normally, he's on guard. But the edge in his eyes seems to burn off. There's more vulnerability than I'm used to seeing. This isn't Bridger the dealmaker. This is the man. "I grew up backstage. I learned stage left and stage right before actual left and right. I did my homework in theater dressing rooms," he says.

That image lodges in my head and heart. A young Bridger, sprawled out on his stomach, pencil in hand, doing algebraic equations amongst feather boas and pancake makeup.

"I can see that," I say, delighted, and I lean forward on the couch, even though there's still a room between us. "That's so you."

"Is it?"

"Yes. It's who you are. Your love of stories came from there. Your passion for entertainment."

"That is true." He takes a beat, twirls his pen once more. "And you? Where did your love come from?"

"My mom. When I was younger, she took me to everything. I barely remember her, but I remember how it felt when she took me to the theater. When the overture would play, she'd say, *Do you feel that? The magic?*"

"And did you? Feel it?"

"I did," I say, breathless, my voice feathery. "I still do."

"Magic is how I felt too," he says, reverently, like we're both cupping that magic in our hands.

And then, because you should always leave them wanting more, I go.

Knowing he's wanting more.

* * *

That night, he emails me the scripts.

Bridger: Just some bedtime reading.

Harlow: Good thing I'm in bed.

Bridger: Then you'll have company. I'm reading them too.

Harlow: In bed?

Bridger: Yes.

He sends me a photo of his tablet, on his duvet. The cover is dove-gray, and an outrageous thrill runs through me at this window into his private life. I run my thumb along the cover like I can feel the cotton. Like I can smell the fresh sheets. Like I can slide under them and then on top of him.

Like I can run my hands down his chest, along his arms, through his hair. A pulse beats between my legs, insistent. Then, I take a picture of my tablet, resting on my bedcover. I send it along.

Bridger: White. With flowers. That's fitting, your duvet.

Harlow: Am I flowery?

Bridger: No. But those flowers are extraordinary.

I feel extraordinary with him.

14

EVERYTHING TO LOSE

Bridger

On Friday, I'm in meetings around the city, stewing on the problem in *Afternoon Delight* in between. I don't bother Ian. He's heading out of town with Vivian on Sunday, but since he punted the script my way, that's a sign he has no fucking idea what's wrong with the story.

But I have a hunch why it's not working. I want to fix it. Right now. Right away. Maybe if I do, I can stop obsessing over Harlow.

If I solve this problem, maybe my mind will let go of its incessant need to talk to her.

Maybe, maybe, maybe.

But I want to tell her too what the trouble in the script is. I'm dying to know if she's spotted it as well.

I shouldn't want to share, but I do.

As I walk to my next meeting in Tribeca, I make myself a promise—I'll only tell her if she brings it up.

There. That's a good limit.

After I finish my meeting, I return to Columbus Circle, my limit front and center in my mind. Once I reach the fourteenth floor, I say hello to Christian at reception, then head down the hall. When I round the corner into my office, Harlow flies in. Vibrating with energy. Looking incredible in that black skirt.

"I know what's wrong," she announces, eyes wide with delight.

I light up with the thrill of problem-solving. "Me too."

"There's no backstory," she announces. "For the hero."

Yes. Fucking yes. She got it.

"I don't know enough about Austin," I add, enthused.

"No wonder the writers said it needs work," she says, equally excited.

"And I want to care about Austin."

"We need more insight into him," she zings back.

We stand inches away, exchanging ideas. This is like foreplay, this back and forth. But I should be boss-like. I should be businesslike. I clear my throat. "Can you write up a report on Tuesday? Since the office is closed on Monday."

"I'd love to. I'll work on it over the weekend."

"You don't have to work over the long weekend," I say.

"I don't mind. I'm happy to talk more about it now too, if you want."

I glance at the clock on the wall. "I have a few calls then I have to go to a thing," I say, the last word tasting sour. "A cocktail party."

"Want me to go with you?" she asks, kind and friendly.

More than you can ever know.

"It doesn't have to be complicated," she adds in a whisper, so no one else can hear. "I could be your wing-woman?"

Am I that obvious with my disdain for events? Perhaps I am to her. Talking to her is easier than talking to anyone else. She's the opposite of my days, of deals, of problems, of negotiations. She feels like a solution to them, even though my feelings for her are the biggest problem of all—a conundrum tucked inside a riddle.

But I want her to solve all my riddles, so I shut the door this time. She moves to one end of the couch. I sit on a chair across from it. "Why do you think I need one?" I ask, desperate to know if she truly sees through me.

If she sees me.

"You don't like parties," she says plainly.

"You noticed."

"I told you. I notice things."

I'm a little amazed at how she lasers in on me. Or perhaps a lot amazed. And completely charmed. "You notice everything," I say.

"I don't drink at parties either. I don't drink at all,"

she says, and I didn't know that about her. I had no reason to know it.

"That so?" I ask, wanting more, always more with her.

"I didn't drink on my twenty-first birthday."

"Yeah?" I don't hide a smile. This is good news. No, the best news. I hardly meet anyone who has the same lines as I do.

"I don't want to be buzzed. It's not my thing. I like control." She takes a pause, her expression vulnerable. "I didn't have it when I was younger."

I hear everything she's not saying. She was raised around uncontrollable situations, a man with a monstrous appetite, a world she had no say over.

"You want to make all your choices with a clear mind. You want to make them for you," I say.

"Exactly."

The more I talk to her, the more I let her in. I don't usually share. I don't like to. But Harlow breaks me down. "That's why I walk around the park before events. To gird myself before I have to face a party. Moving around, walking, often the same path, helps me do that."

"Why don't you like parties, though?"

"My mom drinks. She's an...alcoholic. I don't tell people that," I admit. But Harlow's not people. I trust her. I don't even know why, except maybe because she's only ever given me reasons to trust her. "She was always throwing parties when I was a kid, having friends over. They all got drunk. All the time. They'd booze around my home, holding bottles, singing, dancing, talking about everything so damn loudly. I hated seeing everyone like that."

"That sounds hard," she says gently. "I get that. I do."

"I don't want to be like that." Each word is a scrape. Dry and harsh. "I want to be..."

"In control?" She doesn't say *like me*. She doesn't have to.

"Yes."

"So, should I go with you?" She sounds hopeful, eager.

My business should be at the top of my mind. My relationship with my business partner. The empire we've built. I have everything to lose, and still, I move to the couch. Sitting closer. "Harlow, I said this before. I need to say it again." The words threaten to stick in my throat, but I press on. "Do you really think that's a good idea? You and me at a party?"

"I like the idea," she says, strong, certain.

I take her strength and swallow it, letting it fuel me. "So do I," I say, quietly, telling the truth. "That's kind of the problem."

Her smile reappears for a second, then she seems to rein it in. "Why is it a problem?"

"You know why. It's complicating things," I say, frustrated again with our situation, with all the lines between us.

"But they're already complicated," she counters.

I stare out the window, Central Park below us, New York beyond. Then I look to the brunette beauty on my couch, my heart pounding mercilessly hard. I could crush her lips in a kiss, cover her body, fuck her till she's lost her mind.

Get it together.

"They're so complicated I can't fucking think sometimes around you," I admit, and it's a wild relief.

"Same for me," she says, breathy. "Same for me... Mr. James."

Her lashes flutter.

It's the first time she's called me that and it's too sexy, too dangerous.

My heart stops then starts again, beating in double time. "You know that no one in the office calls me Mr. James, right?"

"Do you like it when I do?"

I clench my fists. "Too much," I rasp out.

She leans closer. I dig my fingers harder into my palm.

Then she whispers my name once more, letting it slide off her lips like she's lingering on every letter. "Mr. James..."

I'm this close to saying *fuck it* to everything. To locking the door and pushing her up against the wall. To tearing off that shirt, and pressing my mouth to her lush, tempting skin.

But my office phone trills.

I want to thank the caller and curse the caller at the same time.

On the intercom, Jules announces that Carlos Mondez is on the line.

"He's a friend who's trying to get me an intro to

David Fontaine. I need to take that call," I say to Harlow.

Her green eyes sparkle, then her lips curve in a wicked grin, like she's just cracked a case.

"Hope the party is short," she says.

Me too, I mouth before she slinks out, whispering, "See you next week."

I can't wait for Tuesday to come.

15

CHECK MATE

Harlow

Since it's a long weekend, I take off for the Hamptons with Layla and Ethan. By her family's pool, I work on my report. I respond to the trust lawyers too, setting up a meeting for later this summer to review the funds I can access now.

Then, lounging on her outdoor couch under the June sun, an Arnold Palmer in hand, we work on my plan to deliver Bridger something he wants.

Allison Tanaka-Fontaine is the way to his business heart, and I know Allison. I know too where she'll be this week. I show the screen on my tablet to my friends, a spark of nerves lighting up in me. I hope this strategy pans out. "What do you think?" I ask.

With a decisive nod, Layla declares, "It's like shooting fish in a barrel."

I laugh. "Is it, though?"

She slides closer, rests her chin on my warm shoulder. "It's honestly brilliant."

Ethan whistles in appreciation. "You are a steely-eyed seductress."

"I don't know if it'll work." But I'm giddy with hope.

"Won't know till you try," he says.

"So try, Harlow. Try," Layla urges but I'm already there.

I've been looking for an opening, and I've found it. I send an email to the wife of the TV writer Bridger wants badly, since I met her at MoMA last year, and I make a request.

That night, Ethan, Layla and I go out dancing, arms high, hips bumping, music thrumming. I'm having the best night, but still I can't wait for this glorious summer weekend to end.

On the way to work on Tuesday, I spot a black rotary phone on the stoop of a brownstone. Odd. Is it headed for someone's vintage collection or destined for the trash? I snap a picture, then post it with the caption: *Coming or going?*

Even though I've already finished my report, I want to read it over again and then send it at just the right time.

I wait till the end of the day, then email it to Bridger. As closing time nears, Jules packs up. "Time to go," she says.

"I've got a little more to do."

She arches a brow. "Suit yourself."

I will, Jules. I fucking will.

Once everyone leaves, including Jules—*especially* Jules—I head to Bridger's office and rap twice.

"Come in," he says, and I stride inside and then shut the door with finality—a loud, declarative click.

"What did you think?" I ask.

He laughs. "You think I read it already?"

"I think you read it as soon as it landed twenty minutes ago," I say, feeling confident and powerful.

"I think your report is brilliant. And I think the phone is going." There's a sparkle in those blue eyes as he confesses he's looked up my photos—a confession that makes me feel bubbly.

"I think it's coming. Or staying, I should say," I add.

"I can see that too," he says, his eyes never leaving mine.

Now I feel more than bubbly. I feel...bold. I move closer, jutting out a hip against the side of his desk.

His eyes travel up and down my legs like he's fighting not to but can't resist. Good thing I like wearing skirts as much as he likes looking at my legs. "Did Carlos get you that intro to Fontaine?" I ask, prompting him.

"He's still working on it."

I smile, but it's a small one so I don't let on how thrilled I am that Carlos hasn't quite come through. "Then, what are you doing tomorrow night?" I ask.

For a second, he startles. I've surprised him. Good. He's most pliable when he's off-kilter. "I'm working," he answers.

I shake my head, then pop up onto his desk, perching my butt on the edge. "No, *we're* going to the Petra Gallery. There's an exhibit. Allison Tanaka-Fontaine is a silent partner in the business."

It's like watching a sunrise, the way his smile spreads, slow and unstoppable. "You're indispensable," he says as if amazed by me.

Good. I want to amaze him.

"I got us on the VIP list," I add.

"You did?"

"I sure did." I go for the kill, crossing my legs and leaning a little closer. "I wanted to do this for you."

"Harlow," he says, a low warning.

"We can go together," I say, pushing more. I'm not letting this chance pass me by.

"Together?" he asks, like he's never heard the word, never uttered it.

I slide my palm farther across his desk. I'm at a sharper angle now. The kind that shows off hips, and curves, and breasts. All the places he wants to touch me. "Yes, like a date," I say, and I should be nervous. But I'm not. I've been working up to this moment for the last year. I'm simply ready for my gift.

"This is a bad idea," he warns.

He's wrong. It's not a bad idea at all. "Are you sure about that?"

Another harsh breath. His eyes close. The man is at war. Well, some men need to chase. I sit up, hop off the desk, head to the door.

The wheels of his chair squeak.

In no time he's up too, grabbing my wrist, yanking me around, and jerking me against him.

My wrist tingles. My body sings.

He glares at me, fire in his eyes. "You have done nothing but tempt me for the last few weeks," he hisses.

An accusation. And also the truth.

"Good," I whisper in a taunt.

"Why the fuck are you tempting me?" He bites it out, but it's not a question for me. It's for the universe. It's rhetorical.

Portrait of a man breaking. It's happening. Before my very eyes. This is art, and I love it.

My pulse beats wildly fast.

But I've been patient. I've waited for my chance. I stay patient.

He will bend. He will break. "Am I, Bridger? Am I that tempting?" I ask.

His nostrils flare. He exhales harshly. "You're destroying my self-control, Harlow."

I hum, like the wicked vixen I am with him. "Then...ruin it. Just ruin it."

He grabs my face, and he takes what he wants—my mouth in one hot kiss.

16

LIKE CHERRY

Bridger

I've done it. I've stepped over the line I swore I'd never cross. But, as I sweep my lips over hers, it's still not too late. I *could* stop.

This could be one hot kiss that's over far too soon, and then I'll walk away.

Nearly exonerated.

I could say it's a mistake.

Write it off as a one-time thing that'll never happen again. If I don't let it go any farther, that is.

But as our lips brush once more, my bones crackle with electricity. Then it's as if the whole city sparks. We kiss like a storm, like thunder and lightning, and the sky breaking open. And in this tempest of a kiss, I know. I just know.

There's no turning back.

I *could* stop. But I won't. And so I will take what I want.

I clasp her face, and I crush her lips, consuming Harlow.

This is so wrong.

Her luscious sighs fill my head.

This is so right.

She's so responsive, melting under my kiss, murmuring sweet sighs and gasps. Her sounds go to my head. Her longing electrifies me.

And I need even more.

Deeper. Closer. I'm unwilling to stop. Uninterested in a thing beyond this office. She's here with me and fuck the world.

Her hands climb up my chest, traveling over the fabric of my shirt. Gripping me tight, refusing to let go too.

A tug from her.

A push from me.

And we are a tango of a first kiss.

Her lips taste incredible. She's like...

I break apart, panting. "You taste like cherry," I say.

"It's my lip gloss."

"It's addictive."

Her eyes twinkle. "So take another hit."

"I will," I say, but first, I indulge with my eyes, savoring the sight of her. Her beautiful face, from her glittering eyes to her pretty lips to her delicate neck.

I want to explore every inch of her body. Want to kiss all the terrain of Harlow, learn how she tastes everywhere—her collarbone, her neck, her stomach, behind her knees, between her thighs.

With that, I kiss her again, and my brain goes haywire. My body overheats.

She grapples with my shirt collar, those nimble fingers clasping tight. A needy moan falls from her lips as I kiss her.

I suck on her bottom lip. She whimpers.

That sound.

That sexy sound is killing me.

I should not know what she sounds like when she's turned on.

But now I do, and now I am consumed with even more want. It runs through my blood. It drives me on. I nibble on her lips, a mix of teeth and tongue, soft and hard, push and pull.

Then, when she ropes her eager hands around the back of my neck and tugs me impossibly closer, it's hardly a kiss anymore.

It's foreplay.

I press my body to hers, letting her feel my arousal, craving hers desperately too.

So much it's driving me mad.

Making me reckless.

One more kiss and I'll stop.

But her lips, and her scent, and her hands roaming over me...

I have to touch her. I let go of her face, drag a hand down her side, brushing the outline of her breast.

She trembles, then murmurs, "*Oh, god.*"

It's enough for me to break the kiss. To stare at her with, I'm sure, wild eyes.

She looks back at me with even wilder ones. "Bridger," she whispers, her voice like smoke.

"Yes?" I ask hazily.

"I want you," she whispers.

Three words and I might as well surrender.

I hardly know what to say. *I want you too* is patently obvious. Instead, I slide my palm along her hip, brushing the outside of her thigh, heading for the hem of her skirt. The whole time she's gazing up at me, lips parted and red, neck stretched long and inviting.

"And you are entirely bad for me," I say at last. Because it's true. And necessary.

She just smiles. Slow, a little wicked. Then she bites the corner of her bottom lip before she says, "But that's not stopping you, is it?"

I grit my teeth, trying, fucking trying, to stop. But then, she tilts her chin. An invitation. "Have you thought about my neck before?"

It's like she can see inside my filthy mind. I breathe harshly.

Walk away. Just walk away.

I don't walk away.

"Too much," I admit. I don't even know what rational thought is anymore. I've lost it with her.

She lifts her right hand, and sensually, seductively, brushes her fingertips along her neck, then down to the hollow of her throat, then just a little farther. Teasing at the top of her breasts. Leaving a trail for me to follow.

I dip my face, and I kiss her there. She tastes so

sweet, so tempting. Soon, I'm moaning as I layer open-mouthed caresses along the column of her throat. My hand plays with the hem of her skirt, and I'm flirting with the red zone of danger.

Kissing her is one thing. Touching her intimately is another.

If I can just maintain that line...

I'll indulge in one or two or ten more seconds, and I won't do it again.

But then she slides one hand into my hair while the other hand wraps around my hand. *On her thigh*. She threads her fingers through mine.

My hand buzzes. Everything tingles. My whole body is vibrating, and I can't stand how good she feels. I break the kiss, meet her lust-struck gaze.

But I don't just see lust in her shimmery eyes.

I see confidence. I see certainty. I see a woman with a plan. She doesn't look away as she moves our joined hands under her skirt.

Warning signs flash, and still...I go.

She's guiding my palm along the silky skin of her inner thigh.

"Harlow, honey," I warn, the affectionate nickname slipping out, unbidden.

"Honey?" she asks, but it's hardly a question. More a dirty delight.

I don't answer her.

I don't need to.

We both know what I just did.

She's like a gorgeous silhouette in a lighthouse, guiding a sailor home. I follow her spotlight as her hand drags mine up her flesh, closer and closer still.

I can feel her heat. I can sense her wetness.

What kind of panties does she wear? How long would it take to make her come? What does she sound like when she loses control?

Wicked thoughts lash my mind. I close my eyes, squeezing them shut as my fingers come *this* close to crossing a terrible line.

For a few tense seconds, I hope for a fire alarm, a phone call, a knock on the door.

But I'll have to be my own knock.

Like I've been burned, I yank away, step back, drag my hand across my mouth. Like I can wipe away the taste of her.

"I can't," I mutter, shaking my head, ashamed.

Or perhaps I'm just shocked I've let it go this far.

I can't mess around with my business partner's twenty-one-year-old daughter.

Her eyes widen in question. "Why?"

It's a valid thing to ask when someone's staring at you like they want to tear off your clothes.

But the answer is too easy.

Resigned and frustrated, I sweep my arm out to indicate the office, then the door, then somehow all of New York. "Because of all this," I say, angry with myself. "Lucky 21, and the business and...everything."

Her eyes shine.

Her lower lip quivers.

Oh, fuck. I can't stand making her sad. I advance

toward her then stop, thinking better of it. *Thinking.* Finally thinking.

"Harlow," I say softly.

"Yes?"

"It's just too risky," I say, imploring her to understand. I don't enumerate all the things that could go wrong—I'm risking my reputation as well as this company, and her father could turn on her too. He could take his support away from her. She doesn't even have a real job yet. I can't risk her future either. "And you. I don't want to hurt you."

She purses her lips and nods. "I understand." Then she draws a breath and seems to erase whatever emotions flickered through her moments ago. "I should go."

I hate the thought, but I nod crisply. "You should," I say, and the look on her face is so tough, so strong.

She reaches for the door, looking wise beyond her years, strong beyond her age.

"Good night," she says in a tone I've never heard from her before. Both sad and cold. Like the tone is a necessity.

"Good night."

She leaves, and when the tap of her shoes fades, the elevator doors ding closed, I slump on my couch and drop my head in my hands, wishing my chest didn't feel so damn hollow.

17

EVERYONE WANTS SOMETHING

Bridger

The problem is I don't feel hollow when I return home later that night.

I feel jangly. Jittery.

I replay those ten minutes incessantly.

I can't stand being in my apartment alone with these rampant thoughts, so I head for a late yoga class. Axel says he'll meet me on the corner.

On the way out of the building, my doorman calls out to me. "Hey, Mr. James. I have something for you," he says from his post at the gleaming black desk in the lobby. He waves me over like he's got a secret to share.

"Hey, Randy. What have you got?"

The mustached man in the navy-blue uniform lowers his voice to a stage whisper. "My cousin Joey has a script. New action series centered around a group of co-workers, and each one has special powers. It's gonna be epic. I'll bring it to you tomorrow," he says with a wide smile.

I flash a smile back. Not because I'm eager to read another script. But because this is my life. Everyone, everywhere has a TV show in them, and they're always asking me to read them. To do to their shows what Ian and I did to *Sweet Nothings*. Make them soar to the top.

That's my fucking job. Find shows, make shows, make them rain down money on Ian, me, and our employees.

"Sounds great, Randy," I tell him, then give a quick nod goodbye as I head out into the warm June evening.

Will Randy's cousin's show be the next hit? Odds say no. But still, the request resets my focus to TV, media, and the business I've built with Ian.

I was twenty-five when Harlow's dad and I started working on *Sweet Nothings*, when we founded Lucky 21 to make it happen.

That show is my biggest hit. *Sweet Nothings* is the reason I've earned the regard I have, and it's the reason we produced the shows that came after.

It's the reason our company is worth millions.

I can't mess with that reason.

As I walk toward the corner, there's a clap on my shoulder. I turn to find Axel. "Superhero co-workers?" he asks, raising an eyebrow. He must have been behind me and heard the whole conversation.

I shrug as we head to the studio together. "You never know where you might find the next big hit."

"Randy gave me tips on how to write a better

escape from law enforcement scene last week. Everyone knows something. And everyone wants something."

"That's the truth, isn't it," I remark.

But I say nothing more, even as Axel chats about a new band. While he talks, I'm seeing the dazed post-kiss look in Harlow's eyes, then the bite mark on her lip. I'm inhaling the scent of her desire.

I'm smelling her cherry lip gloss all over again.

"Want me to send them to you?"

I have no idea what Axel's talking about. "What?"

Axel laughs. "I was just telling you about some new tunes."

"Sorry. I was...distracted."

He rolls his eyes as a bus rumbles by, spewing a plume of exhaust. "I figured as much."

There's a strange silence between us for the next block, and then a clearing of his throat as we near the studio. "You okay, Bridger? You don't seem like yourself."

I sigh. "No, but I'll be fine."

I head into the studio and try to will away these feelings for an hour.

* * *

But back at home, I'm still wound tight. Every thought in my mind comes back to those ten minutes by the door in my office.

I strip out of my clothes, head to the shower, and turn it to scalding. The bathroom steams up, and in no time, I've slammed a palm against the wall and I'm working myself in a frenzy.

It's been a while since I've jerked off like this.

Frantic. Urgent.

Images snap before me. Her hand on mine. Mine dangerously near her panties. Her wanting me there.

Just fucking wanting me with this same, wild abandon.

I come on a guttural groan, then pant, breathing hard, hanging my head under the water.

Maybe I just needed to get her out of my system.

Maybe one good jerk will erase today.

* * *

Ten minutes later, I'm restless in bed, something gnawing at me.

Of course something would gnaw at you. You touched Ian's daughter.

I turn off the light, annoyed and pent up. I'll just mentally review my plans for tomorrow, and maybe then I can sleep.

I start my review with my meetings in the morning, then my calls in the afternoon, and then...

Tomorrow night. Wednesday evening.

That's it. That's what's eating at me.

I bolt upright, grab my phone from the nightstand.

I didn't confirm the plans. She might think I won't go with her after how I left things. Or she might think I'd go without her.

I send her a text.

.   .   .

Bridger: Thank you again for the VIP tickets. Maybe we should meet there.

Harlow: Good idea.

My gut churns.

That's so not her. That's not her at all. She's bright and sharp as a knife. I should leave well enough alone. Truly, I should.

So I do one right thing today—I turn my phone off so I won't start up again with her.

18

THE VIRGIN SOCIETY

Harlow

Honey.

He gave me a nickname.

A delicious, sexy one.

Honey's not a name you give someone you only kiss once. I've read enough, seen enough, know enough. I am his honey.

And I'm not going to let one setback get me down. I'll simply...find a new way to solve the puzzle of Bridger.

I want what I want, and I'm not done getting it —*getting him.*

The next morning, I do what any smart, Upper East Side girl would do. I call for reinforcements. On the way to work, I send a text to Layla and Ethan asking if they can meet for a quick lunch at a nearby diner that Layla loves.

A working lunch at Neon Diner, I add.

Naturally, they both say yes.

Until then, I'll be the best damn intern there ever was. I walk into Lucky 21, and I do everything that's expected of me and more in the morning. I write excellent reports. I take orders from Jules. I don't even see Bridger, talk to him or text him.

As noon ticks close, I grab my phone with the built-in lip gloss case—purses can suck it—and swing by Jules's desk.

"I'm going to grab lunch. I'll be back in forty-five," I say to the stony-faced woman.

Without even glancing up from her pristine desk, she replies, "You can take an hour. It's standard for *everyone.*"

Even princesses.

"Forty-five minutes is fine. I don't mind," I say, upbeat. I don't want to look like I'm taking advantage of my connections.

Though I can't see her eyes, I have a feeling she's rolling them. Then, she raises her face. Her mouth is tight. Her dark eyes, piercing. "Are you going to stay here at Lucky 21 at the end of your internship this summer?"

I'm taken aback by the question and the intensity with which she asks it. "I don't actually know," I say, trying not to stumble on my own surprise. I didn't think she was interested in my plans.

She straightens her spine. "If you're going to apply for an open position, I'd like to know. It'll help me to focus my...*resources.*"

Jules, I'm here for one reason, and it has nothing to do with a job.

But she doesn't need to know I have no desire to work in media. "Thank you. I've been thinking about my fall plans a lot. I'll let you know."

"You do that," she says, then returns to typing, tap, tap, tapping away on her noisy keyboard. There's no dismissal, no goodbye. But that's no-nonsense Jules for you.

I've turned to go when she clears her throat and says, "And if you're not keen on sticking around, you don't have to stay late."

A prickle of fear slides down my spine.

Does she know what I did last night? Or has she noticed me hanging around Bridger's office at other times in the evenings?

No idea. I swallow back the nerves, then face her once more. The more I seem like a bad girl, the more she'll think I am one.

"Thanks, but I was that way in school too. Working late. Coming in early," I say with a *what can you do* shrug.

Look it up, Jules. I was the valedictorian at Carlisle Academy and I attended a top twenty-five ranked university, earning a double major in French and art history. I'm not a slacker who leaves work early.

On that salvo, I head out to lunch, doing my best to shed my worry over her. I'm allowed to spend time with Bridger. In fact, it's expected. My dad made it clear Bridger would be the point of contact for my internship. I've done nothing wrong with my office visits.

Still, as I leave, I don't even look at Bridger's door. I won't give Jules any bait.

* * *

Sixties music plays overhead at the diner. Servers in mint green and pastel pink skirts scurry by. A jukebox offers Elvis tunes.

And from her side of the booth at the retro diner, Layla fans herself. "Holy shit. That sounds hot," she says when I finish telling my friends the tale of last night.

Layla waves her jeweled hand in front of her face, her collection of silver skull rings catching the afternoon light. Next to her, Ethan whistles at me, with a "Damn, girl. Can you tell that story again?"

I preen a little, pleased they've enjoyed my escapades. I sure did.

"I'm going to need to hear it again too since my love life is more nonexistent than mermaids," Layla adds.

I hold up a hand as a stop sign. "Wait," I cut in. "I thought you were going out with that guy? The one your mom thought was perfect for you?"

"Mom thinks he's perfect because his family's like triple-yacht wealthy, and he won't try to steal her makeup empire," Layla says.

"The important metric of your romantic life, of course," Ethan puts in.

"So I went out with him once. He was all *let me tell you about my stock portfolio* level of boring," she says. "Ergo, my sex and love life is mermaid level."

Ethan grabs a fry from Layla's plate. "Sidenote: My last date thought she was a mermaid."

Layla frowns. "Did she have a fishtail?"

"Or is she one of those *I want to be a mermaid* girls?" I ask, snagging a fry too.

Shaking his head, Ethan waves a hand breezily. "Like, in a past life she was a mermaid." Then he leans closer. "Enough about me. Tell us about that kiss again and don't leave out a single detail. Layla needs to use that story when she tests out her new toy tonight from Date Night For One."

Layla smacks Ethan's shoulder. "So do you."

"I'm not testing your toy, girl," he says.

But I don't want to tell the story again. I *need* insight. "Guys, help. I feel like I'm at an impasse. I don't know what to do next. To convince him we could be good together," I say.

Good in bed for sure.

Maybe even good out of bed.

But one thing at a time.

Layla furrows her brow, takes a minute. "Look, odds are nothing will come of this," she says, ever pragmatic.

I nod, taking the truth on the chin. "I know." Do I ever know.

"But maybe he needs something from you," Layla offers helpfully.

"Yeah, he needs her panties removed and her body spread out before him," Ethan stage whispers.

I snort laugh.

Layla slugs him again. "I meant something… emotional, philosophical, you ball-carrier."

"Oh, right, *that*," Ethan says, then shrugs helplessly. "Testosterone. What can you do?"

That's the question, though. "What can I do?" I press, staying the course.

Layla taps her finger against her chin, and I think hard too, replaying last night for the millionth time.

But I focus on the words this time, not the intimacy.

His *This is too risky.*

Bridger's worried, understandably, that someone would find out about us. "He must need reassurance that I'm trustworthy," I say, like I've just answered the right question in class. "That I will keep not only his secrets, but *this* secret."

Layla's blue eyes brighten. "Oh yes, that's it, baby," Layla says, offering a palm for smacking.

Ethan does the same.

"And I can definitely keep *our* secret," I add. After all, I've spent the last several years of my life amassing an absolutely pristine track record of keeping things to myself. I've never once breathed a word of Dad's affairs beyond the vault of my two best friends, who I met all the way back in grade school. We've seen each other through our parents' divorces and my mother's death, through family addictions and disorders, and through good nights, bad mornings, joys and victories.

"So you need to let him know you're not about to blab," Ethan adds.

Except, am I such a good secret keeper? I wince, a little embarrassed over how I just disproved my point here at this lunch. "But I told the two of you," I say, like a confession.

Layla pulls a *you've got to be kidding me* face. "We rent space in your brain. We don't count."

"This is the vault," Ethan says, drawing an air circle around us. Then he drops that hand onto the Formica. "We could even be a secret society, the three of us."

"Yes!" Layla says, enthused. She slams her palm on top of Ethan's.

"I want in," I say, adding my hand to theirs.

"You've been in," he adds. "And now we swear allegiance to...what's our society called? Do we use The Virgin Club? After our favorite dating column?"

We've all grown addicted to a helpful, sex-positive dating column under that name. We share it with each other every week, along with our comments on positions, ideas, approaches, strategies. But I have a name unique to us.

It's perfect. With a sly smile, I whisper, "We're the Virgin Society."

Layla regards me with mischief. "And I nominate you to be the first one to break her virgin vows," she says with a devilish smirk.

And I want Bridger to be my first. "I accept your nomination."

Tonight at the gallery, I'm going to steal Bridger away, tug him into a nook or alcove, talk to him, reassure him, and let him know I'll look out for his *honey* and him.

19

VERY DIFFERENT SOMETHINGS

Harlow

I won't give Jules the satisfaction of thinking I'd stay late for *any* reason tonight. At six on the dot, I pop up, grab my things, and say breezily, "See you tomorrow. I'm heading out with friends tonight. Shopping and all."

I contemplated telling her I had volunteer work at the children's hospital but the more you say, the more it's clear you're lying. I've learned that from Dad.

"Of course," Jules remarks as she gathers her bag.

She doesn't ask for more. Because she thinks I'm a privileged brat anyway. There's nothing I can do to convince her otherwise.

"Oh, and I started that new database you wanted," I add. "The one with the list of all the agents. I added their favorite gifts too," I say with a breezy shrug, "in case we ever need it."

Her eyes flicker with a hint of surprise, but she erases it quickly. "Cool," she adds, then rises too, and before I know it she's walking down the hall with me to the elevators. Christian from reception is already gone for the day.

I squint ahead.

Oh.

Is that Isla with Bridger? Their backs are to us, but they're talking by the elevator banks.

That's odd. I hardly ever see Isla over here near Columbus Circle. She's usually at the writers' room on-set over on Eleventh.

"But do you know when he'll be back?" I hear her ask Bridger.

"I'm not sure," Bridger says, his tone professional, a little distant. "He and his fiancée are busy planning the wedding."

It's pointed, the emphasis on fiancée.

"Okay. So he'll be here all next week?" Isla asks, almost like a plea.

"I believe so, but Isla, you're the head writer for *Sweet Nothings*. You know what you're doing. We trust you with the storyline," he says, firm, not placating. It's a reminder she doesn't need my father for work.

"It's just that I wanted to run this one scene idea past him. With Sam and Josie and the lawyer character too," she says, and there's a break in her voice. A slight tremble.

But once we near them, Isla straightens her spine, spins around cautiously. Her blue eyes widen, then she flashes a plastic smile my way. "Oh, hi Harlow. How are you?"

"Great," I say.

"How's everything?" she asks again, like she didn't just make that same inquiry.

Jules clears her throat. "Hello, Isla. Is there anything I can help you with on *Sweet Nothings*? I have the latest revisions, as well as a report from standards and practices approving the legal issues in the storyline."

Jules might as well pee to mark her territory.

Isla shakes her head, her red hair whipping fast. "No, I'll be fine. I'll just…"

But when she doesn't finish, Jules must lose interest since she lasers in on Bridger. "Do you have all the research I sent you on the upcoming CTM meeting to finalize the TJ Hardman deal?"

"I do. Thank you. That was quite helpful," he says, uber professional.

I fight off a smile. I don't let on that I helped him win that deal. Jules would lose her mind.

"If there's anything else you need, I can do it," she says.

"Thank you," he answers as the elevator arrives and the four of us step inside—the woman looking for my father, the woman wondering what I'm up to, the young intern studying them all, and the man everyone here wants something from.

Very different somethings.

Bridger stands at the back of the elevator. He doesn't look at me. I'm not bothered. I don't want him to reveal himself to them. I'm glad he's not letting on he wants to slide his hand between my legs.

Jules tilts her head toward Bridger. "Where are you off to tonight?"

"I'm heading to an event," he says with finality.

I wonder if Jules knows he dislikes events, but then she says, "How fun."

Ha. She doesn't know. But I do. I know things. I notice things.

"It's work," he says crisply, like it couldn't possibly be fun.

For him, it won't be.

But I can help him. I can be his wing-woman tonight.

As the elevator chugs down, Isla fiddles with her phone, her fingers flying like she's sending texts at Mach speed. Her lips twitch in a grin. Probably a lover she's texting.

"I'll be working tonight too. On some research," Jules puts in, and this hardly seems like the blasé executive assistant I've seen before. More like she's sucking up to him. Something I've never seen her do before.

Once we reach the lobby, we fan out toward the big revolving doors where Jules breezily calls to me, "Have fun shopping, Harlow."

Right. Naturally, she needed to point that out.

But I don't break character. Waving at her, I flash her a *vapid rich girl without a care in the world* smile. "Can't wait to get new shoes," I say, then I take off first, leaving them in my dust, cutting across Columbus

Circle and heading for the subway to go downtown to the art gallery.

When I'm a block away from the entrance, my phone buzzes. I grab it from my pocket. A text flashes across the screen.

Bridger: Get in the car. For your shopping trip.

My heart skids as I turn my head and catch sight of the sleek, black town car ten feet away from me, idling at the curb.

My heart rockets.

I close the distance. The door opens. I slide into the back, next to the man who crushed his lips to mine last night.

"Shopping, really?" he asks wryly.

I stretch out a leg, the one with the scar on the ankle. "Well, maybe I need new shoes."

20

THINGS WE IGNORE

Bridger

I wasn't about to let her ride the dirty subway.

Not when I have a plush town car to take her in.

Not when we're heading to the same destination.

And not when she secured VIP tickets to an event *for me*.

So, yeah, I'm only being gentlemanly.

That's all.

The partition's up as the car pulls into traffic, heading west. It's just Harlow and me in the backseat, the hum of the air-conditioning and the weight of last night surrounding us.

Her wavy chestnut hair shines in the fading day as she rolls up the window, sealing us into our private corner of Manhattan. With lush pink lips, she smiles at me. Her knowing eyes are an invitation.

And mine follow her lead, roaming to her ankle.

"So, on this shopping trip, what kind of shoes should we get you?"

She taps her chin, in mock deep thought. "Let's see...would you like me in slippers?"

Yes, slippers. You'd wear them in the morning, in my kitchen, when you're all sleepy, sexy and morning soft, skin dewy and kissable from a night next to me in bed.

"Or perhaps rain boots," I suggest as the antidote. They're so not sexy.

"Good idea. They'd look good with," she says, stopping to stare at the ceiling of the car, before she fixes me with a smirk, "cute little shorts."

Check. Checkmate.

Laughing softly, I shake my head, then lean back against the headrest as the driver maneuvers us onto a congested Ninth Avenue en route to the Village. "You win," I say softly.

This admission covers...everything.

I'm not merely being gentlemanly. I want to be near her. I want to stay in her orbit, feel its pull.

"Or maybe we both win?" Her voice pitches up with hope. A desperate, pleading kind that tugs on my heart, which is already clay in her hands.

I wish we could both win. As the car slogs downtown, the last few weeks at Lucky 21 snap into shape.

She's been vying for me.

Maybe the whole time.

Do I like that?

Yeah. So much.

It's heady to be the object of this woman's attention. I want to just enjoy the shine of it.

But I can't. Instead, I shift gears with a nod toward her right ankle, the once pink scar faded to white now. "Nice scar," I add.

"Glad you like it, Mr. James," she says.

I like it so much I want to kiss it. I want to kiss her calf, the back of her knee, her thighs. But before I can linger on this dangerous hunger in my chest, on the rapid pace of my pulse, and what the hell to do with it all, Harlow tilts her head, studying me quizzically.

"What is it?" I ask, a little unnerved.

"Your shirt," she says.

I glance down at it. A deep rich orange. Not a Halloween shade, but more like orange sapphire. I pluck at it with mild concern. "Something on it?"

"No. I just like it. You look good in rich colors. Jewel tones," she says.

Warmth spreads through me. She's sunshine and desire all at once. "Do I now?"

"Yes, you do, Bridger."

I tear my gaze away, the knot in my chest tightening, the ache intensifying. Do I tell her I bought it a few weeks ago? The weekend before she started at Lucky 21? That when I held it up in the men's store in the Village, the one I go to regularly, I imagined the times when she held up shirts, snapped pictures, sent them to me?

But I just choke out a strangled *thank you*.

Then I run my hands through my hair. Being near her is so fucking hard. I wish...

I just wish...

"Bridger," she says, and that's a new tone. It's an *I have something important to say* tone.

"Yes, Harlow?" I hope I'm hiding the nerves in my voice. What the fuck am I even afraid of? Except...

Losing the thing that's kept me centered.

My business.

My whole life I've wanted to tell stories. I never had the talent to write them on my own, or the interest in performing them. But I always had an eye. A sharp, astute eye for spotting a diamond in the rough.

After an unsteady childhood, moving around from city to city, following Mom's tours, whiplashing from New York to Los Angeles, from Miami to Sacramento, no one but her and me, I don't want to lose my anchor.

My stability.

My Lucky 21.

It feels like a part of my soul.

"I would never let on about us," she says, answering my question in a calm but impassioned voice. "I won't say a word at work. The only ones who know about..." she stops before she says *us*, but I hear it, and more so, I feel it, "are Layla and Ethan."

I startle at the mention of her friends. "They know?"

Her lips twitch in a grin, but she seems to fight it off. "I told them. They know how I feel," she begins, and my heart skitters too fast. I barely have time to recover from those three words flung at me—*how I feel*—since she continues. "They love me. Unconditionally. We don't tell each other's secrets. We protect each other. We always have. And you have to know, Bridger, you just have to. I would never tell my..." she stops, correcting to, "Him."

"Okay," I say, since I'm not even sure what to say next, at the mention of that...pronoun.

She inches closer, her hand moving near mine. My fingers ache to hold hers.

But she sets her hand in her lap. "You need to know something else," she continues.

"What is it?"

"When I was thirteen, *he* told me to never say a word about the things he did. And I never did," she says, her voice trembling with hurt. "I never said a thing to Mariana, or to Joan. Through all of high school and college, I kept it quiet like he asked me to. All of it. I don't reveal secrets. I'll protect you."

Oh, god. Oh, fucking hell. She shouldn't protect me. I should protect her. I should look out for this incredible woman. Unable to resist, I reach for her, curl a hand gently around the back of her neck, and whisper, "Come here."

In no time, she's next to me, thigh to thigh, our bodies turned, our faces near.

"All day I couldn't wait for tonight," I tell her, and it hurts saying those words. Because we can go nowhere.

"I counted down the hours," she whispers.

"And you should *never* have to protect me," I tell her, emphatic, pressing my forehead to hers.

"But I want to. And I can," she says.

My heart squeezes. She's so young and so strong at the same damn time. It doesn't take a genius to know why. She had to sculpt herself into this young woman with her own tools. Had to do it with no role model while her one living parent chased his narcissistic, selfish desires.

"No, Harlow. Don't protect me," I murmur into her hair, drawing an inhale of her shampoo and I'm lost. Just lost in the vanilla scent of her.

I inch back, look at her eyes, gleaming with passion.

Then I drop my lips to hers and kiss her once more. It's a whisper of a kiss. We're both holding back, perhaps acutely aware that we can't tumble out of the car, looking kiss-drunk and bruised.

But I know in the soft press of our lips, in the hands on arms, hands in hair, hands so eager to touch, that I can't protect myself from what's happening either. Because this is the kind of kiss that erases everyone before it.

Soon, though, I find the will to pull away, looking at her dazed eyes as I say, "What are you doing to me?"

"I thought that was clear," she says, that naughty smile returning.

I laugh lightly. "Fine, then what am I supposed to do with you?"

She tugs on the neck of my shirt. "I have some ideas. It might involve getting this shirt off," she says, and she's playful and fun.

Smart and vibrant.

Kind and bold.

She's like Joan of Arc of Manhattan, spurred on by her vision. And I think I'm falling terribly for her.

Change of topic. I need one, stat. I glance out the tinted window. Times Square is nearby.

"Who would you cast in an *Ask Me Next Year* revival?" I ask.

"Oh, I have so many ideas."

We spend the rest of the ride casting the revival, choosing the three leads. I ignore the fact that the musical doesn't have a happy ending.

When we reach the Village, the driver pulls the car over, cuts the engine. I brush a hand down my shirt, check my reflection. No evidence.

Harlow's reapplying lip gloss using the camera on her phone.

"Shame," I mutter.

She cocks her head. "That I don't look well-kissed anymore?"

"Yes. That."

"I know," she says.

Then we get out, walking down the block together, but apart.

The sun falls low in the sky, casting long beams of light between red-brick buildings. When I turn the corner onto Jane Street, the sign for Petra Gallery comes into view.

Focus, James.

Get Fontaine. That's my only mission tonight.

21

TIGER

Harlow

A banner sprawls across the glass window of the gallery. *Reread,* it says. That's the name of this exhibition of confessions of love from some of history's greatest writers. The photographs of the correspondence are paired alongside stunning black-and-white images that capture the theme of each letter's romance.

It's surreal to walk up to an art gallery with the man who just kissed me in his town car.

For a few heady seconds, I play pretend, imagining this is us. This is how we do New York. We attend exhibits together. Maybe we go to the theater, check out quiet bookshops. Together, we'd imbibe art and culture, devouring stories, being dazzled by a show.

After, we'd walk around the city. We'd talk and we'd understand each other implicitly.

Right now, I have to fight the urge to look at Bridger with all these expectations in my eyes.

Because we're not that couple.

We're not *a* couple at all.

I let the daydreams die as we cross the threshold into the gallery.

Servers in black slacks and crisp, white shirts circulate with trays held high, while art lovers in plaid shirts and Converse, in motorcycle boots and Manolo Blahniks, admire the letters and the photos.

We're here for business, but when I catch a glimpse of Bridger adjusting his cuffs, my heart squeezes.

I make a move to touch his wrist in reassurance, but then I clasp my hands together instead. I can't do that. Here or anywhere.

He stops fidgeting, and his eyes scan the crowd with speedy efficiency. He's a man on a mission. He's not here to mingle.

"I don't see him yet," I whisper.

"I don't either."

"He'll be here," I reassure him. I hope—I really hope—I'm not wrong about Fontaine being here to support his wife.

Except...there has to be an easier way to get to the man. "Does he not take your calls?" I ask.

Bridger scratches his jaw, a little pensively. "He has in the past, but recently, no. I've been trying to get an intro, but he's old school. An in-person type of guy. So..." Then Bridger leans the slightest bit closer to me, not inappropriate, not too much, but just enough for me to catch a hint of his cedar scent.

Different from when I ran into him at MoMA in December. It's subtler now. There are new notes of faded soap and rain. My stomach zings.

"I've been working on some concepts that I think might impress him," Bridger says.

I'm eager to hear them. I love it when he lets me into his world, his mind, his thoughts. "Can you tell me what they are? Or are they secret?"

His deep blue eyes twinkle. "I trust you," he says, low and barely audible. Just for me.

They mean even more after our talk in the car. "Good. You should," I say.

"I read every single one of his humor columns from years ago. He used to write for the *New York Press* before the paper was shut down. I want him to do something with those. He never has, but I can see a path through them. A story he was trying to tell in his witty observation."

"Oh nice," I say, then my gaze catches on the silver fox I spotted at the MoMA sculpture garden in December. It's Fontaine, and once again, his arm is wrapped around his wife. Once again, they're laughing, but like it's a private joke between just them. "There they are. He really seems to make her laugh," I whisper encouragingly. "Go get 'em, tiger."

"Tiger," he repeats, lifting a brow in appreciation. He likes the nickname. "Wish me luck."

I want to rise up on my tiptoes and kiss him. Instead I say softly, "Good luck, tiger."

He heads straight for David, cutting through the press of people with purpose, ambition, and a plan.

God, that's so fucking hot, the way he goes after what he wants. In this case, David's ideas. I want him to win David.

Badly.

Once Bridger reaches the man, Allison cuts away, joining another group.

I let out a satisfied sigh.

I did that.

I engineered that meeting.

Bridger didn't need Carlos Mondez.

He only needed me.

I can't stop a private grin, and I don't have to because I have a few minutes to myself. And I use them to do one of my favorite things—admire all the pretty things.

As I head toward the first installment of letters, my mind wanders briefly to the ones my mother wrote me when I was a girl.

Like the last one where she wrote about our day together in the Village.

Dear Harlow,

Can I tell you a secret?

When we went to that ice cream shop in the West Village tonight, I remembered how I felt the first time I moved to New York, long ago, before you were born. It was just Cassie and me. My sister and I had come from Florida after wanting to make it to New York for so long.

We were overwhelmed. At first, the city was daunting, from the subways to the skyscrapers, from the smells to the speed. But New York doesn't hold your hand, so I had no choice but to learn my new home.

Today, as I watched you walking down Christopher Street with a certain ownership in your step, I thought, that's my city girl.

She doesn't need New York to hold her hand. She owns this city.

As my throat tightens, I finger the *I* on my necklace, breathe in, breathe out, and let the memory lap over the shore of my mind. Then, like a wave, it's pulled back out to the endless sea.

It fades away, and the knot of emotions loosens.

I reconnect to time and place, here in Petra Gallery, in this sliver of the West Village that I once visited with her. I stop at a letter from Diego Rivera to Frida Kahlo, reading their correspondence. It's desperate, deep, and laced with lust and words like *Nothing compares to your hands, nothing like the green-gold of your eyes.*

I gaze at the photo next to it, a black-and-white close-up of a pair of eyes. Probably not hers or his. It's impossible to know who they belong to. But even in black and white, I can somehow believe those are Frida's green-gold eyes. I stare a little longer, my mind drifting into the image, into its beauty, its shapes.

When I take a step toward the next installment, a

feminine voice floats past my ear. "So if a sculpture is just a sculpture, is a letter just a letter?"

It's Allison Tanaka-Fontaine, looking sharp in a pantsuit, her hair styled in a twist. And she remembers our conversation from MoMA when she said *sometimes a sculpture is just a sculpture*. "It hardly seems so, reading this letter. But I suppose letters are a different type of art."

"Fair point. They're written art. At least *I* think these are," she says with a touch of pride. Understandable.

"They definitely are. Can you imagine writing one like this today? We just send selfies and texts instead. But these letters are sort of pure and primal in a way we don't see anymore. They're like a raw look at how people were. A window into the past. Into the ways we *don't* communicate these days."

"Exactly." She says it like she's been desperately wanting someone to make that observation all night. "By the way, thanks for coming. I saw your name on the VIP list and remembered our brief conversation at MoMA. I thought of it when I was curating our part of the exhibit."

"You did?" I can't quite believe I made that much of an impression on her.

"I wanted an installment that attendees would *experience*. I wanted them to see the letters, read the letters, but also *feel* them. That's why I sometimes say a sculpture is a sculpture and art is art. Because it's about a feeling art elicits more than anything."

I'm the same way, and I feel bubbly, a little excited

over our shared connection. "That's so nouveau. So formalist," I tease.

She faux gasps. "I've got a formalist in me," she says. "Don't tell a soul."

Then I latch back onto what she just said. "You said *your part* of the exhibit. Is there more to this?"

"Yes. We're partnering with two other galleries. Bettencourt tomorrow night. Ashanti the night after. They both have letters. Each one hits a different theme."

"Like a pub crawl for art. And your theme is longing?" I ask.

Her bright brown eyes spark with awareness. "It is," she says, then nods toward her husband and Bridger. "He's trying to woo my husband, isn't he?"

For a split second, I'm tempted to say *how would I know*?

But that's a defensive stance. She's not asking if we're having a thing—are we? Are we having a thing? God, I hope so—so I swallow the reaction.

Then I consider her question carefully before I ask, "Don't most people in the entertainment business want to woo your husband?"

"That is true." She sighs, a little resigned. "Most fail."

"I hope Bridger doesn't," I say, since that's a reasonable thing for me to want as a Lucky 21 intern.

"I suspected that since you came with him," she says.

"We work together," I add, not quickly, not defensively. Just proving my point. We are nothing in public. "At Lucky 21."

"What do you think he has to offer my husband then?"

I definitely didn't think she'd be quizzing me about Bridger, but the answer rolls easily off my tongue. "He's tireless. He's driven. He's passionate. And he understands what your husband wants to accomplish with his stories. He wants to make people laugh." Then, what the hell. I go for it. "And he wants to surprise them with an unexpected love story," I add, taking a little liberty there, but I'm pretty sure I'm right based on how David dotes on his wife.

Allison smiles, impressed. "Good to know," she says as the curator from MoMA arrives by her side, this time with her braids curled at the ends.

"We meet again," Amelie says to me, playfully, in French.

"We sure do," I say, answering in the same language.

"And what do you think of the exhibit? Does it have enough theory for you?" There's a wink in her tone. A reference to our past conversation in the sculpture gardens.

"Or perhaps never enough," I volley back, then with a nod toward the black-and-white shot of a woman on a bridge, I say, "Black-and-white is a clever choice. It's like the photographic complement for the letters."

The curve in her lips says she's pleased with that observation. "Yes, a perfect pair. Wine and fruit."

"Olives and cheese," I toss back, then the three of us chat for another minute about the installation until a man strides up behind Amelie, dressed in black, and he whispers in her ear.

"Of course, Serge," she says to him, then to me, "There's someone I need to talk to. Allison, come with me."

We say goodbye and they take off, two power women in the art world, making deals perhaps presiding over *feelings*. As I make my way to check out more letters, I spot Bridger shaking David's hand. David flashes a small smile at him, then spins around, smiling bigger when he sees his wife. He beelines for her. Bridger strides across the gallery to me.

"Thank you," he says, soft, just for me.

"I don't think I did anything."

He shakes his head adamantly. "You did everything. You unlocked the door. Hell, you kicked it open with a steel-toed boot."

Well, I won't turn down the compliment. "And, tiger?"

Bridger dips his face, then raises it, like he's trying valiantly to erase the evidence of how *tiger* makes him feel.

Pretty damn good, by the looks of it.

I glow.

"I made some inroads," he says. "He likes the idea of the columns and how I suggested structuring them in a story. But there's something getting in the way for him. I don't know what. But I can sense something stopping him from a yes."

"Any idea what it is?"

"No. But I told him I'd do everything to make our show the biggest hit in the world."

I tingle from his confidence. I love that he went for it. That he put himself out there for Fontaine.

I glance around at the press of people, the noise and the buzz, the chatter and the music. Bridger doesn't like this many people. They make him uncomfortable. They bring him back to a place that hurt him when he was younger. "Do you need to go?"

"I bet you'd like to look at the exhibit," he says, letting me know he'll stay for me, he wants me to enjoy myself.

I love the gesture and so, I take it. "I would."

He lifts a hand, as if to put it on the small of my back. Then he must think the better of it, since he lowers his arm. I miss that hand terribly, but I file away the impulse, tucking it into a folder of moves he's made toward me.

We circulate, wandering past other letters, stopping at the original of one Zelda Fitzgerald wrote to her husband, F. Scott Fitzgerald, tell him there's nothing in all the world she wants but him and she'll do anything to keep his heart for her own.

When I finish the letter, my chest twinges for the sender, then I say, "It's a beautiful letter, don't you think?"

"It is, even though they had a complicated relationship."

I want to ask: *But do we?* But now's not the time nor place—not when I'm still cultivating an *us*. Instead, I ask, "Do you think these letters are all lies?"

"No. I just think we see what we want to see. People show what they want to show. But every letter has some other story behind it."

Story.

That word reverberates.

It echoes in my bones.

Maybe in Bridger's, too, since he adds, almost reverently, "And backstory."

Then, I swear I can see ideas flicker in his blue eyes. A puzzle solved. "Harlow," he says, like he's found buried treasure. "That's what we were saying is missing from *Afternoon Delight*."

"Right, yes." Where is he going with this?

He glances around. We're surrounded by people. Too many ears. Then he tips his forehead to the door.

I follow him, spilling out into the New York night, away from the crowded gallery, then he calls his driver, motions for me to join him—like I'd go anywhere else. I'm breathless with anticipation. When the car pulls over, he asks the driver to head all the way up to Central Park.

Oh, yes.

That gives us plenty of time alone together.

22

A CHAMPAGNE KISS

Harlow

The second the driver closes the door, Bridger blurts out, "What if every episode of *Afternoon Delight* starts with a letter. It's framed around a letter, a love letter that reveals some of the protagonist's past?"

The hair on my arms stands on end. "That's brilliant!"

"You like it?"

"I love it," I say, and as the car weaves through the Village, we trade ideas for the *Afternoon Delight* story. Then, when I explain the *pub crawl* style of the love letters exhibit, he says confidently, with not a shred of concern, "We should go together tomorrow night. To the next exhibit. And to the last one."

Together.

He's made a move.

Toward me.

A huge one.

"Yes. Yes," I say again, giddy on ideas, on us, on this night.

Bridger looks the same. Lit up, a little high.

"Is this how it feels to drink champagne?" I ask in a whisper.

He's quiet, his brow knitting, his eyes darkening. Then he says, "I think *you're* what it feels like to drink champagne."

My heart stutters.

His jaw clenches. Then he takes a sharp breath through his nostrils. Closes his eyes. He's working through the problem of me again.

Let him. Let him solve the problem. The only solution he'll find for me is, well, *me*.

When he opens his eyes, they're wild and fiery.

He beckons. One finger. That's all. I'm so there. I move in seconds, climb on top of him, hiking up my skirt, straddling his lap.

His hands curl around my hips in no time.

God, this feels so good. Me on him. His hands on me. Us touching. Everywhere.

"Harlow," he says, like my name is his breath.

"Have some champagne," I say.

Then, he wraps his hands around my waist. I rope mine around his neck. There's a pause, heated, fragrant. I can smell both of us wanting.

Needing.

My stomach whooshes. I ache as I wait for him to

kiss me. But no kiss comes. Instead, he lifts his hand from my hip, then traces my bottom lip with it.

Then my top lip.

Next, he brushes his finger along my chin, my jawline, over the shell of my ear.

Somehow, it's both more tender and more thrilling than a kiss. It's like he's memorizing me with his hands. Drawing me, remembering me.

For when he can't do this.

But I ignore that voice of doom as best I can.

Here and now, in this car, cruising through the Manhattan night on some avenue, some street, in some time, I'm his to have.

As he runs two fingers down my cheek, he regards the path they're traveling. His fingers return to my lips, and it's like they're kissing me. Then, he is. His lips are on mine, but they're softer, gentler than they have been before.

Who knew Bridger was such a tease?

He's barely touching me. He's hardly kissing at all. And I just *want*.

And I squirm, then sink down on his lap. Feeling the outline of him.

He groans, bordering on a growl.

I rock against the ridge of his erection. The growl turns more carnal, and I feel wicked. "You're teasing me," I say, a simple observation.

"And you like it," he says.

"Love it," I counter.

He nuzzles my neck. "Mmm. Me too."

His hands explore me more, traveling down my arms, over my thighs, along the fabric of my blouse. He doesn't undress me. But he returns to my mouth, taking little hits. A tug on my bottom lip. A sip of my mouth. A taste of me.

If this isn't a champagne kiss, I don't know what is. I am bubbly. I am intoxicated. And I've never been so aroused before.

Soon, I'm rocking against him, and when I let out a long, breathy moan, he grunts.

Then he grabs my face. Hard. He jerks me against him, kissing me relentlessly for several hot, mind-bending seconds. As he devours my mouth, he drops one hand down to my legs, where he grips my right thigh.

Tightly. Like he's handcuffing himself.

Oh, Bridger. Let me help you along.

I grab that hand, break the kiss, and meet his gaze. "Touch me," I say, then guide his hand under my skirt.

"Yeah?" He's trembling with desire. He's breaking and it's exhilarating to watch.

"Please," I say, and I'm both begging and in charge at the same damn time.

He closes his eyes, like he's offering a prayer to the gods of restraint. But they don't answer him. Desire does, because when he opens his eyes, he lets his hand travel up my thigh, mercifully heading for my center.

Then, his fingers graze my soaked panties.

And we both groan.

"Oh fuck, honey," he rumbles.

That's all it takes. In a second, his fingers slide

under my panties, and his mouth crashes down on mine, and I'm in dirty heaven.

I sigh into his mouth, kissing him back, but it's messy because I can't focus. I can only *feel* the exquisite pleasure between my thighs as he strokes me.

Breaking the kiss, but not the contact, he rasps out, "Look at you. Just fucking look at you."

I can't, of course, but that's not the point. *He's* looking at me. Staring like I'm precious and filthy at the same time.

"So wet, so fucking beautiful," he praises, then he buries his face against my neck, laying desperate kisses all along my skin as he slides his fingers across my center, faster and faster.

His thumb finds where I'm pulsing for him.

I cry out. It's never been like this, not alone, not by myself. Ever.

"God. Please. Yes," I say.

Until the words spill into each other.

Until I'm shaking, trembling everywhere.

Until the agony of pleasure becomes excruciating.

I rock faster, ride harder, and then I shatter. I moan so loud, he cups a hand over my mouth. "Shh, honey," he urges.

But I can't stop crying out, even with his hand quieting me.

I can't because I'm buzzing, floating, blissed out beyond words.

And when I open my eyes and look at him, he looks drunk too. "Better than all the champagne in the world," he says. Then he kisses me.

It's a soft, firm kiss, almost like a promise.

Then he licks off his fingers, sending another after-shock of pleasure through me before he grabs a tissue from the console. When he's done, the car's near my home, the familiar buildings mocking me as my night with him ends.

"Can you come up? I want to..." I lean in close, whisper, "Return the favor."

He sighs, then shakes his head. "I can't," he says.

My heart aches.

It's not even the loss of...touching.

It's the way we keep ending.

The car idles. He strokes my hair. "I wish things were different," he says.

"Me too," I say. I lower my gaze to his shirt and reach for the cuffs, fiddling with them, wanting to delay time.

"It's just so many things. Like, how hard it is not to look at you at the office," he says, resigned. Then, he cups my cheek, his voice gentle. "I don't want you to get in trouble. *With anyone*. And I don't want to be boycotted."

I wince at that last, terrible possibility. "I won't let that happen," I say, and he laughs once, humorlessly. "I'd never say anything.

"I know, honey. It's not you I worry about," he says, then shakes his head. "It's others, and then where would you be? Where would I be? I'd have to start over."

I wish this situation were a passage in French I could translate, a piece of art I could analyze. Something I know how to handle intrinsically. But this is harder, and it'll take a new level of strategy to overcome.

I should go. "I'll see you tomorrow night?" I ask, choosing to believe I will. Choosing two more nights for now.

"Of course," he says. "The Bettencourt."

It's not a date, but it's a promise. We at least have two more nights. Time for me to devise a new plan.

I slide off him, grab my phone, adjust my skirt, and reach for the handle.

"Wait."

My pulse sings. I turn to him, eager.

"I have something for you," he adds.

"What is it?" I ask, but he's already unbuttoning his shirt, revealing his white T-shirt underneath. It fits him like a dream, stretched tight across his strong chest.

Then my gaze strays to his arms. I haven't seen him like this before—where I've had permission to look *freely*. Where I've been able to stare at the muscles, the ink on his forearm. Where I've been able to touch. I reach for him and trace the lines of the tattoo on his right arm. Quietly. Wordlessly.

He shudders as I travel along the vines drawn on his skin, curling around a small stack of books. Why does he have this? Sure, I can guess, but I want to know *his* reason. But now's not the time to ask about his ink. I've been given a gift just to touch it, to touch him.

My heart skids against my rib cage. He is beautiful.

And he will be mine.

I let go, and he blinks like he's floating back to

earth. Then he hands the crisp orange shirt to me, and I press it to my nose, inhaling him, inhaling our secret.

After another searing kiss, he strokes my cheek. "Take a picture in it. Send it to me."

I will.

23

A THANK YOU GIFT

Bridger

Twenty minutes later, I'm home, my mind at war with my body. Or maybe my brain's simply fighting with itself.

My emotional mind says, *run to her*.

And my rational mind says, *run from her*.

But my heart, my stupid fucking heart, just says...*her*.

Over and over, as I stare at my phone, and wait.

I can't let go of the damn device as I walk to my closet, sit on the stool, take off my shoes and neatly set them on the shoe rack. I put my phone on the cushion as I strip off socks and then slacks, folding the pants neatly, setting them in the dry-cleaning pile. I toss my T-shirt in the laundry.

I grab the phone once more, checking again.

This is me—down to boxer briefs and my phone.

Dear god, who have I fucking become?

I have to stop, and yet I'm strung out on mere hope for a photo.

Get a grip.

Leaving the phone on my nightstand, I shed my boxer briefs, step into the shower, and let the hot water sluice over me until it washes away tonight.

Soon, my business partner will be back in town.

Soon, I'll have to look him in the eyes.

Soon, we'll do another deal.

We'll talk about *Afternoon Delight*, we'll work on the concept, we'll deal with *Sweet Nothings*.

I can't do that if I'm fucking his daughter.

You're not fucking her.

Yet.

"God," I mutter, slamming a fist against the tiled wall in the shower. Like the technicality matters. I shut off the faucet, step out, grab a towel.

As I dry off, I remind myself that there's so much more at stake than Ian.

Hundreds of employees.

The shows we own.

The productions we oversee.

All of those people around the world who depend on the two of us for paychecks. All those productions. All our plans. How the hell can I lead this company if I'm sleeping with the other guy's daughter?

Ian would never forgive me. He'd never trust me. And he wouldn't want to work with me anymore.

I can't keep doing this with her. But when I pull on

a pair of gym shorts to sleep in, then head to bed, I lunge for the phone, checking it once again.

My heart slams ruthlessly when I see her name. Taunting me.

I sink back onto the mattress, gripping the phone like it's a precious artifact. It is. It holds the key to her. I slide it open. My mouth is dry as I click on her name, then I open the message.

There's nothing, not a single thing, sexier in the world than this.

Harlow, in the mirror, her whole body this time.

She wears nothing but my shirt.

Her legs are bare, the cuffs are rolled up twice, and the top few buttons are undone, giving me a peek of the curve of her breasts.

Her lips are parted slightly.

I trace her outline adoringly. Then I tell myself not to look again, not to reply. But I can't ignore this photo or the words she sent—*Thank you for my gift.*

I tap out a note, then hit send.

You deserve all the gifts.

A few seconds later, three dots appear. But before she can send a response, I sneer at my reply. *You deserve all the gifts?*

My reply is not worthy of this photo.

At the speed of sound, I write back again.

I can't stop thinking about you.

I hit send.

Her dots stop dancing. Then start again.

You know it's the same for me.

* * *

In the morning, I go to a breakfast meeting near Grand Central with a casting director. Then, I swing by the Chrysler Building to see a brand marketer we work with. In the late morning, I'm finally on the way to the office when my mother texts. As I head toward the revolving brass doors, I open the message.

Mom: Darling! I'll be in New York next month. Can you believe it? I'm doing a cabaret with some friends. And we're throwing a party at Sardi's that night. You must come!

I have no interest in Sardi's. No interest in a boozy night out with her pals. But I should go. She is my mom. It's only ever been us.

Bridger: I'll be there. Can't wait.

That's a lie, but it's not the worst one I've told lately. When I reach the black building, I brace myself for more lies. Bigger lies. I put on my armor so I can pretend I'm not losing my mind over my partner's daughter.

As I ride the elevator, my phone pings. It's Harlow.

My breath hitches. Annoying, my reaction. But I click open the note instantly.

Harlow: Hey! Jules sent me to the set today. I've been here all morning. She said they needed me over there more than at the office today.

Hmm. That's unusual, but I suppose she should go where she's best able to be used. I reach the fourteenth floor, then head down the hallway when another message from Harlow lights up my phone. The preview says something about a lunch she's trying to set up with Jules.

But I don't open it since my assistant is waiting for me in my office.

Jules stares at me, her eyes like bullets. "I know what's going on with Harlow."

24

JUST SOME BOOK

Harlow

My dad called me from Cape Cod a few minutes ago, asking for my help. Now, phone pressed to my ear as I talk to him, I'm hunting through the books in a library on the set. A ladder rests against tall shelves of tomes, spines sticking out, inviting hands to touch.

And many hands have touched the books here.

Backs have too.

And let's not forget butts.

Since my father and his writing staff have written countless make-out sessions that take place in this studio.

This is the library in Cruz's penthouse on *Sweet Nothings*. The rich playboy who can't be tied down. He's a fan favorite on the show, so he has a new romantic arc every season.

I don't want to think too hard on whether my father

imagines he's Cruz or not. I don't want to think too hard on my father at all.

Especially after last night.

I simply want to help Dad so I can get off the phone with him stat and connect with Jules about some things that have been on my mind. I sent her a text seconds ago to see if she could meet me for lunch shortly, but then my dad called so I haven't been able to check if Jules has responded.

I'm antsy to see if she wrote back. Antsier to talk to her.

At the moment though, my father desperately needs me to find a certain book in the library. But he can't remember which book he wants. It's on the shelf closest to some paintings, Dad says. So I'm his ears and his eyes while he's out of town.

Alone here, I scan the shelves nearest the character's collection of modern art, reading off the names to Dad on the phone. "*Anna Karenina. The Pelican Brief. Carrie.* This is an odd collection."

"Cruz has wide and varied tastes."

"Or he likes to show off," I say, then read the next one. "*Romeo and Juliet.*"

"That's not the one. That's tragic," Dad says with a laugh. I can hear birds chirping off in the distance, then the faint sound of ocean waves. Bet he rented a fantastic beach house for his getaway with Vivian.

"I know it's tragic. I did read it," I point out, then continue on, reading more names of more books. With each, I'm met with a *no*, or a *not that one*, or *definitely not that one*.

Dad's so focused on finding a book whose name he can't remember that now seems as good a time as any to drop in a question. Being with Bridger is just easier with Dad out of town.

"How long will you be on Cape Cod?" I ask him, as blasé as I can muster, as run-of-the-mill as I'd normally inquire about his whereabouts. He's been on the Cape for a few days now—last weekend and into this week.

"Oh, you know. As long as I need to," he says, airily, and if that's not evasive I don't know what it is.

I don't push though, since, well, I don't want to appear too interested in his life. That might make him think I'm up to something.

But I'm not up to anything he needs to know about. Right? I'm twenty-one. I'm an adult. I don't need to tell him about my evenings out.

It's none of his business.

But as I search through the shelves, my gut churns viciously.

Here I am, on the set of their show. Interning at their company. What I'm doing is *their* business.

Too much of it.

I need to fix this problem I've made. I need to do it stat. But first, I have to deal with Dad's request to find *some book*.

I read more names to him, and when I'm at the end of the last shelf, hardly any books left, I flick a finger-nail against a book of poems. "Pablo Neruda?"

"That's it!"

Finally.

I run my hand along the slim volume. "Do you want a photo of it?"

"No." There's a pause over the phone line. "Take it," he whispers, even though he knows I'm the only one on the set. "They'll never miss it."

"What?"

"Poppet, no one will even notice you nicked it."

Great, I'm a liar and a soon-to-be thief. "Dad," I chide softly.

"I promise it'll be fine."

Irritated, I roll my eyes. But he's right. I know he's right. Still, I glance around at the empty set. If Ollie, the stage manager, sees me walking out with this book, he might be pissed one of his props has gone missing. After all, Ollie let me in because I said it was a favor for my dad. "Dad, Ollie will be annoyed."

"Only if he sees you," Dad says, so clever, so devilish.

I quickly assess my options for cat burglary. I'm wearing a pencil skirt. I'm not going to stuff it into the waistband. Briefly, I wish I carried a purse. But I don't. Gritting my teeth, I grab the book, tuck it under my arm. Best to just look innocent.

Shoes muffled by the maroon Turkish rug, I head out, book in hand, phone plastered to my face. Then, I've escaped into the hall.

"Okay, now what?" I ask.

"I'll text you the address where I'm staying. Pop it into FedEx overnight please. I need it tomorrow morning before we leave."

"Where are you going to?" I ask.

Dad laughs. A chuckle that says he's charmed himself. "I'm taking the rest of the week off. Viv and I are having too much fun, and we're going to tool around New England."

Ah, that makes sense. An extended vacation. "Well, you deserve it. I'll take care of this." I say goodbye, head to the office supplies room, and pack up the book in an envelope. Then I drop it at the studio's mailing room to go in the overnight shipping.

I return to my messages, ready to check in with Jules when my attention snags on a handsome man heading down the corridor. Empirically handsome that is, with tanned skin, a chiseled jaw, and a lopsided grin fans adore. It's Dominic, the award-winning actor who plays Cruz. He's chatting on the phone, but when he spots me, his eyes light up. He covers the phone. "How is the art world coming along, Harlow? Have you taken over MoMA yet?"

I'm impressed Dominic remembers anything about me from our brief chat at MoMA at the silver and gold party. "Not yet, but maybe soon," I say with a smile, one that I hope covers up any betrayal that reveals *I stole a book from your character's library for my father.*

He waves goodbye and heads on his way, and I return to my phone.

Oh!

There's a text from my brother, asking if I'm free on Saturday morning for breakfast at our favorite diner on Third Avenue.

I stop in my tracks and clasp my mouth. Oh my god. He's going to extend his San Francisco trip to visit me!

. . .

Harlow: Are you serious? Does this mean you're coming to New York? For real? Don't tease me!

Hunter: Well, someone made it clear I needed to see her. I'm off to Chicago tonight for a meeting tomorrow morning, so I figured I could extend my trip by spending one night in New York. BUT...any chance I can stay at your flat tomorrow night? I'm leaving on the last flight out of New York on Saturday.

Harlow: As if I'd let you stay anywhere else! I love you madly!!!! Can't wait to see you! And you picked wisely —Dad won't be here!

Hunter: I'm pretty much brilliant. Can't wait to see you, Lo. Will email you the flight info.

Harlow: I can't wait to see you either.

But as I turn back down the echoey corridor, returning to the set to work, it's as if a small stone is wedged in my shoe. An annoyance, a trifling thing. But it starts to dig into me.

I'll have to lie to my brother when I see him tomorrow night since I can't breathe a word about Bridger.

I shudder involuntarily, a wave of shame and guilt cresting over me.

But then, it's early days. I wouldn't tell Hunter anything this soon even if Bridger were, say, some guy I met online.

Only, Bridger's not some guy I met online. He's someone I met in my home years ago.

Guilt nips at my heels. But one thing at a time.

First I need to deal with the problem I've created. Screw making plans with Jules for lunch.

I call her.

25

MY BOYCOTT GRAVE

Bridger

Earlier this year, I went to lunch with Ian shortly after running into his daughter on the East River path. I put on my best poker face then for our meal.

A few months later, when Harlow marched into my office and asked boldly for this internship, I somehow found an even better mask so Ian wouldn't be able to see through me.

Now, with Jules standing in my doorway saying she knows what's going on with Harlow, I feel like I've just walked into a world championship round of Texas Hold'em in front of millions when I've never played the game before.

Time to bluff the fuck out of this.

"Yeah?" I ask, evenly. So damn evenly she won't hear a hint of crack in my voice. She won't spot a fissure in me at all.

"I do," Jules says, nodding, a quick huff in her breath.

Underneath my stone facade, my heart is sprinting, my mind racing. Did Jules follow us last night? See Harlow get in my car?

I've got to be more cautious.

But there's no time to wonder *how* she knows. She just knows. Ready to bullshit my way out of this, I head to my desk, carelessly set down my phone like it's any other day, any other moment.

Like Jules is inquiring about something other than where my hand was last night around nine pm.

Like I'm not about to lose the thing I love most —Lucky 21.

All because I'm obsessed with a woman I can't have.

"Harlow's very good," Jules continues, in her clear, crisp tone, the one she uses to tell me an agent's on the phone, my lunch is here, she's finished a project.

The same voice she uses for literally everything.

The woman is unreadable.

And sure, I could say *yes, Harlow's good*, or I could shut up and let Jules just keep talking.

I stay quiet. I want to know what evidence she has. Coolly, I sort my jar of pens on my desk, like my life's work doesn't hang in the balance.

Jules takes the silent bait.

"She stays late. All last week she was here late," Jules continues.

Shit. Fuck. Hell.

Jules knows about those times Harlow stayed late?

Talking to me here in my office about life, New York, family?

I take a seat, tilt my head, wait for the blade to drop. I ignore my speeding pulse, approaching Mach 10.

"And I know she knows French. I know she's an art student." She stabs her chest with her finger. "But I know things too," Jules says, and there's not a trace of *gotcha* in her voice, but it's coming. I swear it's coming. Why else would she be piling on the compliments?

"I'm sure you do," I say plainly, but inside I'm screaming *What the hell is she getting at?*

"But if one of us is going to get the junior producer job, it should be me."

What???

What the hell did Jules just say?

I nearly furrow my brow and blurt out *What are you talking about?*

But I bite down my surprise. "Ah, the open one. Right, right," I say, like I've been contemplating who to hire when I have not. Not at all. That's not my role.

It is my fucking pleasure to contemplate hiring her right now. But just to be certain I'm reading her right at last, I ask, "You want the job?"

In my head, I ask, *You're not here to dig my boycott grave?*

"I've been here longer than Harlow," Jules says, methodical, making her case. "I'm devoted. I'm focused and smart. And to be honest, I don't even think Harlow wants to work in TV. But I do. This is my life. This is my goal. I know she's been trying to impress you by working late and coming up with plans for shows, but I want a chance too," she says, then lifts her chin. "I want you to give me a chance to show I'm the best one for the job."

I stifle a grin of *I got away with it*. Instead, I give my best boss nod, then say, "I'd love to see what you can do, Jules."

She shares ideas and plans for Lucky 21's shows, and they're good. Truly, they're good. But then Christian rings through and says Mia Liu from the LA office is on the line. She's a VP, handling our marketing from the West Coast, and we're heading to Paris together next month before shooting begins.

"You should take that and discuss the marketing plans for *Afternoon Delight*," Jules says, like a damn good assistant.

Or maybe like a junior producer.

"I will."

I pick up the phone and chat with Mia, relieved, utterly relieved the entire time. It might even be the best call of my life.

When we're done, I'm about to text Harlow when Jules raps twice, then pops back in.

"Did you want to chat more about the possible job?" I ask. *I could chat all day about it.*

"I'd love to," she says, then breathes out deeply and smiles for the first time in, well, ever. "By the way, Harlow just quit."

26

CAN I TELL YOU?

Bridger

At ten minutes till seven, I'm pacing outside the Bettencourt Gallery as the sun streaks lower, playing peekaboo behind skyscrapers on the Upper East Side.

I haven't been able to reach Harlow all afternoon. Meetings and phone calls ate up my day. Text is entirely unsatisfying for the conversation we need to have.

When I wrote to ask **What happened?** her only reply was **It's all good and I'll explain tonight.**

Then, she'd added, **I'll walk to the gallery. It's only four blocks from my home.**

I'm hoping—make that fucking praying—that she's early. I need a minute alone with her. No, more than a minute.

And I need to *not* see a soul I know here.

Good thing not many of the agents, producers,

casting directors and writers I court are likely to be at an art gallery event.

I'm not trying to avoid them because of Harlow. I want to avoid them because our idea for the show's backstory excites me. The love letters as a way to frame the hero is like a whole new level of market research I'm conducting with her. *Only her.* Story research. Clandestine research.

I don't need a Mia type, or an analyst, or anyone else showing up.

I check my watch. Two minutes till seven. Harlow's never late. The gallery is at the end of this ritzy stretch of Madison Avenue, populated by shoe stores with four-figure price tags, and boutiques peddling maybe eight items apiece surrounded by so much empty space it's a real estate sin. On the corner is a chichi bar named Opal. I pass it, then stop, turn around, peering this way and that, staring at my phone, waiting.

Still waiting for her.

Then, the back of my neck tingles. Somehow, I sense her before I see her.

Is it the sound of her shoes? The memory of her scent? Can I even smell that vanilla perfume or bodywash in the midst of Manhattan rush hour with buses trundling by and garbage cans on corners, needing attention?

I don't know the answer. But I *feel* her somehow, and it's entirely disarming.

I turn around, both gratified I'm not losing my mind and gobsmacked at the sight of her walking toward me on Madison.

Her chestnut hair is clipped on one side with some kind of shiny, silver barrette. Tendrils fall from it. That's a new look. A little boho, almost. I drink in the rest of her. She wears short ankle boots, a black leather skirt—vegan, I bet—and a silver top that slopes off one shoulder.

My mouth goes dry.

This is not office Harlow.

This is some other version of her.

And I am here for it. Which is a problem. I am here for all the versions of Harlow.

I shove aside all the reasons she's a bad idea for me. Immediately, I go to her, since I am caught up.

But the second I reach her, a cab pulls to the curb. A quick glance inside tells me all I need to know. It's full of art types. I don't need anyone to hear us discussing her job.

Correction—*her former job.*

"Grab a drink with me?" I ask quickly before anyone spills out of the taxi.

"Of course."

I tip my forehead to Opal. Two minutes later, we're in a corner booth in the quiet bar, nursing iced teas.

"What happened? Why the hell did you quit?" I ask in a hush.

I don't want to say *did you quit for me.* That's presumptuous. But I'm thinking it. I'm absolutely thinking it.

"Bridger," she says, then glances around, taking the temperature. Hardly anyone is near us. "What you said last night on the way home, about how risky this is, it stuck with me. I was foolish not to think of those things before. What *this* might mean especially for you. How *this* could hurt you and your career."

I grit my teeth. Then grumble, "I told you not to protect me." Though maybe it's a hiss.

"I know," she says, her shoulders squared like she owns what she did today, like it's her choice only, and really, it is. "And still, I don't want you to get hurt. I don't want you to have to start over."

"And I don't want you to lose a job you love," I say sternly since she can't, she just can't, give up things for me.

"But see...the internship? It's not my dream job." There's an apology in her tone.

"What?" That does not compute. "You...seemed like you really wanted it. That day when you came into my office. You said it was your birthday wish."

A soft shrug. Almost a confession unto itself. "It was...expected of me. I knew it would make...*him*... happy." Her eyes look a little guilty. "And honestly, there are probably a ton more TV and film students who'd be better at it than I am. Who deserve it more. I shouldn't have a plum internship just because of my last name."

I disagree. "You wouldn't have lasted if you weren't smart and sharp," I point out. "Don't discount what you brought to the table. You're one of the best."

"Thank you. But it's because I'm good at school. I can learn. I can figure things out." She reaches for her glass of iced tea, runs a finger along the condensation sliding down it.

"But what will you do for work?" I ask, though the second those words come out, something occurs to me for the first time. She's not making much as an intern. We don't pay a ton. No one does.

"Can I tell you a secret?" she whispers.

God, tell me all your secrets. "Yes."

"My apartment?"

"Yes?"

"It's paid for. My mother's royalties on her last *Sweet Nothings* made it possible."

I drag a hand over the back of my neck, absorbing that. Her life is so different to mine. I had to fight for every cent growing up. My mom didn't make much, and what she made went to booze, parties, and sequined dresses. I never had anything unless I worked for it. I went to college on scholarships and loans.

Harlow attended a top university...well, on her parents' many, many dimes. She probably lives loan-free.

Nothing wrong with that. We're just from different worlds. But that doesn't bother me. She's learned how to use her head, not simply her privilege. She's sure as hell used her brain in the last few weeks at Lucky 21.

As I sort out my thoughts, untangling the practical aspects of her quitting from the emotional ones, I take a drink then ask, "What will you do? What do you want to do?"

"I have some time. But I think I've figured it out, Bridger," she says, and my name comes out full of excitement. Like I'm the first one she's wanted to share this realization with. And, hell, do I ever want to be the first one to hear it.

That's why her decision makes me feel emotional too. Because I desperately want to be privy to her future plans. "Tell me," I say, eagerly.

"Turns out, I do want to work in the art world after all. I just don't want it to be theory or education or history. I want to curate things that make people think and feel," she says, her green eyes bright, sparkling. All at once, she seems young again. Or rather, she seems her age. "Is that...silly?"

"God, no. I think it's great. I truly do." It's a gift to discover your passion. To learn what excites you.

But it's also a weight off my shoulders.

For a couple of hours there today, I'd thought she was giving up everything for me. And I didn't know how to deal with that kind of gesture. Mostly because I don't want her to make sacrifices for me. I want her to experience the world. To find her own way. "I guess I just thought you'd really wanted the internship," I say, relaxed finally.

She dips her face, turns the glass around, then looks me in the eyes, a softness around her mouth. She holds my gaze as she says, "I did. I really did."

My breath catches. My heart stutters. Yeah, I'm pretty sure I know why she wanted it now.

"I'm glad you did," I admit, quietly.

Then I check my watch. We *should* go, but I don't want to. Not when we've escaped into this quiet corner of a bar where no one's knocking on the door, no one's asking where we're going.

I nod to her hair. "That's a new look."

She lifts her hand, touching the silver barrette like she's just remembered it's there. "You noticed."

"I notice things too."

She smiles. "Like my barrettes?"

"Yes. Like your hair and how you style it. Like your skirts. How you're wearing something I've never seen you in before. Is this Art Harlow I'm seeing tonight?"

Her cheeks flush at those last few words—*seeing tonight.*

Yes, they fit in the context of the question, but maybe there's a Freudian slip in there too.

"I guess I need to look more gallery chic than office chic," she says. "Am I pulling it off?"

"It's a good look," I say.

"I want to look the part," she says, then a little breathlessly, she adds, "I'm having coffee on Saturday with the MoMA curator. I met her at the *Sweet Nothings* party and saw her again last night. I reached out to her this afternoon."

Damn. That's the way to take charge of your career. "You're a go-getter."

"Should I have given two weeks' notice? When I told Jules I was quitting, she said I was free to go immediately. That I didn't even need to come back to the office."

I'm not surprised at all. "It's fine. Jules said this afternoon she'd found someone else to hire." I don't add that Jules felt threatened by Harlow in the first place. Nor do I add that Ian and I basically invented an extra intern position for his daughter. Harlow doesn't need to know that now.

"Okay, but I feel like I've left you high and dry. Can I still help with *Afternoon Delight*? I want to, Bridger. Can we still work on the idea for the hero's backstory?"

"Of course," I say, immediately since it feels like *ours*. "It's our idea."

Besides, working with her like this is safe. Ian wanted me to solve the script problem. And he's shared story ideas with Harlow for years. The *Afternoon Delight* project is a natural extension of the nights I've spent at Harlow's home when she was younger. Nights working with her father.

And...nope.

I can't go there. Not now. Not with her sitting across from me looking so very lovely.

I fight off the thoughts of my partnership with her dad. I only want to think about these nights with this woman, visiting art galleries, checking out love letters.

"Besides, the show needs it," I add, like dammit, come hell or high water, we'll fix *Afternoon Delight*.

"Good. I want to help," she says.

That gives me a plausible excuse to see her in the evenings. An excuse for Ian if he saw us or called. It's not as if I can reveal to anyone else that we're dealing with a story problem.

I'll take whatever I can get with Harlow. Even with her off the team, there's no way we can last. There's too much still at stake. We're an impossibility. A few nights though? Yes, please.

The server swings by and asks if we'd like a tapas

menu. It's tempting, utterly tempting to order a meal with her.

"Harlow? Are you hungry?"

"Starving," she says.

We order a few small plates, and it feels like playing hooky as we stay a little longer and nibble on appetizers. Like we're closing the place down, even though it's barely past happy hour. "Tell me more about your meeting with the MoMA curator," I say as I dig into a portobello mushroom.

"I'm going to spend the day tomorrow prepping for it. But I feel ready. I've been following her collections ever since I met her. She has an amazing eye," she says. "And it turns out we both love The Frick."

"The museum on Fifth Avenue? That used to be a house?"

"Yes! Have you been?"

"Never."

She gasps playfully, lighting up as she tells me more about the collection, then takes a bite of her tofu satay. When she's done, she says, "You'd like it there. Maybe someday...you can go," she says, almost swallowing the *we* to say *you* instead.

Like she knows that *we* won't happen—her and me at The Frick.

"Maybe I will," I say, resigned, since realism is easier right now than giving in to the drumbeat in my heart.

As Harlow sets down her fork, finished with the meal, she says my name, firm but a touch desperate. "Bridger?"

"Yes?"

She glances around once more, as if she's making sure we're still safe. Her eyes lock with mine. "I meant it when I said I don't want anything to happen to you."

My heart slams painfully against my rib cage. Like it's throwing itself at her. "I know, honey."

"I thought about it last night. I can't let something bad happen to you because of *this*."

But something already *is* happening to me. *She's* happening to me.

I should stop moving closer to her. Truly I should. She might have removed one jagged rock that could have sliced me. But there are plenty of others below us hidden under the raging river. There's no way to cross these rapids safely.

There's her father and the company, and I won't get past those without getting cut apart.

For now, though, at least I'm not the guy who's fucking an intern.

On that bitter thought, I push away from the table. "We should go. Because you have to experience some art."

Her smile is magnetic. It says I understand her completely and in this moment, that's all we have—our understanding of each other. "I do," she says.

I pay the bill. I wish I could do this every night for her. And I suppose, I do know how to deal with the gesture she made by quitting.

I want to wrap her in my arms, kiss her for a good, long time, and take her home.

But I can't.

27

LOST AND FOUND

Bridger

I barely say a word as we wander through the Bettencourt Gallery, past the stark white columns, checking out the letters on the wall. These missives are paired with paintings from modern artists, both capturing the theme of long-distance love.

A surreal painting of a lonely typewriter hangs next to an image of a James Joyce love letter.

Harlow reads it quietly aloud. "*You have me completely in your power. I know and feel that if I am to write anything fine or noble in the future I shall do so only by listening at the doors of your heart...I would like to go through life side by side with you, telling you more and more until we grew to be one being together until the hour should come for us to die...*"

She side-eyes me. "Dramatic much?"

I laugh. This is a new side of her. Irreverent, poking fun at art, the thing she loves.

I hold up a thumb and forefinger. "A little bit."

"But I love the typewriter. I keep looking for one outside on the streets. I have this wild dream that someday I'll spot a typewriter as I wander the city."

"Why do you want to find a typewriter?"

"It has to have a story, right? Or many stories, if you think about it. I'd love to find one somewhere on a stoop, like that rotary phone. And I imagine the type-writer would whisper all the things it's recorded. In the dark, as the curtains close and the lights go down," she says, then sighs contentedly, painting a vivid image.

"We'll find that typewriter someday," I say, and our typewriter hunt feels like a promise I can keep, though I know I can't and we won't.

But tonight, everything feels a little possible.

Especially as we walk unknown amongst the crowds. I feel like we're in a foreign country, slipping past locals, no one spotting the tourists who are checking out the alleys and quiet side streets. That's us, visiting this land of love letters and paintings, unnoticed.

No one stops to gladhand. No one asks me to read a script. Not a soul asks how her dad is.

Instead, Harlow moves freely and fluidly, stopping in front of a painting of a vintage rolltop desk done in broad, mirage-like strokes. A woman stands in front of the desk, holding a pen poised above a piece of paper but she's written nothing. Instead, she's staring out the window at the river. Maybe even the Seine. It's lined with trees. A couple walks along the water, wrapped up together.

Everything is a little silvery, a little like a memory.

"That's a Zara Clementine," she tells me. "She's a little melancholy, but she understands longing so well."

I don't have to ask Harlow if she loves the painting. I can tell in her eyes, enrapt. In her lips, slightly parted. And her expression. A little lost and found at the same time.

Harlow points to the tag and snaps her fingers, *aw shucks* style. "It's sold. Too bad."

I laugh. The price is many, many zeroes.

We move on, and as we go, I return to the mission of the night. "I think our hero had a long-distance love affair. Maybe with a woman who wrote him letters from a vintage desk," I suggest.

"Yes! That's why he won't give in to love. He hasn't made peace with the past. There's someone he left behind."

"Someone he misses too," I say.

We write a new backstory for our guy and it's the best time in public I've ever had. We're swimming in a crowd, but I don't feel that familiar tightness in my chest, that usual sense that I don't belong.

I don't want to push my luck though. It's nearly nine, and I do want some time alone with her, so I steal a chance, lean in close. "Want to get out of here? I have my car."

Her breath catches. Her eyes say yes. But before she can answer with words, a voice, strong and confident and all too familiar from more than five seasons on TV, hits my ears.

"Bridger!"

Like glass shattering, the moment splinters into a thousand pieces. I turn to face the actor from our show.

Dominic Rivera is here, and he's looking curiously from Harlow to me.

28

BROWN PAPER, THAT'S ALL

Harlow

Thank you, Dad.

For teaching me to think on my feet.

"Hey, you!" I say brightly to the man I ran into mere hours ago on the set. "When I saw you earlier, I was going to ask if you were coming tonight."

Dominic's rich brown eyes spark with questions. "You were?"

"I didn't want to interrupt your call though. But when we met at MoMA last winter, didn't you talk about how much you adored the nineties school?" I ask, bullshitting, utterly bullshitting about the nineties school of painting that Zara Clementine typifies.

Dominic said nothing of the sort, but I've learned a thing or two about art collectors. They love to show off their knowledge. And I've learned a thing or two about

Dominic. He's picked up most of his art knowledge from his character on *Sweet Nothings*.

Guess who helped Dad with Dominic's art?

This girl.

"Yes. Yes, we *were* talking about that," Dominic says, then with some of his questions dismissed, he leans in and gives me a hug. "Good to see you again."

When he lets go, he shakes hands with Bridger. "Hey there," Dominic says. "I still want to talk to you about a spin-off."

"Anytime," Bridger says in a cool, even tone as he gives a quick hello.

Before he can say anything more, I set a hand on Bridger's arm. "I should go. I'm meeting my friends for that *thing*," I say, rolling my eyes. "Some VIP blah, blah, blah," I say to them both, like *can you believe what I have to do with my ride or dies.*

Dominic laughs. "Sounds so thrilling."

I just shrug and smile. The Upper East Side girl, so jaded with it all.

Bridger jumps into character immediately. "Have fun, and thanks for the tip on the nineties school. It'll help with *Afternoon Delight*."

"I'll let my dad know," I say, then blow them both kisses and hightail it out of there, without looking back.

There's no way we're leaving together now, so it's best to act like we're...*nothing* to each other.

That thought nicks away at me, little knife jabs at my heart. But it has to be like this. It just does.

Once I'm outside on Madison Avenue, I don't look back even though I'm dying for a final glimpse. I resist, marching forward, off to see my friends for my blah, blah, blah thing, leaving Bridger behind to handle our unexpected gallery crasher.

The whole time, as I put distance behind me, my pulse is spiking.

Even when I circle around and head back down Third Avenue, I'm still aware of the fumes of lies I'm giving off.

They're like a cloying perfume, chasing me, clinging to me.

They don't leave even when I reach my building, head inside and give Bridger's name to the doorman.

"He's dropping something off for me. So you can just put him on the list," I say, thinking ahead, planning.

Then, I reach the elevator, and I blow out a huge, stuttering breath. It rushes to break free from my lungs.

Anxiety swirls up inside me, but then my phone pings with a text.

Bridger: You're a genius. I've been roped into dinner. But you're a brilliant genius. And I owe you.

Then I'm laughing, wildly laughing as the elevator rises. Holy shit. We pulled it off. We are one hell of a team. When I'm inside my home a few seconds later, I write back.

Harlow: Come over later if you want…You're on the list. I just added you.

Bridger: I wish. We're going downtown. To a private club. He has a whole pitch for a new show. I don't think I can get out of it. Wish I were going to see you.

I swallow a knot of emotions.

Maybe I was a fool to give up the job.

Maybe I was stupid thinking I'd finally gotten Bridger after wanting him for so long, chasing him for so long.

Maybe I was never meant to have him.

* * *

In the morning, I'm hunkered down on my couch, researching Amelie's collection while batting away thoughts of Bridger and where we're going—nowhere, probably, just nowhere—when my phone rings with the building's number.

I grab it and answer.

"It's Andy," says the building's handyman. Andy the handyman. "Henry gave me a package for you. To bring up."

Oh. I haven't ordered anything. Maybe it's something fun from my cousin? A necklace? "I'll head down," I say.

"It's pretty big," he tells me. "I'll bring it up. Just wanted to make sure you were home."

When he knocks a few minutes later, I'm up and at the door already, swinging it open. I gasp when I see the size and shape of the package.

My insides jump, but I tell myself to calm down.

It's probably something else. Something other than what I'm imagining. My daydreams are too dangerous, and I try to snuff them.

"Thank you," I say, then take the rectangular package from Andy, letting the door fall closed with a soft thud.

I carry it to my couch, breathless with anticipation, then set it down. I step back and stare at it. Brown butcher paper covers it, and my name is on the front.

There's no way.

There's just no way.

Carefully, I undo the tape on one corner, then the other, then one more.

I peel off the paper.

I freeze.

Then, in slow-motion, I unfreeze, clasping my hand to my mouth.

I can't believe it. Bridger bought me the painting from last night. The Zara Clementine. And there's an envelope in the corner with my name on it.

With eager fingers, I open the envelope. Inside is a sheet of stationery from the Bettencourt Gallery.

I'm sorry for the way last night ended, but now you can look at this anytime. You've never looked so beautiful as when you were gazing at this with longing in your eyes.

xo
B

29

YOU ARE JUST

Harlow

After Andy hangs the painting that morning, I call an impromptu meeting of the Virgin Society for late Friday afternoon in Abingdon Square, a little triangular patch of park atop the Village. It's an oasis in Manhattan, with benches and trees and so much greenery.

Another benefit? It's right next to Lulu's Café, an extension of the chocolate shop.

The three of us nurse iced hot chocolates in the park while Layla preps me for tomorrow's meeting with Amelie, and I try to stay in the moment and not jump ahead fifteen minutes to when I'll see Bridger.

Layla issues me a stern, no-nonsense stare. "And where do you see yourself in five years?" she asks, roleplaying Amelie, while Ethan snags her iced chocolate drink to take a sip.

Before I can answer *and* before he can drink, he mutters, "Between Bridger's legs, sucking him off."

I smack him. "Shut up."

Layla simply stares at Ethan, her eyebrows saying *well played*. Then, she clears her throat. "As I was saying, in five years, do you see yourself giving him a humdinger under his desk, or in your living room while your firstborn naps?"

"You're both fired!" I shout.

"From friendship? Because it seems like you'll be firing yourself from the Virgin Society soon," Ethan points out, then finally takes that sip.

"That was always my goal," I say, then I look at Layla. "Stop distracting me from work talk with sex talk. This was your idea. You wanted to prep me for tomorrow."

"And I also enjoy naughty tales. So sue me," she says with a shrug.

She asks the five-year question again, I answer eloquently, and with that done, I declare that I'm ready for tomorrow.

Ethan pats my thigh. It's mostly bare. Well, I *am* wearing a short, blue plaid skirt. "So, does your dad know you quit?"

"I haven't told him. He hasn't asked either. He's probably too busy with Vivian. I'll tell him soon, though."

"Speaking of, what happens with you and the birthday present," Ethan says, wagging his eyebrows, "when Daddy's back?"

My stomach twists. I'm not sure when my father's

vacation is ending, but he can't stay away forever. He loves work too much. That's the problem. He'll always work with Bridger. "Bridger and I haven't talked about that. I don't even want to broach it yet. Everything is so...fragile and dangerous."

"Ooh, that sounds like lyrics to a new Ethan song," Layla says brightly.

Ethan knits his brow and nods to a beat in his head, getting a rhythm. "Like, my heart is fragile with you... but dangerous to us," he improvises in a beautiful tenor with a touch of gravel.

"Stop showing off your talent," I tease.

He checks the time on his phone. "I should return to the rehearsal studio. The guys will be back."

I perk up. "How is it going?"

Ethan's been riffing with his new band, and he stole away to meet us while they ran errands.

"Oh, you know how it goes. You love it and hate it and beat yourself up all at once," he says.

"So...it's like any other type of art."

"Exactly."

Layla hops up too. "I should go. Mom has a charity thing for me tonight. Wish me luck."

I say goodbye, and once they head out into the Friday rush hour, I check the time. Bridger will be here in ten minutes.

I can't wait to see him. And to *finally* get the details.

I asked him earlier how he pulled off the gift, but he said he'd tell me when he picked me up on the way to the Ashanti Gallery in Brooklyn. *Patience, honey*, he'd written.

How can I have patience when you gave me this beauty?

Then I sent him a photo of the art hanging on my wall. Andy the Handyman worked fast.

Right on time, Bridger's town car pulls up, and he steps out of the back, looking sinfully beautiful in dark slacks that hug his legs and a shirt the color of rich red wine. Fine stubble lines his jaw.

His eyes twinkle—he looks so damn pleased. Maybe he's been grinning wickedly all day after pulling off his very own art heist for me.

I nearly can't stand how good I feel right now. How fizzy my body is. I head toward him, but he's faster. With purposeful steps, he strides across the park to meet me. When he reaches me, he looks down at the cup in my hand. "Anything good?"

"It's an iced chocolate," I say as if I'm floating—on the whole damn day, on the possibilities of tonight. Since my brother's arriving later, we have little time together this evening, so I want to savor every second. I offer him the drink. "Do you want to try it?"

"Yes," he says, watching me as he takes a sip from the same metal straw my lips touched moments ago.

It's heady.

When he lets go, his gaze drifts to the lip gloss remnants on the straw. "I can taste chocolate and your lip gloss."

My skin tingles. My body aches. "Do they taste good?"

"Exquisite," he says, his blue eyes darker than I've ever seen them, full of heat and unabashed want. A rumble comes from his throat as he tilts his head toward the car. "Let's get in the car, Harlow. *Now*."

Holy shit. This man just turned all the tables on me.

For the whole month—no, for the entire year—I've been wanting, hoping, craving.

Then chasing.

Now, he's taking the reins. He's in this too—whatever this is.

Quickly, I toss the cup in the park's recycling bin, then stuff the metal straw in its pouch.

He holds open the car door, and I slide into the backseat—our private ride in Manhattan. Once he shuts us inside, he turns to me, looking ready to take me. But I'm faster. Setting my things down on the console, I grab his cheeks, holding his face. "Thank you for the painting. Thank you so much," I say, wanting him to know how much it meant to me.

"It was my pleasure—" He swallows that last word as my lips capture his.

I try to tell him with my kiss that no one has ever given me something like that before.

But a kiss can't say everything.

I break apart. "Bridger, I love it. And I love your note too," I say, vulnerable, totally open with him.

He smiles—a warm, relaxed kind of smile that's all new on him. I imagine that's his vacation smile, the one he wears when he's lounging on a chair on a tropical island under the warm sun, the ocean lapping the shore.

It's the smile of a content man.

But it's not in his nature to be content. He's busy,

always moving, striving, yearning. In this moment though, he seems satisfied.

With me? With us? With this night? Maybe all of it, all at once.

As the car cruises toward Brooklyn, I ask again, "But how did you do it?"

His grin is wicked. "Do what? Get this car?"

I play along, sliding a palm over the black leather seat. "Yes. The car. It's so nice."

"You like me for my town car?"

"That's it exactly."

"Say it," he teases. "Say you like me for my town car."

"Never," I taunt.

"C'mon. Just a little?" he prompts. But I wonder if he truly craves reassurance.

Maybe he needs to hear that I like him for him, not for the town car, not for the trappings of his job, not for the accouterments of wicked success.

Not even for the painting.

Maybe I'm the only one he interacts with who doesn't have an agenda. Or rather, perhaps my agenda is the one he wants too—*us*.

I grab his shirt. "I'd walk with you to the gallery in Brooklyn."

He covers one of my hands with his. "All right, we're pulling over now."

"Okay, maybe I didn't mean it," I say, laughing. Then I meet his gaze again, my smile disappearing. I draw a quick breath for courage, then I leap. "I care about you deeply," I say, as I test out those words, the start of an admission. But it barely covers this coil of emotions knotting tightly in my chest. Desire, want, hope, and then, something else. Something new. Something delicious. "And I love the painting because you gave it to me. That's why I love the gift."

He takes my hand from his chest and curls his fingers through mine. "I had to get it for you."

"Yeah?"

He presses a soft but terribly sexy kiss to the corner of my mouth. "Once I saw you staring at it, I was determined," he says, breaking the kiss.

I nearly bounce. "Tell me. How did you pull it off?"

With a confident shrug, he says, "I negotiate for a living. I negotiated for it."

"But when?" I ask.

"Before I left, while Dominic was chatting with the curator, I asked the owner about purchasing the piece. Bettencourt himself. He said it had sold. He wouldn't disclose the buyer's name. Told me he couldn't sell it out from under someone." Bridger takes a storytelling pause, building suspense. "But there's more than one way to get what you want. So I mingled with Dominic as he chatted with attendees—making small talk with guests, seeing if anyone knew the buyer."

"You did all that?" I ask in a whisper.

He despises mingling. It stresses him out. Makes him feel out of control. Borderline anxious. But he did it for me.

He just nods, then continues. "And I found a lead while Dominic was talking to Bettencourt. There was another gallerist who said she'd heard a guy bragging about having bought the Zara Clementine. As Dominic and I headed downtown, I looked up the guy. Turns out he works at a hedge fund."

"Wow," I say, and impressed barely covers it.

"I didn't make an offer then in front of Dominic. But I called the buyer this morning shortly after the markets opened, told him I wanted it, and then I made him an offer he couldn't refuse."

"Bridger," I say, swept up in the magnitude of his gift.

"It worked out for everyone. He's an investor. He made a terrific ROI in less than twenty-four hours. You have the work of art you want." He cups my chin and strokes my face. "And I was able to give you the thing you wanted most."

I have chills everywhere—sexy, gorgeous chills. My heart is caught in my throat. "Thank you," I manage to say past the tightness.

"I just wanted you to have it," he says, then he dusts a kiss onto my lips. "Especially after what you did for…"

He's this close to saying *us*.

I can hear it on the tip of his tongue.

I don't know if there will ever be an us, but right now, tonight, it feels like we can't be anything else but an *us*. Especially when he lays kisses on my neck like he adores me. Then when he nibbles on my earlobe, like I belong to him.

Intimacy feels inevitable, whether tonight or another time, so I slide a hand between us, press it to his chest. "I've never had sex. I want you to be my first."

He stops, blinks, then asks carefully, "You do?" It's

full of wonder, naked excitement, and not an ounce of judgment.

"I do."

He shudders out a breath. Licks his lips. Then just nods. "Yes."

That's it. It's done. A promise that some time, we will.

Right now all I want is to get closer to him, so I lie down on the seat, stretch across it, and pull him on top of me.

He covers me with his strong body, and I wrap my legs around him.

"You are just..." His words fall to pieces as his lips find mine.

He doesn't have to finish the sentence.

I feel the same.

He is just...

Like that we kiss, with our whole bodies, the entire way across the city.

30

DON'T FALL

Harlow

I float through the last love letter exhibit barely aware of anything but the prospect of more time with Bridger.

Somehow, in this haze of wishes and hunger, we manage to plot a solid concept for the hero's backstory for *Afternoon Delight*.

When we're done, he says, "That feels strong enough to share with the writing staff next week."

Next week looms.

What will we be doing next week? I won't see him at the office, of course. We won't have a show concept to play around with. I want to ask him what the future holds for us but now hardly seems the time.

It doesn't seem the time either when we leave the gallery, and Bridger scans the block, spotting a sign for the Brooklyn Botanic Garden nearby.

He checks his watch, a hopeful look in his gaze. "Summer hours. They're still open?"

It's a question that says *will you go out with me tonight?*

Quickly, I check the flight alert. Hunter's plane is on time, but he won't arrive till a little later, so I can steal more of the night. "My brother won't be here till nine-thirty."

We walk to the garden and head inside, with Bridger buying tickets to enjoy the last fading light of the day. It's like last night, when he asked to grab a meal and I seized the chance.

We wander through the lush gardens, checking out the orchids blooming by the lily pool terrace. Surrounded by blankets of flowers in succulent reds and delicate pinks and blinding oranges, I'm tempted to pull him into a secluded section.

But that's too risky. Instead, we stroll through the Shakespeare Garden, bathed in green, with its lush bushes, trees, and shrubbery. "It would be funny if Shakespeare really wrote here," I say.

"The Bard in Brooklyn," Bridger says, as if musing on the words.

"That sounds like the name of a musical," I say. "You should produce *The Bard in Brooklyn*. That could be your next career move. Backing musicals."

He laughs. "That's not risky at all."

"TV's risky and you do that," I point out.

"Fair point."

"And then you could have a kick-ass one-line bio in *Playbill*, like the one Davis Milo has," I say, referring to the award-winning director. "You know what his *Play-bill* bio says?"

"Of course. *Davis Milo directs*," he says.

We say the next line in unison: "Bridger James produces."

"See? How much better does it get than that?" I ask.

"It doesn't." But he shakes his head. "Except I think I just want to see shows. Know what I mean?"

"I understand. I never wanted to work in theater. But I do want to gobble it up."

"Me too. I would love to take you to see *The Un-Gentleman*," he says.

I light up at the mention of the musical opening in a few weeks. "I can't wait to see that."

"Same here," he says wistfully, then he shifts gears. "My mom is coming to town next month."

Or maybe it's not such a shift. His love of theater comes from her. But his unease with crowds comes from her too. "You don't want to see her?"

He takes a beat, blows out a breath. "I do want to see her. But she's throwing a party and she wants me to come. She'll be at Sardi's." He winces on the word.

I stop in the middle of the garden, my hand itching to touch his. I lock my fingers together so I don't touch him in public. "When?"

I ask it like there's some time in the future, the near future, when I could go as his date. When I could be his shield for real.

"A couple weeks," he says, resigned, clearly knowing I can't go with him then.

I'm not sure I ever can. But I can give him *this* much. "I'd go with you. You know that, right?"

Instantly, he answers with, "I'd take you. You know that?"

I nod, barely able to speak past the emotions in my throat. "Bridger?" I begin, and I can't wait any longer. "What happens after tonight?"

He sighs, smiling sadly. "I'm not doing a very good job staying away from you, am I?"

"Do you want to get better at that?" I ask, a little coy.

He inches closer, a tease of a smile on his lips. "I should want to, but I don't."

"Me neither," I say.

We're only grabbing onto pieces of the present, but for now, he's not letting go either.

"Your brother won't be here for a bit, you said?" he asks.

I check my phone. A text from Hunter says he just landed. "He should be at my place in an hour."

"That gives us *some* time," he says.

I know exactly what I want to do with it.

There's not time for *that*.

But the second the elevator doors close in my building, Bridger's all over me. Pressing me to the wall, holding my face, devouring me.

This is what I longed for way back when I was in Paris.

This is what I imagined every time I was alone.

I pictured this man wanting me with this wild abandon.

When the doors creak open on my floor a few seconds later, Bridger's breathing hard. I scan the hall. There are ten apartments on my floor. The hallway's empty. I grab his hand, and together we walk down to 8E.

Quickly, I unlock it.

The door's barely closing when he crowds me up against the wall. Kissing me fiercely. With sighs, and lips, and touches. His murmurs wind me up. His touches turn me on. And his body grinding against mine exhilarates me.

He's more pent up than he was in the car *before* the gallery.

He's a jack-in-the-box, and every push and pull of our bodies makes him coil tighter, higher.

Harder.

God, he feels incredible, and I want so much more of him. I maneuver a hand between us, sliding down his flat stomach, heading for his waistband.

My breath catches as I near his erection, pulsing, thick.

He breaks the kiss, sucks in a breath.

The awareness that my hand is traveling to his hard-on hits him.

He pulls back, looks at me. "Harlow," he says, like a warning.

"I want to," I say, stripped bare and hungry.

He closes his eyes, then covers my hand. He's not stopping me yet. Maybe just stalling me.

When he opens his eyes, he keeps his hand locked tight on mine, poised on his belt. "I want you so much," he rasps out. "I don't even know how to handle this. I don't know what's right anymore. I don't know a goddamn thing. But when I'm with you, I just...*want*."

I'm on fire. "What do you want to do to me right now?"

His eyes darken. "Taste you. *Everywhere*," he says.

I shudder. *Everywhere*. In my knees too.

With his free hand he grabs my hip, steadying me. "Don't fall," he murmurs.

Too late for that.

"I won't," I mutter, then I glance at the time in the kitchen. My brother will be here way too soon.

There's no time to be Bridger's dessert. But I have to ease this ache. I can't survive the night this wet, this aroused. I'm desperate and needy so I ask, "Can you—"

In no time, his hand slides up my skirt, into my panties, and he's easing this ache.

Oh god, is he ever.

Up against the wall, he strokes me, fast, expertly. It won't take long. Not tonight. Not with me this wired.

When I'm close, I gasp out, "Can I please touch you too?"

"Fuck," he curses.

I don't know if that's a yes, so I ask again. "Please?"

"Yes, fucking yes," he bites out.

Then, my hands are flying, and I'm unzipping his slacks, tugging at the waistband of his boxer briefs, and curling a hand around his hot, hard length.

I gasp, stroking him as he fucks me with his fingers.

He shakes as I touch him. Then growls something rough and incoherent. It's the sexiest sound I've ever heard, and it flips the switch in me. In seconds, I'm crying out, and it's intense as pleasure whips through my body.

But I don't let go of him. I keep going, moving my fist, thrilling at him rocking into my hand.

Then, I'm whimpering when he stops. Covers my hand. Backs away.

"I should go. You need to see your brother," he says, and his pupils are dilated, his lips are bruised and his clothes are a wrinkled mess.

I can't stop looking at him. He's in my home. And it better not be the last time.

On his way out, he tosses a glance at the Zara Clementine above my couch. "It's perfect."

My heart thunders as I say, "I love it."

Then he goes.

31

ANYONE IN PARTICULAR?

Harlow

It's a perfect summer morning, Central Park whooshing by as I go on a bike ride with my brother.

Hunter rounds the sparkling lake ahead of me, the boathouse off in the distance presiding over the water. I'm a few paces behind him, but I'll catch up.

It's energizing to bike with him like we did when we were younger, chasing each other around our favorite place in the city—*here*.

I never beat him then. But I'm tougher and battle-scarred—literally—now.

Determined too.

I picture my ankle. The scar on it.

I pump the pedals harder and faster, and soon I'm passing Hunter, shooting him my most devilish little sister grin.

"Race you to Bethesda Terrace," I shout.

"You're on."

Then, I bend low, tucked over the bike. He's a racer, and he loves his adventure bike rides, but I'm fueled by the adrenaline of my wild life. By getting away with moments like I did last night with Bridger, from the gallery to the garden to my apartment. No idea when I'll see him again. No clue either when I'll hear from him again.

The uncertainty makes me push a little harder, working my muscles. Like if I ride harder, I'll see him again sooner.

With that goal fueling me, I roar down the bike path, but when we're fifty feet away from our destination, Hunter pulls ahead, badass that he is.

He finishes before me, panting hard, but victorious.

When I stop a second later, I faux grumble at him. "I know you had your bike turbo-charged last night," I tease, like I did when we were kids.

"Yes, that's it exactly, Lo. I juiced my rental bike late last night when you were sleeping," he says drily.

"Knew it," I say, then we lock up our bikes on a rack, and helmets in hand, we walk toward Bethesda Terrace, home of some of our most mischievous excursions years ago when Hunter spent his summers here.

We stop at the terrace overlooking a fountain made famous in movies, and I point to some trees beyond. "Remember when we tried to build a tree fort there? We bought wood at a hardware shop, tools and everything," I say, picturing that adventurous day when we'd thought we were both explorers and builders.

He laughs. "Wherever did we come up with that mad idea?"

"In a book, I'm sure," I say.

"And then the police came by and were basically like *well, kids, you can't very well build a tree house in Central Park*," he says.

"But it seemed like such a good idea at the time," I say.

"The best idea."

I laugh at the lovely memory, then rest my elbows on the terrace, soaking in the sun. I'll be meeting Amelie a little later, but for now, I'm gobbling up my morning with my brother, especially since he was too exhausted to hang out when he arrived last night. We both crashed hard. Maybe that was for the best, given what I'd been doing moments before he arrived.

Bridger texted me from his car last night, saying, **Hunter just walked in.**

I didn't bother to say *close call*. We both knew it was.

I focus on my guest now. "So, tell me more about the trip to California." He'd traveled to San Francisco for work. "How's everything going with Webflix?"

His cheeks pinken, his dimple appearing in full force. Ohhhh. That's quite a tell. "I guess something more interesting than work happened?" I stare at him purposefully. *What are you hiding from me*?

"Why would you think something happened?" he asks ever so innocently.

"Hunter! Who did you meet in California?" I stomp a foot, exaggerating indignation.

"Nobody." But he can't keep the smile off his face,

and he rolls his eyes. "Ah, fuck it. Somebody. Somebody totally fantastic." He drags both hands through his thick hair. "Lo, this guy. Holy fuck. He was just..." He can barely speak, he's so...infatuated.

I can barely do anything but shriek because I'm already infatuated with his story. "Details," I demand.

"We went to his place, and it was amazing."

"Did you...?" I whisper.

He shakes his head. "Not yet. I mean, I've only ever kissed a man before, but we did *a little* more than kissing, this guy and me."

Or maybe a lot, I wonder, reading his expression. But he'll share when he's ready.

He drops his voice even lower. "He's a football player in San Francisco. And just wow. The whole thing was just...wow."

"That's great," I say, giddy for my brother. He sounds all caught up in his crush. "So will you see him again?" Once I ask, I realize it's unlikely. This guy lives in San Francisco. My brother lives in London.

"I don't think so," he says sadly. "What with the whole continent plus an ocean thing and all. But maybe I'll see him next year if I go there again," he says, with the hope that only intoxication can bring.

"Sounds like you already miss him."

Nodding, he winces, like it hurts to acknowledge. "Weirdly, I do. It was one day, one afternoon. But we got on so well. He was sort of sexy but vulnerable, know what I mean?"

An image of Bridger from last night flashes before my eyes.

The clench in his jaw. The heat in his eyes. The restraint in his voice.

But the giving in too.

The way he wanted me with reckless abandon. Sparks rush through me as the memory turns more visceral.

Bridger is sexy but vulnerable.

"I do know," I say as evenly as I can, hoping the heat doesn't leak through in my voice.

Hunter arches a curious brow. "Yeah?"

He doesn't have to say *anyone in particular*?

It's an unspoken question, but it makes me queasy.

I can't let on about Bridger. Not even a hint.

Hunter knows Bridger. Bridger signed his paychecks for two years when Hunter worked as a junior producer on *Sweet Nothings*, before he joined Webflix earlier this year. But I promised Bridger I'd keep us a secret. And even though I knew I'd have to swallow the truth, it still hurts as the lie slides down my throat.

"I mean, I imagine *what* you mean," I correct, saying it as breezily as I can, channeling my inner actress, the one Daddy coached for years with his lies. Then I grab the steering wheel and yank the conversation back to him. "So this guy. Are you sure you can't see him again? Lots of love affairs have started as long-distance ones. Maybe it's not insurmountable."

He chuckles a resigned laugh, rather than a happy one. "Not really. I live within my means. I don't live on Daddy's dime."

I straighten my spine, saying sharply, "I don't either."

Hunter blanches. "Oh shit. Lo, I didn't mean anything about you," he says, apologetic. "I know you don't."

"My apartment is from my mom," I add, hurt in my voice.

"Lo, I know."

"And I'm going to find a job," I add, more defensive than I should be. "Maybe even today."

He pulls me into a conciliatory hug. "I'm on your side. I understand. I wasn't saying you're a daddy's girl. I'm just saying I have to live like I don't come from *Sweet Nothings*."

Reality is, I have it easier. The apartment, after all, is a game changer. I sniffle, then pull away. "Sorry, I'm just nervous. About the interview later today," I say.

"You're going to do great. And I'm glad you quit Lucky 21. It wasn't you. And I don't want you to be so tied up with Dad. He was toxic when I worked with him."

My stomach churns. Hunter had hinted at that, but hearing it tugs painfully on my heart. "I'm sorry you went through that."

"He was always putting me down, belittling me for not being as good as him, and at the same time trying to entice me to work in his world. It was like a hug, then a slap in the face, then another slap, then another hug. I'm happier now that I'm doing my own thing," Hunter says, clearly relieved to be free. "That's why you quit, right? To do your own thing?"

Once again, I wish I could be fully honest with him. I wish I could say *I quit for me. I quit to follow my passion, but my passion also is our father's business partner.*

"Of course," I say and that's very, very close to the truth.

Back at my place, I shower and change into something business-y, but still Saturday-ish. I choose a red summery dress with the tiniest white polka dots and pair it with a short-sleeve white cardigan. It's festive and fresh, and the dots on the dress are small enough to give a pointillism vibe. Always a plus to put on an outfit with an art reference.

Hunter and I leave together. Out on the street, I give him a kiss on the cheek. "See you tonight? We'll do dinner?"

"We damn well better," he says, then heads off to meet a friend for an afternoon beer while I go to a coffee shop in Gramercy Park.

It's a little odd that we're not meeting at or near MoMA, but then it's a Saturday, so I suppose that makes sense.

The Lyft whisks me down to Twenty-Seventh Street, and I find the café quickly, then spot the stylish curator at a table by the window inside. After quick hellos, I sit across from her.

"Coffee, tea, LaCroix, or some shake with some mix in it that makes you feel something?" she asks archly.

I laugh at Amelie's dry humor. "Tea is great. No shakes with things in it for me."

After we order and return to the table with mugs, she deals me an intense stare. "You may be wondering why I didn't ask to meet you at MoMA."

"The thought occurred to me," I admit.

"Look, here is the deal," she says, glancing behind her, then around, then cutting to the chase. "I gave notice the other week. My last day is Tuesday."

Oh, wow. That's huge. "That's a change."

"MoMA is a wonderful place. I am glad to have cut my teeth there. But," she says, in a conspiratorial tone, "Allison gave me permission to tell you this. She's convinced me to come to Petra Gallery. They have some very exciting installations coming up, and we're expanding the space to bring on more new artists," she says, then rattles off details on the type of art they're chasing—art that showcases passion, emotion, love. "We're looking for some associates to work their way up as we build our client base."

"Where do I sign up?" I ask, unafraid to show every ounce of enthusiasm I feel. And I feel all the ounces. All the gallons. All the drums.

"Are you sure?" she asks coyly. "I never got the impression you were that excited about theories of art."

I roll the dice. I go out on a limb as I say, "And I have a feeling that's why you want to hire me."

She shrugs, but there's a smile in it. "You're not wrong."

We talk more, then she tells me she'll need to speak

with Allison for final approval. "I'll get back to you this week," she adds.

"I look forward to it," I say, and I leave, floating on a career high.

For the first time ever, this feeling of buoyancy is all mine. It comes from my head, and my heart, and my work. The time and energy I poured into art—when I learned what I liked and didn't like—has *almost* paid off.

When she heads downtown and I head uptown, I finger the *I* on my necklace, then whisper, "Can I tell you a secret, Mom?"

Then I imagine telling her about the rest of today, knowing she'd be proud of me.

I gaze heavenward, then back down to earth, taking a deep, excited breath. Time to tell my friends and my brother, but first I spot a sneaker on the sidewalk, near a grate. A lone purple Converse. I snap a photo and post it, asking the question: *Lost or found?*

When I open my texts to share the news with my friends, there's a new message blinking up at me.

From Bridger.

And once I read it, I hail the next cab I see.

32

INNOCENT AND SEDUCTIVE

Bridger

A few minutes ago

I often spend Saturdays working. It's not unusual for me to be holed up in my apartment poring over scripts, contracts, deal memos.

So switching between finalizing the streaming terms for a script we acquired late last year, *Anti-Heroes Unleashed,* and prepping the details of the *Afternoon Delight* rewrite should keep me in the zone all day.

Operative word being *should.*

These twin projects ought to occupy me well into the evening when I can grab a bite with Axel, or maybe connect with some producer colleagues.

Trouble is, it's late afternoon, and I've made seriously shitty progress on both fronts. I'm alone in the

Lucky 21 office, staring blankly at the laptop, the terms turning blurry.

What the hell am I even reading?

Maybe I'm just distracted today.

Maybe I should turn off the *Card Game* soundtrack.

There. Done.

Surrounded by silence, I try once again, but my mind is wandering. To last night. The night before. Then the one prior.

I curse, then pace, stare out the glass fourteen floors below, watching New York stroll by on a Saturday. Peering farther, into the park. Harlow loves the park. Did she go there today with her brother? Did they wander around the lake? She's told me of their adventures when they were younger. Others I heard about on my own, just from being in her home, working late to launch this company many years ago.

Working with her dad.

I jerk my gaze away from the window, like I can flip off the reminders of our twisted connection.

Then I turn the other way, but I'm still a treacherous ball of nerves.

I could do yoga to let go, but I'm wearing tailored slacks and a button-down. I'm not going to be that jackass in an office doing yoga in his work clothes.

Pass.

I blow out a long stream of air, then flop down on the couch. Maybe I just need a break from work. Maybe I've been too go-go-go lately.

Except...

I've worked a little less than usual the last three nights because I've spent them with Harlow.

All at once, my body feels lighter as I think of her. A feel-good drug works its way through me.

I close my eyes, slipping into the most delicious memory of last night. Up against the wall. The way she moves as I touch her. The sexy whimpers that fall from her lips.

That's the answer to all this cranked-up pressure inside me.

I want to see her soon.

I just want to see her. Hold her. Talk to her. *Be* with her.

Pretty sure she said her brother was leaving tonight. In a flash, I pop up, stalk to my desk, grab my phone. She's in her interview right now though. So I start with a simple text: *Hey there...thinking of you. Hoping the meeting with Amelie goes well.*

Then, I tap out another, *What are you doing tonight? Can I see you?*

There. I can breathe, I can work, I can focus. I stretch my neck from side to side, crack my knuckles, and dive back in.

But I keep reaching for my phone on my desk to see if she's replied.

I keep checking the time to see when I can check in again.

It's nearly five.

I can be patient. I won't push her.

But when I close my eyes, I see her, I feel her, I smell her.

I wish she were here right now. If she were, I'd...

I groan, unbidden.

I know what I'd do if she were here.

After I open my eyes, I send one more message.

When you're done with your interview, I'd like to see you. I'd like to kiss you. I'd like to put you on my desk, slide my hands up your thighs, and then taste you. Everywhere.

I'm at the office. No one's here.

The second she walks through the doorway, I tug her to me, kicking the door closed as I lift her into my arms.

I greet her with a deep, passionate kiss. I don't stop kissing as I carry her—her legs wrapped around my waist—to my desk.

Then, I set her down on it.

With a naughty grin, like the vixen she sometimes is, she leans back, pats the oak, and says, "It *is* a really big desk."

"Let's see how well it works," I tell her, then I lock the door quickly and return to her. I slide a hand down her bare leg, traveling to her right ankle, the one with the scar. "Put your foot on the desk."

She places the spike of her high-heeled foot right on the edge of the wood.

Lust shoots down my body.

"Beautiful," I murmur, then I sit down in my chair, pull it closer to the desk, and I bend to kiss the scar. I do it gently, adoringly, treating her like the gift that she is.

A shuddery breath greets my ears.

My hand wraps around her ankle. I brush my lips along her skin. Then up her calf. That tempting vanilla scent of her lotion drifts into my head, intoxicating me. I reach her knee, traveling to kiss the side, then the back.

A soft gasp.

A wriggle.

I smile and set my other hand on her other leg, slowly, luxuriously, spreading her legs open for me. I raise my face, needing to look at her.

She's watching me, her green eyes glittering with want.

"I've thought about this before," she says in a soft confession. Heat spreads down my back as I turn my face to her left leg, brushing my stubbled jaw along her soft, delicate skin.

"And how does this compare?" I ask.

I can feel her smile more than see it as she says, "I don't have enough data yet."

"We should do more research," I suggest.

She leans back. "I like research. Lots of research, Mr. James."

"Me too." I kiss her thigh again. She's like a treasure, and I want to discover every precious facet of her.

The way she gives herself to me is such a privilege.

She trembles as I kiss up her inner thigh, closer, and closer still. Her scent drives me wild.

"Please."

That word tugs on my heart and makes me impossibly harder at the same damn time.

With a groan, I devote myself fully to my mission, teasing her with my mouth, then I push her skirt up higher, bunching the fabric at her waist and revealing her panties.

Tiny, white lace.

I stop. I'm trembling too. I need a fucking moment.

I lift my face again, craving eye contact. She must be as well, because she's looking at me with expectation in her gaze. I think she's been looking at me the whole time.

"Do you like?" She sounds hopeful.

I rush out a throaty, "I love." Then I cover the white lace with my hand, pressing the heel of my palm against her heat.

She cries out. "Yessss."

Jolts of pleasure shoot through my body all at once. I don't know if I can survive this. I'm more aroused than I've ever been in my life.

But I'm willing to try.

"I almost don't want to take these off," I tell her, running a finger along the seam of her panties. "They're innocent and seductive at the same time. They're just like you."

In a feather of a voice, she says, "I think you're seducing me."

I answer first with action as I play with the lace, running a finger along the outline of the fabric.

She lifts her hips, her body begging.

Then, I answer her with a question. "Do you want me to seduce you, Harlow?"

She pushes up higher on her elbows, pinning me

with her vulnerable gaze. "I've always wanted that," she says, then she sweeps a hand down her body, over her breasts, along her belly, and pushes her fingers inside her panties.

My mind spins with lust. Her hand slides farther, then out, and she lifts her fingers to my face, offering herself to me.

I grasp her wrist, then lick off the heady taste of her.

"Take them off. Now," she says in a trembling command and it's a reminder too—that I am at her mercy.

I comply, slowly, torturously slowly, pulling them down, over her thighs, then off.

I set her feet back on the edge of the desk.

Then, I spread her legs wide, and it feels like going to church.

Unholy, wicked, church where I intend to worship this goddess.

33

___

AN INDECENT KISS

Harlow

I'm shaking with lust.

Desire.

And so much emotion I don't even know if there is room inside me for all of these feelings.

It's like I'll burst with all this exquisite newness.

Especially since Bridger gazes at me with fire in his eyes. I can barely withstand how good I feel right now, spread out on his desk like dessert, my skirt hiked up to my waist, my body revealed to him.

He can't stop staring. He won't stop touching.

I feel adored.

Is it foolish of me to think this is more than sex? It feels that way to me. I don't have many benchmarks. I can't even compare him to anyone else.

But his hands touch me reverently. His eyes regard me worshipfully. And when he kisses his way along my thighs and at last, at long last, presses an absolutely indecent kiss where I want him most, I swear I can feel his storm of emotions too.

I gasp, arching my back, grabbing his head, then lacing my fingers through his soft, dark hair.

I want to close my eyes and bask in these gloriously wicked sensations as he kisses me. It's like a filthy French kiss, chased by his hungry noises. But I don't dare close my eyes. I've dreamed about this. Far too much. I've longed for this too many times. I've pictured *us* just like this.

And he's eating me like I am breakfast, lunch, dinner, and dessert.

His soft lips kiss and then devour. Graze and then suck.

Pleasure radiates from my center, through my bones, under my skin. My whole body sings.

My hands rope through his hair as I rock against his mouth.

He kisses me more deeply all while his possessive hands travel up my belly, then around my waist, then down to my ass.

He squeezes my cheeks. Gripping hard. Then harder still. Like he won't let go of me. God, I don't want him to ever let go of me. I don't want him to stop. Not the kissing. Not the going down on me, and not the seeing me.

I don't want to stop anything. I want so much more of him.

He groans. Carnal. Possessed. He stops, looks up at me, his expression savage and lust-struck. "You taste fucking incredible. I just don't want to stop," he says, urgent, pleading.

Reading my mind and my body all at once.

It's dark and dangerous the way he says *I don't want to stop*.

Like he means so much more than this moment.

Than this act on his desk.

It's like he's offering a risky promise to me—that *we* won't stop. I swallow roughly, hunting for words to match my emotions as I curl my hands tighter in his hair. "Please don't stop. You have no idea."

His lips quirk up in a wicked grin. "No idea what?"

"How much I want you," I say, my whole body shuddering.

He lifts his chin, his smile confident, determined. "You want to come, honey? You want to come on my face?"

Who is this man? With that dirty mouth, the filthy eyes, the hungry hands?

My man.

He is my man right now. And we are seducing each other at last. "So much," I murmur.

He slides his hands under my ass, cupping me then lifting me back to his mouth.

And I am just lost in this deep, passionate indulgence.

From the sounds of it, he is too. His groans are filthy and beautiful.

I'm so close that the twist of pleasure coils in my belly. All our carnal sounds mingle together.

And then, I hear a ring.

Sharp, abrasive. Too loud.

He ignores his phone, licking me more fiercely, determinedly. Thank god. But my phone goes off next, seconds later. Like a braying cow.

Then his phone barks again.

It's enough noise to break the moment.

I push up higher on my elbows. I turn toward mine first, but I can't see who the missed call is from. Then we both turn toward the offending sound coming from his phone, rattling on his desk, inches away from my naked legs.

And the name flashing on the screen is *Ian*.

34

PARTNERS IN CRIME

Harlow

I scramble.

Hopping off the desk, jerking down my skirt, hunting frantically for my panties.

Where the hell are they?

"Are you going to answer it?" I whisper hiss as I search for a white scrap of lace.

"Yes. He might be *here*," Bridger says, cool and calm.

How the hell does Bridger do that? Stay centered like that? My heart is exploding. If my dad's in this building...

I will die.

I have to get dressed. As I smooth my skirt, I scan the carpeted floor of his office, then I spot them.

I seize my undies like they're contraband. Bridger draws a breath then answers the phone. "Hey, Ian, what's going on?"

His normal voice. His normal greeting. I've heard it before. At different times over the years. Right now, it makes me feel like I'm the one who's been caught cheating.

There's a pause.

I yank on my damp panties. I'm surprised I'm not tripping on my freaking face. It's a miracle.

I adjust my clothes, try to calm my racing heart as Bridger's eyebrows rise. "No kidding? Congratulations."

But I don't hear an exclamation point in his tone. Still, I'm racing to puzzle out what the congratulations is for. Then, with an all too familiar awareness, I'm certain.

That's why my father called me too, seconds ago.

As my dad talks to Bridger, I mouth, *He married Vivian?*

A nod.

I knew this was coming. I absolutely knew this was coming. And still, I hurt for her already. I hurt for the inevitable end that's probably coming sooner than she can even imagine. I picture Isla searching for my father earlier this week with worry in her eyes, emotion in her voice. She wasn't merely looking for her boss. She was looking for...

I can't even say the words *her lover* in my head.

This marriage will be his shortest.

But then, I stop thinking of them, since it's time to plan my own exit from this building right now.

Just in case Dad's here.

With the phone pressed to his ear, Bridger asks, "Tonight? Now? Aren't you going on a honeymoon?"

Another pause. My stomach is an upside-down amusement park ride.

"Right. And yes, of course I want to celebrate with you," he says, placating the beast. "That's fantastic. I just didn't realize you were back in the city."

I dart my gaze around the office, heading for the door. But Bridger darts out a hand, stopping me. He curls his palm around my arm. But it's not affectionate. It's...calculating. We are partners in crime, and we need to plan our getaway.

"You're home?" That's a few blocks away. "Yeah. Why don't we just meet at McCoy's? I can be there in an hour." A shorter pause. "Sooner. Sure, I can be there sooner. Ava's Bistro instead." A pause. "Right, right. It's closer and Hunter will be there shortly," he says, and I hope my father doesn't realize why Bridger's repeating this info—for my sake. "Yes, that makes sense. And have you talked to Harlow?"

I press my palm to the door, needing something to hold onto.

"Hopefully, she'll call you back soon."

My dad's chuckle is loud enough for me to hear.

"Yeah, I'm sure she's more of a texter," he says.

Yes, that generation and all.

Another reminder of the age difference.

Bridger closes his eyes. Shame and shock wash over his features. Then, he drags his hand over his mouth.

I swallow, roughly. *I'm* on his mouth. He's wiping me away while he talks to my dad.

He opens his eyes. "See you soon and congratulations again."

Then he hangs up. Lets go of my arm. Stares vacantly out the window. Then back at me. "They eloped yesterday. They're back in New York. Vivian has to work this week at the agency. He wants to take all of us out to dinner to celebrate," he says, telling me everything I've already figured out. "When you didn't answer, he called Hunter. And Hunter's going to dinner too. Before his flight."

Bridger's tone is laced with guilt and self-loathing.

Like he just came this close to being caught.

Terrible thoughts prick at my brain.

This can never work.

This company will always come between us. My father will always come between us.

How the hell could we ever be something for real?

Lucky 21 is where I am right now.

Lucky 21 is where I seduced him.

Lucky 21 belongs to the two of them.

And I can't ask Bridger *can we ever be a real thing*?

We aren't there yet. We aren't at that level. We are at the panties-on-the-floor level, the tryst-on-the-desk level, the cover-up-quickly-and-get-the-hell-out-of-there level.

I need some control. I need it fast. My life is spiraling.

I raise my face, hold my chin up high, and I blurt out the first thing on my tongue. "I'm freaking out. I'm seriously scared. This is so risky."

He winces but only for a second. "I know."

That's it? *I know*? He's supposed to reassure me. To tell me we'll figure this out. We'll face it together.

My throat tightens. "You think so?" I ask, my eyes stinging. But I don't want him to see me cry. Not over *this*.

Maybe he'll change his mind, say this isn't risky after all. Or maybe he'll say we can handle it.

But the most strategic man I know is thoroughly flustered as he glances around his office, flapping his hand at his desk, sputtering, "What are we even doing?"

Me? I'm falling for him. But what the hell is he doing? I'd like to know the answer. I kick away all the trembling emotions as I lift my chin and cross my arms. "I don't know, Bridger. What *are* we doing?"

He sighs heavily, full of awful resignation. "I'm not sure. It's just..."

Here it comes. I brace myself for the end. "So you think we should...?" But I swallow down the word *stop*.

I can't bring myself to say it. No matter how tough I think I am.

His jaw tics. His eyes almost...harden. "Harlow..."

I wither.

In one word, in my own name, I've been pummeled. There it is, and I can't bear to hear the words *we can't do this*. I can't bear to hear him say *stop* after all.

I hold up a stop-sign hand. "I have to go."

Then before he can say another word, before he can grab my wrist, before he can implore me to understand, before anything else at all, I leave.

Even when he calls out my name, I just keep going. Faster than he is.

Once I'm safely outside, walking along Central

Park, I fight off all the emotions swirling up inside me. I have to text my father after all.

Because that's what he expects.

But seconds later, he's calling me and I'm answering, and I'm faking it all over again, with enthusiastic *congratulations* and *oh my gods,* and *that's so wonderful.*

All to cover up the lies twisted like vines inside me.

* * *

As I march down the block to the restaurant, I run my finger over the *I* on my necklace. I need all my bravery tonight.

I need all my toughness too.

I can't let anyone see how much I ache right now.

I walk into the private room at Ava's Bistro off Park Avenue. When my father sees me, he beams, brings me in for a huge hug. Then he pulls Hunter in on the other side.

"Lucky me! We were returning to New York anyway since, well, I can't stay away from Lucky 21 forever, and it turns out I'm lucky again since both my children are here to celebrate with me," he says, like our presence in the city on this day in history is *only* because of him. I catch Hunter's gaze like *can you believe this.* His eyes say *yes, yes I can.*

As a server walks in, Dad lets go of us.

Even though I'm ripped up inside, I owe my brother a huge apology.

While Dad and Vivian chat with the server about wine, I grab Hunter and pull him aside. "I'm sorry I dragged you into this," I whisper. "I know you didn't want to spend your last few hours in New York with him."

"It's fine," he reassures me, his voice low. "And I didn't tell him where you were."

I go ramrod straight. Picturing the desk. My legs spread.

"The job interview," Hunter prompts. "I wasn't sure if Dad knew you quit."

Right. Of course. That's where Hunter thinks I was.

"Thank you."

"Did you get it?" he asks eagerly, happy for me.

"I think so. I hope so. I haven't told Dad I quit."

"Good luck. You'll need it," he says, then hugs me once more.

I'll need all his strength, especially when, a minute later, the click of wingtips signals it's time for me to be tough again.

The man who *Harlow'd* me walks into the room. The man who doesn't even know what we're doing.

I knew what I was doing.

Falling.

My heart thumps too unevenly for him, too painfully. Too much is happening inside me all at once. I try valiantly to quash all my emotions, but it's impossible with Bridger so close to me.

My dad beams at his business partner. "And of course I had to have my best friend here to celebrate as well."

For one of the first times ever, Bridger doesn't pull a poker face. Instead, he looks confused. He lifts his brow. Question marks flood his eyes. But he doesn't say the obvious—*We're not best friends, Ian.*

Because he knows how to read a room, and now is not the time to burst my father's friendship bubble.

Not when my dad greets him with a clap on the shoulder and an embrace. "My best mate," he says again, like he's driving the point home.

"You're like family," Vivian coos to Bridger.

I just blink. What the hell? *Several months ago, she wanted Bridger for his money.*

Then, my dad sweeps out his arm toward the table. "Let's have supper before my son has to leave town."

We sit down for the most awkward family dinner ever. I'm seated next to my new stepmother, who's nine years older than I am. On the other side of me is my brother, who I can't tell the truth to. I'm diagonal from the person who taught me how to lie. And I'm sitting across from the man I was stupidly falling in love with and can never ever be with.

I can barely look at Bridger throughout the entire uncomfortable meal.

But the good thing is, I don't have to.

Because the narcissist is in the room. And Dad's leading the conversation, regaling us with the story of how he gave the Pablo Neruda book to Vivian at their beach house.

"We bonded over Pablo Neruda on our first date," he says, so pleased with their romantic tale.

The book he could barely remember.

"And then we stole away to get a marriage certificate

and tie the knot in City Hall," he adds, saying that they'll plan a honeymoon for later this summer when Vivian can schedule another week away from the agency.

"We just couldn't wait to get married though," Vivian puts in.

Maybe she's pregnant.

I don't fucking care if she's going to give birth to my half-sibling.

When dinner winds down, Dad clears his throat. "There's a new musical opening this month. *The Un-Gentleman*. I know you two love Broadway so much," he says to Bridger and me.

My breath catches and for a few hopeful, dangerous seconds, I imagine Bridger saying *yes, I would love to take your daughter to the theater*.

But then, what would I do if he said that? Would I tell my father what's happened? That I've fallen for his partner? How would my dad handle that?

Badly.

Dad keeps going. "I thought the four of us could go." He turns to Hunter with a *you lost* shrug. "I would invite you if you lived in New York, but you've left me for London once again."

Hunter doesn't take the bait. "Yes, Dad, I did." Then he checks the time. "And I have to leave again. My flight is taking off in two hours."

My father doesn't wait for me to RSVP to the theater. He doesn't wait for Bridger to either. "Great. The four of us will go," he says like *Make it so.*

I don't want to cause a scene. I don't want to be a

problem. I'll just tell my father sometime this week I can't attend.

There's nothing for me to say here. Or do. And since Hunter is leaving, that's as good a time as any for me to go as well.

I walk out with him and say goodbye to my brother on the street, our hug lasting longer than usual, me not wanting to let go, him seeming to understand how needy I am.

Then he's gone. I almost wish I could hitch a ride in his luggage.

Instead, I walk home alone. Drops of rain start falling on my head. And a lonely pair of tears streak down my cheeks.

35

PEDESTALS AND PRINCESSES

Harlow

Ten blocks and an elevator ride to my floor later, my dress is clinging to me. My cheeks are wet too, but not from the rain.

Once I'm inside my apartment, I strip out of my damp clothes, toss them listlessly in the hamper, and trudge to the shower.

I didn't bring an umbrella today. Didn't think I'd need one. That was a rookie mistake. New York loves to surprise anyone who gets too complacent by dumping a truckload of water from the sky.

Rain in New York is a shadow, lurking around the corner. You can't escape it. You just have to let it hunt you down.

I turn on the shower and wash away the last few hours of lies and hurt. I scrub off my own deception, along with my heartache. There was pleasure too, but that's long gone. And for a while in his office, when he was kissing me like I was the only thing that mattered in the universe, I felt...hope and possibility.

Maybe that's foolish of me, to feel so much from sex.

Maybe it was only ever sex to him.

An image of the Zara Clementine on my wall flashes before my eyes. I was never just sex to him. I know that.

What was I then?

I may never know.

When I get out of the shower, I run a towel over my hair and pull on a pair of black sleep shorts and a white tank top.

Freshly scrubbed, I head to the living room, sink down on the couch, and grab my tablet. I should read some news in French. Study up on the new trends in art galleries. Do something productive as an antidote to all my dangerous choices. Find something enriching so I don't wallow in this...*breakup*.

Can you even break up with someone you were never truly with?

Yet another question I have no answer to. Instead, I go to Webflix and I tune into *The Ultimate F Boys*, a mindless reality show. Before I can get too lost in the world of beefy, bleached blond boys and bling-wearing, bosomy, bratty girls, my phone trills.

And my ridiculous heart scampers. Maybe Bridger's calling to say he can't stand being away from me. That he meant to say he's wild for me. That he's not scared—he's bold and brave.

But when I grab the device, my shoulders fall. Hope is having a field day, smacking me tonight.

I pick up. "Hi Dad," I say.

"Poppet, why didn't you tell me you quit?"

I knew this was coming, and I should have gotten ahead of this one. Add that to my list of mistakes. "I'm sorry, Dad. I didn't want to bother you when you were away with Vivian or take away from your celebration tonight."

"What happened? Was someone mean to you?"

My heart squeezes. I can't believe that's where he went first—to defend me from schoolyard bullies that don't exist.

Times like this, it's hard to hate him.

I'm not even sure I do hate him. Hate is too strong a word. I'm frustrated. Conflicted, disgusted.

But right now, I'm none of those things. I'm just his little girl. He's only ever put me on a pedestal. If he knew that Bridger put me on a desk this afternoon, he'd be so disappointed in me.

A fresh, sharp pain corkscrews up my body.

If my father knew what I'd done, he'd cut me off. And I don't mean financially. He'd excise me from his life.

I'd be an orphan, for all intents and purposes. I've already lost one parent and even though my relationship with my living parent is more complicated than a ten thousand-piece puzzle, do I want to lose him too?

Maybe Bridger saved me from a future I'm not ready to handle.

With my stomach roiling, I say, "I'm really sorry. I

just realized that I want to work in the art world after all."

I feel better than I'd thought I would for saying something to him that's wholly true. Maybe, after all the lying by omission tonight, I need to just tell the truth, so I unspool more of it. "I learned so much while I was there at Lucky 21. I'm so grateful for the opportunity you made possible. But I realized how much art calls to me, and I want to work in a gallery. I truly didn't want to bother you while you were prepping for your wedding. I'm sorry to disappoint you."

"Harlow, you could never disappoint me," he says, warmth in his tone, like a hug. "I just wish you had told me. I would have helped you."

There was nothing he could have helped with. There's no point in saying that though. "Thank you," I say. "How did you find out?"

He chuckles. "Isla told me on the phone a few minutes ago."

My radar beeps. "On a Saturday night?"

"She was calling about something in the script. She's also working on a show of her own, and she wants me to look at it. It better be brilliant. I don't want to waste my time on drivel," he says.

He goes on for ten minutes about writing skills, and talent today, and storytelling.

Clearly, he's not bothered at all that I quit. Part of me wishes he were. It would be easier to let righteous rage fuel me.

Instead, I'm twisted up in knots.

When he says goodbye, I feel lonely once again, with only *The Ultimate F Boys* for company.

I wallow on the couch. Wishing I knew what to do next. Wishing I didn't feel so foolish. As Brayden says brazenly to the camera that no woman can ever pin him down, a knock on the door startles me.

I turn off the show, then pop up and peer through the peephole.

My breath catches. Bridger's on the other side. And he's drenched.

36

TEN TIMES

Bridger

I've been pacing back and forth outside her apartment. Debating whether to knock.

Wondering if she'd even want to see me. This *thing* with Harlow is completely uncharted territory. I don't have the map to navigate it.

I should have handled that moment in my office so differently when she confessed she was scared, then when she asked what we were doing.

My bright answer? *I'm not sure.*

But I know this much.

I should have insisted Harlow leave with me.

I should have told her that yes, this is terribly risky, but she's worth the risk.

I should have said I'd figure something out.

Even though I have no answers to anything...except for the too-fast, too-frantic beating of my heart.

No answers...except I walked around the block ten times in the pouring rain, trying to talk myself out of showing up, figuring she'd be with friends, she wouldn't want a visitor, she was over this *thing* already.

No answers except...

She swings the door open, her eyes narrowed, her brow knit. "What are you doing here?"

I take that on the chin. Her defenses are all the way up, and I deserve that. But I can't let her go. I just can't. Without thinking, I ask, "Should I have said something to him? Tonight? Did you want me to?"

Speaking that harsh possibility—hell, acknowledging the huge challenge, that's only a first step, that doesn't even solve the problem—unlocks something in me. It turns the door on my own emotions for her, the way I've tried to keep them tamped down. I'm not sure I can any longer.

"Tell him?" she repeats, looking thoroughly confused, like I've spoken a dead language.

"Do you want me to? Because I'm so sorry for what happened in the office," I say, afraid she might kick me out. She might slam the door. But I have to try.

"What part?" she asks fiercely, challenging me.

I can't let her think I regret touching her. Not for a second. "For the part where I made you think I was willing to let you go."

She's still for a few seconds, frozen in place. But her eyes flicker with hope.

Before I can say anything else, she opens the door for me. "Come in."

Somewhat relieved, I step inside, drag a hand

through my wet hair, and look down at the tiled floor. There's no puddle, but there are a few drops.

"Do you want a towel?"

No, I don't want a fucking towel. I want you. I want to talk to you. I want to see you. I want to touch you.

But I ruined things earlier.

And I have to fix them. I have to earn the right to touch her again, to hold her again, to deserve her.

The second the door shuts, I waste no time. "I'm sorry for what happened after the phone call. When I didn't kiss you goodbye. When I didn't tell you it'd be okay. And at dinner, when I didn't steal a moment with you," I say.

She swallows like there's a knot in her throat.

But she just waits.

"This *is* risky," I say, my eyes locked with hers. "This is the riskiest, scariest, most dangerous thing I've ever done. And it's true that I don't have a clue what we're doing, Harlow," I say, desperation clinging to me. Fitting, since I am desperate for her.

"But are we doing something, Bridger? It didn't sound like we were when I left your office," she says, not yet bending, not yet forgiving.

"I was...thrown off then. But the truth is...I just don't want to stop whatever this is. And I don't mean the physical," I say, imploring her as I try to put my heart on the line, hoping she'll have it. "I mean this thing happening between you and me." I stop, then clarify, "Between...*us.*"

Her lips twitch in the hint of a smile, but then it vanishes. Still, it gives me hope, especially when she softens, saying, "When you said *what are we even doing...*" She stops, shakes her head. "I thought you were ending things. But it's okay."

But no.

She doesn't need to make this easier for me.

"I can't stop," I admit, helpless to these feelings for her. I step closer, lift a hand to reach for her, but then drop it. I've still got more to say. I bunch my hands into fists at my sides. My emotions might be galloping away from me, but I've got to get a handle on the situation. Start small, not big. "Are you okay? The whole night must have been awful."

"I was really hurt. But I'm okay now. I'm tough," she says softly.

"I know you are, but I was worried about you at dinner."

"You were?" It comes out with a touch of wonder.

"Of course. I always worry about you. I always think about you. And I knew seeing your dad after the way the afternoon ended, and the things I said, couldn't be easy. You're so strong. So tough. And I shouldn't have let you go into dinner thinking anything but the absolute truth of what's happening."

"What's the truth?" she asks, sounding desperate too. "What is happening?"

My hand aches to touch her cheek, to hold her face. "I want to spend the evening with you. I want to spend the next night with you, and the next, and the next." I draw a soldiering breath. "I am absolutely enchanted with you."

On those words, a smile shifts her lips. Spreads to her eyes. Takes over her whole face. "Enchanted?"

With a small laugh, I stare down pointedly at my soaked clothes. "Yes. So enchanted I walked around the block again and again in a downpour." I exhale roughly. "Harlow, I don't have a plan. I don't know what we're doing. I don't know a thing. But...do you want me to tell your father?" I ask again.

Her eyes pop. "Oh god," she says nervously, perhaps finally processing the scope of what telling her father means, the sheer scale of that mountain. "I don't know," she adds slowly, weighing each uncomfortable word.

"If you wanted me to right now, I would," I say, offering something I have no idea how to deliver.

"I don't know how to handle that yet, Bridger," she says, a touch embarrassed maybe over her answer.

"It's okay. I don't know how to either," I admit.

More relief. More deep breaths, this time from both of us.

At last, we've voiced the big issue.

Maybe that's what we need for now. To breathe it out loud, even if we can't solve it tonight.

I take a small step closer. "Once they left, I started to go home. But I couldn't even bring myself to hail a cab. For the last hour, I've just been wandering around New York, thinking about you, trying to figure out what the hell to do. I didn't want to text. I didn't want to call. I just wanted to see you. But I didn't know if you'd want to see me."

She softens, her eyes shining. "I always want to see

you." She steps closer, gazing up at me, then she cups my cheeks.

Tingles race down my spine. Her touch is everything I can't give up. "Always," she repeats, soft, but confident. She lifts a hand, slides it up my damp shirt. "Even when you're drenched. Maybe especially when you're drenched."

And with that, I have permission to hold her. That's all I want in the world. I curl my hands around her hips, lift her up. She moves with me, wrapping her legs around my back.

Enchanted barely covers the way I feel for this woman.

My mouth crashes down on hers, and I kiss her like she's all I've thought about all day.

Like she's all I need tonight.

And like I'm falling so far, so hard, so fast for her, and the last thing I want is to scare her away.

She kisses me back hard. Powerfully. Emotionally. And deeper than she has before.

Here in her foyer, in my rain-ruined clothes and her dry ones, we come back together with a kiss that sends my world spinning out of focus.

Spinning closer to her.

All I want is to get closer to her.

Somehow, we find the will to stop, coming up for air, both panting.

She plucks at my damp shirt. "You look really good after a rainfall, Bridger."

I laugh. "Glad you like the look." Then I let go of the laughter, letting it die as I gaze at her with want, with desire, and with the start of a wild hope. "Let's finish what I started on the desk."

She nibbles on the corner of her lips, then shivers, arching a brow. "I want that, but you're a little cold and clammy."

"Well, we can't have that."

She hooks her thumb toward the inside of the apartment. "Go get in the shower. Warm up quickly. *Really quickly.*"

I take off my shoes and walk to the bathroom, Harlow right behind me.

Once inside the small white room, she hands me a towel. "Hang your clothes up on a hook." Then she shuts the door.

I take the world's fastest shower, warming up my cold body so when I touch her, she'll feel the heat.

I turn off the water, dry off, and wrap the towel around my waist. When I open the bathroom door, she's perched on the edge of her bed, wearing only her white tank and panties—no more sleep shorts.

I growl in appreciation. "You look incredible."

"Same to you," she says, her eyes traveling over my bare chest, then to the towel cinched around my waist. She points at me, circles her finger. "Strip."

I love her command, but first...*this*.

"In a second." I close the distance, stalk over to her, cup her chin. Bending, I bring her face to mine. Kiss her once—a firm, declarative kiss that says I'm here and I'm not leaving. When I break it, I say, "Thank you."

"I'm really glad you're here."

"Me too," I say, then I let go and take off the towel, dropping it to the floor.

Her breath comes in a staggered gasp as she stares at my naked body.

Stares with a hunger that matches mine.

I reach for her hand, tug her up, and strip off her tank. "Now lie down and spread those beautiful legs so I can feast on you properly."

With sparkling eyes, she obeys. I crawl between her thighs, tug down her panties, and kiss her once more.

And just like that, we're back.

She is naked before me and I am in awe.

It is such a privilege to touch her like this. It's like being given a Stradivarius, something precious and rare, and you must treat it with reverence.

I start slow, listening to her cues. Soon, I am touching her and tasting her again. She responds like a dream, moving like water, sounding like pleasure. She becomes a blissful mix of noise and motion, and then complete abandon as her hands grip my hair and my lips consume her. She arches, then cries out, and nothing, nothing, nothing has ever been better than this.

I feel like a king as I move next to her while she comes down. With a woozy, giddy look on her face, she turns to me, then glides her hand down my chest. "Finally," she whispers.

"You wanted my mouth on you that badly?" I ask, laughing and ridiculously turned on all at once.

She shakes her head, naughty and seductive. "Finally, *this*."

Wedging her body next to mine, her fingers trace

the artwork on my pecs, then travel through my chest hair. I'm not furry, but I don't manscape. She seems to like it, her fingers nimble as she explores. "I've wanted to touch you for so long," she says, and she is fearless as she spreads her hands across my chest, then my waist.

My desire is a tightrope stretched as far as it can go. But I will wait for her as long as she needs. "I love your hands on me, but I can wait for you, Harlow."

She meets my gaze, her eyes wide and not at all innocent. "Don't wait. Fuck me now," she says in a desperate plea.

My body burns.

I move over her, grab her wrists, and pin them above her head. "I'm going to fuck you whenever you want, but I'm always going to make love to you too."

She nibbles on the corner of her lips, then says all lingering and bold, "Start now."

37

MY GIFT

Harlow

An hour or so ago, everything felt wrong.

Now, everything about tonight is right once more. From the way Bridger holds my wrists tight to the way he gazes down at my face, sweeps his lips along my neck, asking, "Do you want to ride my cock, honey?"

His mouth.

His beautifully filthy mouth.

I shiver.

I turn wetter, hotter.

Breathless, I answer him with, "I want it all."

He gives a soft chuckle. "You can have everything, but not all at once."

I collect my thoughts. "I want you like this," I confess, looking up at him, his strong arms braced over me, his firm body covering mine. This is my fantasy, and yet... "Only, it's supposed to feel better if I'm on top of you."

In a flash, he lets go, shifts to his back, and pulls me over so I'm straddling him. He covers my stomach with his palm. "Mmm. How about you take your time like this? Make sure it feels good," he says, then travels a hand to my right breast, squeezing. I moan loudly. He groans faintly, then seems to shove off his own desire. "I can touch you," he says, with another squeeze. "And you find your pace."

The man loves my tits. And I love watching him play with them, so I help him along, reaching for his other hand, so he can cup and squeeze both.

Like that, I rock gently against his erection, my wetness coating him, a preview of what's to come.

Most likely, *me*.

Any second.

I'm that turned on. That aroused. That wound up.

He seems to be too. His eyes go dark. His jaw tightens. He's a picture of coiled restraint. A man about to snap with lust. And yet, he's waiting for me. I reach for the nightstand, grapple around for a condom, then hand it to him.

He sits up, opens it.

I can't take my eyes off him. Seeing him like this makes my throat dry and heart pound.

He rolls on the protection, then holds the base of his cock for me. And...wow.

That's so wickedly sexy.

So deliciously dirty.

The man I've craved for the last year of my life, the

man I've pictured taking me, is here in my bed. In my home. Under me.

Offering his dick to me like a gift.

Like the present I wished for when I turned twenty-one.

And now, a few months later, I'm unwrapping the present the rest of the way.

I rise up and rub my center against the head of his dick.

Yes, happy birthday to me.

Gripping him, I guide his length to me like I'm his north star tonight. Maybe I've been his north star for a while too. The thought stirs wild emotions in me.

Slowly, luxuriously, I sink down on him.

I press my palms to his chest, adjusting to the stretch, the intrusion.

The wonderful, wicked intrusion.

It hurts at first, and the pain stretches to my belly as I adjust to all this...newness.

He reads my reactions as he slides a hand up my chest, to my neck, into my hair. His hand is tender but passionate. "My beautiful woman," he says, like he can't take his eyes off me.

If any word could turn me fiery tonight, I wouldn't have picked that one.

My.

But said in his gravelly voice, with reverence, with lust, that word thrills me.

Tonight, he *can* be mine.

And now, nothing hurts. The pain washes away, and in its place comes something incredible.

Him and me, moving together.

His hands on my hips, gripping me.

Mine on his chest, owning him.

His eyes roaming over me, adoring me.

Our lips coming together as we kiss while we fuck.

Then, as I lower myself, my breasts pressed to his chest, my fingers in his hair, his hands come down on my ass. Curling around me. Possessively.

So damn possessively. Like his voice, too, urging me on. "Did you picture this?" he asks, calling back to my admission earlier in the day.

"So much."

"Me too," he says, hot and urgent.

"Yeah?"

"A few nights ago. A week ago. A month ago," he rasps out in quick succession, and with each confession, another fire ignites, burning brightly.

He's wanted me the same way for some time too.

And he shows me with how he fucks me, with deep, passionate thrusts.

I gasp. A sharp, fevered intake of breath as he hits someplace inside me that bathes my brain in pleasure.

We fit perfectly, legs and hips twined, lips and breath tangled. He slides a hand between my thighs, his thumb finding my center, and I'm chasing the climax that's hunting me down.

My toes curl, and my spine tingles. He looks in my eyes, and the intensity of his gaze is almost too much to bear.

I close my eyes, the world turning black and beautiful as I cry out.

Then, seconds later, his fingers dig into my flesh, and he's pumping, thrusting, and grunting as he comes undone too.

A few minutes later, after we straighten up, I tense, standing stock-still in the bathroom hallway, expecting him to get dressed, say goodbye, and take off into the night.

But then, his clothes are still wet and hanging on the rack in my bathroom.

I glance at them. "I guess you're stuck for a little while."

With a *you know it* grin, he just laughs. "I'm stuck, Harlow. I'm definitely stuck."

He slides back into bed with me, his warm, naked body pressed to mine. He's not staying because he has nothing to wear. He's staying because there's no place he'd rather be.

I'm light-headed, buzzed on the new sensations still rippling through my body. I trace my fingers down his chest.

He reaches for my hand, kisses my fingertips. "The shoe you found today?"

I still for a moment, cycling back to this afternoon. Oh, right. The purple Converse. "The one on the sidewalk?"

"Yeah." He takes a pause, holds my gaze importantly. "It's not lost. It's found."

I try not to read too much into the *found*.

Truly, I try.

But I fail.

38

FIND ME IN THE RAIN

Harlow

With fresh laundry in a bag, I step off the elevator, head down the hall, then open the door to my apartment on Sunday morning. Even though he's on the couch, I teasingly call out, "Are you decent?" But I don't wait for Bridger to respond. "I know the answer. You're indecent until I give you these back."

As I shut the door, I dangle his pants from my arm like I'm waving a red cloth before a bull.

With a casual grin, he looks my way. He's lounging on the couch, wearing the orange shirt he gave me and his boxer briefs from last night. Those, obviously, weren't soaked from the rain, so they're dry enough, but I tossed his dress pants on an air-dry cycle in the laundry in my building this morning. He's drinking a cup of coffee, steam wafting off the top of the mug. "Yes, Harlow. I'm incredibly indecent."

I shiver. "And I like it."

"I noticed," he says, his grin spreading.

"Trade you? Pants for coffee?" But then I tap my chin, checking out his bare legs, his strong thighs on display. "Except, you are cute pantsless."

He lifts one eyebrow. "Cute? I'm cute?" he echoes, incredulous.

I bob a shoulder as I flop next to him on the couch, cuddling right up against him. "So cute," I say, vamping it up.

"Hmm. For that, you might not get coffee."

"You'd never deprive me of coffee."

"You're right. I'm not that cruel." After he sets down the cup on the coffee table, he tugs me close, presses a kiss to my hair, then inhales me. "Vanilla. You smell like vanilla."

"Does it make you hungry?"

"You make me hungry."

"You have quite an appetite," I say.

"I do," he says, but then he scoots away and heads into the small kitchen, returning a few seconds later with another steaming mug.

He hands it to me, and after I indulge in a life-affirming swallow of the good stuff, he pulls me against him once again. "Thank you for drying my pants," he says like that is the height of generosity.

I smile, feeling at home with him on a lazy Sunday morning. Doesn't matter that this hazy, floaty feeling won't last for long. Doesn't matter that we're living in a bubble inside my apartment. For now, this bubble is the entire world.

I thought I'd lost him yesterday, but he's still here after a night together, after waking up together, after unhurried, sleepy morning sex for the first time ever.

I like this bubble.

But sun streams through the window, casting brighter rays across my home, a reminder that the day is passing by.

I don't want to delay the inevitable. So I gird myself, asking, "Do you have to go? Now that you have clothes again?"

"That's a good question," he says, deep in thought.

Setting my coffee down on the table, I turn to him, curious. "Why is it a good question?"

He runs a hand down my arm, purposefully, but also easily. Like this is just a thing we do. Hang together on my couch, drinking coffee, touching freely as the day unfolds. "Do you have any plans for today?"

"Not really. I'll probably see my friends or go for a bike ride or go to The Frick," I say, automatically before the weight of his question registers on the scale.

Oh.

He's not asking what I'm doing simply to make conversation.

"Do you want to get out of New York with me? For the day?" he asks.

Sounds like a dream. "Yes. I do."

"We can do that, don't you think?"

I understand everything he's asking. "I think so," I say, giddy already from the possibility. "We're still working on that *Afternoon Delight* thing."

There you go. We have our cover story—not that we'll likely need it. Escaping from New York means escaping from the tight quarters of the sardine city, from the probability of bumping into someone we know on the subway, in the park, on the street.

"Let's go to Wistful. It's not far from here. I'll call my car service." He takes another drink of his coffee, checks his watch. "Can you be ready in an hour?"

My heart flies to the moon. "Yes."

* * *

A little later, we step out of the car and onto the quaint, quiet stretch of Main Street in the little Connecticut seaside town, so far away from everything and everyone in New York.

I feel like I've stepped into a story, especially when Bridger sets a hand on my back and keeps it there as we wander down the streets.

Together, for the first time.

We pass a hardware store, a shop peddling vintage signs and garden gnomes, then I stop in front of Various and Sundry when the window display catches my attention.

An umbrella—clear, with a map of the world on it. "You need an umbrella, tiger."

"I thought you liked my emerged-from-the-lake-like-a-Jane-Austen-hero look," he deadpans as I push open the door, the bell tinkling above me.

"That's true. I did. But what if you get stuck in the

rain before an important meeting? Like, with David Fontaine," I suggest as we head toward the umbrellas, blue with polka dots, gray with cartoon dogs, red with music notes.

A woman behind the counter looks up from behind cat-eye glasses. "Let me know if I can help with anything."

"I will," I say, then beeline for the rain gear. "So you'd rather show up to a meeting soaked than carry an umbrella?"

Bridger pretends to consider this, then nods. "I would."

I roll my eyes. "You really don't want to carry an umbrella?"

"I don't. I don't want to lug a bunch of things around. Too much to carry in New York already. You need to be nimble in the city," he says, then he moves deliciously closer, his nose near my neck. "Besides, you don't carry one either."

"Touché," I say, feeling a little fluttery, a little tingly with him next to me.

A little distracted too from my mission.

But I shake off the fizz of desire, spin around, and search through the store till I spot a simple dove-gray notebook. Small, nearly pocket-size. I grab it and a pen, then head for the counter and buy them.

Once we're outside, Bridger gives me a quizzical look, clearly waiting for me to explain the purchase.

I don't indulge him yet.

Spotting a bench along the sidewalk, I head to it, sit

down, and flip open the cover. He sits next to me, curious eyes on me the whole time as I write.

Closing it, I hand him the notebook and the pen. "It's a gift."

My stomach cartwheels. Nerves spin through me. I've never given him a gift before. I hope he likes it. "So you can think of me when you're in the office this week," I add.

"I would anyway," he says, then, with the hint of a smile, he opens the notebook.

Heart beating in my throat, I watch as he reads the words.

Find me in the rain.

When he closes it, his eyes glimmer darkly, deeply. "I will, Harlow. I will."

He moves closer to me, and it's like we're poised, riding the possibility of a public kiss on the streets of a small town.

Far, far away from our New York life.

He stays there.

And it's enough for me.

Later, we stop in a jewelry boutique at the edge of the town square. It reminds me of my cousin's store in San Francisco. As we amble past a display of necklaces, Bridger stops, stares at me, his gaze drifting down to my neck. "I've never asked what this is for?"

He brushes his thumb gently against the *I* on my chain.

"My mother gave it to me once upon a time," I say, memories of her flashing before me. But they don't hurt now. In this moment, I feel like she'd understand me and my choices, every single one of them. I've read her books. I know what her religion was. Romance was her one and only church. "It's *intrépidité*."

He repeats it, not quite getting the pronunciation, but valiantly trying. Then he lets go of it, his fingertips dusting across my chest.

"I've always wondered," he says softly.

That thrills me. "Have you?"

"Maybe not always," he corrects with a slight shrug. "But definitely since that party."

I know exactly which one he means. "Last December? In the brownstone?"

"That one," he confirms.

"When I learned olives were your guilty pleasure?"

"Yes," he says.

"I almost didn't go to that party."

"I'm so glad you did," he says.

"That was one of my brighter decisions," I say, laughing, but then the laughter fades. That night was a turning point. When my future came into focus. All because I said yes. Bridger and I – we are invitations accepted. We are yeses and more yeses with no regrets.

"But I learned other things that night," he says. There's a hint of vulnerability in his tone.

"What did you learn?" I ask, like I'm on the cusp of something big, something meaningful.

His gaze lingers on me for a good long time in the

store. "*You*," he says at last. "I learned you. Like how you knew all the lyrics to *Ask Me Next Year*."

It's as if gravity doesn't have a hold of me.

I'm drifting back in time to that heady moment when he said that was what he wanted in a woman.

When we traded lyrics and looks.

When we started, for all intents and purposes, making a plan for each other.

"And so it began," I murmur.

"And it didn't stop," he adds.

He blinks, like he needs to recenter himself. To shake off the haze of desire curling around us. He turns away from me, heads to the counter, purchases a brushed silver barrette. As we leave, he hands it to me.

"It's for your first day. At your new job."

"I haven't gotten it yet."

"You will, Harlow." He links his fingers with mine. "You will."

He's right. On Tuesday, an offer lands in my e-mail. On Thursday, I begin at Petra Gallery. Before I leave my apartment that morning, I send him a photo of me on my first day at work. I stand in front of the Zara painting. The side of my hair is clipped back with the silver barrette.

Art Harlow is in the house.

A few minutes later, when I'm out on the street, heading to the subway, he responds with a photo.

It's a picture of the notebook I bought him. It's

opened on his desk. On the first page, he's written me a message.

Miss you at work. But I'll see you tonight. Can't wait.

I touch the *I* on my necklace, look at the message from Bridger, then click over to my group text with my friends, who are wishing me well.

Today feels like the start of the rest of my life.

39

WIN SOME, LOSE SOME

Bridger

With his brow knitted, Ian stares over the piles of scripts on his desk, the stacks of dog-eared books, the souvenirs from places he's been.

I'm seated in a chair across from him in his Eleventh Avenue office. Waiting for an answer.

His feet are on the desk too, the scuffed soles of his shoes like a statement. It's certainly his prerogative to put his feet on his own desk. But who wants to look at the bottom of somebody else's shoes?

He steeples his fingers together. Hums. Gazes beyond me here in the chair to the books on his shelves, the complete collection of Felicity's stories.

Ian's quiet, and this is rare for him.

"So, do you want to hear the idea?" I ask again. Maybe he's forgotten why I'm here.

Why do I feel like he's the king and I'm his subject?

Like I've come before him to ask him to please consider my idea for *Afternoon Delight?*

He takes a deep breath, then tears his gaze away from the books. Meets my eyes at last. "So, let me get this straight. You've been working on a concept for the backstory? For the Austin character on *Afternoon Delight?*"

"*Yes*," I say succinctly, trying to strip the frustration out of my tone.

I've told him this. He knows this is why I'm here.

He asked me to work on the story problem. Hell, he asked his own daughter to work on it too.

But I try to wrestle away the word *daughter* from my thoughts. I'm trying so damn hard not to think about her when I interact with him. How I've spent the last few nights with her. The early mornings too.

"With Harlow," I add, hoping it's the last time I need to mention her name with him today.

He hums again. "Right. Right. Got it now. And so?"

Does he truly not remember? I try again. "The concept we came up with was to frame a backstory around—"

He drags his feet off the desk, pops up from his chair. "Let me just cut you off right here. Isla and I took care of it."

I nearly lunge out of the chair to make sure I've heard him right. "You and Isla?" I ask, standing.

He paces around his desk, heads to his bookshelves. "Yes. She'll come to Paris too. When we go there the week after next before shooting begins. It'll be good to have the head writer there."

I grit my teeth. I want to believe that's why he's bringing Isla on a business trip to visit our next big production site. But I don't.

I stay silent as he keeps going, saying, "We've been working on it since I've returned. I suppose I should have told you. But we were actually working on it when I was on the Cape too."

Is he for real? "I thought you and Vivian were busy planning the wedding?"

Ian just chuckles. "Well, there wasn't *that* much planning going on, if you must know."

No. I must not know. How about you don't discuss your sex life, and I won't discuss mine?

I ignore his comment. "So, what's the idea, then?"

He stops in front of his bookshelves, his eyes bright, but just shy of sad. Rapping his knuckles on the wood, he says, "I think backstory is the answer too. Austin lost the great love of his life. That's why nobody else compares," he says, emphatic, certain. "That's his wound."

Wow. Can we hit the nail on the head even more? But he's the creative lead, not me. I was merely pitching in when he needed it. "That's the direction that you want to go with Austin?"

A crisp nod. "That's the direction we *are* going," he says as if issuing a royal decree. "We spent a lot of time reframing some of his scenes. This is what drives him. I have no doubt. He will find someone. Goddammit, he *will* bloody find someone." He stops pacing, huffs. "Finally, once and for all, he will."

My heart lurches in sympathy. I've never heard this

kind of intensity from him, but I've suspected this is his pain. This is *his* wound. This is why he spins like a top from woman to woman to woman.

"I hope he does," I say. I do want my business partner to be happy. To be whole.

And, I suppose, I want the father of the woman I adore to find some stitch of happiness again.

Ian's jaw tics. "He will. He absolutely will."

He takes a long breath. Seems like he's finished, so I close out the conversation with a "Sounds good. It's your department."

He checks his watch then blinks, like he's just realized I said something. "But do keep your idea handy, Bridger. We can use it on the next show we work on. The one we're trying to acquire from David Fontaine, for instance. You're talking to him?" he asks.

Without even saying so, Ian has made one thing crystal clear. He's the creative producer. I'm the business producer. We don't cross those lines.

Perhaps because of that, I don't feel like telling him about David Fontaine yet. Or that I'm still chasing him. That I'm brimming with ideas for the elusive writer.

For the first time in a long time, I don't tell Ian I have a plan. "He's a long shot. I don't think it'll happen," I say, then shrug. "Win some, lose some."

I head to the door. Before I exit though, Ian's eyes light up with a familiar glimmer.

An almost salacious one.

He's turned his gaze past me, and he's looking down the hallway, then he's bent over his phone, muttering, "Good chat, mate."

As I leave, I find Isla walking toward me, a smile on her face, tapping away on her phone.

Are you fucking kidding me? This is dangerous. This is so damn risky. I should know.

I clear my throat. "Good afternoon, Isla," I say, perhaps pointedly.

Startled, she snaps her gaze away from the screen. Wipes that smile right the hell off her face. "Oh, hello Bridger. How are you?"

"I'm great. How are you?"

Her lips twitch in a smile she tries to banish. "Good. Very good."

She keeps going. I slow my pace, backing up against the wall, out of sight of the doorway.

As she nears it, I double back, walking along the wall like a spy. I'm twenty feet away when she heads into his office, closes the door. I lean in just in time to hear the distinctive click of the lock.

Part of me says *I have no room to judge him*. But another part of me—a stronger part of me—says *we are not the same*.

We are not the same. At all.

40

SPECIAL GUEST

Harlow

I could get used to this. I'm curled up with Bridger in his bed, and we're reading.

It's a Sunday night. My first two days at work were incredible. So was this weekend, especially since we slipped away again today, heading to another Connecticut seaside town for the second Sunday in a row. "We're creatures of habit," I'd teased.

"Yes. That's us," he'd said.

Us.

I want to figure out how to be an *us*, but I'm still a little terrified of what that means. So I return to my book.

A chapter later, my phone trills. I glance at it on the nightstand. My Dad's name flashes on the screen.

My chest twinges briefly, a reminder of a week ago

in Bridger's office. But I hit ignore. I won't be summoned this time.

Seconds later, there's a text from him.

I read it. Oh. Wow. "Huh," I say, surprised.

Bridger sets down his book, then his reading glasses too. "What's going on?" he asks curiously.

I read the note out loud.

Poppet, would you like to go to the Annual Critics' Award Gala next month? Vivian and I have a VIP table, of course. We would love to have you as our special guest! First year that you can go!

I set the phone down and look to Bridger. "I wanted to go so badly when I was younger."

He nods in understanding. "Ah. There's a rule that attendees have to be twenty-one and up," he says.

"I remember when I was ten, my mom and dad were going. They were guests of her agency, since *Sweet Nothings* was just a book series then. I begged them to take me." I'm a little embarrassed at my young antics. "I said I'd clean the house for a year if I could go. I'd sweep the floors, clean the toilets, anything." I laugh at the memory. Then turn to Bridger. "I assume you're going."

"I'll be there."

I play with the neck of his T-shirt. "In a tux?"

A cocky grin curves his lips. "Of course."

"Mmm. I guess I'll go then. I've always wanted to see you in a tux," I say.

He reaches for my hand. "And then you'll come over after, and I'll take you while you're still wearing some gorgeous dress."

Pleasure curls through me.

And so does an idea.

"Actually, there's something else I want to do to you when you're wearing a tux," I say, my hand traveling down his chest, covering his abs.

"And what's that?" he asks, his voice going dark, a little dirty.

I sit up, then tug at the hem of his T-shirt. "Take this off."

He sits up and in one swift move, he does that ridiculously sexy thing where he takes off his T-shirt one-handed.

I slide down his body, pulling at his shorts, then his boxer briefs. His cock springs free, already hard. Ready for me.

"I need more practice, Mr. James," I say teasingly, then dust the faintest kiss to the tip.

His hand comes down to my hair, curling lightly through the strands. I swirl my tongue over him as I settle between his spread legs.

He moans, low and restrained.

I've only done this once before to him. The man's so focused on my pleasure. He's such a giver that I hardly have the chance. But I want to experience all the things with him. I am ravenous for intimacy with this man.

So I practice once more, circling a hand around his length, bringing him farther into my mouth.

He's quieter than he is during sex, barely talking.

Just grunting.

Moaning.

Murmuring as I take him deeper.

Even though we've been naked together so many nights already, it's like there's a part of him that's still restrained around me.

The other time I did this, he didn't let me finish. He fucked me instead when he was close.

This time, I'm determined to last. So, I suck deeper, more fervently.

"Fuck, Harlow," he groans.

Instantly, I'm wetter.

Hotter.

I show him with my mouth how much I like turning him on. When he's shaking under me, his hand curls tighter in my hair, and he mutters. "Let me touch you."

I let go, look up. "Please. I want to."

He gazes at me, like this is hard for him, but then he growls, "Then finish me."

I sizzle at the command. Taking him back in my mouth till he's groaning loudly, incoherently, then coming down my throat.

A few seconds later, I move off, settle next to him in the crook of his arm. He seems happy, sated. His woozy look tells me so. But still, I'm concerned. I've got a sinking feeling this is an age thing. "Bridger, do you not want me to do that to you?"

He blinks in surprise. "What?"

I woman up. "Is this because I'm younger? Like, you think you're taking advantage of me if I give you a blow job? If I do something totally centered on you?"

He laughs incredulously. "No, Harlow." Then he hedges. "Fine, maybe at first I felt that way. Before we started spending every night together."

I relax a little bit. But not completely. "And now? Do you still feel that way?"

He smiles devilishly as he grazes a hand down my arm. "That's not the reason."

"Then what's the reason?"

"I'm obsessed with your pleasure. So why don't we stop talking and you can sit on my face?"

With a shiver, I obey.

* * *

Later, before I turn off the light, I RSVP to the gala. I'll see Bridger in a tux that night in a few weeks. I'll go home with him after. Like we will too when we go to *The Un-Gentleman* next weekend.

That's more than I ever imagined I'd have.

Only, I can't help but want the before too.

And the during.

It takes me a long time to fall asleep as I lie there thinking of the consequences of my choices.

41

HOW TO ROB THE BANK

Bridger

As Harlow places the leftovers in her fridge, she's still beaming. Glowing, even, from talking about the new installation at Petra that she's working on. It's a Friday night in June, and we celebrated her first full week on the job with a special dinner ordered in. There's a slice of her favorite cake on the counter for later.

"All week long, I felt like I was using my brain and my heart at the same time," she says.

It's an absolute thrill to hear the genuine joy in her voice, to see her experience the pleasure of a job well done. "You're where you belong," I say, proud of her as I set the plates in the sink. It's our routine from spending the last few weeks together too—nearly every night.

"After all that, who knew that I would wind up working in art?" she says, amused with her own career path as she arranges cartons on the top shelf in a tiny New York fridge.

"I guess I was wrong with my predictions back at MoMA," I tease.

"I don't think you were wrong," she says, closing the fridge door, then leaning against it. I'm standing opposite her in the galley kitchen. "But hearing you say *how* you used your degree and how you *didn't* use it actually freed me. It made me see—eventually—that I could work in the art world. Just differently than I'd imagined."

"It's your passion. Art is your passion. And sometimes it can be your profession too."

"So I'm having my cake and eating it too," she says, her eyes drifting to the slice of decadent chocolate cake, but a crease forms in her brow. "Then again, it's just the first week. First weeks are supposed to feel good, right? Like first kisses?"

I can't resist proving her wrong. I lean in, press a lingering, tease of a kiss to her lips. A faint sigh greets my ears. Her fingers curl around my waist.

With her melting into me, I break the kiss, tilt my head. "What were you saying about first kisses being better than tenth or one hundredth kisses?"

"I was saying research. I need more research," she says in a breathy voice.

We conduct kissing research for another minute or two, and when we stop at last, she nods to the stack of plates in the sink. "Dishes or sex? I know you hate messes."

"That's a trick question."

"So, sex then. Got it."

I shake my head, tsking her under my breath. "Harlow, with you and me, dishes are foreplay."

She smiles mischievously. "Is that so?"

Feeling a little cocky, a lot confident, I say, "I'll have to roll up my sleeves to do dishes."

I start to unbutton the cuffs of my shirt.

Her jaw drops. "Now you're playing dirty."

"Like, I said...*foreplay*," I say as I flick open another button. She draws a feathery breath.

"Let me do it," she says, then turns down the lights in the kitchen. Her home is doing its own impression of dusky twilight, setting the mood.

I hold out my wrists. She unbuttons the right cuff the rest of the way, folding it up once, then another time. She moves to the left cuff, slowly freeing the metal button from its holder, then she grazes her fingers along my arm, over the ink curling around the books.

"You wore a sapphire-blue shirt the day my crush began," she says, like she's narrating the story of how we began.

"Yeah?" I ask, hungry for more of her tale.

"And then there was a ruby-red shirt. An emerald one. I noticed them all. I used to think about what shirt you might be wearing if I ran into you. If you came over. If there was a party."

I'm about to say *the clothes do make the man*, but that's a throwaway comment, and this is not a light moment. Instead, I say nothing. I just listen since she's telling a story. "I noticed all these things about you last summer, Bridger. And then the day I broke my ankle," she says, looking up at me, with so much tenderness my heart can barely handle it. "You wore purple and you carried me."

"You were hurt. I wanted to help," I say, truthfully. That's all I'd thought then.

She runs her hands up my chest, eager fingers fiddling with the top button. "I thought about you that summer. I pictured you when I was in Paris. I RSVP'd to that *Sweet Nothings* party to see you," she says, a hitch in her voice as emotions seem to rise up in her.

As she takes a beat, I add my own layer. "And then I looked for you on the running path. My favorite days were the ones when I saw you."

Her eyes glint, the gears turning in her mind. "And then I asked for the internship for you," she says.

An image of her blowing out the candle in my office, meeting my eyes, holding my gaze, taunts me. Tantalizes me.

Just knowing what she wanted is such a wicked thrill.

"I don't think I figured that out at the time. But just the other week, it hit me that you had," I tell her, my hands curling tighter around her, desire ratcheting up in me.

"And what did you think?" she asks, guileless, pure innocence as she revisits the story of how we came together.

"I think I was your birthday wish," I say, rolling the dice.

She lifts her chin, shooting me the sexiest smile. "You're some birthday gift." She leans into my neck, dusting her lips against my throat, kissing her way up to my jaw.

I sigh greedily, craving more of her. "You wanted to seduce me," I murmur.

She nods against me. "Did it work?"

She damn well knows the answer. But a little show and tell never hurt.

I grab her hands, take them off my chest, then back her up and prop her on the counter. My fingers find their way into her hair as I kiss her neck, leaving a trail of hot, needy kisses along her throat.

"Mr. James," she murmurs, and the seductive tone sends lust curling down my back.

My sexy, sweet vixen. "Say it again," I command.

It's risqué like this as we lean into the ten years between us. She likes those years, I've learned.

"Take me, Mr. James," she says, turning me on impossibly more. "Fuck me into the mattress, Mr. James."

Need her now. Right now.

"The bedroom is too fucking far away."

* * *

Gripping her ass, I jerk her harder onto my cock. She digs her nails into my biceps, holding on tight as I fuck her on the kitchen counter, her skirt hiked up, her blouse undone, her tits bouncing free.

Savoring the tight heat of her body, I swivel my hips, stroke into her. "You love it like this. When I fuck you deep. Don't you, honey?"

Frantically, she answers, urging me on with, "Harder. Deeper."

I give her everything she wants.

Soon, my sweet, sexy girl is losing her mind. She's grabbing the back of my neck, scratching my shoulders.

Lust barrels down my spine. But I stave off my own release. I crave hers. Her noises, her sounds, her pleasure.

Most of all, I crave her sweet, reckless, abandon. She is fearless in bed. She's a woman who chases desire shamelessly, and who deserves it completely. And I'm the lucky man who gets to give it to her.

She's close, so close and still, she pants out, "Please, please, please, Mr. James."

"You're so fucking good at begging for it," I praise.

She shudders everywhere. "I'm begging you. Make me come."

My circuits overheat. They sizzle. "Always. Every fucking time," I say as I maneuver a hand between her legs, circling her clit with my thumb. She's shaking and shuddering, then falling apart, breaking so beautifully into bliss.

My thighs shake. My cock throbs. And I'm right there with her, filling her with a soul-deep orgasm that blots away the city, the night, the time.

There's nothing else but this ecstasy. And *us*.

* * *

A little later, I'm lying next to her in bed, still feeling the effects of the orgasm drug.

The side effects of *her*.

Absently, I run my fingers through her hair. "Where do you want to go on Sunday? Maybe we could try Brooklyn again," I suggest, picturing the last time we were there at the gardens.

"Brooklyn," she says, like she's trying out the word. "That's getting closer, isn't it?"

She means closer to the city of course.

I kiss her bare shoulder. "Manhattan soon," I say, hopeful, making a promise I don't entirely know how to keep. But I want to.

"Soon," she says, then takes a beat. "There's so much to see in this city. Always something to discover and to uncover. I've never lived anyplace else, and I'm not sure I want to."

I clear my throat. "Ahem. Are you forgetting Paris?"

She gasps in faux shock. "You're right. How could I forget Paris? I do love it there."

"I'll take pictures for you when I'm there this week to remind you. I can picture you in the city of light perfectly. Wandering down some passage, ducking into a boulangerie, finding a hidden garden where there's an art gallery."

She hums happily, and I wonder if she's imagining

the same thing—doing that together someday. "I'm a city girl at heart," she says, shifting to her side, propping her head in her hand. "My mom said that about me."

I scoot up in the bed. She doesn't talk about her mother much. When she does, I want to listen. Intently. "When did she say that?"

Harlow takes a moment to answer, like she's weighing what to say. Then she moves away, leans toward her nightstand, and grabs something from the lower shelf. A wooden box with an unlocked latch. She flips open the top. A stack of small envelopes sits inside. "She wrote me letters when I was a kid."

"Did she send them to you?"

She shakes her head. "No. She'd leave them on my pillow actually. They were just little observations. Not even lessons. But thoughts about our day," she says, running her fingers along the stack, curling at the corners from age. "Want to hear some?"

"I'd love to."

She takes out a handful, flips through them carefully, then reads one about oranges, another about being a city girl, and one more about a day they spent at the library. My heart glows a little hearing these bits of unexpected advice, observations, or anecdotes.

Then, she puts the stack neatly in place, closes the box, and returns it to the nightstand. When she lies back down, there's a contented look on her face.

"They make you feel connected to her," I say.

"They do."

"Thanks for sharing. I'm glad you have those," I say.

"Me too," she says, then she traces the artwork on my arm. "When did you have this done?"

I glance down at the vines that curl around a small stack of books. "After college. When I figured out what I wanted to do for a living."

Her fingers journey down the curves of a black vine, then along the cover of one of the drawn books. "Because you love books?"

Makes sense why she'd assume that. I let others assume that. The full answer isn't one I've ever given. It's too revealing. "I've never told anyone before."

She edges back a bit, like she's giving me space to say something hard. Saying this is only hard because it makes me feel vulnerable, and I don't like to feel that way. Vulnerability makes it hard to do my job.

"When I was younger, I played sports, as you know. But they didn't quite do the trick in turning off all these thoughts I kept having. Worries, you know?"

"About your mom?" she asks gently.

"Yes," I say, and I'm this close to saying *I don't have the fond memories that you do*. But all she has are memories. So I don't need to make a comparison. "I never knew if she'd show up at a game. If she'd come home drunk. If she'd stay out later than she'd promised. Sometimes, if she came home drunk, she'd ground me for no reason. Then, the next day she'd say she was sorry and didn't mean it. She'd *unground* me."

Harlow winces in sympathy. "That must have felt like being on a ship out in a storm."

"Exactly. I didn't realize it at the time, but I kept looking for something to...*hold onto*. Something that felt reliable," I say, then drag a hand across the back of my neck. God, I hope she doesn't think this is ridiculous. But fuck it. I push past the nerves. "I found it at the library. I found it in books. And I started spending my time there instead."

Something dawns for her. She tilts her head, staring at me anew. "You said the day I broke my ankle that you'd stopped playing sports. Was that why?"

"I think I was always trying to escape," I say, admitting something out loud for the first time. "First on the field. Then in stories."

"You really love what you do," she says, a little sad perhaps as she states the obvious. But sometimes the obvious needs to be said.

"I do," I say, and I'm pretty sure we both know the subtext of her observation. We both know too that soon we'll probably need to talk about what's next for us. How long we can keep seeing each other after dark. It's been a wonderful two weeks, but is it sustainable? Soon, we'll need to discuss the things we weren't ready to talk about the night I found her in the rain. Maybe this is the start of that conversation.

"I don't want you to give it up," she says earnestly but with a hint of a frown. She presses a kiss to one of the vines on my arm.

When she lifts her face, I run my thumb over the corner of her mouth. "I know you don't want me to lose anything," I say, and even though the *what's next* is borderline terrifying, even though the plans I probably need to make will require a new kind of armor, I still feel a sense of calm when I'm with her.

This is what I've wanted my whole life. Passion and peace. But I didn't know that until I came to know her. Can I really have it in one person? It's wild to think that, but it feels possible with Harlow.

"Maybe there's a way," she adds, her tone bright.

That's a relief to hear her say. I've held back from broaching the topic since the first time we did that night two weeks ago. She wasn't ready then. Perhaps she is now. "Maybe there is," I say.

She pulls back, studies my face. "Do you think we'll find it?"

My heart thumps louder. Can she hear it? She has to. "I want to," I say, laying my wishes on the line. "Do you?"

She gives me a soft nod as she returns to tracing the lines of the books. "I do. Especially because you have an art soul too."

"Just like you."

"Maybe that's why we're good together," she says with hope in her eyes—the same hope I feel when I'm with her.

"There are a million little reasons we're good together. You worship coffee, you like my shirts, you love the gifts I give you..."

"You send me photos of your day. You have great taste in music. You forgot to do the dishes when I distracted you with sex."

I laugh as she busts me. "You did distract me." Then I turn more serious, brushing some strands of hair from her face. "There are a few big reasons too," I say, cracking open the conversation. I don't want to hold back any longer with her. I want to find a way. I want her to know how I feel.

"What are the big ones?"

Now that we're here though, I don't entirely know how to say *you fill the empty spaces inside me* without also saying *when the hell do you want me to tell your father*? I don't want to push her without a plan, but I'll make one if she's ready. I press a kiss to her shoulder. "You make me stronger. You make me better. And you make me happy," I say, starting that way, laying out the stakes.

She wraps her leg around mine, our calves curling together as she whispers, "And you see me for who I am."

I run my thumb along her chin. "I want to keep seeing you...for who you are," I say, with all its implications.

Then, screw *implications*.

There are metaphors and there are words. Clear, direct, meaningful. We both know what's happening. We're both adults.

I brush a kiss to her lips then pull back, feeling bold and ridiculously happy even before I say, "I'm in love with you."

Then I'm happier to have said it.

Her breath catches. The look in her eyes is incandescent. They shine with tears, but really, emotion. "I'm so in love with you."

I feel free. I feel *unwound*. I feel like I'm exactly where I should be, no matter how risky our choices are.

I only feel rightness. Truth. Possibility.

And a new kind of joy. I know we'll find a way.

I gaze down at her ankle, staring a little longer than usual at her scar, remembering the day she had me sign her pink cast. "I have another reason we're good together."

"Tell me," she says eagerly.

"How about I show you?"

* * *

She's lounging on her couch in a tank top and panties, the chocolate cake on a plate in her lap, her feet across my thighs. As she takes a bite, I dip the brush into a bottle of mint green nail polish and spread it across her big toe, then her middle toe, then her little toe.

She offers me a bite from her fork, and I take it.

Then I switch to lavender nail polish, painting the other nails in alternating colors just like they were painted on the day after her bike accident.

When I'm done, I blow on the polish. "Skittles toes."

Harlow sets down the unfinished slice of cake on the table, then looks at her toes, then me. "I love my Skittles toes," she says, a touch breathless.

She's not talking about the pedicure. "I love spending nights with you, Harlow," I tell her, returning to the topic.

Her eyes lock with mine. "It's my favorite part of the day too," she says.

The nights are wonderful, but I'm hungry for days too. "I want them both," I say.

"Me too," she says with emotion in her eyes.

I need to make a plan. Stat.

The tickets for the *Un-Gentleman* are for tomorrow. I take a deep, fortifying breath. "Maybe tomorrow night will give us an idea of how hard it'll be," I suggest, carefully, ever so carefully, opening the topic.

"When we go to the theater with them?" she asks. "What do you mean?"

I'm still working through the details. "Maybe we can just see how he is with us."

"With us together?" she squeaks.

"Not like this," I say, shaking my head as I gesture to us on the couch. "More like...we can feel him out. Try to get a sense of how he reacts to the two of us. Next to each other. Walking down the aisle to the seats together." Then, an idea flashes, fully formed. I'm a genius. "We could even arrive together."

"Oh! Like we shared a car?" she asks, enthused.

"Exactly. We both live on the east side of the city. It makes sense."

"So we went together to the show," she adds. "This is like subliminal messaging."

"Exactly. We can test the waters that way," I say, and this feels smart.

Strategic.

Her clever grin widens. "We could even ask Vivian to take a picture of us," she suggests, getting in on the planning too. That's my brilliant woman.

"Yes. We'll get some data."

"Do some research."

"And we'll get a better sense of how he'll handle...*things*."

"And then, for how to do it eventually," she adds, and I can hear the excitement in her voice.

The eagerness.

The determination.

We're a team, we're in love, and we're planning perfectly for how we're going to pull off this great heist.

42

THE BEST-LAID PLANS

Harlow

The next night when we reach the theater, we step out of the car and onto the sidewalk.

I'm wearing a little black dress. Bridger's wearing black slacks.

His shirt is wine red. So are my shoes. We look like we belong together.

This is our subliminal messaging.

It's like we're casing the joint, studying all the potential points of failure in our plan to steal our happy ending.

We walk through the glittery crowds toward the St. James Theatre, the marquee lit up brilliantly against the New York summer night, inviting us to take a step into our future as a couple.

"I feel good about this," I say. Then I grab his wrist and squeeze it.

He takes mine and squeezes back and then we let go. "We've got this," he says, confident, assured.

Like two badass and brilliant thieves, we stride past the brass doors, showing our tickets on my phone to the ushers, searching for my father and Vivian inside the busy lobby.

I scan through the opening-night crowds of theater-goers dressed to the nines. At the edge of the bar, I spot my father with his slicked-back hair, his Gatsby grin, and his new wife.

Except.

Wait.

Who's that with them? There's a guy with brown hair and a nice smile. Maybe a few years older than I am.

I steal a glance at Bridger and even though it's crowded, and even though they can't hear me, I still whisper as we go, "Who's that? Did my dad say anything about bringing someone?"

Bridger's brow knits. "No idea. Probably just someone he ran into."

But Vivian's chatting animatedly with a pretty blonde woman by her side. And my gut says no, they didn't just run into these two.

When we reach them, my father doesn't seem to notice that we came together.

"Harlow," he says, upbeat, and that's another sign something's amiss. He normally calls me poppet.

But he's calling me by my name instead. Treating me like a woman, rather than like his kid.

"We wanted you to meet Vivian's brother," he says,

then he introduces me to the guy with the nice smile. "This is Jack Waters. He works in the music business."

"At a record company," Vivian adds. "So he's in the art world too."

"Nice to meet you." Jack extends a hand.

I freeze, momentarily forgetting how to interact with people as our plan crumples spectacularly.

This is not a recon opportunity. This is a triple date.

I take Jack's hand, recovering my manners. "You too."

Seconds later, Vivian introduces the blonde to Bridger.

"And this is my best friend, Francesca. She works as an agent too."

"Nice to meet you," Bridger says, like a perfect gentleman.

A few minutes later, my father and Vivian, holders of the tickets, guide us to the seats.

Bridger's at one end of the six of us, sitting next to Vivian's best friend. My father and Vivian claim the middle seats. And I'm sitting next to some guy named Jack who's probably very nice. Who's possibly a lovely man. But he's not the man I'm in love with.

We make meaningless small talk for a few minutes. When the overture begins, I feel like a complete and absolute idiot for thinking any of this would be easy.

43

SOMEONE

Harlow

There is no Sunday getaway after all.

Bridger's colleague Mia is in town. She flew in from LA already and she wants to have a working breakfast meeting before they travel to Paris to deal with *Afternoon Delight*. Their flight is this afternoon. My father and Isla are taking the same one. I don't even want to think about what the sleeping arrangements will be like in the city of light.

In the early morning in Bridger's apartment in Gramercy Park—my boyfriend's apartment?—I get dressed as sun streams through his bedroom windows. The sun feels like a lie though. We can't go out in it, not really, not fully.

I keep a change of clothes here but as I pull on a summer dress and then loop my hair into a messy bun, I feel seedy. Like I'm preparing to escape before the city stretches its arms and wakes up. Is this what my father's lovers felt like all those times they left early in the morning?

Like a secret?

But of course it's not the leaving early that's the problem—Bridger has a breakfast meeting. I do understand that.

It's that we only exist behind closed doors.

With my phone and lip gloss in hand, I go to leave. Bridger's right behind me, walking me to the door where his carry-on waits, packed and ready.

Perhaps sensing my mood, he reaches for my hand. "I'm really sorry about last night," he says.

That nearly knocks me from my funk. With that gesture, my heart turns a little squishy. We did try last night. Sure, we failed, but at least we tried.

We haven't talked much about what happened at the theater. Or about how to regroup. I think we both feel foolish for thinking we could subtly *market* our romance to my dad.

"It's not your fault," I say gently. I don't want him to worry about me or us when he's in Paris. "Don't think twice about it."

"We'll figure it out, Harlow," he says, a touch of desperation in his voice. "I promise. We'll come up with a real plan. I land..." He stops to do the time-zone math, "...late tonight our time, but tomorrow morning Paris time. And we can—"

I shut him up with a quick kiss. "Bridger, you have a show to deal with. The time zones and work and everything will be hard." I thread my fingers through his.

"We'll deal with it when you return. You don't need to worry about this or me."

Narrowing his eyes, he growls at me, clearly disliking my assessment, but perhaps knowing I'm right. He holds my face. "I like worrying about you, Harlow. You're worth worrying about."

I smile faintly. "Worry about work. We won't figure this out in Paris anyway. It's going to be hard," I add heavily. Then I admit the truth of last night. "It was silly to think it would be easy."

His expression turns serious. "I know. As soon as I return, we'll figure out how to tell him. No testing the waters. No subliminal messaging. Just the truth. No matter how hard it is," he says, strong and certain, but underneath his tough exterior, his no-nonsense tone, I hear fear and uncertainty.

Understandable.

"Of course."

He gives me a quick kiss, like he's stealing it. Like we're not going to see each other again. "When I get back, then? Maybe even before the gala. That day?"

"Sure," I say, wanting to speed up time to Friday. Till we can roll up our sleeves and figure this out.

"I've been thinking too about what's next—"

He's interrupted by his phone barking. After he grabs it from his pocket, his blue eyes light up. Like the caller is a Christmas gift. I glance down at the screen. David Fontaine flashes across it. It might as well be a billboard.

"Take it, take it!" I urge, excited for him.

Immediately, he answers. "Hey there, David. Can

you hold on just one second? I have to say goodbye to someone."

I wince inside. I'm only *someone*. I get this. I know why. But I want to be Harlow. I want to be his girlfriend. I want to be the one he declares in public.

Be patient. This was never supposed to be easy.

After he mutes the phone, he leans in, kisses my cheek. "I love you," he tells me, and love whooshes down my body all the way to my toes.

Why then do I feel so unsteady? Just because I want this kiss on the street? At a restaurant? In the park? In a museum? Outside? Here, there, everywhere?

Settle down. Settle all the way down.

"I love you," I say. "I'll see you Friday at the gala."

"I can't wait."

But we have to.

Now isn't the time to make a blueprint for telling my dad we're together. For what we'll say. How we will say it. Besides, I finally realize that Bridger always faced the bigger obstacle.

I'd thought I did. For the longest time, I'd thought my obstacle was huge. *Bridger* was my obstacle.

Now I'm here with him, and he was worth the chase. This love was worth the pursuit.

I still don't have any idea how my father will handle the news that I'm in love with him. But if I could withstand losing my mother, I could handle losing him.

Though I think, in my heart, I know my father won't disown me.

It's not in his nature.

My heart aches for the man I'm in love with. There's no way he can escape without major collateral damage.

But now's not the time to warn him. I wave goodbye since he needs to focus on his phone call.

* * *

Later, he texts me that he's at the airport, the call was promising, and that he'll miss me. But it feels strange writing back knowing that he's with my dad, Isla, and Mia, boarding a flight, so I send a quick **Miss you too,** and leave it at that.

Everything feels weird and uncomfortable as I straighten up my apartment. Like there's a cut in my mouth and my tongue keeps working away at it.

That feeling chases me all day—when I ride my bike along the path, soaking up the summer rays, when I go to The Frick alone later that afternoon, trying to get lost in the art, but failing. My mind is getting lost, instead, in the details of Friday, the gala, the *what's next* and all *the what-ifs* and *how-tos.*

I try to shuck off this funk, but the weirdness dogs me when I head to meet Layla and Ethan for dinner in the West Village.

I do my damnedest to ignore the feeling, peppering Ethan with questions about his bandmates—including the new drummer who, in Ethan's words, has *serious rhythm.* Then, I zoom in on Layla, catching up on her job and listening as she talks about office politics and the woefully out-of-touch dudes in the skyscraper where she works. Then she casually drops a mention of her sexy new silver-fox boss. "I just want to run my hands through his hair. And I might have to blackball my libido from going to the office with me."

"Silver foxes have always been your downfall," Ethan says.

"I'm getting that as a tattoo," she replies.

Somewhere between the kale salad they teased me for ordering and the polenta that's coming next, Layla clears her throat dramatically. Stares at me importantly. "Did you think we wouldn't notice?"

I arch a brow curiously. "Notice what?"

Ethan sniffs, lifting his nose in the air. "The smell of sadness. It's wafting off you." He waggles his hands near me, like he's inhaling the scent.

Dammit. I wanted to focus on them tonight, but I guess I've done a terrible job.

"'Fess up," Layla says, wriggling her fingers like she's telling me to serve it up.

I draw a fortifying breath, then tell them everything. Last night at the theater, the night before, the words we've said to each other.

They know we've been seeing each other. But now they know we've said the L-word

And the P-word, too, for *let's make plans*.

They both ooh and ahh.

"And now we need to tell my dad," I say, the weight of that sinking into me.

Layla's smile disappears. Ethan sighs heavily.

"You're really in love," Layla says, kind of amazed.

"I seriously can't believe you went from seducing him to falling in love with him," Ethan adds.

I drop my head in my hand and groan, like that'll help me find the answer to how to have it all. But I'm laughing too. "I kind of can't either," I admit softly.

Early on, I was driven by attraction, ambition, and conquest. Then, over time, those crumbled away, replaced by something deeper—this great love.

I lift my face, shrugging helplessly. "I don't know what happens next. I don't know what I'm supposed to do."

Layla inhales deeply. Lifts her glass of water and takes a drink. When she sets it down, she says, "There's no magic bullet. Sometimes we just have to get through the hard things. We can't game them. We can't even always plan for them. You just have to march into it and say the hard thing."

She knows these difficult truths as well as anyone.

I suppose in some ways I do too.

Maybe I've been preparing for them for the last several years.

My stomach dips, but I try to ignore the fear. Anything worth having is worth fighting for.

I'm pretty sure I'm going to have to fight for my happy ending.

44

LOVELY LITTLE LIE

Bridger

I scan the lobby one more time, tugging on the cuffs of my shirt, peering at the elevator.

I'm still hunting for my business partner as the clock ticks well past ten. Ian, Mia, and I are showing brand partners around the *Afternoon Delight* locations today in Paris. Easily a half dozen Parisian ad execs cluster around us in the lobby.

But only one of the two Lucky 21 owners are present.

Tension climbs up my spine. But I do my best not to show it as I say to the VIPs, "Ian should be here any minute."

I try to inject lightness into my tone I don't feel.

Where the hell is Ian?

"It's not a problem," Philippe says. He's with the

perfume maker, and I appreciate his effort to smooth over the annoyance of waiting.

But Ian's absence *is* a problem. I fiddle with the collar of my shirt, then glance at my watch. He's fourteen minutes late.

I swallow down my annoyance and paste on a smile. "It's probably just the time change. I'll just go round him up," I say, since they don't need to wait any longer.

Mia pulls me aside and sidebars, "I'll keep them busy."

"Thank you," I tell her, then I cut across the lobby, turn down the hallway, and push open the door for the stairs. I take the steps two by two up to the third floor, speed down the hall. Then I rap on his door.

If a rap could be angry, mine is livid.

"Come on," I mutter under my breath. Not quickly, not quickly at all, I hear the click of the door unlocking, then opening. Ian smiles, wide-eyed. He's wearing jeans and a white button-down that he's currently buttoning up.

Thank god he's ready.

Except...

He doesn't usually wear jeans and casual button-downs for work meetings.

"We have a meeting right now. With our partners. We're taking them around the city," I remind him.

He tosses his head back, laughing. "Right, right," he says, all chipper. "We do."

With a sly shrug, he gives that look that people flash when they don't give a shit. "But I'm going to nip off. I think I'll head to Giverny for the day."

My jaw hangs open. Did he just say that? "What are you going to do?" I ask, because he needs to repeat that for me to believe it.

"Giverny. It's fantastic this time of year. Just tell them I had..." He waves a hand as if he's hunting for a reason, then snaps his fingers. "Food poisoning," he says, clutching his stomach as if that will help sell the lie. "Will you, mate?"

I don't try to hide my irritation as I drag a hand through my hair, peering briefly into his room.

I catch a glimpse of a pair of black flats on the floor. Like the ones Isla wore to dinner last night.

A ball of rage lights on fire in my gut. Are you fucking kidding me? He's asking me to cover for him? In all the years we've worked together, he's occasionally used me as an excuse, he's claimed he's had meetings with me, and I've shrugged it off since he's never asked me to lie.

I've simply been his alibi.

Now he wants me to be his enabler.

I grit my teeth. I grind them. But now is not the time to argue. "Fine," I bite out. "But I'm not doing it again."

He rolls his eyes. "Young people. I swear. So right-eous. It's just a lovely little lie. Surely, you've told them," he says off-hand. There's no dig. There's no sucker punch to it. It's not as if he knows I'm involved with his daughter.

And yet I feel a thousand razor cuts slicing me up.

I can't do this any longer. I can't lie by omission. I can barely hold back any longer. The truth wells up inside me—*I'm in love with your daughter.* It threatens to spill out right now on the floor of his suite, with all its consequences. Namely, the end of all trust—the trust we've had as business partners.

But with our brand marketers waiting downstairs, I swallow the truth, instead saying, "We need to talk when we're back in New York."

"Of course. My door is always open for you."

Then he turns around to join his lady, and I go downstairs and cover for him while he spends the day with his newest affair.

That evening I walk along the Seine, heading to meet the Paris production team for dinner at a brasserie by Notre-Dame. As I walk along the water, passing bouquinistes peddling old and new books, I catch up with Jules in New York on the phone.

"And I sent you coverage of Isla Moretti's script," she says, as businesslike as she's always been.

I'm caught off-guard though. "Isla, as in our writer Isla?"

"Yes. She wrote her own show. It's called...*Happy-ish*."

"Good title," I say begrudgingly.

"Bad story," she says.

"Yeah?" This delights me. This should not delight me. "What's the storyline?" I ask, getting down to business.

"A woman in New York goes on dating quests," Jules says crisply.

That nags on my brain. It sounds a hell of a lot like a show that's already on Webflix. "Like Ellie Snow's *The Dating Games*?"

That show launched to fantastic reviews and ratings. It's already been renewed for another season.

"As a matter of fact, it's exactly like *The Dating Games*. It's completely derivative. Also, the lead is unlikeable. Ian sent it to me. I think he didn't want to turn her down himself."

I seethe as I cross the bridge nearest to the famous cathedral.

He wanted the rejection to come from me. I'm not going to play his game. I'm going to knock on his suite tonight and tell him to do it himself.

Except...no.

My game needs to be truth. My game needs to be honesty. My game needs to be standing up for who I believe in. For myself, for the woman I love, and for the people I work with.

Like Jules. My badass, no-nonsense junior producer. I trust her judgment. If she thinks the script is derivative, then I will stand by that, and my office will do its job—saying yes or saying no.

That's what I do—I make those decisions.

"You can go ahead and pass on it," I say. "Make sure it's clear the decision is coming from *our* office. We work as a team."

There's an audible gasp. A rare display of emotion from my stoic former admin. "Great," she says, and I can still hear the thrill in her voice before she tamps it down, sliding into full professional mode again. "I'll take care of it tomorrow afternoon when I send out all the replies to agents. And don't forget, your tickets to the gala tomorrow night will be waiting at reception outside the ballroom at the Luxe Hotel."

"Thank you," I say. Then I hang up, go to dinner, and turn my focus completely on my production team here in Paris. They're working hard on this show. We've turned it around. I want nothing more than a terrific launch for *Afternoon Delight*.

If it goes well, it'll pay a lot of people's bills for a long time. That's what I need it to do.

* * *

When dinner's done and I've said goodnight to everybody, Mia tells me she's going to catch up with friends in the city. "They convinced me to grab a glass of wine in Le Marais."

"Gee, so sorry to hear. That sounds terrible."

"The worst," she says. "See you in Los Angeles next time you're there. By the way, the marketing for this show is *magnifique*."

"My marketing VP is brilliant."

She waves goodbye, then heads on her way.

I'm alone again. Walking through a city. Just like I do in New York when I need to reset. To think.

And, also, to clear my anxiety. To erase the tension that's chased me my whole life, since I was younger and felt the uncomfortable press of too loud, too boisterous, too intoxicated crowds.

I've shucked that tightness off through sports, through exercise, through control, through stories.

But especially through work. My relentless quest for excellence is a pursuit that's defined my days and my dreams. Lucky 21 has woken me up in the morning and put me to bed in the evening.

It was all I ever needed in my twenties.

Until Harlow stormed into my heart.

Until she peered over my walls fearlessly, then knocked them down brick by brick, moment by moment, insisting that she noticed things. That she noticed *me*.

Then, insisting I notice her.

Day by day, I did.

Now, she's all I need.

And more so, she's what I want. Even if wanting her changes everything else in my life, like the relationships I have from nine to five. Because it does. There is no easy solution to being with her. Only hard ones. But she's worth it.

That same sense of calm I felt with her the other night tiptoes alongside me as I walk by the river, the moonlight reflecting off the water.

I pass a magazine stand. Then another one peddling postcards of Paris. I take a moment to assess what I'm feeling now that I've made my decision, waiting for the familiar knot of tension to tighten.

I don't feel it at all.

I know what I want.

I know what I'll give up.

I'm ready.

I take a picture of the last bouquiniste, framed by the faint glow of a nearby streetlamp. Then I send it to Harlow with the caption: *Want to go here with me? How about for Christmas?*

Her reply lands quickly. *Don't tease me. You know I want to.*

I write back. *You know I want to take you. Come with me.*

My phone pings once more. *Oui.*

When I'm back in my hotel room, the clock ticking close to midnight, I text again to see if she's free. She tells me she just left work.

As I toe off my shoes, I call her, and I waste no time. "We need to come clean as soon as possible. Let's set a time to tell him," I say, then I lay out the whole plan. The one I've been working on this week in the city of light. "What do you think? I return tomorrow just before the gala. I think we should do it on Saturday morning. Together. I want to look him in the eyes and tell the truth."

I can hear the gulp in her voice, but I can also hear her strength as she says, "And he needs to hear it from me too. Should we take him out to breakfast or lunch?"

"Breakfast. Wait. No," I say, running through scenarios as I pace around the suite. "He might make a big scene in public. We don't want that."

"Good call. I'll invite him over for lunch at my place. And then you'll be here too."

Finally. "Yes."

She shudders out a breath though, full of nerves.

"Are you sure you're ready for this, honey? We can wait. I'll wait for you," I say.

"No, we're not waiting. We're doing this," she says, emphatic.

Good. I need her *intrépidité*. Telling Ian will be the biggest thing I'll have done in my whole life.

"This is huge," I say, struck by the magnitude of what's happening in my life, in my heart. I sink down in a chair by the window, Paris stars winking in the sky.

"Are *you* sure, Bridger?"

It takes nothing for me to say, "Completely. In every way." I glance at the time. I have a plane to catch in the morning. "I'll see you tomorrow, honey."

"And on Saturday, after we talk to him, we're going out. We're going to hit the town, and I'm going to kiss you on the street like you're a sailor returning home."

I'm RSVPing for that kiss right now. "Anything for you."

45

RIDE OR DIE

Harlow

I'm counting down.

All day at work, I tick off the hours in my head. Then, I do it as I head home in the evening to get ready. As I finish my makeup, Layla comes by, banging on the door, declaring she's here to help.

"What else are friends for but to help get you ready for a gala?" she asks as I swing open the door.

"You're right," I say.

She sweeps into my apartment and closes the door behind her.

I'm already in my red dress. I gesture to the back of it. "I can't zip this up without you."

She smiles slyly. "I knew you'd need me." Layla spins me around and zips up the sheath dress.

I turn back to her. "How do I look?"

She eyes me up and down, assessing. "You look twenty-one and sexy."

I laugh, like I'm dismissing the compliment. But that's a damn good way to look when I see Bridger again.

I can't wait. It's been too long.

Layla dangles a pair of chandelier earrings from her fingers and holds out a tiny purse. "Wear these earrings tonight. I wore them when I landed my job. They'll give you good vibes."

I snatch them and the purse. "I need *all* the good vibes."

"So is everything all set for tomorrow?"

I nod, nerves rushing through me as I put on the earrings. But even though I'm nervous, I'm also resolute. "I texted my dad. He's coming over at noon."

She gives me a *you've got this* look. "It's all going to work out in the end."

I swallow past a lump in my throat. "I hope so."

One more night to get through. One more night, and then we'll be free to be together.

Layla walks out with me, crossing through the lobby and to the street. I do a double take when I spot the red sports car at the curb—Layla's ride. Ethan's at the wheel, aviator shades on. He waggles them. "Hop on in, gorgeous," he says. "Think of me as your chauffeur."

I shriek, and I'm not even embarrassed by the high-pitched sound that comes from my mouth. "You guys are driving me to the gala?"

Ethan winks. "What else are friends for?"

"Everything," I say seriously as I slide into the car, emotions climbing my throat. "You guys are for *everything*. And I love you so much."

"You better, especially since you left the Virgin Society," he teases as he peels out into Manhattan traffic.

"I'm sure you'll find a way to uphold all its values," I say.

Ethan snorts. "Like getting out of this society," he says, then licks the corner of his lips salaciously. "With a hot babe or a hot dude."

"You go," I say, and we cheer him on as he weaves expertly through traffic.

Soon, we reach the hotel, and they drop me off in front. I can't think of a better way to enter.

Inside, I'm strung tight with anticipation. I'm wildly eager to see Bridger again. But I also want it to be tomorrow so I can kiss him in public already.

A quandary indeed.

I make my way through the bustling lobby, up the escalator, then down the hallway. When I'm ten feet away from the French doors, my phone buzzes in my clutch.

Grabbing it, I slide it open.

I'll be there in five minutes. Xoxo

I glow a little inside. Maybe a lot. After tapping out a quick reply—***Prepare to be impressed as I resist flinging myself at you when I see you***—I head to the ballroom, tucking the phone back in my clutch.

We're almost there. Tomorrow isn't far away.

I lift my hand to touch the *I* on my necklace for strength. But then, I gently tap the chandelier earrings instead, picturing Ethan and Layla. No matter what happens with my dad tomorrow, I'll always have my friends. They are my family now.

Feeling strong, I follow the sound of *Unfinished Business, Sweet Nothings, The Dating Games.*

My ten-year-old self would have floated to the moon to have waltzed in here. It's as sparkly as I imagined more than a decade ago when I begged my parents to be their plus one.

Servers in white shirts and crisp slacks circulate with silver trays of fancy hors d'oeuvres. Gorgeous guests in reds, golds, fuchsia, and sapphire smile dazzlingly bright. Men in tailored tuxes—probably ones they own rather than rent—look polished and sharp. There are even a few women in tuxes.

I devour the sights—actors like Jude Fox, writers like Ellie Snow, and then, wow...is that Davis Milo over there, holding court with his Tony Award-winning wife Jill Milo? I shiver in excitement. In another corner, I spot Nick Hammer, the creator of a popular late-night animated show that was adapted into a Broadway musical.

But my father taught me better than to stand and gawk, so I weave through the crowds, scanning for Table Twelve in the center of the room. I move past the A-list of the television industry and spot my father there, his arm curved around Vivian's waist, grandly entertaining some agents from Astor Agency, I presume.

Vivian chimes in, it seems, laughing, then saying something I can't make out. She seems...happy.

Ignorance is bliss, I suppose.

Dominic from the show is with them, with his red-carpet grin.

I keep my focus on my father as I walk, but my stomach churns. My chest aches too with a new pain, a new fear.

I'm going to be the instrument of his hurt.

Even if he doesn't disown me, he's going to be so disappointed in me.

Maybe even angry.

But I do my best to shove those emotions to a far corner in the back of my mind as I near the table.

Out of the corner of my eye, I catch a flash of red hair a few tables away. Isla's here. *Sweet Nothings* was nominated for an award, and she's the head writer.

Weird that she's not hanging around Table Twelve. She's talking to a man at another table. No idea what that means—if it means anything at all. But I have enough trouble of my own; I don't need to borrow it from others.

When I reach my father, he turns to me, beaming. "Harlow! At long last, my princess," he says.

I wither inside. He has no idea. Of course he has no idea that tomorrow I'm going to blindside him.

Maybe I'm the selfish asshole.

Words well up inside me, and I'm dying to spit out the truth right now.

But for one last night, I'll play the role I've played my whole entire life. The good daughter.

"Hi, Dad," I say and give a kiss to his cheek.

"I'm so glad you could be here. Tell me everything

about the new job," he says, playing the part of the doting papa. Only, neither one of us is acting. My father does adore me. And I am a good girl.

But he is also a liar and an addict.

As for me? I'm not a princess. I'm just a flawed young woman.

We are all good and bad in our own ways. But the difference is who we hurt with our shades of gray.

I'm faithful. He's not.

"It's going great." We make small talk for the next few minutes, and it's the most surreal moment of my life. All I want to do is blurt out the truth.

"And the installation will be done on Monday," I finish. Then my skin tingles, and I just know.

Bridger's here.

I spin around. My heart thunders at the sight of him moving through the crowd, his tux hugging his strong frame, his jawline shaven, his eyes locked on me.

I'm sure he can't help the way he can't stop looking at me. My smile grows dangerously wide as he nears us.

It takes all my willpower not to run to him, to fling myself into his arms. I've missed him so much. I want our future so badly. But I've spent a year being patient. I'll spend another few hours doing the same.

When he arrives, he tears his gaze from me like it pains him.

"Hello, Ian," he says.

But it's different from any greeting I've heard him give my father before. It's tight. Clipped.

Did something happen in Paris between them?

If so, my father doesn't let on. He simply claps

The RSVP

Bridger on the shoulder and says, "Let's hope we win Best Show for the fifth year in a row. It'll make it even sweeter when we present the final award of the night."

Bridger doesn't answer. He simply says hello to Vivian, the guests from Astor, to Dominic and then me.

Here we are, at the gala I longed to attend when I was younger. I'm in the center of all the festivities. Everyone is lovely, but I'm not a part of this world. I belong in SoHo, or Tribeca. I'm at home in The Frick, or the Ashanti Gallery. My heart lies in the St. James Theatre, and the rest of the theaters on the Great White Way where I can get lost in a musical.

With that man.

The one across from me. The one I'm pretending I'm not with all throughout dinner, all throughout dessert, all throughout these conversations.

Even though Bridger keeps stealing glances at me.

Finally, there's a break before the awards start, so I grab my purse and head for the ladies' room.

Inside, I touch up my lip gloss and check the time. I half wish we were at a diner, Bridger and me, eating French fries, gabbing about his trip.

Maybe tomorrow.

Once I leave and turn down the hall, Bridger's walking toward me.

With purpose. With intensity.

With desire in his eyes.

My stomach swoops.

He's where I belong too.

I turn around, head back down the hall, scan the area. There's an alcove off to the left—a quiet nook with a chair just past the ladies' room. I nod to it then turn in. He's there seconds later, and I'm vibrating. He balls his hands into fists so he doesn't touch me, and I do the same.

"Hi," I whisper, fighting every impulse to kiss him, to hug him, to touch him.

"Hi," he says, his dark gaze raking over me. "This whole time, I've wanted to take your hand. Kiss you. Touch you. Tell you that you look beautiful."

My heart beats wildly. "So do you."

Then, with *fuck it* in his eyes, he leans in, brushes his lips to my cheek, whispering, "Missed you so much."

"Missed you too," I say against his stubble. "Come over tonight."

"As if I'd go anywhere else but home. *With you*."

Home. That's what he feels like. My home at last.

Then he leaves, and when my hummingbird heart settles down, I exit the alcove and head back along the hall.

But all the air vacates my lungs when a redhead pushes on the door to the ladies' room in front of me.

I go still as a rabbit.

Maybe Isla didn't see us.

But then she casts her gaze over her shoulder at me.

And she looks smug.

46

AND THE AWARD GOES TO...

Harlow

No big deal.

Maybe she didn't see us after all. Maybe Isla's face just looks like...*that.*

Maybe she did and she doesn't care.

She hasn't been around the table yet tonight. Everything will be fine. But as I return to the ballroom, my pulse is spiking. Prickles of sweat form on the back of my neck as I walk past the French doors again while the host takes the stage.

It's Jude Fox, the British charmer who broke out on TV in *Unfinished Business*. He strides to the center of the stage as I scurry back to my seat.

"So lovely to see all of you tonight, and just remember if you enjoy your host, it's custom to tip extra on the way out. I'll pass a hat around," he says.

The crowd chuckles softly, and my pulse starts to calm.

That was nothing with Isla. That was nothing at all.

I reach my chair and sit down, then let out a huge breath. She saw nothing. She knows nothing.

I glance around the table, reorienting myself. Someone from Vivian's agency must have left for the restroom since there's an empty chair next to Dad. He's holding Vivian's hand. Bridger is across from me. Dominic's next to him. A few other agents are here. All is fine.

I breathe steadily again, settling back into the night, trying to focus on Jude's monologue when I hear the sharp stab of stilettos against the floor.

The sound stops, and she's here.

With a flick of her swishy hair, Isla drops into the empty chair and snaps her gaze to my father. "Derivative?" she hisses. She sounds like a snake.

My skin crawls. I tilt my head, listening as dread worms through me.

"Isla, I have no idea what you're talking about," my father says to her in his most placating, charming tone.

She whips out her phone, waggles it like a weapon, then she shoves it into his face. "It's a pass, calling *Happy-ish*...derivative."

Even while holding her loaded gun of a mobile phone, she manages to sketch angry air quotes.

Jude's melodic voice booms from the stage, filling the ballroom. "And now for the Best Actor category. The nominees include Dominic Rivera from *Sweet Nothings*..."

Isla doesn't stop. She doesn't seem to care that one of the actors she crafts scenes for has been nominated for an award. What is she doing? Is she about to break up with my father in front of the ballroom of his contemporaries?

Holy smokes. I actually feel bad for him.

"I can't believe this. After all I did for you," she hisses to my father. But it's a stage hiss, designed for the whole room to hear. "After all we shared, after Paris, after you broke my goddamn heart...You did this."

She's not dumping him. He's already dumped her. My married father broke it off with his lover.

I drop my face, embarrassed for him. His affairs have gotten messier by the year, by the month as his ladies overlap increasingly.

Vivian jerks her gaze from my father to Isla and back. "Ian?" she asks. And that one word contains every question a wife could ask in this moment.

He squeezes her hand, like he did to Roselyn way back when. When Roselyn checked into the *spa.* "Nothing to worry about, Vivvy love."

Isla huffs haughtily as she brandishes that phone like it's evidence in a trial. The people against Ian Granger in the case of rampant infidelity. "There's plenty to worry—"

Bridger clears his throat, lifts a hand as a stop sign, and cuts in. "Isla, now is not the time and place."

His cool voice seems like it could soothe a wild beast, but Isla whips her gaze to him. Red fumes billow from her eyes as Jude rattles off the other nominees for

Best Actor. "Oh, you're one to talk about time and place," she says to Bridger.

But he remains calm, trying to keep the peace. "Yes, I am the one to talk because that pass came from my office." His volume low, but his command high. "You can take it up with me after the event. *Not during*," he says, laying down the law.

Only Isla is evidently lawless tonight.

She glares at Bridger, shakes her head. Then, her smug smile from the ladies' room returns. "But won't you be busy after the event?"

He narrows his eyes. "Not. Now," he bites out.

Isla's grin turns wickedly wider. "No, I think now is the perfect time to discuss where you'll be," she says, then points at me. "*With her.*"

My heart stops beating. My cheeks flush. The embarrassment I felt for my father moments ago reverses. Now, it blankets my entire body as Isla busts us in front of the table.

In front of one man in particular.

My father blinks, startled and confused. But then, he would never believe his princess would do such a thing. He deals Isla a sharp stare. "Let's stop this. You have no idea what you're talking about."

With fire in her green eyes, the scorned woman—scorned by love, and scorned by business—lashes out for the entire ballroom to hear. "Don't gaslight me, Ian Granger. You know damn well what's going on."

With an amused chuckle, he shrugs. "I have no idea why you'd bring my daughter into this. I'd love to know."

It's a challenge, spoken as if he holds the winning cards.

I brace myself for more bullets.

Isla tosses her head back and laughs, almost like a beautiful villain in an animated flick. But not that cartoonish. She's all real and vitriol.

I can't let this go on, so I seize the chance to control the story. "Dad, I can explain," I say quickly. I'm not a teenager anymore covering up affairs before someone might go insane.

Bridger jumps in next with, "Let's go into the hall, Ian."

But Isla will not be vanquished. With a contemptuous eye roll, she spits out, "I brought your daughter into it—"

"Please stop," I beg to no avail.

Isla stares at her former lover, ready to deliver a fatal blow. With a devilish grin, she starts up once more, but nope. No way. I'm not going to let her cheapen me.

"I'm in love with Bridger," I blurt out right as Isla says, "She's fucking the man who turned down my script."

Then, I'm shaking. Breathing hard.

I think this is shock.

No one speaks.

Not even the host.

Not a single guest.

No one.

Then, a glass shatters in the silence. I jerk my head toward the sound. Across the room, a server must have dropped a glass of champagne, the flute shattering on the marbled floor.

But the show must go on. From the stage, Jude tries to wrestle control of the rubbernecking and the ten-car pileup. "And on that dramatic note, the winner for Best Actor is Dominic Rivera from *Sweet Nothings*."

It takes several seconds to register, and then Dominic blinks, but he doesn't move from his chair. He's riveted by the table and the scene unfolding before all our eyes. Then he recovers, stands, and weaves through the crowd toward the stage.

But no one is looking at the star actor who's nabbed a statuette for his work on a nighttime soap.

Everyone is staring at Table Twelve as we steal the spotlight with our real-life soap opera.

47

MY DINER DREAMS

Bridger

I need to get Ian out of the ballroom, stat. Harlow doesn't deserve to have this happen in public. I push back in my chair right as Ian rises, like he just grew ten feet tall.

In slow motion, as if he is still processing every shocking detail, he turns first to Isla, an outrage in his eyes, before he erases that, rearranging his features expertly. Then, he laughs softly, like he needs to reassure a child. "Clearly, you're even more creative than you were before. Because that's quite a fable." Then he looks to his daughter gently, calmly, like he's a different person with her, and says, "You don't have to cover for Isla just because Bridger turned her down."

No, just fucking no.

I head to Harlow as Jude once more tries to clean up the mess from the stage. "How about Dominic?

Have you seen his character's library? I fantasize about libraries like that."

Dominic laughs and says something in reply, but I don't care.

None of that matters. Nothing matters but Harlow. Not even the too tight feeling in my own body. Not even the way my business, my world, my reputation is spinning out of control.

No, *imploding.*

Not even the way I can feel the press of bodies. Heavy. The weight of the room. Oppressive.

When I reach her, I take her hand. She laces her fingers through mine. My heart settles. My anxious mind quiets.

I need her more than I need anything or anyone in this room.

I lift my chin and look straight at Ian. "I was going to tell you this tomorrow, but there's no time like the present. Tomorrow, you're buying my shares at the price we agreed to when we started the company. I'm exercising the buyout clause in our contract. After that, Lucky 21 is all yours and we won't be in business together."

Silence coats the room for another few seconds, then Dominic laughs from the stage. "And they say all of the action happens on TV. I guess sometimes art imitates life," he says, trying valiantly to detract attention away from us once again.

He's not the only one aiming to steal control. As Harlow rises, squeezes my hand, Ian stalks over to me, getting in my face. "Where the hell is this coming from? Are you fucking delusional too?"

I'm not sure I've ever heard him swear. He doesn't rely on curses. He relies on charm.

But tonight, his smooth, affable persona has burned to smoke. He's livid. And I just don't care. He's not my priority. I've said my piece. I'm done having this conversation in public.

I turn to my brave woman. "Can I take you home?"

"Yes," she says, breathing hard, like she's run a race.

We leave, cutting through the ballroom hand in hand, all eyes on us. I don't tug on my cuffs. I don't practice steadying breaths. I simply go, feeling more centered than the moment calls for. Because she is with me.

Trouble is, Ian is right behind us, stalking us beyond the French doors. "What in the bloody hell?" he asks, his eyes flickering with both fury and utter bewilderment.

Fine. We'll have tomorrow's talk now. Out in the hallway, away from our colleagues, where I asked him to take this conversation moments ago.

I turn around and grab the conversation before he can take over. "We planned to tell you this tomorrow. That's why Harlow asked you to come to lunch at her place. I was going to be there to tell you—"

"—That you've been fucking my daughter?"

"Watch your mouth," I spit out.

"I won't watch my mouth. I brought you into my world."

I scoff at his revisionist history. "We're equal partners. We built this together."

"And then what did you do? You seduced my
daughter—my *daughter*—behind my back," he
lashes out.

Harlow steps closer. "Not that it's any of your business, but I pursued Bridger."

"Poppet," he says, softening. He'll probably always
have a soft spot for her. "You don't know what you're
talking about."

She levels him with an intense gaze. "I know exactly
what I'm talking about. I'm twenty-one. This is my
choice. Bridger is my choice."

He holds out his hands and huffs like this is all
unbelievable. "How can you even know? You're too
young."

She lifts her chin high. "Mom married you when
she was twenty-two," she says. *Take that, Dad*.

I want to cheer her on. My woman could be a
badass attorney right now. I also want to tell Ian where
he can shove his opinions, but for better or worse, he'll
always be her father. He'll be in her life, and by extension, he'll be in mine. So, I wait, patiently, as she continues. The floor is hers right now.

"I know what I want." She reaches for his arm,
squeezing it. With both strength and grace, she says, "I
didn't want you to find out like this. I wanted to tell you
in private at my home, tomorrow. We wanted to talk to
you then. Not in public like this. I never imagined Isla
would storm in."

Ian flinches at the mention of his lover, or perhaps

at his own culpability in the meltdown tonight. "Nor did I," he says, then he purses his lips like he's holding in his own thoughts about Isla. He didn't expect this from her either. Usually, he's able to juggle like an expert street performer, tossing knives in the air and catching them all.

Then, he shakes his head, parts his lips like he's hunting for more words, but nothing comes. Maybe our fortitude has thrown him completely off.

Or maybe not. He snaps his gaze to me, finding a new head of steam. "I trusted you. I relied on you. I can't believe you'd do this to me," he seethes. "I can't believe you'd go behind my back while we were working on deals, refining scripts, wooing business partners and do...*this*."

He says it like it's a dirty act.

Like it's unforgivable.

"To my *daughter*," he adds, to emphasize his point. "I can't believe you'd go behind my back and take my daughter."

That's my unforgivable crime. She's the one he adores. She's the one true thing in his life. She's his pure love, especially once Felicity was gone.

I crossed a line he'll never forgive.

I saw this coming. I saw the end when Harlow and I began, and I did it anyway. Ian is who he is, and I don't believe he will ever trust me again. We certainly won't be friends since we were never truly close to begin with.

So, here I am, exactly where I was once terrified to be. There is no choice but the nuclear option.

But I'm not scared of the consequences.

And I don't need his forgiveness or his permission.

I stay cool and calm and focus on the facts. "We've had a good run, but it's best we move on. I hope you understand that the buyout benefits you much more than me, and I'm willing to do that. Because I love Harlow, and I plan to be with her," I say, using her name rather than saying *your daughter.*

He drags a hand through his hair. "Really, Bridger? You're really leaving the company?" he asks, like he doesn't believe I'd ever leave. But staying isn't an option now. That's my other unforgivable act—the company is the next most important thing to him. It's his connection to Felicity. It's the way he understood the world after she left it. *Sweet Nothings* has become more than her successful series. It's become *his* tales of sex and affairs twined on top of her love stories.

It's his, and he can have it.

"Yes. Yes, I am," I say.

But Ian's still desperate, borderline begging. "We run it better together."

Huh. He needs me. In this moment, he needs me. But he can't have everything he wants. He'd always remind me I'm with his daughter. He'd always needle me that I took her from him. My love for her would always be between us.

Once again, I choose her. "You'll do fine on your own," I say.

Another groan. Another bitten-off curse. "You're going to blow up what we've built for something that might not—"

"Don't go there," I bite out, cutting him off. He'd never say something cruel about her, but I don't need him to insult how he thinks I'll treat her or how committed I am. "Whatever you were going to say next, don't."

He huffs through his nostrils, turns to Harlow, and pleads. "Come back. Stay for the rest of the awards, at least."

She smiles sadly. "I appreciate the invitation for tonight, and I'm sorry I can't stay. But it's really time for me to go."

He sputters, trying to say something, anything, and finally spits out, "Where in the bloody hell are you going? We have to present an award."

Like that matters.

With Harlow's hand in mine, I take a few steps to go, then I toss back, "Feel free to present the last award solo. I have a date. I'm taking out the woman I love."

I let out a long, deep breath. Of relief. Of possibility. Of a future that I want. Not one that I chase to fix the past. One that I embrace for the present. "I hope your show wins. Felicity wrote some seriously great love stories, and *Sweet Nothings* owes everything to her."

I turn around, and we don't look back.

Ian doesn't follow. It's just Harlow and me, hand in hand, escaping from the glitter and the crowds, from the drama and the noise, from everything and everyone.

Down the escalator, through the lobby, out the revolving door we go. "It's going to be all over the industry trades," she says, a little amazed. A lot concerned. "You know that, right?"

I shrug, truly not caring. I've worked hard. I've made plenty. I've saved well. I'll start over. "I don't care. I love you."

Then finally, we're outside on Fifth Avenue and I do the thing I've longed for more than anything in the world. I cup her cheeks. I kiss her mouth. We come back together for all of New York to see. She ropes her arms around my neck and holds on tight.

No matter what happens tomorrow or next week or the week after, I have no regrets.

When I break the kiss, Harlow smiles at me, happier than I think I've ever seen her, and that's saying something. "Want to go to a diner and get French fries?" she asks.

"More than anything in the world."

With that, we go on our first date.

48

DEFINITELY FOUND

Harlow

The second we sit down at the booth at Neon Diner, Bridger's phone goes wild, rattling across the Formica counter like a windup toy.

He side-eyes it.

Then my phone buzzes. It's the group text with Layla and Ethan. They saw a video on social, and pictures from a distance of Isla's confrontation. Layla asks if I need anything at all, and Ethan offers to come pick me up—in Layla's car—and escort us to a private getaway in Vermont.

I write back quickly, telling them all is well, and there'll be more to come tomorrow.

Then Bridger finishes typing a message and smiles apologetically. "Jules. She asked if I needed any help with projects this weekend."

I laugh. "*She's* the go-getter," I say.

He waggles his phone. "And everyone else wants to know what's up, so my answer is *this*."

He makes a show of turning off his phone. I do the same with mine. Then, we order.

A few minutes later, I swipe a French fry through the ketchup, then offer it to my date.

Bridger takes it, pops it into his mouth and chews. "Best fries ever," he declares as Sinatra croons overhead about this city.

"Best meal ever," I say, one-upping the man sitting next to me in the mint-green upholstered booth at the diner a few blocks from my home.

"Best night ever," he says.

"You win the negotiation," I concede.

"Excellent."

I twirl the straw in the metal milkshake container then suck on the cold beverage. When I'm done, I lift my chin, offering my lips to him like I did that day in Abingdon Square. "Do my lips taste good?"

He takes my challenge with a firm, confident kiss under the bright fluorescent lights. "They do."

I kick my high-heeled foot back and forth under the table. I feel frothy and daring. I can't wait to tell my friends about tonight. I can't wait for Bridger to truly meet my friends. "I want you to meet Ethan and Layla."

He shoots me a look like I've got that all wrong. "I have met them."

"Sure. At parties. In passing. I mean, meet them, *meet them*. Like this. As my...boyfriend?" I say, but that word comes out awkwardly and as a question.

He laughs. "Was that hard for you to say, honey?"

I grumble a yes. "You don't seem like a boyfriend."

"Am I a man-friend?" he asks drily.

"Well, kind of," I admit.

"I'm definitely not a boy," he says. "But please don't call me your man-friend either."

"What should I call you?"

His gaze holds mine, his eyes full of love and passion. "Just call me, Harlow. Just keep calling me."

My heart twirls once again. "Always. So, how was Paris?"

"It was good. But it's going to be so much better with you," he says.

"Because you need a translator," I tease.

He shakes his head, not taking the bait, and tucks a strand of hair behind my ear. "No, Harlow. I need *you*."

Now, my heart flips. It does that a lot with him. I fiddle with the end of his undone bow tie. "I like you in a tux. But I like you here in this booth in a tux the best."

"You look good. Here with me. In the light."

We finish, leave, and head into the summer night.

When we reach my apartment, it doesn't take long for me to strip him out of his shirt, for him to undo my dress, for the rest of our clothes to vanish.

Then, there are no words, only a crashing together. His lips meet mine, and we kiss in a mad frenzy, desperate for each other. As we stumble toward the bed, we are a tangle of lips and teeth. A chorus of sighs and gasps. I wrap my arms around him tighter, and he grasps my back.

We can't get close enough.

On my bed, I pull him against me, thrilling at the

feel of his chest against mine, his skin against mine, then him inside me.

I pull him deeper. Move with him. Whisper and murmur and groan, and we lose our minds together once again.

* * *

In the morning, we do something for the first time—we leave my apartment, hand in hand. With the summer sun rising in the sky, we go to get a cup of coffee at a shop around the corner.

The coffee is incredibly average, but even so, it's everything. As I lift my cup by the crowded counter, I tap the rim of the mug. "Found," I say.

He smiles. "Definitely found."

When we leave the shop, I stop at the end of the block. Bridger's heading home to catch up on work, and I have someplace to be—*alone*.

"Are you sure you don't want me to go with you?" he asks.

I shake my head, resolute in my new plan for this morning. We no longer need to tell my dad we're together. Isla got the ball rolling for us last night, and we pushed it the rest of the way down the hill. Now, Dad knows. The whole industry knows—yes, last night's spectacle was all over social, but c'est la vie.

Still, there's something else I need to talk to my dad about.

Bridger leans in to brush a kiss onto my forehead,

then my cheek, then my lips. "I'll see you tonight. You're going to be fine."

"I will."

Then we part, and I mentally prep for a tough conversation as I walk several blocks along Fifth Avenue, head a block over, then stride up the steps of the brownstone where I used to live.

I brace myself as I knock on the door.

In some ways, I've been preparing for this moment for years. But you can't truly be ready. You have to take life as it comes.

I don't have a clue what's coming. But I know what I want to say.

Vivian answers, and that surprises me.

So does her warm greeting. "Come in," she says, sweeping out her arm.

My heart lurches. She believes him. She believes whatever lies he's spun.

She invites me into the living room, then nods to the front door. "I'll give you some space," she says, then leaves.

When the door snicks shut, my dad emerges from his office and joins me on the couch.

He wipes his hand across his brow theatrically and says, "Tell me that was all a dream last night."

He offers a cheeky grin.

I don't smile. Instead, I find the courage to say the hard thing. "I love you, and I think you need to get help for love and sex addiction." I'm grateful to have finally breathed those words out loud.

To his credit, he doesn't flinch. He doesn't feign

surprise. And he doesn't brush me off or call me young. He simply nods. "Thank you for your advice."

For a few weighty seconds, a tantalizing hope winds through me—the hope that he could change, that he could turn his life around.

So I push once more.

"I mean it," I say desperately, imploring him. "I want you to get help for your addiction."

"I know you do." But then he shrugs, his expression unbearably sad, and completely revealing for one of the first times ever. Like he knows who he is. Like he knows why he does what he does. "I just don't want to."

I remember my mother's words about help. We can rarely help people. Either we don't have what they need, or they don't want what we can give.

"I hope you change your mind someday," I say.

He takes my hand, squeezes it. "Thank you." Then, like it costs him the world, he whispers, "I just want you to be happy. So did your mother."

My throat swells with emotion. Tears prick my eyes. "I am."

On that note, I go. I walk down the block where I grew up, stop at the corner, cross the street. I head straight into Central Park. A place I went with my mother, my brother, and a place I like to go by myself.

I wander around, stopping when I spot a tattered paperback on a green bench. A bookmark pokes out from the pages. Someone must have left it behind. I snap a picture and post it with the caption: *Time for a new story.*

49

OPENING NUMBER

Bridger

It's Friday morning in mid July, and I leave my new office in Chelsea with Jules by my side, rattling off our plans for the rest of the day. "We'll have lunch with Ellie, and then after that we can meet with—"

But her words are cut off by a jackhammer ripping through asphalt. That's New York for you. Construction is everywhere all the time.

When we pass the workers, I turn to Jules. "It's okay. You don't need to brief me on my schedule. Christian does that. You're a junior producer now. You're coming to the meeting in that capacity."

My no-nonsense co-worker seems to fight off a smile, then dives right into business for our walk and talk, discussing the details of the courting we're doing of Ellie Snow. After she won her Critics award for Best New Show, I called her agent, and asked for a meeting.

Then I pitched her on a concept.

She was keen on it, and now we're going to refine it.

We reach the lunch spot Ellie picked out and head inside. After quick hellos, the upbeat showrunner turns to me. "So, love letters. That's a brilliant concept," she says.

"Thank you. Harlow and I thought so too, and we want you to helm it."

"And I want to helm it," she says, then she shares where she'd like to take a show where the hero's backstory is told through love letters. "And we frame his current arc around a letter he's writing. But we don't know who it's to. But we'll find out over the course of the season."

I never shared the concept with Ian. He wasn't interested. So it wasn't his or Lucky 21's to claim. It was mine, and it was Harlow's.

Now, my hope is that it'll belong to Opening Number, my new production company that I launched immediately after the awards ceremony.

We're lean, but we're fierce. I hired Jules the first day. Though *insisted she join me* is more like it. "You need to work with me. You're sharp and talented, and I want you to learn the business from me," I'd told her over the phone.

"Yes. The answer is yes," she'd said, and then she jumped ship.

Lucky 21 now belongs to Ian. Or it will soon. It takes time to unwind a partnership, but our lawyers are handling the details, and soon we'll be...professionally divorced.

Our soap-opera scene from the gala was indeed all over the trades and the gossip rags. Lots of agents and writers and actors don't want to work with me. But lots don't want to work with Ian either.

And honestly, enough *do* want to work with me. Besides, I only need a few. And I still have my best asset.

Taste.

I have excellent taste and a strong gut instinct.

This love-letter story can be a hit with Ellie leading it. "We're going to need a star though. Someone to lure the fans," she says. "Anyone in mind?"

Jules squares her shoulders. "As a matter of fact, we happen to know someone who's very keen on having his own show."

"Do tell," Ellie says.

"Dominic Rivera," I say.

Ellie's big eyes widen. "I like where this is going. Tell me more."

"We have a meeting with him after this. He'll be perfect for the role."

* * *

A week later, I head to another meeting. One I've been seeking for a long, long time. I go to lunch with David Fontaine, eager to learn what's on his mind at last.

Over iced tea, he says, "So, I've been thinking about your idea about the humor columns." Ah, I'd been hoping he'd marinate on that after the gallery. Maybe this is why he arranged this meeting the day he called me. He keeps going, saying, "But it's not just supposed to be funny. There's a love story."

"There always should be a love story."

Then he tells me his idea, finishing with, "What do you think?"

He wouldn't want me to blow smoke. So I point out a few small holes, and he nods thoughtfully. Then I say, "But that's easy. I can sell it on a concept if you want to work together."

He's quiet for a few seconds, then he scratches his jaw. "I heard you left Lucky 21 because of...love?"

Not because of a *blowout*. Not a *meltdown*. I appreciate the word choice, and the distinction. "You heard right," I say, but I don't add any details. The industry trade mags reported the basics for a hot minute, then moved on. I'm not a star. I'm just a producer. Ultimately, a consensual relationship between two adults isn't that newsworthy.

"Love can be vexing. Didn't I tell you that at the exhibit?" David asks rhetorically and wags a finger at me, like he's admonishing me as a father would do. But he doesn't seem pissed or annoyed.

He also still hasn't said yes to us working together.

"You did. You're not wrong. But it can also be the reason you get up in the morning," I reply.

"I won't argue with you there." He stares at the ceiling then looks back at me, his expression suddenly intense. "I like the concept. And interestingly enough, I agreed to meet with you to tell you I'd consider working with you under one condition."

I'm damn curious what that could be. "What's the condition?"

David smiles slyly. "I was going to tell you I'd work with you if you were solo. So, yes, Bridger, I'd like to work with you on the show."

"Let's do it," I say, excited to have nabbed him, and excited too, I suppose, to know why he was elusive for so long.

David's eyes twinkle and he continues. "Good. Let's just say I like to work with honest men," he says.

Let's just say I get it.

I lift my iced tea and clink it to his, finally understanding why he didn't take my calls for so long. I was never going to win him before. I was radioactive by association.

Guess the starting over has been worth it already in so many ways.

* * *

As I hit the third mile on my morning run the next Monday, the sound of wheels whooshing faster comes from behind me.

Her voice comes next. "Hey, runner."

"Hey, rider," I say as Harlow slows her pace on the silver bike, pedaling alongside me on the East River Greenway.

"Fancy meeting you here," she says.

"What a coincidence."

"Exactly. Nothing planned at all."

I keep running as she rides slowly, her brow knitting like she's deep in thought. "I was thinking about this coming weekend. When your mom comes to town."

"Yeah?" I'm not dreading Sardi's like I have in the past. I'll go with Harlow, and it'll be fine. Not my first choice, but it's only one night. "I already said yes. I'm not worried anymore."

"I know. But why should you go at all? It's a party she's throwing for her friends. Let's take her to lunch instead. Just you and me. Then I'll spend the afternoon with her, shopping."

"You'd take my mom shopping?" I want to make sure I've heard that right.

Laughing, Harlow rolls her eyes. "You say that like it surprises you. I like to shop—especially for you—and you've told me that Mama James does too. This way I can spend time with her. And you can—I don't know— go brood in a library or something. Write dark poetry. Scowl," she tosses back at me.

She loves to knock me down a peg or two. And I love to let her. "That sounds fantastic," I say, and a lot better than a party.

Lunch is the middle of the day. She usually only drinks at night and with friends.

Yes, Harlow's plan sounds like a way for me to enjoy time with my family. That's a gift. One I've been seeking my whole life.

But one I couldn't find until now.

* * *

On Friday, I head into the elevator at the Lipstick Building to meet with Webflix executives about Ellie's new show when someone calls out, "Hold the door, please," in a charming British accent.

I brace myself. It was inevitable I'd run into Ian again. I press open, and seconds later he strides in, nearly stumbling in shock when he sees me. "Oh."

"Hello. What floor?" I ask politely.

"Nine, please."

But I should be more than civil. Gracious is a better way to behave. I press the button, then turn to him. "Congrats on *Afternoon Delight*," I say. "I heard the shoot went great."

He doesn't answer at first, just furrows his brow. Maybe deciding if he's going to deign to answer me at all. Then he says, "And I hope it launches well."

"Me too," I say, since the show won't premiere for a few more months. I clear my throat and say another hard thing. "Your revision was good."

A nod. A quiet thanks.

But I'm not done. "Best of luck, Ian. Truly," I say as the elevator slows at the seventh floor.

"Thank you, Bridger."

Then I step out and the doors shut behind me. I doubt we'll ever exchange more than pleasantries, but for Harlow's sake, the pleasantries are necessary.

After all, she'll be in my life always.

I just know it.

* * *

On Saturday, Harlow and I walk across town to the Chelsea Market, where I reach for the door and hold it open for her. A familiar voice, brassy and big, calls out from down the block. "My baby!"

Harlow's jaw drops, and she shoots me a *that's so adorable* look.

I grumble, "Don't tell anyone she calls me that."

"I won't tell a single soul at all," she says in the tone of someone who'll tell the world.

Then, I take a second for the familiar curl of dread to twist through me at the thought of seeing my mother, but it doesn't come.

I'm not bracing myself to see her. I'm surprisingly grateful.

That's a welcome change. My mother closes the distance between us, her arms out wide, a red silk scarf wrapped around her hair, white sunglasses on. "Bridger, it's been too long," she says in that throaty voice that has graced microphones and stages for years. She throws her arms around me.

When she lets go, she turns to Harlow, immediately beaming. "And...you! I've been dying to meet you, sweetheart."

"Helena, this is my girlfriend, Harlow," I say.

Mom grabs Harlow's shoulders. "You're an angel for tolerating my moody, sarcastic, complicated son."

"Way to sell me, Mom," I say.

"I would say I do a little more than tolerate him," Harlow says.

As we go inside, Mom breezing ahead of us, Harlow

turns to me and whispers, "Her name is Helena? Like Helen James, the First Lady of American theater?"

"Well, there is an *a* at the end of Helena. So it's not exactly like it."

"But it's close. Bridger! Show business is in your blood."

"Yes. It is."

Over lunch, Harlow chats with my mom for most of the meal, and I relax as I listen to the two ladies talk about music and theater and art.

I don't have an apple-pie home, or a white-picket-fence story. Few of us do. But right here, right now, I'm at peace with where I came from and with everything I have.

50

UNFINISHED BUSINESS

Harlow

I finish the article I've been reading on the train—on trends in art buying—then close my tablet and stare out the window, content to watch the seaside towns rush by for now.

Soon, the train slows as we near our destination. And my contentment slinks away. I hope it's not a mistake to bring all my *found family* together. I hope my friends and my guy have a good time.

Bridger closes his tablet. He's been reading scripts the whole train ride.

"Anything good?" I ask.

"As a matter of fact, the first episode of Fontaine's show is fantastic," he says, then he lowers his voice and brings his finger to his lips. "But don't tell a soul."

"I'll keep all your secrets," I whisper.

It's a Saturday morning in September and after a

long work week, we're going to spend one night in the Hamptons. Once the train stops, we grab our bags and make our way through the station. Outside in the late summer sun, Layla's looking thoroughly New York with her black tank top, big black shades, and her hair looped in a messy bun. She's behind the wheel of her little red ride, while Ethan's shotgun.

As we head down the steps, butterflies race through me.

I hope it's not weird.

I hope he doesn't think we're too young for him.

I hope they all like each other.

But then I talk back to my worries. It's just one night. Plus, his friend Axel is in the Hamptons for the weekend, researching his next book. They'll slip off to do guy stuff—play golf, grill on the deck, hoist sails on boats, I guess. Stuff like that.

Bridger and I hop in the backseat of the car.

After quick hellos, Bridger hits Ethan and Layla up with a critical question. "So, how's the scene this weekend?"

As she pulls onto the road, Layla answers authoritatively. "We already spotted William Halifax and his boyfriend down by the beach playing volleyball."

"I wish William was playing a concert here this weekend," Ethan says, wistful.

"You're a big fan of his music?" Bridger asks.

"Absolutely," Ethan says over the breeze. "He's my inspiration."

Bridger strokes his chin thoughtfully. "Yeah, he definitely rocks, but I've been kind of interested in hearing this new band, The Outrageous Record?"

Ethan whips his head around, gawks at Bridger, then at me. "Your dude's a keeper."

"I know," I say, then Ethan hits play on the single his band recorded just last week.

I close my eyes, the sun warming my face as we listen to a tune about longing as we drive to Layla's home. I know the weekend's going to be great.

And it is.

* * *

The next weekend, when I'm back in New York and Bridger's working late to wrap up Ellie Snow's new deal, I have lunch with my father. We catch up at Neon Diner—my choice. He wanted something fancy, but I said diner food is better.

Over sandwiches and fries, he tells me about the new season of *Sweet Nothings*—it's great—then how Vivian is doing—she's great—and then how he's doing —also great.

"I'm glad to hear that," I say. I still wish he'd make new choices, and I'm determined to help him see his struggles. "And I hope you'll keep considering what I said at your house."

He smiles, but it's rueful. "And I hope you'll keep having lunch with me."

"I will." Maybe someday, somehow, these lunches, these talks, these reminders will be enough.

I'll keep going. I'll keep trying in case he ever wants the help I can give.

Later that night, my friends and I head out again to meet up with my brother. Hunter's in town for work, so the four of us grab tapas then cab it to our favorite dance club in Tribeca.

Inside Rapture, we beeline for the middle of the floor, grooving and grinding under the purple lights, dancing our asses off till we're sweaty and breathless.

"Refuel," Layla shouts above the noise.

At the bar, I grab a water while Layla and Ethan replenish their dancing electrolytes with mojitos. Hunter asks for a bourbon. "Bourbon makes me dance better," he explains, and I hug him again because I've missed him.

When we're done at the oasis, Layla tips her blonde head to the dance floor to suggest we all return but my vision snags on a familiar silhouette.

Someone I did not expect to see.

Someone I just realized I have unfinished business with.

"I'll be right there," I say.

They rush back into the crowd while I make my way to the woman who thought I was a brat.

At least, I think that's how Jules saw me back when I worked at Lucky 21 at the start of the summer. Leaning against the bar, she's nursing a drink and watching the crowd. She sure doesn't look like office Jules, though. Here, in downtown Manhattan, she's After Dark Jules. She has smoky black eyes, cherry-red lipstick, skinny jeans, and a tight black corset, along with a choker necklace.

Wowzers.

"Jules?" I ask loudly when I reach her.

She turns, and the second she registers it's me, her professional face comes on. Her poker face. It's understandable. I'm involved with her boss. She's surely going to be cautious with me.

"Hi, Harlow," she says.

"Good to see you, Jules," I say, and it's a little awkward, maybe because she works for Bridger, or maybe because of what went down earlier in the summer.

That's my unfinished business.

Except...did anything really go down? Or was it all my perception? Was I just assuming that she had it out for me when really, she might have just been looking out for herself?

I move closer and cup the side of my mouth, trying to talk above the thump of the bass. "Hey, I'm sorry that we didn't always get along when we worked together," I offer.

Her eyes widen in surprise. "Oh. Well. I'm sorry too. I was just trying to be super businesslike," she says, then shrugs a little sheepishly. "It's just easier for me that way in the workplace."

"I get that. And I'm sorry if I ever made you feel uncertain about your job."

She shakes her head. "I'm sorry if I wasn't always friendly."

With that, we put the past behind us.

I lean in once again. "Bridger really values you. He thinks you're smart."

"Thank you. I appreciate hearing that. All I've ever wanted is to work in TV," she says above the thunder of the music.

"It sounds like a perfect fit," I say as a busty redhead with big hips slides up next to her.

Jules pats the woman's shoulder. "This is my friend Camden," she practically shouts. "We're going to head out to the dance floor." Then, in a stage whisper, she adds, "My dirty little secret is I absolutely love to dance."

It comes out salaciously. Like there's a whole other side of Jules at night. "Want to dance with us?" she asks.

"I'd love to," I say, and I'm swept up in the crowd in the middle of a club, dancing with my brother, my two best friends, and perhaps some new ones too.

EPILOGUE
CAN I TELL YOU A SECRET?

Harlow

The next week, I finish my day at Petra Gallery, showing a collector the newest sculpture from an artist she admires. When the client leaves and we lock the doors, I tell Allison and Amelie I'm taking off.

I have a meeting with my trust attorney at last.

She leads a busy practice, and with my gallery work schedule and the rare few evening appointments the lawyer had available, this is the first time I could see her.

After I say goodbye to my fabulous bosses, I head to the Village to the law offices of Gupta & Wong. They're located on Jane Street, in a beautiful red-brick brownstone with a white door. It's almost too warm and cozy for a staid family-law attorney.

I head inside, taking the stairs to the second floor where I give my name to the receptionist.

"Great. Prana is looking forward to seeing you," the man behind the desk says.

I'm sure he says that to everyone, so I simply smile and thank him as he escorts me along the hallway to a corner office.

A forty-something woman with electric-blue glasses and silky black hair rises from her desk, and says, "You must be Harlow Dumont." She realizes her error and shakes her head, correcting herself. "Excuse me, I meant Harlow Granger."

"That's me," I say, but I don't mind the mistake.

She strides around the desk, and we shake hands. "Prana Gupta," she says, then gestures to a blue couch. I take a seat and she sits on a chair across from me.

"I want to review the details of the trust your mother set up for you before she died." She goes on to explain how and when the money comes due. It's perfunctory, businesslike, and about what I expected from this meeting.

Prana takes a beat, purses her lips, and then, like she's trying to strip emotions from her voice, says carefully, "But your mother also asked us to hold onto something for you."

I startle, then tilt my head. "What do you mean?"

Prana takes another breath. It seems this is a big deal for her, like these kinds of meetings don't happen every day for her. "It's not uncommon for family members to want to give something to a child when she comes of age," Prana explains.

Instinctively, I finger my necklace. "Like jewelry? A locket?" That doesn't entirely sound like my mother.

Despite the necklace I wear, she was never big on baubles.

"Yes, and family heirlooms or art," Prana explains.

Maybe Mom collected art I didn't know about?

Prana reaches for a binder from the table then takes out a slim envelope. Instantly, my eyes well with tears.

I know exactly what that is, but still I have to ask, even as my voice breaks. "A letter from her?"

Prana nods with sympathy in her dark eyes. "Yes, but there's more. The letter explains it all."

She hands it to me reverently, a touch of pride in her eyes. Maybe even anticipation.

With trembling fingers, I open the envelope, but I'm not even sure I'll be able to read the words past the sea of tears.

I didn't walk in here expecting to receive a letter from beyond.

This wasn't on my bingo card at all.

Prana hands me a box of tissues. She must be well stocked. I grab one and wipe my cheek. Then, delicately, like it'll crumble, I take the sheet of paper from the envelope.

My throat tightens. That's my mother's handwriting. I don't even try to stop the waterworks as I read.

Dear Harlow,

Can I tell you a secret?

I've always wanted to take care of you. Even when I knew it would be difficult, I tried to find a way. The only way I knew how.

And it's this—I've saved something special for you.

Just you.

I was working on a new story when I became ill. It's nearly done. It only needs an epilogue. I asked my lawyers to hold it for you until you could take it under your wing completely.
When you read this, it'll no longer be a secret, undiscovered last manuscript. It'll belong to you to do with whatever you want. It's something we will have created together.

There's something else I want to tell you, but I'm pretty sure you already know.

I love you.

I still love you.

I'll always love you.

XOXO Your mom

. . .

My shoulders shake. My sobs rain down. The tears don't stop. I go through a box of tissues, blowing my nose, wiping my face, drying the endless tears as Prana tells me she kept digital copies of the book. That it's safe and sound. That she's now sent it to me in a password-protected file. That she can help with whatever I plan to do with it.

I thank her profusely.

Somehow, I make it out of her office, my cheeks tear-stained, my heart aching and wrung out.

But I'm also overjoyed.

Not because of the book.

The true treasure is the letter and the realization that dawns, bright and clear, with it.

The people we love stay with us.

FINAL EPILOGUE
ASK ME NEXT YEAR

Harlow

A week later, on the couch in my apartment, under the Zara Clementine, Bridger hands me a tissue as I type the final words of the epilogue.

Once I wipe away the evidence of my latest waterfall, I attempt to speak past the lump in my throat. "I tried to match her voice," I say. "I think it'll do the job. Want to read it?"

He nods solemnly. "I do."

He sits next to me. I hand him the laptop. He reads the words I wrote. It's short, but it wraps up the characters' love story that started with an invitation to a masquerade and ended with a proposal, and the last words—*And I say yes.*

Watching the smile slowly form across his face is everything.

When he's done, he turns to me and kisses my cheek. "She'd be proud of you, Harlow."

I nod, knowing he's right, feeling the truth of his words in my soul. "Yes. She would."

* * *

On a Friday night in November, a little over a year later, I slip into a silver dress and black heels at our apartment. We live together now—Bridger moved into my place a few months ago.

He holds my coat for me, and as I button it, I admire his clothes—charcoal pants, emerald shirt, and a suit jacket. No tie though. "You and your shirts. I still love them."

"Good. I'll keep wearing them for you."

"Deal."

"Wait," he says before we go, and I comply as he reaches for a small box on the end table, then takes out a small gold picture frame.

He hands it to me and I gasp. "You found the typewriter," I say, studying the photo of a Smith-Corona on a stoop in the Village.

"It has lots of stories in it," he says. Then he sets the frame down on the end table. "It'll look good here, don't you think?"

"Yes. It looks great in our home."

He takes my hand and we leave, heading for the theater. Maybe it's fate, or maybe it's just coincidence, but Davis Milo revived *Ask Me Next Year* and we're going to the opening night.

I. Can't. Wait.

Along the way, we walk past my favorite bookstore

in the city—An Open Book. We stop to admire the window display of the country's new, big best-seller.

Bridger wraps an arm around me and tugs me closer. "Look at what you did, Harlow *Dumont*."

I hardly did anything. I simply found an agent, handled the publication, and wrote the epilogue.

The story did the rest.

My mother's final romance sold out its first printing, hit number one on all the lists, and made her readers happy.

Also, Opening Number bought the TV and film rights.

Well, I guess I did one more thing—I gave it a title.

I snap a photo of the window display, the image catching the reflection of Bridger and me and a love story I named.

The RSVP.

* * *

Do you want more from these characters right now? Be sure to turn the pages for an extended epilogue! Want something to keep you captivated while you wait for the Layla's story in **The Tryst** to come to KU next? You'll love THE VIRGIN NEXT DOOR. It's a crossover, set in the same world in New York and it's also **FREE in KU**!

Turn the page for an excerpt!

EXCERPT - THE VIRGIN NEXT DOOR

Veronica

I Shall Call Him Mister Sexy Pants

I know a thing or two about fetishes thanks to my super-secret dating-in-the-city column, but I didn't know about my own fetish until it began a few months ago. I'd just landed the column gig, so I took myself out to celebrate, as one does, with cake.

The guy who served me the slice at Peace of Cake was sexy and clever, and we flirted over frosting for a few minutes, talking about nerdy things like fractions and synonyms. But then, a pack of teenagers swarmed the shop. I had to go, and I never got his name. He called me Miss Polka Dot. I called him Mister Dessert.

I returned a few days later, but he wasn't there.

Turned out he'd just been helping out a friend. I had no idea where to find him.

C'est la vie.

But a month after that, I was sitting on my third-floor balcony of my apartment in the Village, watching New York go by in the spring, when I spotted him walking down the street. And what a view. This specimen of bearded, inked modern man wasn't picking his clothes from the conventional dude-drobe of baggy pants, loose jeans, or Boring-with-a-capital-B khakis. He was clearly dressing for my delight in those trim, checked pants that hugged his legs.

Thank you, Mister Sexy Pants.

I, Veronica Valentine, had discovered a brand-new kink. I had a thing for men wearing trendy, tight trousers, as I went on to detail the following week in my anonymous column, *The Virgin Club*.

But then, a little while after that, life happened, things happened, trouble happened, and my crush crashed into the middle of my life, where I'd have to see him every single stinking day.

The plan? Make sure he never, ever knows he's the one and only Mister Sexy Pants.

Keep reading: THE VIRGIN NEXT DOOR!

Get your Harlow and Bridger extended epilogue by clicking here or using this QR code!

And stay tuned for more romances later this year featuring Layla, Axel, Jules, Ethan, and Hunter! I'll share all the details on these books in my newsletter and my Facebook group!

MORE BOOKS BY LAUREN

I've written more than 100 books! **All of these titles below are FREE in Kindle Unlimited!**

The Virgin Society Series

Meet the Virgin Society – five great friends who'd do anything for each other. Indulge in five forbidden, emotionally-charged, and wildly sexy age-gap romances!

The RSVP

The Tryst

The Tease

The Chase

Front Man

The Dating Games Series

A fun, sexy romantic comedy series about friends in the city and their dating mishaps!

The Virgin Next Door

Two A Day

The Good Guy Challenge

How To Date Series (New and ongoing)

Three great friends. Three chances to learn how to date

again. Three standalone romantic comedies full of love, sex and meet-cute shenanigans.

My So-Called Sex Life

Plays Well With Others

The Anti-Romantic

Boyfriend Material

Four fabulous heroines. Four outrageous proposals. Four chances at love in this sexy rom-com series!

Asking For a Friend

Sex and Other Shiny Objects

One Night Stand-In

Overnight Service

Big Rock Series

My #1 New York Times Bestselling sexy as sin, irreverent, male-POV romantic comedy!

Big Rock

Mister O

Well Hung

Full Package

Joy Ride

Hard Wood

Happy Endings Series

Romance starts with a bang in this series of standalones following a group of friends seeking and avoiding love!

Come Again

Shut Up and Kiss Me

Kismet

My Single-Versary

Ballers And Babes

Sexy sports romance standalones guaranteed to make
you hot!

Most Valuable Playboy

Most Likely to Score

A Wild Card Kiss

Rules of Love Series

Athlete, virgins and weddings!

The Virgin Rule Book

The Virgin Game Plan

The Virgin Replay

The Virgin Scorecard

The Extravagant Series

Bodyguards, billionaires and hoteliers in this sexy, high-
stakes series of standalones!

One Night Only

One Exquisite Touch

My One-Week Husband

The Guys Who Got Away Series

Friends in New York City and California fall in love in this fun and hot rom-com series!

Birthday Suit

Dear Sexy Ex-Boyfriend

The What If Guy

Thanks for Last Night

The Dream Guy Next Door

Sinful Men

A high-stakes, high-octane, sexy-as-sin romantic suspense series!

My Sinful Nights

My Sinful Desire

My Sinful Longing

My Sinful Love

My Sinful Temptation

Hopelessly Bromantic Duet (MM)

Roomies to lovers to enemies to fake boyfriends

Hopelessly Bromantic

Here Comes My Man

Men of Summer Series (MM)

Two baseball players on the same team fall in love in a forbidden romance spanning five epic years

Scoring With Him

Winning With Him

All In With Him

MM Standalone Novels

A Guy Walks Into My Bar

The Bromance Zone

One Time Only

The Best Men (Co-written with Sarina Bowen)

Winner Takes All Series (MM)

A series of emotionally-charged and irresistibly sexy standalone MM sports romances!

The Boyfriend Comeback

Turn Me On

A Very Filthy Game

Limited Edition Husband

From Paris With Love

Swoony, sweeping romances set in Paris!

Wanderlust

Part-Time Lover

One Love Series

A group of friends in New York falls in love one by one in this sexy rom-com series!

The Sexy One

The Hot One

The Knocked Up Plan

Come As You Are

Lucky In Love Series

A small town romance full of heat and blue collar heroes and sexy heroines!

Best Laid Plans

The Feel Good Factor

Nobody Does It Better

Unzipped

You might also enjoy the following romances! Available on all retailers!

The Gift Series

An after dark series of standalones! Explore your fantasies!

The Engagement Gift

The Virgin Gift

The Decadent Gift

The Heartbreakers Series

Three brothers. Three rockers. Three standalone sexy romantic comedies.

Once Upon a Real Good Time

Once Upon a Sure Thing

Once Upon a Wild Fling

Always Satisfied Series

A group of friends in New York City find love and laughter in this series of sexy standalones!

Satisfaction Guaranteed

Instant Gratification

Never Have I Ever

PS It's Always Been You

Special Delivery

Good Love Series of sexy rom-coms co-written with Lili Valente!

The Caught Up in Love Series

A group of friends finds love!

The Pretending Plot

The Dating Proposal

The Second Chance Plan

The Private Rehearsal

Seductive Nights Series

A high heat series full of danger and spice!

Night After Night

After This Night

One More Night

A Wildly Seductive Night

If you want a personalized recommendation, email me at laurenblakelybooks@gmail.com!

CONTACT

I love hearing from readers! You can find me on Twitter at LaurenBlakely3, Instagram at LaurenBlakelyBooks, Facebook at LaurenBlakelyBooks, or online at LaurenBlakely.com. You can also email me at laurenblakelybooks@gmail.com

Printed in Great Britain
by Amazon